A Redoubtable Citadel
Book Four of the Peninsular War Saga

By

Lynn Bryant

To my sister, Patricia
With all my dearest love

About the Author

Lynn Bryant was born and raised in London's East End. She studied History at University and had dreams of being a writer from a young age. Since this was clearly not something a working class girl made good could aspire to, she had a variety of careers including a librarian, NHS administrator, relationship counsellor and manager of an art gallery before realising that most of these were just as unlikely as being a writer and took the step of publishing her first book.

Two of Lynn's books have been shortlisted for the Society for Army Historical Research fiction prize.

She now lives in the Isle of Man and is married to a man who understands technology, which saves her a job. She has two grown-up children and two Labradors. History is still a passion, with a particular enthusiasm for the Napoleonic era and the sixteenth century. When not writing, she walks her dogs, reads anything that's put in front of her and makes periodic and unsuccessful attempts to keep a tidy house.

Acknowledgements

There have been many people who have helped me since I rashly embarked on a career as a writer. Some of them, I did not even know when the first edition of this book was published in 2017 but since then I've received so much help and advice, and what I've learned has gone into the new edition of this book.

Research is a huge part of the writing I do, and I'd like to thank various historians and writers who have helped me with the maddest questions, especially Jacqueline Reiter, Rob Griffith, Rory Muir, Andrew Bamford, Zack White, Charles Esdaile, Gareth Glover and many others on social media and in person. There will be some I've missed out and I'm sorry but thank you all.

As always, I'd like to thank Mel Logue, Jacqueline Reiter, and Kristine Hughes Patrone for reading sections of the work and making helpful suggestions.

Thanks to Richard Dawson, my husband, for his amazing cover, for technical help and for endless support and patience during the writing of this book.

Thanks to my son, Jon and his girlfriend Rachael, for sharing my study during lockdown and completely ignoring my historical mutterings and to my daughter, Anya, for helping to keep me on track when I was really struggling to motivate myself.

The re-editing of this and all the other books would never have happened in the way it has without the intervention of Heather Paisley, my editor, proof-reader, and partner-in-crime for more than thirty years.

Finally, thanks to Oscar and Alfie the stars of *Writing with Labradors* for sharing my study and bringing me joy.

And in loving memory of Toby and Joey, my old Labradors who have died since I first wrote this book and broke my heart. You will both always be with me in spirit.

Chapter One

It was early evening, and the skies were growing darker. The guns had fired all through the day, a deafening bombardment of the city walls which left men with their ears ringing even after the noise had stopped but it was becoming quieter now, with longer gaps between shots. The men of the 88th Connaught Rangers stood immobile, so quiet that it was possible for each man to hear the breathing of his neighbour as they waited for the order to begin the assault. This band of men were all volunteers and would form the Forlorn Hope, the first men over the breaches. Survival would bring glory and in some cases promotion, but survival was very unlikely.

Sergeant Nathaniel Higgins was not one of the volunteers, but these were his men, and he ran an experienced eye over them and approved their steadiness. At the front of the line were two officers, also volunteers and neither were from the 88th. The older of the two was a dark haired captain of thirty-five and Higgins had been told that he was facing a charge of killing a fellow officer in a duel. If he was convicted, he would probably be cashiered and disgraced, and Higgins thought that he was lucky to have been offered the chance to lead these men to death or glory.

The other officer was very young an ensign of no more than twenty, and his youth bothered Higgins. He was pale and sweating but seemed surprisingly calm. The Sergeant wondered what had driven the lad to this desperate end. Debt or a woman, Higgins supposed. Sometimes the young fools did not realise what they were doing when they volunteered for this or how unlikely they were to survive, seeing only the prospect of glory and quick promotion. Looking at this boy, Higgins decided that Ensign Jackman knew exactly what he was doing. He was looking up at the walls with intelligent grey eyes and Higgins felt very sorry for him.

Reaching into his coat Higgins took out his battered flask and drank, then touched the boy on the arm and offered him the rum. The young officer looked surprised but took it and drank with an attempt at a smile, then handed it back.

1

"You all right, sir?" Higgins said, and the boy nodded, his eyes still on the fading bulk of the citadel of Ciudad Rodrigo, looming up in the falling darkness.

A sound broke through the silence and Higgins jumped. It was a shout, a bellow so loud that every man of the Forlorn Hope also jumped and turned, peering through the darkness. A tall figure was striding from the waiting lines towards them, and he did not appear to be in the least concerned at the stir he was causing.

"Oh bloody hell," the young ensign said and Higgins thought he sounded more terrified than he had seemed to be of going over the wall.

"Mr Jackman. Am I seeing things or are you actually standing there with the Connaught Rangers when you should be back in line with your men?"

The tall figure resolved itself into an officer, fair-haired and hatless with a long legged stride. Close up Higgins was aware of a pair of startling deep blue eyes which were fixed with ominous intensity on the young ensign. Jackman snapped to attention and saluted, and Higgins did the same realising that the man wore a colonel's insignia on his red coat.

"Yes, sir."

"Don't give me 'yes, sir' you bloody idiot. What the hell are you doing here?"

"I volunteered, sir. Sorry, thought you'd know. Sergeant said commanding officers would be informed..."

"I was informed, that's why I'm bloody well here chasing after you when I ought to be back there putting the fear of God into my men. What made you think you had the right to volunteer for this suicidal piece of lunacy without my permission? Get your arse back to your company before I kick you so hard you'll scale that breach without your feet touching the ground."

Higgins cleared his throat. "Excuse me, Colonel. But the lad...I mean, the young gentleman... is right. He's entitled..."

"Not when he's nineteen and being a bloody imbecile he isn't," the Colonel said decidedly. He looked at Higgins. "Are you going over with them, Sergeant?"

"Not with this lot, sir. With my men afterwards."

"Good man." Suddenly the Colonel smiled. "Sorry, I should have introduced myself. Colonel Paul van Daan, 110th."

Higgins stood to attention and saluted. The extraordinary scene suddenly made more sense. Higgins had heard of Colonel van Daan who had been given command of the recently formed third brigade of the Light Division. There were many legends in the army, most of whom, in Higgins opinion, fell woefully short of their reputations but he was already beginning to see why men spoke of Paul van Daan with something bordering on awe. The Colonel looked at the Captain commanding the troop.

"Name and regiment?"

"Captain James Harker, sir, of the 9th."

"Ah. I rather see why you're here." Van Daan studied him. "I was hoping to get myself onto that court, but I presume they've offered you an alternative way out of your difficulties."

"Yes, sir."

"Bastards," Van Daan said dispassionately. "I hope you make it, Captain. If you do, come and see me, would you? I asked around and I've heard very good things

2

about you. You might feel that a change of scene would do you good if you decide to carry on in the army. I'm always on the lookout for good officers."

"Thank you, sir."

Van Daan's gaze shifted back to Ensign Jackman. "Captain Manson has informed me that you are in debt, Mr Jackman."

"Yes, sir."

"Cards?"

"Yes, sir. In pretty deep. Can't pay. Debts of honour, sir."

Paul van Daan studied him. "To whom? Don't tell me any of my officers are fleecing their juniors, I'll skin them alive."

"No, sir. I owe most of it to an officer of the Highlanders, a major. Got into a game up with a few of the headquarters' staff."

"Mr Jackman, when you were offered the chance to serve in my regiment, did anybody give you any information about my rules on gambling?"

Jackman's face was visibly scarlet even through the fading light. "Yes, sir. Not to gamble above our means and never with a senior officer. Sorry, sir. But it's not in the army regulations."

"Fuck the army regulations, most of them are bollocks anyway. You're in the 110th and the only regulations that matter are the ones I tell you matter. And it serves you right for dining with the staff officers anyway, the food's dreadful and the wine is worse. No wonder Wellington tries to avoid it. I will deal with the Major who thinks it is a good idea to flout my rules and gamble with my juniors at a later date. If he is fortunate, he'll get his head blown off before I catch up with him."

Higgins was unable to suppress a choke of laughter. "They're in reserve sir, I don't think they'll be engaged today."

"He bloody will when I get hold of him. Captain Harker, can you manage without this young fool? Despite his evident idiocy in matters of finance, he's a surprisingly useful officer and I'd like him to go over with his men."

Harker did not hesitate which confirmed Higgins' favourable first impression of him. "Gladly, sir."

"Thank you, Captain. Jackman, if it becomes necessary, I will settle your blasted debts of honour myself and you can pay me back gradually. And if I ever see you near a card table for anything greater than a penny a point, I am going to shoot you in the head and display your bloody body as a warning to others. Now piss off back to your company and be thankful that I don't have time to kick the shit out of you as you richly deserve. Move."

He stood watching as the young ensign took off back towards the lines. Several of the men were laughing, and one at the back raised an ironic cheer. Paul van Daan turned and surveyed them.

"I thought the 88th could make more noise than that," he said, and they cheered again. The sombre mood had lightened. The Colonel moved forward, speaking to one of the men. Higgins stood with Harker, watching as the tall figure moved along the line. He heard laughter and an exchange of banter and there was a new atmosphere among the men as though they stood a little taller and held their weapons with new determination.

"Sir!"

3

A voice called out of the darkness, and Paul van Daan turned. "What is it, Jenson?"

"Compliments of General Craufurd, sir. He'd like to know if you're planning on joining the assault today or if this is just a social occasion for you."

Paul van Daan broke into laughter. "Sarcastic bastard," he said. "I'm coming, Jenson. These lads have work to do anyway, I'm holding them up."

He turned back to Harker. "Good luck, Captain. You've good lads there. Make sure you look after them." The blue eyes moved back to the men. "All of you are invited for a drink up with us once this is over and you know my lads only loot the best wine and brandy so stay alive and don't miss it. I need to get back before General Craufurd starts threatening to shoot me again. Good luck."

He saluted, and they stood to attention without an order, to return the salute. Paul van Daan headed off into the darkness back towards his men. Higgins turned back to the Forlorn Hope and found Captain Harker smiling for the first time.

"That was unexpected."

"You met him before, sir?"

"No although I've heard of him, of course. One of Lord Wellington's rising men. He must be five years younger than me and brigade commander already. But on that performance, I can see why. I'm not sure I've ever seen an officer that easy with the men."

Higgins passed his flask again. "His men think the world of him, sir. You can't criticise him in front of one of the 110th they'll punch you. And of course, he's got that wife, which can't hurt."

"His wife?" Harker sounded puzzled.

Higgins grinned. "You not seen her, sir? Can't have, or you'd remember her."

"Pretty?"

"Very. She works with the surgeons. I got taken in after Fuentes d'Oñoro with a bayonet wound. She didn't treat me, but she was working at the next table. Pregnant, she was, if you'd believe it, and she was digging shot out of a corporal of the rifles. It must have bloody hurt because the air was blue with his language. After about five minutes she puts down the scalpel, looks him straight in the eye, and says 'Corporal, if you need to swear that much, use a different word, I'm tired of you bellowing the word fuck into my ear every thirty seconds.' Swear to God, sir, he didn't make another sound."

Harker began to laugh. "You're not serious?"

"As I stand before you. She must have had that baby by now. Loveliest looking girl I've ever seen, apparently Lord Wellington's all over her. That can't hurt his promotion chances."

"Somehow I doubt that's why he got promoted, Sergeant. Looks like our orders coming up." Harker regarded Higgins steadily. "Thanks. You've helped."

Higgins was suddenly angry. He knew nothing about the affair of honour which had caused this man to throw his life away to avoid the disgrace of a court martial and he did not care. He did know a good officer when he met one, and he thought wistfully of a number of officers whom he would happily send over with the Forlorn Hope, secure in the knowledge that their men would not miss them at all. Captain Harker would be missed.

4

"Look after my lads, sir. The Colonel was right, they're good. Try and make it out alive."

"I'm not sure I've got much reason to."

"Rubbish. If you make it over and survive, sir, that court martial will go away. If that happens, I'd go and have a chat with Colonel van Daan."

"Do you seriously think he meant that?"

"I doubt he'd have said it if he didn't, Captain, it's not his way. Looks like you're off. Good luck."

***

Paul van Daan heard the call of the bugle as he arrived back at his lines. He waved up at General Craufurd and saw his commanding officer's ironic salute through the fading light. There would be some time before the order came for the Light Division to advance and Paul paused to drink from his water bottle, surveying his men. They were quiet now, talking softly, if at all. Paul knew that for each of them it was a moment to quell the knot of fear in his belly, to review weapons and orders, to speak a word to a good friend, and to think of the people they had left behind them, their wives, sweethearts, parents, or children.

Paul looked up at the citadel and thought of his wife. He had left her several hours ago, holding their three month old son in her arms, smiling at him as he kissed her goodbye. They had been married for more than a year now and he had loved her for two before that. The memory of Paul's first wife, who had been Anne's friend was still bitter-sweet between them and the memory of Anne's brutal first husband cast no shadow on their happiness.

Paul knew that by now Anne would have deposited Will with his nurse and would be waiting in the surgeon's tent with her Spanish maid and her orderlies ready to assist her. The other surgeons regarded Anne van Daan with a mixture of admiration, disapproval, and exasperated affection. She should not have been there, doing what she did, but her undoubted talent for her unofficial role as assistant surgeon to the 110th had become well established over the past few years. Dr Adam Norris, who had first taken the monumental step of training her after she had volunteered to help with the nursing, had never wavered in his faith in her abilities. Anne had the support of both Dr Franck the surgeon-general, and Lord Wellington who commanded the army but some of the older surgeons complained bitterly that she was allowed to continue. Since Anne was unpaid and unqualified, they could not report her to the medical board and her success level was high, causing men who knew of her to beg to be taken to her table when they were carried in. The shortage of medical staff at all levels along with Anne's position as wife to a senior officer meant that nobody was willing to take the step of forbidding her to enter the hospital.

"Thinking about your wife?" a voice said, and Paul glanced sideways at Major Carl Swanson who commanded his first battalion and had been his closest friend since childhood.

"Yes. I'm hoping she'll have the sense not to overdo it. Not that she'll even consider resting more, but Will is still so young."

"I see Ensign Jackman is back with his company."

5

Paul grinned. "Silly young bleater. Thank God for Leo Manson. When I get out of this, I am going to get hold of Captain Kent and ask for an explanation as to why he didn't know what was going on there."

"Kent is mostly pretty good, sir, but I imagine Jackman was too ashamed to come forward."

"So why did Captain Manson know about it?"

"Because he's an interfering young bastard who knows too much about everything."

"Exactly what I like to see in an officer." Paul studied his friend. "Are you all right?"

"Yes. I'll be glad to get moving, I hate this waiting. Look, sir..."

"What is it, Major?"

His friend took a deep breath. "It's about Keren."

"Is she all right?"

"Yes. No. It's odd. I used to watch you saying goodbye to Rowena and then to Anne and some part of me was envious that you had a girl to kiss you and wait for you to come back. Now I realise it's actually quite painful. Keren is very good, she doesn't cry or make a fuss. Only..."

"What is it, Carl?"

"Look, this might sound a bit mad because I should have dealt with it before, but it's really bothering me. I don't have a will. I've never had that much to leave, although I've invested my prize money and it's doing all right. If I die up there, I suppose what I have will go to my parents. They won't care about it, they've never had any money and never really noticed the lack. But Keren...will you make sure she's all right?"

"Carl, you didn't have to ask."

"My parents don't know anything about her," Carl said. "He's a parson for God's sake, I can hardly write and tell them I'm engaged in a liaison with a miner's daughter. But I can't help worrying about her. She has nothing. She's asked for nothing. She even made a fuss over a couple of new dresses because she doesn't want to feel like a prostitute."

Paul was surprised. "Did she? I'd no idea she felt that way about it, Major. Are you going to draw up a will in her favour?"

"Yes. Once this is over, I'm going to borrow Lord Wellington's man of business and get it done properly. I want to know that she's provided for. I want her to have a choice what she does next."

Paul studied his friend. Carl's relationship with Keren Trenlow had surprised him from the start. The girl was from a humble mining family in Cornwall and had followed her sweetheart when he joined the army only to watch him die of fever before he ever saw a battle. Alone and desperate, Keren had taken up with a man from Paul's third company who had beaten her regularly until one of Paul's NCOs had intervened. Anne had taken the girl under her wing and Keren had worked for her, doing laundry, and mending to earn her keep. Anne had become very fond of her, teaching her to read and write and treating her with the same easy affection as she treated her Spanish maid, Teresa.

6

At some point during the last campaigning season Paul had been surprised to discover that instead of finding herself a husband among the enlisted men, as he had expected, Keren was sharing the bed of his oldest friend. Paul had assumed, along with the rest of the army, that the affair would be short-lived, but Carl was showing no sign of tiring of the girl. If anything, their relationship seemed to be developing into something far more stable.

Paul had watched in some concern to start with, but what he saw reassured him. Keren was bright and practical and very adaptable, and Paul did not think she was with Carl for money. With no means of his own, Carl lived off his pay and prize money like many of Paul's officers, and marriage to a girl of his own social class would have been difficult if not impossible. Paul was beginning to wonder if Carl had found a different solution to the problem and now that he was getting to know Keren better, he approved.

"I'll see to it," he said quietly. "Don't worry about her, Carl. Nan loves her dearly, we'll make sure she's taken care of. Look, there's not a particular reason…?"

"Not yet. But if this carries on, sooner or later she will be. And God knows how we'll manage that, because I don't think she'll want to leave, and I wouldn't want her to."

"You're not going to get yourself killed, lad, that's an order," Paul said. "But in case you're worrying, if there's a child on the way that you don't know about yet, it will be my responsibility and so will Keren. I'm not letting her end up with the camp followers or taking up with another arsehole like Simpson because she's desperate. Don't worry about her."

Carl glanced over at him with a smile. "Thank you," he said quietly. "Do you think I'm mad?"

"No. I think you were looking for one thing and are beginning to wonder if you've found something else. And you know what, lad? You might have. Personally, I don't give a damn where she started, she's a thoroughly good girl." Paul nodded towards an approaching figure. "It looks as though we're on our way. I wonder how it will go up there with the Forlorn Hope?"

"It's never good, sir. You shouldn't have gone up there, it only pisses you off, and someone has to be first."

"I know. I liked the look of Captain Harker. I could give Wellington a list of officers who could go over instead of him and would never be missed. General Sir William Erskine, for example. And if he were still here, Major Longford. Although curiously I don't feel quite as bad about him as I used to, I must be mellowing." Paul surveyed his friend. "Look after yourself. You know how I hate storming a bloody city. And remember…"

"Are you about to give me instructions which would insult a greenhorn?" his friend demanded, and Paul grinned and turned to Wellington's ADC who had arrived with orders.

Wellington's army had marched on the fortress town of Ciudad Rodrigo immediately after Christmas after an unusually short time in winter quarters. Wellington had received intelligence that Bonaparte had ordered Marshal Marmont to send 10,000 troops to help Suchet capture Valencia along with another 4000 to reinforce the central reserve and the time seemed right for an attempt on the border

7

fortress. Paul had been present the previous summer when Wellington had been forced to abandon his siege at the other great border fortress of Badajoz and although the French had been driven out of Almeida, their garrison had managed a daring escape under the noses of the Allies, a subject that it was still unwise to raise in Lord Wellington's presence.

Wellington's forces had marched in terrible conditions including the worst snowstorms Paul had seen in many years. He found himself fuming at the state of his men's uniform, particularly their footwear, as they battled through the appalling weather, shivering in threadbare coats and trousers, and patching their shoes as best they could. Some of them had boots looted from dead Frenchmen and they did rather better, but Paul was angry at how badly equipped they were. Most of the army did not have tents and were to be found huddled under makeshift blanket tents or sheltering under trees. The men of the 110th and 112th were all equipped with tents and Paul was amused and a little touched to see them offering shelter where they could to the Portuguese and KGL of the third brigade, cramming six men into four man tents during the freezing nights. Paul had ordered tents for the rest of his brigade using money saved in other areas, but they had not yet arrived.

The cold weather and poor conditions had been a source of anxiety for Paul given that Anne had only recently given birth and was nursing their young son. He had seriously considered insisting that she stay in Freineda or even go back to Lisbon until the weather improved, but he had hesitated, knowing how upset she would be. Shortly before their departure he had been surprised and touched when his Commander-in-Chief had approached him and placed his carriage at Anne's disposal. Knowing that if conditions proved too difficult, she could return to their excellent billet on an estate near Freineda in the comfort of a carriage and along good roads, reassured Paul, and he loved the panache with which Anne settled herself and their baby into a tent. Their son slept warm beside them on their mattress and Paul awoke each morning with a sense of well-being despite his disturbed nights.

On arrival at the fortress on the sixth of January Wellington and his chief of engineers, Lieutenant-Colonel Fletcher had surveyed the approaches and made their plans. The main wall of Ciudad Rodrigo was more than thirty feet high and appeared to be in poor condition, but the French had built a redoubt on the Grand Teson, a small hill to the north. Intelligence reports suggested that the garrison consisted of around 2000 men which would make it difficult to mount an effective defence of the whole fortress.

Two days later Wellington sent Major-General Robert Craufurd's Light Division, which included Paul's brigade, to storm the Grand Teson. The attack came as a complete surprise to the French and the redoubt was taken with very few losses. The allies began digging trenches to the breaching batteries. It was a hazardous enterprise at night as the picks hitting a rock resulted in sparks which made it easy for the French to direct their fire, but a few days later the trenches were complete, and batteries were installed.

By then, Wellington had received further intelligence concerning Marshal Marmont's movements and was determined to speed up the siege. Over the next few days, he sent troops to storm both the San Francisco Convent and the Santa Cruz

Convent. The French retaliated with a sortie of their own, but the Allies successfully defended their position.

The batteries opened fire on the fourteenth of January and work began on the second parallel, to provide closer batteries and a safe covered route for assaulting troops. Within five days, the guns had opened two effective breaches, one in a wall and a smaller one in an exposed tower. Paul, whose last experience of a siege had been the frustrating failure to take Badajoz the previous year was surprised at how effective the bombardment had been and felt cautiously optimistic about the storming.

Paul disliked siege warfare and his hatred of storming a town was legendary in the 110th. Officers and men who had served with him from the start of his army career ten years earlier could tell a variety of entertaining stories about his bad temper when his regiment was called upon to take part in siege warfare. Paul laughed with them, but he knew that they were right. He had immense faith in Lord Wellington's command on a battlefield and even more faith in his men's fighting skills but when storming a citadel, these advantages counted for little.

The Light Division had been instructed to storm the lesser breach, while Picton's third division had been given the greater breach to the northwest. Paul walked up to meet Craufurd and found the two commanders of the other brigades already with him. Both men were relatively new in post although both had commanded brigades before. Colonel George Drummond had died of fever the previous September and Colonel Sydney Beckwith had been invalided home in August which meant that Paul was now the longest serving of the three brigade commanders albeit the youngest.

The change had cemented his position in the division. Paul was known to be close to both Wellington and Craufurd, and while Beckwith and Drummond had tended to look upon him as something of a young upstart, neither Vandeleur nor Barnard had not been present when he was surprisingly raised to command a brigade at the age of thirty making relations far easier. Paul had met both men before but did not know either of them well. Vandeleur was the older of the two, an experienced officer approaching fifty whom Paul remembered from his time in India. Andrew Barnard was a dark-eyed Irish rifleman in his late thirties with a lively manner which appealed to Paul.

Robert Craufurd glared at Paul as he saluted. "There you are. What the devil was that racket about earlier, I thought you were going over to the French?"

"I considered it, sir," Paul said, straight-faced. "Fortunately, I remembered in time how badly they tend to overdo the garlic in their cooking."

"Van Daan?" Craufurd growled.

Paul grinned. "I was retrieving one of my ensigns from an ill-judged attempt to join one of the Forlorn Hopes."

Craufurd gave a crack of laughter. "Ha! Wish I could have heard what you had to say about it. What was it, a shot at early promotion?"

"He was looking to avoid gambling debts to some Highland major who's been fleecing him at the headquarters mess," Paul said grimly. "I don't know who, but I'll find out."

"It'll be Brodie," Barnard said. "He's known for it. Cards and swordplay. He's a devil with a blade and he keeps up his lifestyle by challenging men to a friendly

9

bout and betting on it. I've heard through the gossip mill that a couple of promising young officers have had to sell out to meet their obligations. I'm keeping an eye on my youngsters with him."

Both Craufurd and Paul turned to stare at him. "Does Lord Wellington know about this?" Craufurd demanded.

"He can't, or Brodie would be up to his neck in it," Paul said briefly. "Thanks for the tip, Barnard. I'll speak to Major Brodie once this mess is over. Trust me it'll be the last time he tries to make money out of one of my junior officers. And if he objects, he can try challenging me to a friendly bout and having a bet on it."

Craufurd gave a bark of laughter and the other two men smiled politely. "I admire your confidence, Colonel," General Vandeleur said. "I believe he's very good."

"I'll be surprised if he's good enough to beat this arrogant young bastard," Craufurd said dispassionately. "I've seen Colonel van Daan fight and he's almost as good as he thinks he is. We'll discuss it when this is over, Van Daan. I have no objection in principle to you kicking his arse, but I don't want Lord Wellington on my back over it. You know how he feels about duelling."

"Yes, sir."

"We're going in over the lesser breach. Call them in around the San Francisco convent, I'd like a word with them before we go in. Vandeleur, your lads will lead us over, Barnard to follow. Colonel van Daan will bring his men up behind to correct all of our mistakes."

Barnard shot Paul a surprised glance and seemed relieved to see him laughing. Neither of the other commanders were entirely used to Craufurd's acerbic tongue yet and were not always sure when he was being genuinely offensive or when he was joking.

"It's what I do best, sir," Paul said placidly. "Do you have any orders you particularly want me to ignore today, or shall we just see how it goes?"

"If you disobey an order of mine today, Van Daan, I will shoot you in the head!" Craufurd said explosively.

"No you won't, sir, you're too fond of my wife. I'll bring them up. Are you going to make a stirring speech? I might make notes."

"You should, Colonel," Craufurd said shortly. "Then you can make another one telling them the best wine shops to loot when they get in there."

Paul heard Barnard give a snort of laughter. He grinned. "I would, sir, but I don't know them, I've not been to Ciudad Rodrigo before."

"I have immense faith that the 110th will find them, they'll follow their noses. Get going."

Paul stood at the head of his brigade, listening to Craufurd's speech. He was aware that not all the men would hear it all, but the words would be passed among them and probably embellished. Craufurd was not popular with his officers, but his men adored him despite his reputation as a strict disciplinarian, and his speech was unashamedly aimed at them, sentimental at times but guaranteed to touch their hearts.

"Soldiers," he said finally, his voice carrying through the crisp cold evening air. "The eyes of your country are upon you. Be steady. Be cool. Be firm in the assault.

The town must be yours this night. Once masters of the wall let your first duty be to clear the ramparts and in doing this, keep together!"

They cheered him with riotous enthusiasm, and Craufurd smiled down at them, black browed and stocky, a man at home in his command and knowing himself loved. "Now lads, for the breach!"

They stirred, checking their arms, ready to move, and Paul stepped forward and stilled his brigade with a yell which surpassed anything his commanding officer had managed.

"Third brigade halt!"

The men froze and snapped to attention. Paul stepped up onto a chunk of broken masonry and looked down over them.

"Wine, ale, liquor – I don't give a damn, providing you bring some back for me and I'm picky so make it good," he said, and there was a gust of laughter through the brigade. "But if I catch any one of you looting houses or hurting the locals and I swear to God you'll wish you'd died in that breach. As for the women – every single one of you bastards knows my views on rape and if you touch a lassie against her will, I'm going to cut off your balls and nail your prick to the doorpost. You have been warned. Officers and NCOs make sure everybody heard that message, will you?"

Sergeant-Major Carter gave an exaggerated salute. "Unlikely to be a problem sir. I reckon they could hear that message in London at Horse Guards."

There was more laughter and Paul jumped down. "Let's get going, Sergeant-Major. You know how I've been looking forward to this. If there is one thing about my job that I hate the most...."

There was a roar of responsive laughter which drowned out the end of his sentence and Paul went to join Colonel Johnny Wheeler at the head of the 112th. "Ready?"

"Yes, sir." Johnny gave a faint smile. "I love the way you manage to make your dislike of storming a town into a regimental legend. I swear they all go over there determined to show you how easy it really is."

"Then they're idiots, Johnny. Because it isn't easy and some of them are going to die. And I actually do hate it. But we need to do it so let's get it over with."

The Light Division storming party was led by Major George Napier of the 52nd who had volunteered for the duty. His request for volunteers to join him had resulted in half the division stepping forward. Paul had run his eye over those of his brigade who had been chosen and observed without surprise that the men who had volunteered were all from his newer recruits. His veterans watched them go with a tolerant eye, preferring to go over with their own officers. Wellington's army was very hierarchical, and the third brigade was a relatively new addition to the Light Division having been formed back in April from the the first battalions of the 110th and 112th, two companies of the 95th, a battalion of Portuguese caçadores and half a battalion of the King's German Legion. Although Paul's men had fought alongside the Light Division for several years he was aware that the men under Craufurd regarded his brigade as newcomers, and the 52nd, 43rd and 95th who comprised the bulk of the division were longer established regiments who did their best to look down on the more recently formed 110th and 112th.

Paul did not care, and his attitude had filtered down to his men. The 110th had been fighting in Portugal and Spain since 1808 and had developed an excellent reputation. They were a particular favourite of Lord Wellington who frequently used them as an independent unit to carry out tasks he considered especially important, and their commander's reputation for unconventionality was legendary throughout the army. Paul knew that his experienced troops would rather be commanded by their own officers whom they trusted implicitly than follow a volunteer whose quest for glory might well get them all killed.

Paul knew that the order of brigades going into the battle had been set purely in order of numerical precedence and he was passionately glad that his was the third and newest brigade on this occasion. He had no desire to be first over the walls and saw no glory or possible advantage in throwing his men against the lethal blast of fire from the French guns. From the rear of the advance he gave orders to his rifles and the sharpshooters of the two light companies to target the defenders on the ramparts. In the darkness and confusion, accurate shooting would be difficult but some of his men were very good and he hoped they would be able to even-up the odds before they reached the bloody melee of hand-to-hand fighting with sword and bayonet in the breach.

The assault began at eight o'clock. Paul stood in line with his men, glancing over at the steady ranks. Through the darkness his eyes sought and found his closest friends. Colonel Johnny Wheeler now commanded the 112th. Major Carl Swanson was at the head of the first battalion of the 110th. Captain Leo Manson, newly returned from brief leave in England was in command of the 110th light company and Captain Michael O'Reilly was in place in front of the 112th light company. There were friends too among the NCOs and men of his regiments; Regimental Sergeant-Major Danny Carter and Sergeant Jamie Hammond of the 110th and many of the others, some of whom had been with him since he was a young lieutenant in India ten years ago. Paul could not bear the thought of losing any one of them although he went into every battle knowing that he might.

The bugles called and Paul stepped forward, drawing his sword. As he began to move, his mind cleared of thoughts of his friends, thoughts of death and thoughts of fear, and focused solely on the breach in the citadel wall, already packed with the red coats and green jackets of the Light Division.

To the left, Napier's storming party had three hundred yards of open ground to clear and moved across it fast, running to the top of the glacis and then leaping down the scarp, a depth of around eleven feet. They scrambled up the fausse braie which was a low defensive wall outside the main walls preceded by a ditch. Once there, the Forlorn Hope headed towards the left while the stormers went straight to the breach.

The opening of this smaller of the two breaches was narrow and had caused Paul some concern from when he had first seen it. He was unsurprised to see, as he led his men forward, that the French had placed a gun at the top which nearly blocked the opening. Looking upwards he could see the Forlorn Hope and the stormers coming together at the top and he swore.

"Christ, there are too many of them up there, they're going to get stuck. Carter!"

"Working on it, sir, but it's bloody dark, we can't see what we're doing, and we don't want to hit our own men."

Paul heard the crack of rifles as his skirmishers dropped into firing position, aiming at the gunners, then there was an enormous crash of French artillery and he saw the first wave of attackers blown away by grape shot and musket fire from the ramparts. Some of the men were firing their muskets back, forgetting in their panic that they were not loaded for the storming. As he made his way out of the darkness of the ditch and up towards the press of men in the breach, Paul could hear Major Napier yelling to his men to use bayonets and he saw other officers scrambling forward. Paul could not actually see Napier although he could still hear his voice and he wondered if the Major was hit.

Paul heard suddenly the bellow of General Craufurd. His commander had gone up to the left of the advancing columns and climbed directly up to the top of the glacis and was yelling instructions to his men. Paul could hear him clearly, the familiar rasp of his voice shouting encouragement and orders. Looking up, Paul could see the short, stocky figure outlined against flashes of fire.

Paul was horrified. Craufurd's reputation for courage in battle was legendary and his men loved him for his willingness to fight alongside them, sharing their danger. Craufurd never commanded from a safe distance, but on this occasion he had misjudged badly. It was obvious that he had not realised the vulnerability of his position, but it was clear to Paul that he had unwittingly placed himself directly in the line of fire from French muskets from two directions, and he was standing high up and alone, a very visible high-ranking target.

"Jesus bloody Christ what is he doing up there, he's going to kill himself." Paul lifted his voice in a bellow of rage which cut through the noise of battle impressively. "Sir, get down from there, you're in two fire lines!"

Craufurd's head turned, and Paul knew that he had heard. He looked around him but before he could move, the French muskets were upon him, firing not only from the ramparts but also from the fausse braie opposite. The ditch was narrow with no cover and at that distance there was no possibility that the muskets would miss.

"Robert, get down!" Paul yelled again. He was frantically trying to push his way through the close press of men scrambling up the breach and he saw his commander take a step as if suddenly realising his exposed position. There was another burst of firing and Paul saw, with sick horror, Craufurd's body lurch suddenly and begin to fall. He fell slowly at first and then rolled faster, tumbling down the steep slope of the glacis.

Chapter Two

Paul stood frozen for a long moment, unable to believe what he had just seen. Around him men continued to fight their way up and he realised that it was possible that nobody else had seen Craufurd fall.

"Johnny, take over," Paul bellowed, and swung around, shoving his way forcefully through the closely crowded soldiers. Above him the gun had been silenced and the men of the Light Division were pouring into the breach, overrunning the French defenders ruthlessly. Major Swanson was passing at the head of his men, face black with powder, and Paul grabbed him.

"Carl, Craufurd is down I'm going to look for him. Tell Johnny he has command, get them over and take the ramparts. Don't let them go haring off until we know what's happened at the greater breach, they might run into something unexpected. If I don't come back up, tell him…"

"I am not telling Johnny Wheeler his job, sir, I don't need to. Get going."

Paul resumed his scrambling run down the glacis, shoving against the press of men until he reached the bottom. He stumbled badly halfway and stopped, swearing as something cut into his leg. It proved to be a rusty sword blade. The ditches were littered with them, set there by the French to slow down the attackers and it had cut a long gash in his calf. Paul tested his leg then set off again. The ditch was empty other than some dead and wounded men and he began to run cautiously over to the left where he had seen Craufurd fall.

Paul found them quickly, apart from the others but still well within range of fire from the ramparts. The fallen man lay in the black shadows while another man struggled, half carrying and half dragging him, desperately trying to get him out of danger.

"Shaw, is that you?"

The man looked up. "Who's there?"

"It's me, Colonel van Daan." Paul ran forward, keeping low. "Let me help you, we'll get him over there to the rough ground out of range."

"Sir, shouldn't you…?" Lieutenant James Shaw, Craufurd's ADC could not hide the relief in his voice.

14

"Get back up there, Colonel." Craufurd's voice was a sob of agony but there were still traces of belligerence in it which broke Paul's heart. "How dare you let your men go over without you? I'll have you cashiered for desertion…"

"I've just decided which orders I'm going to ignore today, sir," Paul said, moving to take the injured man's head. "Where are you hurt?"

"Gone through my arm and into me. It's bad, Paul, I'm not getting up from this. Look…"

"Sir, we are not having this conversation with Frenchmen shooting at me, I can't concentrate. Take his feet, Shaw, I'll manage this end. Sir, I'm going to put your arm across your body, but I'm afraid this is going to hurt like hell."

Between them it was easier, but Craufurd was unconscious with pain when they laid him gently down on the uneven ground out of range of the French guns. The firing was dying away now. The storming had gone well so far although Paul had no idea what was happening at the other breach. He knelt beside Craufurd and took his uninjured hand, and the General opened his eyes.

"I'm dying," he said.

Paul did not reply. In the darkness, with no way of inspecting the wounds he did not know if Craufurd was right, but instinct told him that the wound was bad. Paul felt a desperate longing for his wife, remembering the calm competence which had saved his life at Talavera.

"I'll get you to the surgeons as soon as I can, sir," he said gently.

"I might not make it. Shaw, is that you?"

"Yes, sir."

"You can stay with me. Colonel van Daan needs to get back…"

"Sir, they're in. It will be fine."

"No, it bloody won't," Craufurd said with more force than Paul would have thought him capable of. "If something goes wrong, I want you in there. They're good men all of them, Barnard, Vandeleur, Wheeler…but they're not you. I want you. Paul, please…"

"All right," Paul said quickly. He could sense that refusal would upset Craufurd even more. "I'm going back up. Shaw, we need a doctor to see him…"

"Wait. Paul – both of you. If I don't make it that far…my wife."

Paul dropped back down again. "Sir?"

"I want you both to hear this. In case one of you doesn't make it through. Tell her I love her. Tell her there's never been anybody for me but her. I love her and I love my boys. They won't remember much of me, but I hope my friends…"

"They'll never forget you, sir. All that we know of you, they'll know, I promise you."

Craufurd reached out with his good hand and clutched at Paul's sleeve convulsively. "You understand, don't you?" he croaked. "Of all the men in this army, you understand."

Paul felt his throat constrict. "Yes, I do. Because you feel about Mary and your lads the way I feel about Nan and my children."

"I don't think I'll see her again in this world," Craufurd said. His voice was barely a whisper. "But will you tell her I'll wait for her? That I truly believe we'll be together again in the next life, and I'll be waiting. Tell her to live long and be happy

15

and raise our boys to be proud of me. And I'll see her again. Not spent enough hours in church in my life but that doesn't mean I don't believe, and I think he'll forgive me."

Paul's cheeks were wet. He lifted Craufurd's hand to his lips and kissed it. "There's nothing to forgive, sir, you're a good man and a great soldier and there's a place for those, I'm sure of it. I'll make sure she knows, and I'll make sure she's all right financially."

Craufurd coughed and stiffened with the pain. "I'm in a mess with money," he said. "Never had much, but I've debts, been waiting for a good prize to pay them off. I'm worried about Mary."

"Look at me!" Paul said, and the dark eyes shifted to his face. "No debts. She'll get a pension, and if they mess about with that I am going to flay them alive and nail their hides to the door. But they won't, she'll get what's due to her, I give you my word. Anything else I'll see to myself, she'll want for nothing. Consider your lads my personal responsibility, sir. And you know I can afford to do it. Now rest, you obstreperous old goat and let me get back to my job. I'll send…"

"Sir!"

Paul turned in relief as four men slid down the slope and ran towards him. "Captain O'Reilly. Did you get bored up there?"

"I'd nothing to do, sir, so I thought I'd see if you were dead yet so that I can propose to your widow first. Do you need help?"

"Yes. General Craufurd wants me back up there. Will you find a stretcher and get him to a safe place? I'm not sure where, but there must be somewhere."

"We'll take him to our lines, and he can rest in one of our tents until we find a billet, sir. Don't worry, we'll see to him. Four of my lads are bringing out Major Napier as well."

"Napier?" Craufurd croaked. "Is he hurt?"

"He is, sir, shot in the arm. But we'll take care of you both. Colonel van Daan, we could do with you back up there. Our lads are holding the breach and the ramparts but the first and second brigades have taken off through the town towards the other breach and there's no knowing…"

They were all looking up towards the town when a tremendous bang shook the ground beneath them. The explosion rocked the town and lit up the sky, silhouetting the walls of the city. To Paul's horror there were men in the air, their blackened and twisted bodies thrown high enough to be seen clearly, before falling back onto their comrades below. He saw Craufurd's body convulse with the effort of trying to move and he dropped down and held him still.

"Stay there, you can't do anything. Let Captain O'Reilly take care of you now, I'm going up to see what the hell is going on, that sounded like a mine."

"It was," Craufurd gasped. "Christ, Van Daan, is it our men?"

"It can't be, it's too far off. That was over at the main breach." Paul hoped that he sounded convincing. He had no idea where the Light Division troops were, but given what Michael had just told him, he was worried that some of them might have been caught up in the explosion. There was no point in worrying Craufurd, however.

"I'm going. Michael, get General Craufurd and Major Napier settled and get them seen. There'll be a field surgeon around somewhere, but as soon as we can, I want Nan with him."

"I'll see to it, sir."

"Good man. Sir, I'll come back and let you know as soon as I can. Don't worry, if necessary I will take over the Light Division and get them out in one piece. It's not new to me, I did it all the time when Erskine was in charge. Get some rest and I'll send my wife to you as soon as I can."

Craufurd managed a smile. "Go," he said, and Paul ran, scrambling back up the glacis over the bodies of the dead and wounded towards the breach.

He found, to his immense relief that his brigade was following instructions and guarding the breach and ramparts. Wheeler came forward, saluting. "How is he?" he asked.

Paul shook his head. "Not good, Johnny. Thanks for sending Michael and the lads down. What the hell was that explosion?"

"I'm not sure yet, Manson just took off to find out."

"Are our lot all right?"

"Yes, they're where they're supposed to be. Some of Vandeleur's brigade didn't stop though, I'm a bit worried about them, they took off towards the great breach. I hope they're all right."

"Christ, why didn't he get them back?"

"He couldn't. He's down, sir, wounded."

"How did we do?"

"Not bad on the whole. My third company took a bad hit in the breach, I'll have lost a few there, but we were lucky today." Wheeler was studying his commander. "Do you need to get back to Craufurd, sir? I know what he means to you."

"I'll wait for a bit, see what Manson has to say. And I want to make sure my men behave themselves."

"They will, sir. What's the matter, you're limping?"

"Nothing much. Gashed my leg on one of those sword blades, it's not deep." Paul nodded. "Manson. And he doesn't look happy."

Captain Manson arrived and saluted, catching his breath. Paul studied him. Leo Manson was his favourite among his younger officers. He had been given command of the light company less than a year ago after a somewhat rocky introduction to army life. The command was prized in the 110th. It had been Paul's company before his promotions, and both Johnny Wheeler and Carl Swanson had led it for a while. Manson had been very young for the promotion, but he had grown into the role like a veteran. He had been briefly absent in England the previous year when his father had been ill and had returned in time to join the siege. To Paul it seemed that something had changed while he had been away, but he had not had time to investigate what had happened. All Manson had told him was that his father had made a better recovery than expected. Paul was aware that his junior had a difficult relationship with his father and had asked no further questions, merely welcomed him back.

He moved forward now to greet Manson.

17

"At ease, Captain. What's going on?"

"A mine, sir. Under the breach. It mostly affected General Picton's division, there are a lot of dead and wounded. General Mackinnon is dead. He was right above it. And some of our first and second brigades…they went through the town so fast they'd joined up with the third at the great breach. They were supposed to stay here and clear the ramparts…"

"Captain, breathe," Paul said gently. "Was it bad over there?"

Manson nodded. He was white-faced and looked sick. "Sir, some of them have literally been blown to bits."

"All right, lad. Listen to me, will you, I need your help. Sergeant Hammond, where's Captain Cartwright?"

"Up on the left rampart, sir, with his men."

"Get him down for me, Hammond. Leo, listen. General Craufurd is down and he's badly injured. We need a local billet for him, somewhere quiet and comfortable. If there's a room there for Major Napier as well he'd probably like that. General Craufurd is fond of the Major and at this point I'll do what I can to keep him happy. Davy is a genius at this. I want you to go with him, find the right place and get both of them in there. And then you need to find my wife and tell her and get her in to him. It might not be easy, he's the commander of the Light Division, the surgeons will be falling over themselves to pull him apart trying to save him."

Manson studied him. "Is General Craufurd dying, sir?"

"I think he might be. And if he is, Nan will know how to keep him comfortable. That's why I'm sending you, lad. They might try to keep her out. I'm relying on you to get her in. Don't worry about your company, Major Swanson will take over and get everybody out of here. Probably with a bottle under each arm but who gives a damn about that? I'd do it myself, but Vandeleur is down and Christ only knows where Barnard is and I've a suspicion if I don't step in, the Light Division is going to be rampaging through these streets getting badly castaway and shooting each other over the last jug of wine. What I ever did to deserve this is a mystery to me, but it seems to be my fate in life. Get going, will you? Tell my wife I'm safe and I love her, and I'll see her as soon as I can."

Manson saluted. "Yes, sir. Sorry. It's not like me. Just a bit…"

"Christ, Leo, if you weren't affected by what you just saw you've no business in my regiment. I'm sorry I'm giving you literally no time to get over it. But I need to be here which means General Craufurd needs you. You up to it?"

"Yes, sir."

"Good lad. Get Cartwright and get going."

He watched as Manson ran off and then turned to Johnny and found his friend smiling slightly. "What?"

"No wonder the premium for commissions in your regiment is going up and up, Colonel. What do you need me to do here?"

"Keep our lads here and keep them busy. Get Carter and a few reliable men down to do their share of looting and get the wine up to our lines and tell Sergeant Kelly to get the women cooking food, they'll be hungry. As soon as you can, get them out of here. I'm off to see if Picton needs help and to tell Wellington about Craufurd, he might not know. And then I'm going to take command of the rest of the Light

Division and kick them out of this town before they take it to pieces. If they really are running riot, I'll send for some help."

"Make sure you do, sir. There are plenty of wine cellars in this town, they'll be drunk within the hour. I'll make sure our men stay sober until I'm sure they're not needed.

"And that is why you are colonel-in-charge of the 112th and my second-in-command, Johnny. Once we've got them under control I want to get back to Craufurd. I've honestly got a bad feeling about this, and if he's…I want to be there. So you might get landed with the clear-up for a while."

Wheeler put his hand on Paul's shoulder. "That's my job, sir. Get going."

As he moved through the remainder of that long and difficult night, Paul thought about the two men he had left behind. Wheeler was in his late thirties and had suffered in the early part of his career at being left behind in the race for promotion due to lack of money. He had been a lieutenant when Paul joined and Paul's early memories of him were of a solid, steady presence at his side as he negotiated the choppy seas of army politics. He had risen steadily behind Paul who had the advantage of both money and talent to take him up through the ranks and Paul felt a passionate gratitude for Johnny's lack of resentment at the young upstart who had walked into his beloved company and taken over. In the early days Johnny had acted as his second-in-command, often without pay or recognition until last year when Wellington had unexpectedly held out the plum of colonel-in-charge of the 112th. He was second-in-command still, but of a brigade of the Light Division these days, a post most men envied, and he had never once let Paul down or given him a moment's concern.

Leo Manson was a different matter. He had seemed to Paul when he arrived with the 112th, to be a greenhorn of the worst kind, stuffed full of antiquated notions of discipline and snobbery by his elderly father who was a former cavalry colonel. Paul had found him stiff and awkward and impossible to work with. He had virtually given up on the young lieutenant until his wife, who was only slightly older than Manson, had taken an interest, and quietly worked to get him to look again at the boy. Paul had looked and recognised with considerable surprise that behind the wooden façade was a young man of considerable talent. Since then, he had rather adopted Manson and his patience had been repaid many times over. He wished he could have spent some time with Manson, who was clearly upset by what he had seen, but he trusted that giving him something useful to do would help the younger man to recover his usual equilibrium.

Paul found General Picton assessing his losses at the great breach. He had not always been on good terms with Thomas Picton although he had always admitted the man's undoubted talent as a soldier. Picton and Craufurd were bitter enemies and Paul knew that Picton saw him as one of Craufurd's supporters. He thought that Picton also envied his easy relationship with Lord Wellington.

In return, Paul had taken exception to Picton's attitude towards Anne. The death of her first husband and her subsequent marriage to Paul had taken place under a cloud of scandal, but most of the other officers had chosen to follow Lord Wellington's lead and ignore the gossip. Picton had been the exception, and for the first few months of their marriage, he had goaded Paul with a series of vulgar jokes and inappropriate remarks which had made Paul want to punch him. The gossip had died down and Picton had been perfectly polite to Anne in recent months. Superficially relations had improved, but Paul had not forgotten.

Picton was filthy, sporting a minor wound on his arm, and looking around in grim horror at the carnage wrought by the explosion of the French mine.

"Van Daan. Your men all right?"

"Mostly, sir. We've taken some losses, but it could have been a lot worse. But General Craufurd is bad, I think. My men are finding him a billet and I'll get my wife over to take care of him as soon as I can. Napier is wounded as well, gone off to the surgeon's tent. Sir, Captain Manson said…"

"Mackinnon? Yes, he's gone. Blown up, poor bastard. I don't see any grey facings in this mess, Van Daan."

"My lads are over at the lesser breach securing the ramparts along with about half of Barnard's brigade. Where is Barnard, I can't seem to find him."

"He's injured too, sent him off to get treated. I don't think it's too serious. The town is ours and the garrison have surrendered and been marched out. We're going to need to get a hold on the men, though, they're running wild in the streets searching for loot. It's worse in the main square, they're roaring drunk down there already and I'm told some of them threatened their officers when they tried to step in."

"Are the French definitely out?"

"Yes."

"Then I'll take the 110th down there and haul them out. Do you know where Lord Wellington is?"

"Speaking to the French commander but he'll be back soon."

"Does he know about Craufurd?"

"I've no idea, but I'll make sure he does, Colonel. I'll let him know you'll be playing policeman, and he can decide if he wants you to continue."

Paul bit back a vulgar response with an effort. Instead, he saluted, giving the General a look which made Picton blink in surprise and take a step backwards.

Paul spent the next three hours taking his battalion through the town, ruthlessly chasing out the drunken soldiers back to their lines to sober up. His own men were patient, knowing that when the time came, he would release them to take their share of wine and move back up to camp. Paul was realistic about his enlisted men. They were well-disciplined and fiercely loyal to him, but they lived and fought and marched in often appalling conditions. They were frequently not paid for months at a time and were far too often short of uniform, shoes and provisions.

Paul chose to draw a clear line between rule breaking which he considered acceptable and offences for which he would give no quarter and they understood him very well. He was very aware of the anger of a prosperous looking wine merchant as his men nonchalantly collected cases of wine from his stock and marched back to their tents. The Spaniard stood uttering insults and imprecations and Paul wondered if he had any idea how many of the men understood basic Spanish.

"Why don't you think of it as a tax of war, Señor," he suggested quietly and the man started at his command of the language and closed his mouth on the next insult. He stared at Paul warily and Paul gave a faint smile.

"If these men hadn't been through and cleared out the worst of the looters you'd have been a lot worse off. Are you married?"

"I am, sir."

"Daughters?"

"One. She is fifteen."

"Well concentrate on keeping her and your wife safe. I hate to be harsh but you're better off letting them walk off with a few boxes of wine with a wave and a smile than letting the rest of the army break into your house, drink themselves silly and get their hands on your women. The worst is over now and considering how welcome you've made the French you've done all right out of it. Get yourself indoors, lock your doors and keep quiet. They'll all be sober by morning and some of them will be down to buy the rest of your stock and be perfectly friendly. Storming a city is hell but they'll get over it."

The man was silent for a long moment. "I suppose you are right," he said finally. "Wine can be replaced. I will do as you suggest."

Paul moved away and was joined by Carl, who was masking a smile. "I bet you didn't tell him some of that looted wine is about to find its way into your tent, did you, sir?"

"It would be wasted on me tonight, Carl. Get back and get to your bed and well done today – all of you. Our lads were amazing. Normally I'd be up there sharing a drink and telling them so but it's your job tonight. I'm going to find Craufurd and hopefully my wife. Will you keep me updated on our dead and wounded?"

"I will. Paul – I am sorry."

"So am I, Carl."

Paul located the house which had been commandeered for General Craufurd and Major Napier after enquiring throughout the town. It was a small town house not far from the lesser breach, undamaged and well-furnished in a quiet location and Paul approved the choice. Captain David Cartwright of the 112th had formerly been with the quartermaster's department and his ability to locate good billets and local sources of supplies since he joined the regiment was already causing some resentment among other brigades and divisions who had managed to overlook his talent for years.

Paul approached the house. Two riflemen were on duty outside and they saluted him.

"Sir."

"At ease, Rifleman. Do you know if my wife has arrived?"

Before the man could reply, there was a sound from upstairs and Paul heard his wife's clear tones.

"Put that damned thing down and move away from him. How much blood do you think he needs to lose before he runs out entirely? It's not helping him. And has anybody done anything to relieve his pain yet? Get out of my way, for God's sake."

"Does that sound like your wife, sir?" the Rifleman enquired with a grin.

"It sounds exactly like her. How's he doing, do you know?"

"Not good, sir, but your lady has brightened him up. You should have heard the racket when they tried to tell her she couldn't come in. Black Bob nearly killed himself laughing."

Paul smiled and mounted the stairs. On the way he passed the surgeon coming down. The man glared at Paul. "I am going to complain to the Surgeon-General about that woman, sir," he said shortly.

21

Paul wondered if he was supposed to reply but the man clattered past, giving him no opportunity. He looked up as his wife appeared at the door at the top of the stairs.

"Paul! Are you all right? What have you done to your leg? You're limping."

Paul caught her to him, kissing her soundly. "A scratch only, bonny lass. Are you all right? Where's Will?"

"He's with Gwen Astor. She'll feed him if he needs it and if it gets too cold, Mary Scovell has found a billet down in the town, she says the women can take him down there."

Paul studied his wife in silence. He had been somewhat surprised, on the birth of William, that his young wife seemed keen to feed the child herself. Nothing in Anne's somewhat eccentric personality had suggested a strong maternal instinct but she had taken to motherhood with an ease which astonished him and so far she had resisted attempts to introduce a wet nurse although they had lined up a young widow who had lost her man at Fuentes de Oñoro who could feed Will at need. So far Mrs Astor's role had been minimal, but it was immediately clear to Paul that the needs of General Craufurd were to be placed ahead of his son.

Putting his arms about his wife he drew her close and held her for a long moment, savouring the feeling of her body in his arms. Anne van Daan was just twenty-two and they had been married for less than eighteen months although he had adored her almost from the time he first met her in Yorkshire when she was seventeen. He had already been married then, with two children and a career on the rise and there had been no place in his life for the slender dark daughter of a manufacturer who was trying to choose between half a dozen suitors in whom she had no interest at all.

Their romance had been brief and passionate and had left Paul with a weight of guilt. He had never been a particularly faithful husband, but he knew that his feelings for Anne were a betrayal of a different kind to his serene, pretty wife Rowena. He had never before fallen in love and he had fallen hard. Leaving Anne behind to go back to his wife and his regiment had broken his heart and the shock of finding her on a transport to Lisbon a year later married to his former lieutenant had shaken him to the core.

They had married just before the battle of Bussaco. Rowena had died in childbirth and Robert had been shot while trying to attack his young wife in a fit of jealousy and the rocky path to their present happiness had made Anne all the more precious to him. His wife's beauty made him the envy of Wellington's army but it was her unusual character that Paul had fallen in love with and he found himself constantly surprised by her.

"It is good to see you, girl of my heart. How is he?"

He read the answer in the sadness of her dark eyes. "Paul, I've examined him but there's honestly nothing I can do and neither of the other surgeons who have been in are any more optimistic. A musket ball went through his arm, broke his ribs, passed through his lung and as far as I can tell is wedged right against his spine. He's in agony. I've given him the strongest dose of laudanum I can, and I'll keep it topped up but there's nothing more I can do. I'm so sorry."

Paul nodded, a leaden feeling settling in his gut. Since his early days in the army, he had learned to adjust to working with a wide variety of officers, but there

22

were one or two he had become very close to, and Robert Craufurd, whom many of his officers loathed for his abrupt sarcastic manner and harsh discipline, was among his favourites.

"Can I see him?" he asked.

"Yes, he's been asking for you endlessly. Major-General Stewart is here. Come in."

Paul entered the room. "How are you, sir?"

"Better now," Craufurd croaked from the bed. "Come in, Colonel. Move over, Stewart and let the boy sit down."

Wellington's Adjutant-General stood up. "I'll be back very soon, Robert. Don't let him tire you out."

Paul smiled his thanks and seated himself. "Has she been giving you laudanum, sir?"

Craufurd nodded. "It helps," he said. "Hurts to talk."

"Don't try. Do you want me to tell you what's been going on?"

"Please," Craufurd said, and the relief in his tone was obvious. Paul looked over at Anne for permission and she gave a little smile.

"General Craufurd's aides have been here helping me with the nursing, but they were concerned that giving him news of the fighting might cause too much excitement for him."

Paul met Craufurd's exasperated dark eyes and despite his sadness, he wanted to laugh. "I'll be guided by you, girl of my heart, but I think not knowing is going to excite him a lot more."

"I don't think it can do any harm. Dr Craddock gave instructions that he was to be kept quiet, but I don't think he's coming back, so go ahead."

Paul gave an account of the remainder of the storming and the subsequent behaviour of the troops. Craufurd listened in silence. Finally he croaked:

"They still in there?"

"Very few, sir, I went through with the 110th and we've cleared them out. I've left Johnny Wheeler in charge down there. It was to be expected, I suppose, but it's almost under control."

"Losses?"

"Around 500 we think but there's not been time to do a proper roll call yet. I'm sorry to tell you that General Mackinnon is dead, sir."

"Sorry to hear that. Bet Picton's still alive."

Paul could not help smiling. "He was when I last saw him. He's surprisingly worried about you."

"Don't blame him. He's probably terrified Wellington will put you in charge."

"That would certainly stir him up. Mind, it would stir me up as well."

Craufurd coughed painfully. "One of these days you will be in charge and God help him then."

"Not just yet, sir."

"No. Don't know who he'll pick now, Paul, but whoever it is, he'll need you."

"I know, sir."

23

"Thanks for getting your lass up here. I've told Stewart to keep the other fools out, she'll take care of me. She told them off for bleeding me, says it does more harm than good. Is she needed elsewhere?"

"No, sir, she's all yours."

"Appreciate it. Won't need her for long but I'd rather she took care of me than anyone else." Craufurd's face twisted suddenly as a spasm of pain went through him and Paul felt his hand tighten. There were beads of sweat on his commander's face as he fought to stop himself crying out. Paul felt tears heavy behind his eyes and blinked them back determinedly, knowing that they would upset Craufurd. He sensed his wife approaching and made to move but Anne put her hand on his shoulder.

"Stay where you are, he wants you there. I've brought another chair for General Stewart when he gets back. Sir, drink this."

Craufurd struggled to drink the laudanum and managed to swallow. Anne bathed his face with a cool cloth and after a few minutes the General seemed to settle. He opened dark eyes and looked up at her. Anne smiled and moved away and Craufurd's gaze shifted to Paul.

"You did so bloody well for yourself, Colonel."

"I know, sir. I'm far luckier than I deserve."

"I need to see Lord Wellington."

"He knows, he'll be along soon."

"Good. Got things to say to him. Hope he's in a good mood."

"He won't be when he sees how you are, sir. None of us are."

"No." Craufurd winced, seeming silenced by the pain. His face was white and drawn and he seemed to Paul to have aged twenty years, all his fierce vitality drained out of him in his agony. "How's Napier?"

"I don't know, sir. Want me…"

"He's doing well, sir," Anne said. "He's in a room downstairs. They've had to amputate the arm but he's resting and seems quiet. I'm going to be taking care of him too so there will be no possibility of infection, I promise you."

"Glad to hear it," Craufurd said. "Ma'am, thank you for this. Your baby…"

"Is fine and being well taken care of. I need to get him weaned anyway, I'm taking him to Lisbon very soon, Paul's brother and his wife are sailing out to collect him. Sir, you need to rest for a bit if you want to be able to give Lord Wellington his orders."

Craufurd turned his head and tried to smile.

"Yes, ma'am."

Anne came forward. "You'll be more comfortable if we prop you up. Your lung is damaged and that's why you're struggling to breathe. I've got some more pillows here. Paul can help me lift you."

Paul looked past her. "Christ, where the hell did you get those from?" he asked as RSM Carter came forward with an armful of pillows and cushions.

"Looted them, sir. Third division thought we was bloody mad. They're looting churches and wine shops and we're stealing pillows. On orders, mind."

Paul glanced at Craufurd who was wheezing painfully. "Stop laughing, sir, you'll kill yourself. Bring them over here, Carter. I'll hold him, you and Nan get them in place."

They settled him eventually and Paul went to the door with Anne. "I'm going to find Wellington, bonny lass. I'm not sure how much he knows yet but the General wants to see him."

"I know. I'm staying here, Paul. I might send a message to Gwen to bring Will down at some point just for a quick feed, this is very uncomfortable. Maggie Bennett tells me I should be weaning him more gradually off me, but I'm not sure the rules take wartime into account. I'll need to do it before Lisbon, so I might as well start now."

"Does it bother you?" Paul asked quietly, studying her face.

"Yes," Anne said honestly. "I'll miss feeding him myself. But we've managed almost four months which is better than I might have expected. I need to let him go, Paul, or decide to go with him. And I can't do that because I'm not leaving you. He'll be all right in England with your family and we'll be back with him one day."

"We will, bonny lass. Nan – you know, don't you, how much it means to me having you with me? Please don't think I'm taking this lightly. It's going to upset me as well, letting him go but it's bound to be harder for you."

Anne smiled and reached up to touch his face. "Not as hard as it once was saying goodbye to you," she said. "I need to think of him, Paul, and he'll be better off in England. They'll take good care of him and he can get to know his brother and sisters as he's growing up. I'd like to meet them too, but I can wait."

"I hope it's not too long, girl of my heart. Thank you. Craufurd is right; I'm not sure I deserve it, but Christ I'm lucky." Paul glanced back into the room where Stewart had resumed his seat beside the bed. "Poor Robert. He'd give anything for his wife to be with him just now."

"I know. Go and see Lord Wellington."

"I will. Now that's a man who isn't in the least bothered about his wife not being out here. As long as mine is."

He dodged past her, ducking to avoid the playful slap she aimed and went in search of Lord Wellington.

Chapter Three

It took Robert Craufurd four agonising days to die of his wounds. Anne remained beside him, leaving only to eat and to feed her son. He received a stream of visitors, including Lord Wellington, but after the first twenty-four hours Anne would let nobody into the room whom she did not know to be a genuine friend of Craufurd. He had not been popular among his officers, but on his deathbed, many seemed to have forgotten their dislike of him. Anne preferred him to be kept quiet and to spend his time with people who cared. He had always been close to General Charles Stewart, who remained beside him along with Paul. Outside, men from his Light Division stood guard on the door with sombre faces.

Craufurd asked for frequent news of Major Napier and Anne was glad to be able to tell him truthfully that her other patient was doing well. He spoke a lot of his wife and family, and when he was able through the pain, he talked with both Stewart and Paul about past battles, almost choking with laughter as he reminisced about how furious he had been with Paul after the battle of the Coa.

On the fourth day for the first time Craufurd sank into a deep slumber and Anne, checking his pulse, suspected that the end was close. He had lasted far longer than Anne had expected and although she wished for his sake that his pain had been over faster, she knew that for both Paul and Stewart, having this time with him would help during their grief. It would help her too. Anne was deeply attached to the irascible Craufurd and would miss him badly.

While he slept Anne sent a message to Mrs Astor to bring Will to her. Her milk was still coming through and although he was feeding very happily with Gwen, whose own daughter was just a month older than him, Anne welcomed the opportunity to relieve her swollen painful breasts. She welcomed even more, the chance to feed him just a few more times. He had already become part of her, the part she had never known was missing until she had held him for the first time, and the thought of handing him over to strangers was more painful than she was prepared to admit to Paul. If he had been Paul's only child, she would have sent him instead to Harriet, the stepmother who had raised her and her brothers and sister and whom she adored. But Paul had three older children and Anne wanted Will to grow up with them, to see them as his brother and sisters from the start. She needed to trust that her unknown brother and sister-in-law would do a good enough job with her son until she and Paul could come home and be with them.

When Will had finished feeding, Anne sat holding him close, loving the warmth of him in her arms. Alone with him, she shed tears both for Craufurd and for the coming parting from her son. She had not realised Craufurd was awake until he gave a painful cough, opened his eyes and regarded her. "The baby?" he said quietly.

"Yes, sir, I'm sorry. He was hungry. His nurse is on her way to take him now he's sleeping."

"No. I'm glad. May I see him?"

Anne got up and brought William closer, her eyes bright with tears. Craufurd touched the child's face very gently. "He's like his father."

"He is. Apart from the hair."

"You're sending him home?"

"Very soon, sir. I'll miss him, but it's the right thing to do."

"Yes. I wish my wife were here."

"So do I, sir."

"The children are so young. They won't remember me well."

"They will, sir. You're fairly memorable. And your friends will tell them about you."

"Yes. Ma'am, will you...?"

"I'll write to them myself, I promise you, and I'll visit them when I'm back in England. And I'm going to tell them all the stories about you that nobody will ever put in the newspapers when they're busy writing about your glorious achievements."

"Thank you." Craufurd smiled tiredly. "Funny, it hurts less now."

"It often does, sir."

"Won't be long, you think?"

"No, sir."

"Better get Stewart and your man back in here then. Are the others still out there?"

"A few officers, sir."

"Let them come in for a short time." Craufurd gave a twisted smile. "Never been this popular with my officers before."

"You have with your men, sir."

"Yes, I've that in common with Colonel van Daan. He's better with his officers, mind. Or luckier." Craufurd gave another distressing cough. "I've made my will. Everything's shared out. But will you go to my pack? There's a black velvet bag in the front pocket. Bring it here, will you?"

Anne rose and carefully lay the sleeping baby on the end of his bed, a pillow on either side. Going to the pack she withdrew the bag and brought it to him. He fumbled with the contents, made clumsy by pain and weakness.

"Here, take this. Give it to him when I've gone. I don't want to make a big production of it, he'll be upset enough."

Startled Anne took the heavy signet ring and looked at the inscription then up at him. "Sir, you can't..."

"Everything else goes to my boys and my other friends. This is new, Wellington got it for me after Fuentes d'Onoro. He's like me, he doesn't like medals.

27

He had it inscribed, just the date, the place and mine and his initials. I value this, it's the closest that awkward bastard will ever get to saying, 'well done'. I told him the other day I wanted Van Daan to have this, and he approves." The dark eyes met Anne's. "I couldn't have done it that day without your man, he's the calmest battle commander I've ever known. He earned this."

"Thank you." Anne blinked determinedly. "I notice you don't care about making me cry, you terrible man."

"You're stronger than he is," Craufurd said quietly. "All women are. Is he here?"

She nodded. "Downstairs with General Stewart and the others."

"Send them up then. But give him that in private later."

"I will." Anne took his hand and raised it to her lips, not attempting to hide her tears. "It's been such an honour, sir. I'll always remember you at my first headquarters party after we married. You took me on your arm around that room and dared anybody to cut me. And not one did."

Craufurd managed the ghost of a smile. "Just as well, I'd have punched them. Look after him, my dear."

Anne bent to kiss him and then went to the stairs to call his friends. Quietly she effaced herself and let them gather around the bed. Craufurd was exhausted and Anne wanted to chase them out, but she knew it would be his last opportunity to say what he wanted to say. Some of the officers were still hopeful, trying to convince themselves that his lack of pain was a sign of recovery, but looking at her husband's white, set face Anne knew that he, at least, understood.

Finally it was quiet, and Anne handed Will over to his nurse and went back to the room. Craufurd had drifted into a peaceful slumber and the others wandered out in twos and threes to wait downstairs and let him sleep. Only Stewart and Paul remained, one either side of the bed. Anne seated herself on a low stool and waited with them, listening to the slow laboured breathing which was slowing further still.

The end came in the early hours. The two men had been so quiet for so long that Anne wondered if they had fallen asleep. She sat very still, waiting to be sure and then she heard Stewart give a sob and knew that he was awake. He bent forward and kissed Craufurd's forehead then got up. Anne rose and came forward, looking at Paul. His eyes were on Craufurd's face and he did not look round. Anne reached to feel for a pulse and as she had expected, found none.

"Ma'am – I must tell the others," Stewart said.

"Give yourself a moment," Anne said gently.

"Will you...?"

"I'll make sure he's taken care of, sir, I promise you. And Captain Manson is outside, he can take the news to Lord Wellington."

"Thank you, ma'am. You've been..." Stewart took her hand and unexpectedly kissed it. "I've had my doubts about what you do, ma'am, and he never did. He never wavered in his support of you and after today I know why. You made this bearable for him and for all of us. Thank you. God help any surgeon who comes whining to me about you after this."

"Most of them don't, any more, sir. And I couldn't do anything for him, I just wanted to be here. He was my friend too."

She watched him leave then turned with a sense of dread to Paul. He was still sitting beside the bed holding Craufurd's hand.

"It always surprises me how cold they get, so quickly," he said.

Anne stroked his fair head. "Yes. Although with the weather out there you'd be hard put to distinguish between my hands and his right now."

Paul turned quickly and looked up at her. "Oh love, thank you," he said softly. "I couldn't have got through this without you. And it meant so much to him to have you here."

"I wouldn't have left if they'd tried to throw me out," Anne said.

"I know. But you're freezing and you look exhausted. You've barely eaten in four days."

"I've not been that hungry, and I've slept when he did. But I'm ready to go now."

Paul stood up and took her into his arms. Over her head he saw Leo Manson in the doorway.

"Some of the lads from the Rifles want to come up and get him ready, ma'am. They'll take over from here. I'm riding over to Lord Wellington. Jenson is downstairs with your horses."

"Thank you, Leo," Paul said quietly. "I can't believe you're still here, but I'm so grateful."

He led Anne downstairs and past the huddle of distraught men out to the horses. It was not far up to the lines, the night cold and clear and as they approached, he could smell fires and food and hear the murmur of voices as his regiment settled for the night. A few of them still sat outside their tents wrapped in blankets and cloaks and they called subdued greetings, knowing what their commander's return must mean. By morning the news would have spread through the lines.

"They're going to bury him in the breach," Paul said.

"I know. It's what he'd have wanted."

"When this bloody war is over I'm going to come back here and make sure there's a proper memorial for him. And I'm going back to that quiet hillside between Viseu and Lisbon to put one up for Rowena and my lads there as well."

Anne felt fresh tears welling up. Paul talked often and freely of Rowena, but he seldom mentioned the pain of her death. She realised it was a sign of how hard he was taking the loss of his General that it should have taken him back to his first wife's death.

They sat beside the fire. Sergeant Kelly had kept it burning brightly for them and must have been on the watch because he appeared with bowls of stew and bread and bullied Anne into eating when she might not have bothered. As they sat eating in silence a figure materialised out of the dark and Sergeant-Major Carter placed an opened bottle of wine beside Paul and set out cups. Paul watched him pour and managed a smile.

"Should I ask where this came from, Carter?"

"Ask away, sir, I've no idea. It's bloody good, mind. Dawson and Cooper turned up with it."

"Is everybody out now?"

"Yes, sir, no problems. Our lads were very good, save the odd crate of wine or two, and I reckon we all earned that. Picton's boys kicked off a bit, but Major Swanson and Colonel Wheeler took our lads back through and cracked a few heads and they soon shifted. I'm sorry about General Craufurd, sir. Can't imagine the Light Division without him."

"None of us can. Thanks for this, Carter."

"You're welcome, sir. Ma'am, Gwen said to tell you she's taken William down to Mrs Scovell's billet in the town, it's warmer for him there. She said he's all right feeding with her."

Anne nodded a little sadly. "It needed to be done," she said. "I'd not planned on weaning him off me until the journey south, but I seem to have mostly done it this week."

"I'm sorry, lass."

"No, it's fine. Paul, I've something to give you."

Carter rose. "I'm off to bed. Night, sir. Ma'am."

When he had gone Paul smiled at his wife. "I'm always slightly bewildered by Carter's tact. He shows no sign of it in normal life, and yet it appears when needed without fail. What is it, girl of my heart?"

"General Craufurd gave this to me for you. With Lord Wellington's approval."

Anne handed him the ring and watched as he examined the inscription in the firelight. It broke through his exhausted calm as she had known it would and he stood abruptly and walked into the tent. Anne rose and saw the bulky figure of the Irish mess Sergeant.

"I'll see to everything, ma'am. Take care of him."

Anne managed a grateful smile and followed Paul. He was sitting on the edge of their mattress, the ring in his hand and his head down. Anne knelt and took him into her arms, feeling the wet of his tears on her cheek. "This is why he wouldn't give it to you himself," she said, and he nodded, unable to speak. She held him as he cried, and cried with him, and it was some time before he recovered himself enough to get into bed. The freezing weather made it impractical to undress fully so she pulled on her velvet robe and went into his arms feeling the soft wool of his comfortable camp shirt and breeches. He cupped her face with his hand and kissed her long and hard and she felt the unfamiliar ring on his finger and recognised that it would soon become a familiar part of his touch.

"Nan, I love you."

"I love you too, Paul. This has been horrible."

"It has. But you've made it bearable. More than ever now, I want Will out of here, where it's safe. I'm guessing my brother is halfway to Lisbon by now. Once the funeral is over, we'll make arrangements. I wish I could come with you. Come back soon, girl of my heart."

"You know I will."

"I am so selfish for keeping you here."

"You'd have a hard job getting me to stay away, Colonel. This is where I belong."

"I keep hearing Craufurd's voice in my head. Yelling, mostly. He was a bloody-minded, bad tempered bastard. Christ, I'm going to miss him."

"I know you are, Paul."

Paul lay still for a moment, then unexpectedly shifted onto his elbow and leaned over her. He kissed her again, harder and with a new urgency. For a moment, Anne wondered if she was really too tired, but she sensed his sudden need, and reached up to hold him closer.

"Nan, I really want you."

"I'm here," Anne said gently. She sat up and pulled her robe over her head and he seemed to hesitate.

"You'll freeze."

"Keep me warm then," Anne said, and he pulled her down, harder than usual. Anne caught his mood quickly and lay back letting him set the tone, her body yielding and compliant under him, her eyes on his as he moved over her. There was none of his usual gentle finesse tonight and she responded surprisingly quickly to the hard urgency of his body beating into her so that her climax combined pleasure with pain and she lay beneath him when he was done feeling aftershocks shivering through her, and aware that both her arms hurt where he had held them.

"Paul," she said gently and he shifted, leaned on his elbow and looked down at her. He studied her face in the lamplight and his eyes widened.

"Christ, Nan, I'm sorry. Are you all right?"

"Of course I am."

"You're bloody not, I've hurt you." He touched her mouth gently and she realised she could taste blood. "God knows what that was about, but I am sorry."

"Oh love, it's fine. After the week you've had…and I can't say it didn't feel good."

Paul kissed her, feather-light. "You say that now, but when you feel those bruises in the morning, you'll be kicking me. Thank God it's winter and you're in long sleeves or my officers would bloody crucify me, you're going to look like I've beaten you, I can see my own finger marks on your arms. I'm never that rough with you. I just lost control for a minute. I'm so sorry, Nan."

Anne reached up to caress his face. "Paul, calm down, it's not as if you've beaten me. I'm not that fragile."

Paul kissed her again. "You look it just now, girl of my heart. Seriously, did I hurt you?"

"No, love, I promise." Despite the misery of the day Anne could not help laughing at his stricken expression. "Although you are a fraud. I thought you brought me back here to tuck me into bed and make a fuss of me after my long hours this week."

"So did I. It turned out I had something else in mind, but I could have been a bit gentler about it." Paul drew her close into his arms. "If I ever do that again, hit me with something."

"What do you suggest?"

"You'll come up with something, you're very imaginative."

"If I weren't so tired, I'd show you just how imaginative I can be."

Paul was laughing properly now, the shadow gone from his eyes. "I will hold you to that when we both have the energy, lady mine."

"Lady?" Anne said provocatively and he kissed her again, harder.

"You do a very good impersonation of it, Mrs van Daan, but I'm not fooled. After a lot of hours spent in bed with you, I'm aware that there's a whole host of ways in which you're not ladylike. And most of them feel pretty damned good."

"Any pretensions you had towards being a gentleman in bed, love, went out the door earlier."

"I will make it up to you, I promise."

"See that you do, Colonel."

"Let me reach your robe, you're going to freeze like that."

He helped her on with it and lay holding her, stroking her dark hair. Anne shifted to look at him. "Are you all right?"

"Yes. I always am when I'm with you, no matter how awful the day has been. I was just thinking that you reminded me just now of that seventeen-year-old girl I kissed in a barn in Yorkshire a few years ago."

"Four years now, Paul. Almost to the week, as a matter of fact."

"Have you been keeping track? I should buy you an anniversary gift. You wouldn't know it looking at you tonight. There is something very attractive about that wide-eyed vulnerability I occasionally see in you, especially since you don't show it to anybody else. You're so lovely, Nan. Sometimes I look at you and I just can't believe you're mine."

"Always and forever, Paul."

She knew it would make him smile. He had first said the words to her as they parted after the retreat from Talavera, he to return to his wife, she to go back to her brutal husband. Neither of them had expected that they would one day be together, and the words back then had brought tears to her eyes. They had said them often since, a validation of the constancy of their feelings for each other throughout all the difficulties and sadness of the past few years.

"Always. Thank you…just for being here with me. Christ, when I think of poor Craufurd, dying out here with his wife and children so far away…"

They lay quietly together in the cold, still air of the night until finally Anne felt him relax into sleep.

***

Leo Manson emerged into the freezing dawn to find the camp grudgingly stirring around him. A number of the officers were congregated around a big fire and there was an appetising smell from the pot suspended over it. A second fire with a bracket over it was heating tea, and as Manson approached, Keren Trenlow got up and went to get a tin cup and fill it for him.

Manson took the cup with a tired smile. He could hear the murmur of voices from his commander's tent. "Is the Colonel all right?" he asked softly. "I didn't see him when I got back last night. Well, this morning really."

"He'll be all right," Johnny said. "Thanks for what you did, Captain, it meant a lot to him. "I've got men out digging graves. It's a hell of a job in this weather, but they're managing. I'll call him when we're ready to bury them, not before. I'm not sure he's slept much."

"He's always like that when he's upset," Carl said, holding out his cup for a refill.

"Always," Johnny said with feeling. "I'm trying to remember what he used to do with it before he had her."

"You've got a short memory, Colonel," Major Gervase Clevedon said affably. "He used to take it out on us."

"What about his first wife?" Manson asked curiously.

"Rowena? No. It was his job to take care of Rowena not the other way around," Johnny said. "She was a lovely woman, mind, I was very fond of her. But she didn't cope well with him when he was in this mood."

"He never allowed her to try," Carl said, wrapping his hands around the cup. "He used to stay out of her way if he was upset or angry. He was so protective of her, you'd have thought she was made of porcelain. I always wondered if they'd have done better if he'd trusted her more."

Johnny glanced towards the tent hearing the unmistakable sound of Anne's laugh, soft and intimate. After a moment they heard Paul laugh as well. Manson felt a twinge of awkwardness, as though he was eavesdropping, but it did not seem to worry the other men, both of whom smiled.

"I honestly don't know how she does it," Johnny said, keeping his voice low. "She's been up for four days looking after Craufurd, feeding and then weaning that baby in between, she's barely eaten or slept in the meantime and now she's in there, probably awake half the night again making him feel better."

"She loves him, Johnny," Gervase said. "I think she'd do pretty much anything for him."

"I know, Gervase, but even so, she's so young. When he first married her, I used to worry about them. She was so different, so unconventional. I used to think she'd be too much of a handful, that she'd be a distraction for him. Now I realise that all I can think of is I hope she doesn't stay in Lisbon too long."

There was a muted laugh around the campfire. "He'll have to come out of there some time today," Manson said. "Lord Wellington wants to see him."

"How is his Lordship doing, Captain. You saw him last night, didn't you?"

"Briefly. He thanked me for bringing the news, that was all. I spoke briefly to Somerset though, and he says his Lordship isn't doing that well. He's lost Mackinnon and Craufurd in one battle and no matter how much they used to argue, he's going to miss Craufurd."

"I wonder who he'll choose to take over," Gervase said.

"I've a suspicion that whoever gets command of the Light Division, some of Craufurd's actual duties are going to fall to the Colonel," Carl said soberly.

"Along with the job of getting yelled at a lot until Wellington feels better."

"That's already his job."

They sat quietly, listening to the sound of the camp awakening around them. After a while, Paul emerged from the tent, his arm about his wife. She was dressed warmly in a dark woollen gown with a fur lined pelisse that Manson remembered Paul had bought her last winter in Lisbon, and the hardy black boots that she had made especially for her by Lord Wellington's boot-maker in London. She was unusually pale and looked tired and heavy-eyed, but she smiled readily and joined the officers who were congregating around the fire in search of breakfast.

"Any news of the losses?" Paul asked, accepting tea.

"Just over five hundred, we think," Johnny said. "Our brigade did surprisingly well. Only two dead, about thirty wounded but a lot of those are minor injuries. It's a good thing the casualties weren't worse mind, given that you had to desert the hospital wards this week, ma'am."

"I'd a good excuse," Anne said, taking Paul's hand.

"What made me laugh is that Norris tells me that the surgeons have been screaming for you all week. They've had to communicate with the French wounded without your translation skills and there has been nobody to sew up a particularly awkward wound or generally hold their hands when it all gets too difficult."

Anne laughed aloud. "That isn't fair, Johnny, most of the surgeons are very skilled and very dedicated. Though they could do with more French speakers, I admit."

"Serves them right," Paul said unsympathetically. "They take you for granted. Half of them moan that you're unqualified and a female and shouldn't be doing this in the first place and then when they need help they start calling for you. Perhaps this will make them appreciate you a bit more."

"Craufurd's surgeon complained about you, ma'am," Carl said, accepting food with a smile at Teresa. "He went to Dr Franck apparently."

"I bet that was funny," Paul said.

"Funnier than you think. Apparently, Lord Wellington heard about it and then Dr Craddock also heard about it from Lord Wellington. Along with a large number of other people in the vicinity."

"Well that should stop Craddock lifting his head above the parapet for a while," Paul said.

Johnny was laughing. "Sir, are you aware your wife is struggling to eat with her left hand because you won't let go of her right?"

Paul looked around, surprised, and laughed, releasing her. "Sorry, lass. I'm a bit clingy this morning."

"That's all right, Colonel, you're allowed to be. Are you riding up to see Lord Wellington?"

"Yes. Nan, why don't you go down and see if you can find a billet in town near to Mary Scovell. You should..."

"Already done, sir," Captain Cartwright said promptly. "A couple of houses away. There's a room for you and Mrs van Daan and one downstairs where we've put Mrs Astor with the children. I can help them move down once we're done with the burials."

Paul studied him. "Davy, you have been with my brigade less than a year and I literally can't remember what we did without you. Thank you."

They finished their food, lingering around the fire. It was cold enough to see their breath in the air, and with no orders today, Manson suspected that most of his men would spend their time in their tents or foraging for more firewood. He reminded himself to issue instructions about not taking it from the locals. Eventually Paul got reluctantly to his feet.

"I should get going, before he sends a rude message. Captain Manson, why don't you ride up with me, we'll be back in time for the burials. And after that, I am going to turn my attention to Major Brodie."

"Major Brodie, sir?" Manson said, suddenly alert. "Do you know him personally?"

He realised immediately that he had responded too quickly. Blue eyes surveyed him with considerable interest.

"Well it's evident that you do, Captain. You can tell me all about him on the way. Go and get settled, Nan, I'll be down to collect you for the burials."

***

Paul waited until he and Manson had ridden away from the lines and were heading towards the house where Wellington had set up his headquarters before raising the subject of Major Brodie. He could sense that Manson was frantically trying to decide what to tell him, which probably meant there was more to tell than Ensign Jackman's card debts. Paul gave him time to stew for a while, then said:

"Well, Captain Manson?"

"Sir?"

"Oh don't sound so bloody innocent. Something is going on in my brigade that I don't know about. Have you any idea how much I dislike that?"

"A fair bit, I'd guess, sir."

Paul could not help laughing. "You're a natural clown, Captain. I do enjoy it, but you have been found out. Cut line and tell me, I don't want to have to beat it out of you."

Manson shot him a sideways glance and grinned. "Sorry, sir. It's just…can I speak to you in confidence, sir?"

"Are you in trouble, Leo?"

"Not me, sir. That's why it needs to be in confidence."

Paul studied him thoughtfully. "I can't make a promise, Leo, without knowing what it is, because I intend to deal with Brodie. But I will promise not to come down too hard on whichever hapless junior officer you're trying to protect. Do I take it that Mr Jackman is not the only victim of the rapacious Major Brodie?"

"It's Davy Lloyd, sir. He's in a bit of trouble financially."

"Is he?" Paul was surprised. "How? I know he struggled with the cavalry; it's why he sold out and bought into us. I thought he'd settled well, he's been paying his mess dues on time. What is it, cards?"

"No, sir, Davy isn't much of a card player. Have you met Major Brodie, sir?"

Paul thought. "I've exchanged a few words occasionally, I think. Wasn't he in India for a long time? It was after my time there, but I think we spoke about it at some ghastly reception. Tell me about him."

"He's something of a swordsman. I've heard he's been involved in several duels, and killed a man."

"Not under Wellington he hasn't or he'd be out," Paul said grimly. "Go on."

"He's a card player, but that's not how he makes most of his money. It's a practice of his to get involved in fencing bouts with other officers and gamble on the

35

results. He makes a tidy sum of money out of it, I believe. I've asked around, it seems that a couple of junior officers have sold out to pay their debts to him after losing."

"That's what Barnard told me. Why in God's name do they agree to fight him if they can't afford to lose?"

"Because he'll put it about that they're cowards if they don't," Manson said. He saw Paul's face and laughed aloud. "Don't look like that, sir, I don't understand it either. If somebody wants to question my courage, he can do it on the battlefield. But that's not the attitude among most of the officers."

"No, I know," Paul said in exasperated tones. "It's one of the things that drives me mad about some of our officers, you'd think they were gallant amateurs rather than professional soldiers and they take their honour and reputation so damned seriously."

"It's a gentleman's profession, sir," Manson said ironically. "Have you ever been challenged?"

"Not by anybody with the nerve to follow it through," Paul said grimly. "The closest I ever came was Nan's first husband. He insulted her reputation in front of the entire headquarters mess in Viseu, and then challenged me to a duel. I'm afraid I accepted. I lost my temper. In fact, I came close to killing him on the spot but that's because I'd only just discovered how he'd been treating her for the past two years."

"I think he had a lucky escape, sir. Why didn't you fight him?"

"He ran for it. He came while I was at the Coa and tried to murder her. Johnny Wheeler walked in on it and shot him dead. I'm sure you've heard the story. But with that exception, I've stayed away from pointless challenges. Fencing is a sport I enjoy but whether I'm good at it or not has nothing to do with my courage on a battlefield. I assume young Lloyd agreed to a bout with Major Brodie and lost? What a young idiot. Why, for God's sake?"

"I'm not sure the Major gave him a lot of choice, sir." Manson sounded more relaxed now that he had decided to tell the story. "He challenged him at headquarters in front of a lot of other people."

"Serves him right for going there. Very mixed company at the headquarters mess. Did he pay up?"

"Yes, but he sold practically everything he owns to do it. He's broke, sir."

"He still paid his last mess bill, Leo."

Manson was silent and Paul knew that he had guessed correctly. "I'll reimburse you," he said quietly.

"You can't, sir, it wouldn't be fair. I offered, he's a friend."

"Then you can win it back from me at cards. As long as you don't expect me to actually play cards, you know how I hate it."

Manson laughed aloud. "Haven't you just blasted poor Jackman for gambling with a senior officer, sir?"

"Yes, but I'm not sure who you think is going to come after me if I break my own rules."

"Fair point. I didn't know Jackman was in debt to him as well, sir, not until just before the battle. I found out he'd volunteered for the Forlorn Hope and it made no sense to me, Jackman's a very sensible lad, he's not the death or glory type. So I asked around."

Paul, who had asked Carl to make his own enquiries during the long hours of Craufurd's passing, surveyed Manson with grim amusement.

"You asked around? Leo, I have already checked these facts and I'm told you lined up the junior officers of three companies and gave them the bollocking of a lifetime until one of them cracked and told you what happened."

Manson looked startled, then gave a sheepish grin. "Sorry, sir."

"Don't be, it's music to my ears. So what don't I know?"

"Giles Heron."

"What is this, some kind of effort to bankrupt my half my regiment?" Paul said explosively. "What's the matter with this bloody Scotsman?"

"Broke again I imagine, sir. He does like cards, and he has a very expensive looking Portuguese mistress in tow."

"Well, he's not fucking paying for her by fleecing my junior officers, I'd rather they paid their mess bills and attended to their duties. What happened with Heron?"

"That might have been my fault, I'm afraid, sir."

Paul was surprised. "What happened Captain Manson?"

"Lord Wellington held one of his parades, just before the bombardment started. You weren't there."

"Wasn't I? Oh no, I remember, it was my turn to sit on the bench at the General Court Martial," Paul said. "I loathe that duty. And surprisingly, they don't seem to like me either."

"Probably not, sir. Lieutenant Smith told me that he overheard Major-General Picton saying that he would refuse to serve with you again. Apart from the incessant arguments about either the verdict or the sentence, he said you kept asking impertinent questions about how he would have dealt with each offence during his time as Governor of Trinidad. Did you actually do that, sir, or was Smith exaggerating?"

"Harry Smith always exaggerates, Captain."

Manson said nothing very eloquently. After a moment, Paul broke into laughter. "I did mention it once or twice. Maybe three times. Craufurd was there to give evidence in one of the cases and he sent me a note saying if I didn't stop it, he'd take my brigade off me, so I very reluctantly desisted. It was a shame, I'd got some very good remarks lined up."

Manson stared at him in appalled amusement. "I've no idea how you get away with it, sir."

"It's a very fine line. Occasionally I trip over it. Tell me what you did to Major Brodie, Leo, so that I can judge how well you're doing with that line yourself."

Manson smiled, acknowledging the hit.

"Major Brodie's man took part in the parade. Musket drill, and some fairly complicated short order drilling. It looked impressive, I must say. I'll just bet he flogs the hell out of those men. They don't jump when he says jump, they flinch."

Paul felt the beginnings of enlightenment. He knew how Manson felt about flogging. "What did you do, Captain?"

"I didn't do a thing, sir, I swear it. Colonel Wheeler was in charge of the 112th and Major Swanson was leading out the 110th. And I think you'll find it was Captain

O'Reilly's idea to replicate exactly the drill just performed by the Highlanders. Only we did it rather better."

Paul started to laugh. "Oh no. The last time O'Reilly did that, we were in Dublin and he was still a sergeant. He ended up flogged and demoted. Thank God he's got a commission now. This is very entertaining, Captain, but you're avoiding telling me how you managed to upset Major Brodie."

"I was standing near him afterwards. Lord Wellington stopped and asked where you were. He said some very complimentary things about the 110th. Colonel Wheeler had gone by then, so the General spoke to me and asked me to pass on his compliments about the 112th. He didn't say a word about Brodie's men. I'd just been sitting with Lloyd helping him to work out what he could sell to pay his debt and how much he could manage to live on, so I was in a bad mood. When the headquarters party had moved on, I made a few remarks to the others about how much easier it was to train men who were fit to fight and not terrified of their officers."

"Ah. Well within earshot of Major Brodie?"

"Yes, sir. Sorry."

"What did he do?"

"He was fairly rude. I was offensively civil."

"You're very good at that."

"I've practiced, sir. He asked if I fenced, I said I did. He offered to show me what a real swordsman could do, for a gentleman's wager once the siege was over."

"What did you say, Leo?"

"I said I'd be happy to engage in a friendly bout but that I'd no money to bet on it and wasn't prepared to bankrupt myself trying."

Paul gave a shout of laughter. "Well done," he said. "Although I'm guessing it didn't go well with him."

"No. He spent a while trying to goad me, and I remained very polite. I quite enjoyed myself, really. He called me a coward and a peasant and made some very rude remarks about the type of officers now present in the army. I agreed with him on that point, but luckily he doesn't get irony."

Paul had tears of laughter in his eyes. "I can't wait to tell my wife this story. So what happened with Heron."

"I left eventually, I was getting bored. I blame myself, sir, I should have realised he'd start on one of the others. I believe he insulted the entire regiment from you downwards. I was told he even mentioned your wife."

"Did he? He's braver than I thought, then."

"Heron is a good man, sir, but I think the provocation was pretty severe. He cracked and agreed to fight Brodie. He's not as hard up as either Lloyd or me, but he doesn't need to be handing over what he has to that bastard. I've tried talking to him, told him to pull out. There's nothing in writing and there's no debt to pay if the bout doesn't take place. But he feels honour bound to go through with it." Manson hesitated. "To be honest, the thing that worries me most is not the money, it's that Heron will get hurt. Brodie was really pissed off, and Heron is angry too. He's got a bit of a temper and he's a borderer, they're all stuffed full of notions of honour. It might go too far."

38

"Yes, I can see that. Wellington would be furious if he knew, he wants his officers to be focused on the bloody French not fucking about with duels and fencing bouts. Leo, thank you for being honest with me. I hope you don't feel your honour is impugned in any way?"

Manson hesitated. "Sir, when Heron told me what he'd said, I was tempted," he said. "I could have gone back to him and said I'd changed my mind and I'd take his bet."

"What stopped you?"

"If I lose, I can't pay, and that could cost me my commission. It's not worth that. But more to the point, if I win, I put a target on myself and I suspect he's a vindictive bastard. I'm still only a captain and a very junior one in terms of experience and length of service. I've not long got rid of Captain Longford; I don't need another one." He shook his head wryly. "I don't know what it is about me, must be the look on my face."

Paul regarded his junior with amused affection. "It's not your face, Leo, it's what comes out of your mouth," he explained helpfully. "Don't worry about it. In my opinion it takes courage to refuse to put yourself in an untenable position because of some outdated ideas about honour. I'm very proud of you. Don't say anything to Heron. You've behaved like a good officer and a good friend. I'll take over."

"Is he in trouble, sir?"

"No. I'm going to thank him for his defence of his regiment and my wife and gently remind him of my rules on duelling, which is what this is, however Brodie tries to dress it up. Let me have the total you lent to Lloyd. We'll have a quiet evening of completely failing to play cards next week. I've got a very nice French and you can fill me in on all the gossip from the mess that I've missed. I could do with some light relief after this hell hole and losing Craufurd."

"Thank you, sir. I'd enjoy that."

"Oh, one more thing, Captain. Do you happen to know what he said about my wife?"

His junior regarded him warily. "Yes, sir. But is it a good idea for me to tell you?"

"It's an excellent idea, Captain, because it gives me the excuse I need."

"Ah, I see. Won't she mind?"

"She'll definitely mind that some arsehole is making free with her good name in public, Captain. I suppose I could send her after him instead of going myself, but that would be a bit hard on him."

Manson grinned though Paul thought he still looked uncomfortable.

"I believe he remarked that the only difference between your wife and his Portuguese mistress was that your whore had somehow managed to get you to put a ring on her finger, which he couldn't understand, given that you'd been getting what you wanted out of her for years."

Paul felt a rush of pure fury coursing through his body. He looked straight ahead of him, breathing deeply until he thought he could manage to speak normally. "Thank you, Captain, that was admirably clear. It's probably just as well that I was on that board after all."

"I'm sorry, sir. I didn't even want to repeat it. As I said, I don't wholly blame Heron. He did try to be sensible." Manson studied his commander. "Are you actually going to challenge him?"

"Not to a duel. To a nice friendly bout of swordplay during which I intend to kick his Scottish arse. Trust me he won't be so keen on trying to fleece my junior officers by the time I've finished with him. Come on, let's go and see Lord Wellington. They're burying Craufurd tomorrow and I rather think I'm going to be expected to play some sort of part, which would have made that old buzzard laugh himself silly."

Manson glanced sideways. "I am sorry, sir," he said gently, and Paul looked back at him, his rage at Brodie washed away in sudden appreciation at Manson's genuine understanding.

"Thank you. There are only a few people in life who are genuinely indispensable to me, Captain Manson. A fairly select group, but you are in it. Don't get yourself killed, will you? You're a mad bugger in a battle."

"I learned that from my commanding officer, sir."

Paul laughed aloud. "Fair point. I'm guessing you're not ready to tell me yet what happened with your father?"

"Not yet, sir."

"When you're ready. But talk to somebody, lad. God only knows why, but it does help."

Chapter Four

General Robert Craufurd was laid to rest with full honours in the breach where he had died. Paul had been appointed one of the chief mourners along with General Charles Stewart and Craufurd's ADC. The funeral passed in a blur for Paul. He would have preferred to walk with Anne and his own men, but he knew Craufurd would have wanted him to play his part. The early storms of their friendship had settled, over the past months of Paul's new command, into something deeper and more lasting and although he would have been happier mourning his General among his men it felt right that he should make some public display of respect

Through the day he was assailed by flashes of memory of their years of service, some of them angry and acrimonious and many of them filled with laughter and comradeship. Above all he could remember Craufurd approaching him at the first headquarters reception he had attended with Anne as his wife. All eyes were upon them, the scandal of her husband's death and the gossip of their previous relationship on all lips, and he remembered her smiling at Craufurd who had taken her hand.

"Ma'am – will you take a turn about the room with me and let's see who dares to cut you when you're on my arm?"

Paul had watched them walk off laughing together with fierce gratitude to the commander of the Light Division. He held the memory with him through the long day, and when the formalities were over, he returned to camp, declining several invitations to join the officers of the other brigades for dinner. Paul was beginning to feel at home in the division, but he knew that many of the officers currently drinking solemn toasts to Craufurd had not liked him at all. Paul was happier celebrating his life with his own officers and with the enlisted men, who remembered Craufurd as a strict and often brutal disciplinarian who had nevertheless cared more about his ordinary soldiers than his fellow officers.

With the dead buried and the wounded treated, Lord Wellington removed himself back to his former headquarters at Freineda and Paul marched his brigade back to their comfortable billets close by. He was under no illusion that they would stay there for long, but even a few weeks of dry accommodation and relative was a relief. The freezing weather gave way to torrential rain and his men settled themselves into barns and farm buildings newly repaired to house them while Wellington made plans for his next move and called a general parade of his army to remind the Portuguese and Spanish why he was there.

Paul had made it his business to make enquiries about Major Brodie and at the end of the parade he motioned to his senior officers. "I thought I might have a chat with the Major," he said mildly. "He's over there, near Lord Wellington."

"I'm surprised you've left it this long," Johnny remarked.

Paul grinned. "I've been waiting until Lord Wellington was well within earshot, Johnny."

"He won't be impressed, sir."

"He'll be fine as long as it's not a formal challenge to a duel. I'm not going to kill the bastard; I'm just going to embarrass him. And clean him out. Let's see how long his lassie sticks around when he can't pay her bills."

Paul strolled forward, flanked by his officers and greeted Lord Wellington pleasantly.

"Colonel. Glad to see you here this time. I heard you were a big help on the disciplinary board during our last parade."

"I do my best, sir. But they still keep asking me for some reason."

"It has me in a puzzle as well," Wellington said ironically. "Is Mrs van Daan not with you today? I hope she's well."

"She's very well, sir. Just tired. My son kept her awake most of last night and she's catching up on some sleep."

"Give her my best wishes, Colonel. She works too hard. When are you planning on sending him back to England?"

"Almost immediately," Paul said. "My brother should be in Lisbon by now, Nan will travel down with one of the convoys of wounded."

"You're not sending her home with him?"

"She doesn't want to go, sir. It's a difficult choice, but Will isn't safe here, he's too young and there's always sickness. Nan doesn't want to be parted from him but she won't leave me. We have to put him first."

Wellington studied him in silence for a long time. "You could insist, Colonel."

"I suppose I could, but that isn't how we do things, sir. It's her choice."

"I wonder what your family will think."

"They'll take good care of Will whatever they think. And he'll be raised with the other three which is what we both want. As for Nan, I hope they like her, although if they don't it's their loss."

"Your wife can charm anybody."

"One would think so, sir. Although I was slightly disturbed to hear that Major Brodie is less than impressed."

Paul turned to look across at the highland Major, who stared back at him in startled surprise. Wellington looked sharply at Paul.

"Colonel?"

"I wasn't here last time so I missed it, sir," Paul said. His eyes were still on Brodie's face and he was not smiling. "But I've been informed by at least three different people that Major Brodie was giving his opinion on my wife very publicly. I wondered if he'd like to share his views with me now that the siege is over and I'm here."

42

"Colonel," Wellington said quietly. "This might not be the best time..."

"It's all right, sir. I'm not about to challenge Major Brodie to a duel. Like you I don't believe in duelling, it's a stupid and destructive custom and especially wasteful in times of war. We should be killing the French not fighting each other. But I am interested to know what made Major Brodie call my wife a whore in front of half a dozen junior officers, including one from my seventh company. As far as I'm aware, Major Brodie doesn't even know my wife."

Brodie's face was scarlet. He looked from Paul to Lord Wellington and back again, and then glanced beyond Paul at the solid phalanx of officers from the 110th. Paul did not look around, but he could imagine their expressions.

"Is this true, Major Brodie?" Wellington's tone was icy.

"My Lord...I was just repeating gossip..."

"What gossip has there been about my wife, Major?" Paul asked genially. "We've been married now for a year and a half and she's back in our billet nursing my four month old son. Why don't you share the latest gossip with me, I'm her husband, I should know."

"Nothing." Brodie's voice was strained and Paul did not blame him, given the expression on Wellington's face. "I mean, nothing recent, of course. But before you married her, Colonel, you are well aware..."

"Exactly what should I be aware of, Major, that makes it acceptable for you to publicly impugn the reputation of a lady? I'm waiting to hear."

"As am I," Wellington said, and his tone dripped ice.

Brodie looked like a trapped animal. "Sir...my Lord...at the time it was said that her husband was driven to his final attack through jealousy. Because he...because you..."

He stammered to a stop, having apparently lost the ability to speak. Paul allowed the pause to become uncomfortable, then spoke in alarmingly affable tones.

"It's all right, Major, I'm not going to challenge you. I don't think you're malicious, just surprisingly stupid. Everybody else in this army lost interest in that piece of gossip a long time ago, but you decide to revive it in the middle of a parade in front of at least half a dozen people who are going to repeat it to me. Of course one of them was Lieutenant Heron, whom I understand rather foolishly agreed to a bout of swordplay against you."

"Are you telling me, Major Brodie," Lord Wellington said in biting tones, "that you are intending to fight a duel against a junior officer over an insult to Colonel van Daan's wife, who by the way is a friend of mine, on the eve of marching up to Badajoz? Have you gone completely mad?"

Brodie could go no redder. "No, my Lord. Not a duel. Colonel van Daan has been misinformed. Nothing to do with his wife, sir. Just a friendly bout."

"For a wager, Major?" Paul asked gently.

"That's private, sir."

"Not in my regiment it isn't, since my junior officers are not permitted to gamble with their seniors. I don't think it's good for morale or discipline."

"I completely agree, Colonel," Wellington said harshly. "Major Brodie, you will withdraw from this immediately, and you owe both Colonel van Daan and his Lieutenant a written apology. As for your insult to Mrs van Daan, you are fortunate that I do not choose to have you arrested for conduct unbecoming an officer and a gentleman."

"Heron doesn't require an apology, sir," Paul said pleasantly. "He knows he shouldn't have agreed, I've spoken to him. And there's nothing wrong with a friendly bout for a bet, providing both parties can afford to lose. Most of my junior officers live on their pay and I'll be damned if I'll excuse them their mess bills because they're funding your lifestyle. But if you're interested in a wager, I'll be happy to oblige. Why don't we meet outside headquarters tomorrow morning? Let's make it nice and public. Name the sum, don't worry about the amount. I can afford it."

The silence was absolute. Brodie looked at the Lord Wellington. Paul did not bother. He could imagine the expression on Wellington's face. He knew his chief would back him completely in public, although he rather imagined he was about to hear a good deal about it privately.

"Well, Major?" Wellington said finally.

"Yes. Of course, my Lord. Tomorrow."

"Shall we say ten?" Paul said pleasantly. "That will give me a chance to get morning drill over with. As to the wager, if you don't want to name a sum, perhaps I have an idea. There's a sum of money that you took off Lieutenant Lloyd a few weeks ago. Not that much, although I believe he's having to accept loans from his friends just now to keep himself and his horses fed. Still, I believe you told him that a man who couldn't afford such a paltry wager had no right to hold a gentleman's commission, so it won't be a problem for you, will it? And then there are the card debts from Mr Jackman. He was so distressed by them that he tried to go over with the Forlorn Hope because paying you will ruin him. Do you know the amount they both owe you?"

Brodie nodded. He seemed unable to speak.

"Excellent. I'll see you outside headquarters tomorrow, Major, and if I disarm you, you'll pay Mr Lloyd his money back and write off Mr Jackman's debt. If you disarm me, I'll pay you the same sum. Feel free to make any other bets on this with the other officers that you want." Paul scanned the avidly listening group with amused blue eyes. "I'm sure you'll get plenty of takers on this one. And when we're done, I'll go away and get ready to fight the French and you can carry on fleecing the junior officers of this army. But not my junior officers, Major. Now if you'll excuse me, I need to get back and see how my wife is. Good morning."

He nodded pleasantly and walked back to his horse.

Paul was unsurprised, when he rode up with Anne and his officers the following morning, to find that large area before headquarters was crowded. Brodie was already there, stripped to shirtsleeves, loosening up his sword arm with a series of passes. He looked up as Paul's party rode in and nodded without smiling. Paul reined in and dismounted, handing Rufus' reins to Jenson with a smile of thanks. He turned to lift his wife down and set her lightly before him.

"All right, girl of my heart?"

"Yes, Colonel. Make sure you win." Anne stood on tiptoe and reached up to kiss him. Amusedly aware of the avid scrutiny of half Wellington's officers, Paul caught her to him and kissed her fully on the mouth. He felt her shiver of response and straightened, noticing her slight flush. She had recovered fast from the birth of

44

William, and now that the child was feeding well with Gwen Astor, his wet nurse, they had moved his crib into Gwen's room. Anne had employed a Portuguese girl to help and there was seldom need for her to get up during the night unless Will was unwell as he had been the previous few nights. Ramona or Gwen had instructions to rouse Anne if she was needed, but Paul was enjoying having her to himself again for the first time in several months. She appeared to have missed his lovemaking just as much, and he was amusedly aware that they were behaving as they had during the first weeks of their marriage when they had spent all day waiting to be together.

Anne reached up to help him off with his coat and he allowed her to do so, enjoying the envious stares of some of the other officers around the square. They might have speculated about his marriage to Robert Carlyon's lovely widow, but he was under no illusion about how many of them would have liked to be in his place. Paul knew that Wellington was irritated by his choice to make a public show of dealing with Major Brodie and his chief had spent ten minutes in private the previous day telling him exactly what he thought. Paul was fairly sure that a public loss would keep Brodie away from the junior officers of the 110th in future, but he also wanted to remind the army that he was not prepared to tolerate any kind of insult to his wife, and he was prepared to accept his chief's displeasure in a good cause.

When he was ready, he took Anne's hand and drew her over to the small group around Major Brodie. The Scot looked embarrassed.

"Major, I'm not sure if you've met my wife. Nan, this is Major Brodie."

"Major." Anne gave him her hand and a smile, which could have illuminated half the village. Brodie took it and bent to kiss her fingers, red to the tip of his ears. Paul thought that the Scot looked so embarrassed at being introduced to the woman he had publicly insulted, they probably did not need to bother with the fencing match. Anne was clearly aware of the effect she was having and enjoying it.

"Good luck today, Major," she said.

"Thank you, ma'am." Brodie seemed unable to decide if he needed to say more but Anne gave him no opportunity to do so. Turning to Paul she placed her hand on his chest then slid it up to his face in a blatant caress.

"Take care, this is meant to be for fun," she said lightly. "I'm going to stand with Lord Wellington, he is waving to me."

"I'll be good," Paul promised, bending to kiss her again. He did not think she could have made her point any more effectively.

As she walked away, he glanced at Brodie and grinned at his expression. "Concentrate, Major. You can't fight with half an eye on my wife."

"I've not seen her close up before."

"If you try to fleece any more of my junior officers, Major, you'll see her a lot closer than you want to, she's furious with you. But you're right, she is lovely."

"You're a lucky man, Colonel. I can see why you'd defend her."

"She doesn't need defending, Major, she's done nothing wrong," Paul said quietly. "Which is why I am inclined to get irritated fairly quickly when people make free with her reputation in public. Come on, let's get this over with, I've got a pile of paperwork to get through and I need to go and give the commissariat a bollocking, they've messed up my men's rations for the third week in a row."

He drew his sword and swished it through the air, loosening his arm. Brodie regarded him in surprise. "Isn't that your quartermaster's job?"

"It is, but when they don't listen to him, they get me. After that, things tend to go more smoothly for a while." Paul regarded him with gentle amusement. "I'm a bit of a perfectionist when it comes to the running of my brigade, Major."

"You're so bloody sure you're going to beat me, aren't you?" Brodie said, suddenly sounding angry. "Do you know how many men I've fought, Colonel?"

"No idea and I beg you won't tell me, it's of no interest. Are you ready?"

They moved into the centre of the square and Paul lifted his sword in salute. He saw his opponent's eyes widen. "Is that what you're fighting with?"

"Yes. Unless you've an objection, Major. If you have, I can borrow a sword from one of my officers. It doesn't make any difference to me."

Brodie was still eyeing the engraved blade of the tulwar. "When were you in India?"

"Before you, I believe; I was wounded at Assaye. If you want, we can talk over a drink in the mess afterwards. Just at the moment you need to concentrate."

"Don't you?"

"Not really," Paul said infuriatingly and saluted then stepped back, his eyes on his opponent. The two men circled each other watchfully, waiting for the first attack.

***

Anne watched as the two swordsmen tried a few passes, feinting and parrying easily, testing each other's range and strength. The other officers of the 110th had come to join her.

"He's good," Lord Wellington said grudgingly. "I have not really seen him fight before, apart from on the field of course and there's not much time to admire technique there."

"He's very good, my Lord," Wheeler said, watching Paul. "He's not really trying yet. I suppose he's testing to see how good Brodie is."

"Not that good," Manson said, with an informality, which caused Wellington to glance at him and then smile. "He's very quick and I'd say his advantage is in his strength, but I don't think he often chooses opponents of his own reach and experience. He's built his reputation on numbers rather than quality. The Colonel could have had that blade out of his hand twice already."

"It's a shame you didn't accept his challenge, Leo," Carl said with a grin. "He would have hated to be beaten by a fairly junior captain."

"It wouldn't have stopped him," Manson said. "It wouldn't have mattered if I'd beaten him. Which I think I would now that I've seen him fight. But he could have won it all back working his way through the rest of the 110th's junior officers just to piss me off, nothing I could do about it. That's why I went to the Colonel."

Lord Wellington shot him a speculative look. "Interesting," he said. "If you ever get tired of his antics, Captain Manson, you should come up to headquarters. I get ten applications a week for staff appointments, but I would happily find a place for you. I don't see many young officers with common sense as well as courage, and it would do Colonel van Daan some good to find out how the rest of the army feels when he poaches their best officers."

Manson looked around startled. "Thank you, sir," he said. "Happy where I am at present."

Anne could not help smiling at Manson's emphatic tone. "You leave him alone, sir, or Paul will be after you with that sword."

There was a sudden clash of metal and a burst of activity. The two men flew across the ground with Brodie pressing hard and Paul moving backwards at speed. Despite herself Anne felt her heart skip a beat, and then there was a sudden movement and Paul was under and past the blade, counter attacking with such force that it jarred the Major's whole body. He stumbled backwards and Paul very obviously gave him time to recover. She heard a murmur of laughter from the men around her.

The combatants circled again and came together in another furious bout. Once again Brodie appeared to be on the attack, and once again found himself unexpectedly swiping at an opponent who had moved nimbly out of reach and counter attacked from another angle leaving him scrambling and breathless. Carl laughed aloud.

"The Colonel is being a bastard, he should end this."

"I think he's made his point," Johnny agreed with a smile. "One more round and I suspect we can all go and get breakfast."

"I do hope so," Wellington said shortly. "This is a considerable waste of my time."

Anne looked up at him. "I am sorry, my Lord," she said. "You should not have come. Although I know Paul appreciates your support."

"I am not supporting Colonel van Daan, ma'am," Wellington said. "Colonel van Daan is showing off. I have seen him do it before, it is not new. He could have dealt with Major Brodie privately; he is a senior officer. He is choosing to publicly humiliate him and it is not because of a few gambling debts, it is because of you." Wellington looked down at her. "And I am here for the same reason. After this I imagine that we will hear no more of this nonsense."

Anne was watching the combatants again. "I am grateful, sir," she said. "And you are probably right. Although sometimes, Paul just shows off because he likes to show off."

Wellington gave a crack of laughter. "Touché, ma'am. I believe you are right."

On the third attack Paul fell back more steadily, giving less ground. Brodie was very breathless while his opponent looked as though he had barely begun. Anne watched in fascination as her husband fought, seeing the strength in wrist and arm, the agility of his body and the surprising lightness of his movements. She had always thought him a curious combination; a tall strong man who could be surprisingly gentle. There was no sign of that now. The blue eyes were steady and watchful, awaiting the best opportunity to break through the other man's guard.

Brodie moved back under the attack, then stumbled, almost falling. Paul withdrew, moving his sword back courteously to allow the other man time to recover. Brodie looked up and suddenly Manson swore beside Anne, his swordsman's eye seeing before any of them what was happening. The highlander moved with astonishing speed, not off balance at all, and brought the sword up and under Paul's lowered guard, stabbing with lethal intent directly towards his unprotected abdomen.

47

There was no concealing his intent to strike and the momentum of his movement coupled with Paul's deliberately lowered guard made the outcome inevitable.

Anne gave a choked cry of horror, hearing the collective gasp of the men around her as the point of Brodie's sword connected with Paul's body. There was a yell and a clash of metal and then Paul was falling backwards, the front of his white shirt stained red. Brodie moved forwards, ignoring the furious shout from the Commander-in-Chief.

Paul landed on his back, continued his momentum, and completed a backwards roll out of reach. Anne realised in a flood of relief that the clash of metal had been Paul's sword connecting with Brodie's at the last minute, deflecting the worst of the blow. His white shirt was stained red, but he was on his feet. Brodie came forward murderously, giving no quarter and her husband straightened and lifted his sword. Anne heard him say something although she could not hear what and then he was moving forward, the sword flashing, and she realised that Manson had been right from the beginning and Paul had barely been trying. Brodie fell back under the lethal assault and there was complete silence around the square as Paul came on, giving no time for anything more than desperate parrying. The attack lasted less than two minutes, and suddenly there was an immense clash and Brodie gave a cry of pain and dropped the sword from lifeless fingers. Paul took three steps forward and placed the point of his sword against the man's unprotected throat and the blood drained from the highlander's face.

There was no sound from around the square. Anne had her hands pressed to her mouth, holding back any sound she might have made. She was conscious of Carl's arm about her shoulders, steadying her, and she was grateful.

Into the echoing silence, Paul spoke in tones he had trained to be heard through the noise of a battlefield.

"This is not a duel, Major. Which is just as well under the circumstances, because if it were, you would now be dead. I'll expect payment to my lieutenant as agreed before the end of the day along with a letter formally cancelling Mr Jackman's debts to you. Now pick up your sword and salute like the gentleman you pretend to be. And then piss off before I lose my temper completely and cut your fucking hand off."

He moved his sword into an ironic salute, and Brodie bent to pick up his blade. He returned the salute looking white and shocked. Paul turned, walking back to his friends. His eyes were on Anne's face and he gave a reassuring smile. Johnny moved forward. "Are you all right, sir? Christ, he should be cashiered for that. He tried to murder you."

"I'll be fine, Johnny. He's not my problem now, it's up to Lord Wellington and he's going to be furious." Love, you're as white as a sheet."

"Sorry. I'm not accustomed to watching you gutted like a herring in front of me. I've a feeling that's worse than you're pretending it is."

Paul pulled a face. "It bloody hurts," he said. "I honestly wasn't expecting it; it didn't occur to me he'd actually try to injure me."

"Colonel."

Paul turned to see Lord Wellington approaching. "Are you all right?"

"Yes, sir, I'll be fine. I brought my doctor with me, though I wasn't expecting to need her."

"The man must have gone mad," Wellington said. The blue eyes were dark with anger. "To do that in front of me..."

"I suspect he lost his temper, sir. He's not used to losing, and I rather imagine it will cost him more than he can easily pay in wagers."

"He will be lucky to recoup the money on his commission. I am tempted to send him for court martial."

"Sir, that's up to you. I've no idea what kind of soldier he is, but I know how short of officers you are at the moment. It's not going to upset me if he stays, I've made my point."

"I am not having him in my army, Colonel, not after that. If he wants to exchange his commission and serve elsewhere that is up to him. Disgraceful behaviour."

Anne was watching her husband's face. "You need to sit down," she said.

"I actually do but I don't want to do a dramatic collapse in the middle of the square."

"Come into my quarters, Colonel, my orderlies can run for bandages and anything else you need," Wellington said. "Colonel Wheeler, perhaps you'll send one of your men to convey a word to Major Brodie that I would like to see him in an hour."

In Lord Wellington's sitting room Anne carefully lifted the bloody shirt over Paul's head and caught her breath at the sight of the wound. "Lie back on the settle," she said. "I need to see how deep it is."

Paul obeyed. Anne examined the wound. The sword had begun to enter the abdomen and Paul had deflected it downwards with his blade. It had torn a jagged wound down towards his groin and it was bleeding heavily. "I think I need to stitch this," she said, studying it. "Leo, can you go over to the hospital and ask if somebody can lend me a medical kit and get a dressing and some bandages?"

"Yes, ma'am."

"And ask Jenson to bring some water to clean it, please?"

"I will."

Carl entered with Paul's coat. Reaching into the pocket he took out Paul's silver flask and handed it to his friend. Paul smiled gratefully and took a long pull of the brandy. His orderly brought a bowl of water, and Anne bent over him, bathing the long gash gently. She could see him gritting his teeth, trying not to think about how much it hurt. After a moment her silence reached him and he opened his eyes and saw that she was crying silently while bathing the wound.

"Love, it's all right, I'll be fine. This wasn't how we expected the day to go, but it's not that serious."

"No but it might have been. I'd like to kill him."

Paul pushed himself up and drew her close, kissing her gently. "I'd let you," he said teasingly. "I feel like a fool for being caught so off guard, but I couldn't have guessed he was that mad."

"Paul, he'd stumbled, it was supposed to be a friendly bout, you were doing what any man would have done," Carl said quietly. "Thank God for your reactions, mind, another man would have been dead at that point."

The door opened and Leo Manson came into the room. "Compliments of Dr Franck ma'am, he says use what you need."

"Thank you, Leo." Anne took the bag. She kissed Paul again gently. "Lie back, Paul, it'll be easier if you're lying flat. And drink some more brandy, this is likely to be sore I'm afraid."

Paul lay silently, visibly trying not to flinch as Anne drew the ragged edges of the wound together. When she had finished, she placed the dressing over it and bandaged it carefully. Paul sat up and picked up his bloodied shirt, pulling a face. "It will have to do."

"Take one of mine," Lord Wellington said quietly. Paul had not heard his chief come into the room. "Will you be all right to go back to your billet, Colonel? We can find you a bed here."

"No, I'll be fine, sir. I'll be better off back there, I've got my own medical team."

"My orderly will bring the shirt through. It might be a bit of a tight fit, but you'll manage."

Paul studied his chief's face. "Sir, I'm sorry. You didn't need this just now. He's an idiot, but I should have found an easier way of dealing with him."

Wellington studied him for a moment. Finally, he said:

"Yes, you should. I understand how angry you get, about what they say sometimes, but this wasn't the time. And you're old enough to know better."

"I really am."

"All the same, you cannot have anticipated this. And this has given me information about Major Brodie that I can't ignore. I will deal with him myself, no need for further involvement from you. But grow up. Your wife has enough to worry about when you go into battle, she does not need this." Wellington looked over at Anne's white face. "Are you quite well, ma'am?"

"I'll be fine, thank you, sir."

"When do you leave for Lisbon?"

"Next week. There's a convoy of wounded going south, I can travel with them."

Wellington studied her for a long moment. Then he looked over at Paul. "Go with her," he said.

There was a startled silence. Then Paul shook his head. "Sir, no. There's no need for that, I..."

"That was an order, Colonel, not a suggestion. Colonel Wheeler can take over the brigade for a few weeks. We are awaiting supplies and reinforcements and hopefully our siege train. Nothing will happen for a month at least. Go with her, let that wound heal and see your brother – you can't have seen him for years. See your son settled with his aunt." Lord Wellington laughed at their stunned expressions. "I am not being entirely altruistic, Colonel. There are one or two people I'd like you to see while you're there. I've no time to go to Lisbon to do the pretty with the grandees and the diplomats and I've nothing useful to say to them anyway. But you..."

Paul was beginning to laugh despite the pain. "Sir, are you sending me on a diplomatic mission?"

Wellington was laughing too, his bad temper apparently forgotten. He looked past Paul and directly at Anne. "I'm sending you as part of one."

"Oh I get it. I wish you'd just stop hiding behind the conventions and pay her a damned stipend, sir, she bloody earns it."

Wellington moved forward and took Anne's hand, raising it to his lips. "I know she does," he said. "Ma'am, would you…?"

Anne smiled. "I will. You'll need to let us know all the details, I'll organise a reception and a dinner or two."

"Thank you, ma'am. Take him home and make your arrangements. I shall go and speak to Major Brodie. He ought to be court martialled."

Paul shook his head. "That may not the best idea for morale among the officers, sir, they hate it when one of their own is court martialled. Besides I'd have to give evidence and then the whole mess with Lloyd and Heron and Jackman would have to be made public. I'd like to avoid that, they're good officers. Offer him the chance to sell out or take a transfer. He'll take it, it's the best offer he's going to get. I'd better get back. I'll let you know when we're setting off."

"Do so. Oh, and given your eccentric sense of humour, Colonel, you will be amused to know that I received notification today that I am to be made an Earl. Along another collection of Spanish titles which I shall struggle to remember."

"An Earl? Congratulations, sir. Who would have thought it back in India? You're becoming very much above my touch, I'll have to start bowing."

Wellington snorted, but Anne thought it had a pleased sound to it. "You could start by calling me by my existing title, Colonel, but I do not intend to hold my breath while waiting."

"Would you like me to, my Lord?"

"Good God no! It would worry me."

"I am pleased for you, sir," Anne said, smiling. "It is good to see them acknowledging what you are achieving, even if we know they will be croaking again next week."

Lord Wellington laughed. "They will. I am naturally very moved, but I would gladly relinquish the honour to have Robert Craufurd back."

"Who do we get now, sir?" Paul asked.

"I have some ideas, I'll know within a few days. I'll write to you as soon as I'm certain. It won't be Erskine, Colonel, be reassured."

"Thank you, sir. And for the shirt. Although if they've increased your income along with the title, you can probably afford a new one."

Wellington rolled his eyes expressively. "Take him out of here, ma'am, and do your best to ensure that he behaves himself in Lisbon. Colonel – rest! I need you fit for Badajoz."

Paul pulled a face. "You know perfectly well how much I am looking forward to the almighty cock-up that promises to be. Come on, bonny lass, let's get home."

Chapter Five

Paul's house in Lisbon was set high up in the town, away from the poorer areas around the docks in an elegant street of elaborate villas. It was large with an inner courtyard and a small garden, and stables at the back and he had first rented it when he had arrived in Lisbon with Sir Arthur Wellesley back in 1808 with his first wife, Rowena. The owner had fled to Brazil with the royal court and had been only too glad to rent his elegant town house to a wealthy British officer. Paul had taken on the staff as well and kept the house on while he was campaigning. He had loaned it out frequently to Lord Wellington when he visited the capital and to other visiting diplomats and a year earlier, he had made an offer to purchase the house which had been gratefully accepted. It was the only home he and Anne had. At some point Paul wanted to find a suitable property in England for them but Anne knew they might well be in Europe for some years to come and at least having the villa gave them a sense of belonging.

They arrived at the villa shortly after noon. They had travelled at an easy pace, giving Paul's wound a chance to heal, and were greeted at the door by Mario who ran the household and who emerged shouting orders in Portuguese about luggage and horses.

"Mario, it's good to see you. It's been a while."

"Too long, Colonel. You look well and your lady is as beautiful as ever. And a new little one."

"This is William, Mario, and be thankful he's asleep because. He is very noisy."

"He looks like his father, Señora."

"Is my family here, Mario?" Paul asked.

"They are, Colonel. Señor van Daan is in the courtyard."

"We'll go straight through and then Nan can take Will up and get him settled with his nurse."

"Yes, Colonel. I will make sure they are unpacking."

Paul walked through into the courtyard with Anne beside him. There was a man sitting at the table reading. He looked up and then rose and Paul stopped very suddenly.

"Father. Oh Christ, I'd no idea you were coming."

52

"Paul."

Anne shot a glance at her husband and saw that there was an unexpected shine to his eyes. She looked across at her father-in-law and realised that he was equally affected. It was not surprising. They must have been angry with each other for so much of their lives, these two towering personalities. But since they had last met, Paul had almost died at Talavera, had lost a wife and married another and had risen to the rank of brigade commander at a very young age. His communication with his father had been limited to writing letters during that time and Anne wondered suddenly how much Franz van Daan worried. She stepped forward.

"You two need some time alone," she said quietly. "Let's do the introductions later. I'm going to take Will up and get him settled with Gwen and I'll change into something that doesn't look as though I've been on the road for a week." She looked over at her father-in-law, who tore his eyes away from his son to return her regard. "It is good to meet you, sir, although we've not properly met yet. But we'll do that later."

She touched Paul's arm and made to go, but he caught her about the waist and drew her back. "Just a moment, girl of my heart. Father, have a quick look at my latest."

His father came forward and Anne held out the sleeping child for inspection. "I am going to give you the benefit of the doubt and assume you meant your latest offspring," she said and Paul gave a choke of laughter and kissed her.

"I did. Go on then, go and get him fed and settled."

***

When Anne had left Paul looked at his father. Franz stepped forward and embraced him.

"Christ, Paul, I know it's not possible, but I'd swear you've grown. Perhaps I'm shrinking."

Paul laughed and released him, blinking back the tears. "You're not, I promise you. It's the uniform, it makes us all look bigger. I wonder if that's why they chose it? Something about scaring off the enemy. I'm sorry about this, you caught me by surprise."

"I'm sorry, I should have written to tell you. It was a sudden decision. I thought about it and realised it had been too long, and there isn't much chance you're coming home any time soon, is there?"

"No. I'm so glad you came. Where are Josh and Patience?"

"Out sightseeing. And that was your wife."

"Yes. Now that you've seen her..."

"Now that I've seen her, boy, it's very clear to me how you came to marry her so damned quickly. You could hardly let her sit and wait, I presume there was a queue?"

Paul laughed, going to pour wine. "There would have been, but I was very fast," he said, handing a glass to his father. "Sir, thank you for coming, I'm so glad I made it down with Nan, now."

He held out a chair for Franz and sat down opposite. "So were you hoping to see me and or were you curious to meet Nan."

53

Franz laughed. "Both. Brigade commander, Paul – how old are you now?"

"You're my father, you're supposed to know that. I'm thirty one."

"Christ, you really took this seriously, didn't you?"

"Very. Although I'm well aware you never expected me to."

Franz gave a wry smile. "No. I thought you were doing it to snap your fingers at me because I suggested the law. I gave it a couple of years and thought you'd be back at home and ready to fall into line."

"When did you stop thinking that Father?"

"After Assaye. I was privileged to watch you those first weeks at Melton and I spoke to Colonel Dixon. It was obvious you'd found where you wanted to be." Franz glanced at him and smiled slightly. "And I'm guessing you found something else as well."

"My lady? Yes. I'm still getting used to it, I suppose. Although I'm not sure I'm ever going to learn to take her for granted."

"I was sorry about Rowena, Paul."

"It still hurts," Paul admitted. "She was so much a part of my life, it was like there was a hole left that nothing else could fill. I have Nan, and had from the first, and I love her in a way I never did Rowena. But I don't think I ever knew what Rowena meant to me until she'd gone. She stood by me through so much. It's been hard at times, so much has happened in the past couple of years."

"It is difficult to keep up by letter," his father said drily.

Paul accepted the implied reproof with a rueful smile. "It's impossible, and I'm not a very reliable correspondent, I know. Once you've got to know Nan properly you'll do better, she's very good. And you can read her handwriting which is more than you can say for mine."

"I'm looking forward to meeting her. How long can you stay?"

"Probably not long. Wellington treats requests for leave like being bled by an over-enthusiastic junior surgeon. And he's especially bad with me, God knows why. Bloody Craufurd got three months in England last year and I couldn't manage a week to get married. I'm here and I'm hoping for a couple of weeks but if one of my ensigns walks through that door in a week's time telling me that Wellington is screaming for me, I won't be a bit surprised. If that does happen, I may leave Nan for a bit longer if you're happy with that. There are always supply columns coming north, she can get an escort back when she's ready. And the way the commissariat feel about her, they'll move a lot faster with our rations if she's with them."

"What on earth does the commissariat have to do with your wife, Paul?"

"More than they'd like, she's my unofficial quartermaster. As well as my unofficial regimental surgeon. You ought to hear the medical board on the subject."

Franz was laughing. "I am more and more glad I came. She's got you somewhere I never thought you'd be, Paul, you can't keep the smile off your face when you talk about her, can you? How long have you been married?"

"About a year and a half. It doesn't seem that long, and yet it's hard to remember life without her."

"How old is she?"

"She's twenty-two. She married for the first time very young, he was killed just before Bussaco and we married soon after that."

"And how long had you known her, Paul?"

Paul could hear the suspicion in his father's voice. He considered for a moment then decided to tell the truth. "I met her in '08 in Yorkshire."

"I see. You've been surprisingly constant then."

Paul looked down at the wrought iron table for a moment, then up into his father's eyes. "You mean given that I was unfaithful to Rowena? Yes, sir. If I could go back, I'd change what I did back then, but I can't. I intend to keep my marriage vows this time around."

Franz gave a faint smile. "This wife of yours seems to have thoroughly tamed you, my boy."

"I don't see that as an insult, sir."

"It was not intended as one. Is there anything she can't do?"

"Well I've yet to see her cook a meal, and if you hand her a shirt that needs mending she's likely to tear it up for bandages. She isn't much like other women, sir. Although she has proved surprisingly adept at motherhood which is a bit of a surprise to both of us. I missed the birth completely but she seemed to sail through it without a hitch, and she's proved astonishingly competent with Will. It's going to be hard for her, he's very young."

"Is he weaned?"

"We've brought a wet nurse. She's an Englishwoman who lost her man at Fuentes de Oñoro and she has a young daughter. She's from London and wants to go home. Once Will is properly weaned, which won't be long, it's up to you if she stays on as his nurse or goes home – just make sure she gets there if that's what she wants. Her name's Gwen and she's a good girl, you'll have no trouble with her."

"We still have Mary who came home with Rowena," Franz said with a smile. "She's proved herself very useful and she married a few months ago, one of our grooms. Paul, there's something I've not told you yet."

"Go on."

"When we decided to come out to collect William and meet your wife, we..."

There were sounds of arrival in the hallway and Paul heard his sister-in-law's gentle tones admonishing. The door to the courtyard burst open and a child entered. He was wearing a white shirt and breeches with a loose jacket, open and with at least two buttons missing. He looked at least nine or ten from his height and manner, but Paul knew it was deceptive, knew he could only be seven, and he stepped forward.

"Papa!"

"Francis." Paul moved forward uncertainly and then the child ran. Paul caught him up into his arms and held him tight, the boy's arms wrapped around his neck in a stranglehold. Paul buried his face in his son's hair, fairer than his, almost white like Rowena's and inhaled the scent of him. Beyond him he saw his brother coming forward, smiling, and then his sister-in-law holding the hand of a girl of around ten, dainty and fair in a pink dress with a white pinafore over it. Paul dropped to his knees, still holding his son with one arm and held out his other arm to his daughter.

"Grace. Oh lass, come here, you're as pretty as your mother!"

Grace ran forward and joined the embrace and Paul knelt holding them and kissing them. Finally he looked up at Patience.

55

"Thank you," he said softly. "You've no idea. I'm revising my plans, if Wellington wants me out of here before two weeks, he can either come and get me himself or cashier me, I can take the loss."

"Oh, Good Heavens."

Paul looked up. His wife was coming into the courtyard from the inner door, laughing. She had changed out of her travelling clothes into a sprigged muslin gown trimmed with blue and she looked very young and very beautiful. "You kept this very quiet, Paul."

"Love, I didn't know."

Anne smiled at her sister-in-law and Joshua, both of whom were staring at her in considerable astonishment. "But there's one missing, and she's the only one I've met before."

"She's here, but she's a little shy," Patience said, lifting the smallest child from her skirts. She was not yet two, as fair as the others. Anne came forward.

"My poor Will is going to look like a changeling in this family if he keeps that dark hair. Although he's got the eyes and the attitude already."

"And what makes you think that attitude comes from me?" her husband said, laughing up at her. Anne thought, her heart unexpectedly full, that she had never seen him look quite so carefree. Reaching out she took Rowena from Patience and settled her on one hip.

"You were very tiny the last time I held you," she said, studying the child. Blue Van Daan eyes looked back at her. Anne kissed the soft cheek. "When he's stopped feeding, which might be a while, you shall all come up and meet your new brother."

"Half-brother," Grace said. She was staring at Anne as if she could not tear her eyes away.

"Grace!" Patience said, horrified. Anne laughed.

"No, she's completely right. There are a lot of half relationships in this family, aren't there? I'm going to sit over here with Rowena because she's heavy, come and sit by me, Grace, you need to help me work all this out. You're the eldest, aren't you, which makes you how old?"

"I'm nine. My mother is dead."

"I know, Grace, and I'm sorry. She died of fever in India, didn't she? Your father has told me about her."

Paul was watching the two of them, fascinated at seeing them together for the first time. His daughter went slowly to the chair beside Anne. Rowena was fidgeting, and without hesitation, Anne took the two combs out of her hair and gave them to the toddler, showing her how to lock them together and slide them apart again. Enchanted, Rowena began to play with the combs.

"Anne, let me take her up for you," Patience said, and Anne looked up with a quick smile.

"Oh not yet, please? I've waited so long to meet them all."

"Father told you about my mother?" Grace said, sounding incredulous, and Paul felt guilt twist like a knife.

"Of course he did," Anne said without a moment's hesitation. "He didn't need to tell me about Rowena because she was my best friend. I never met Nell but your father told me she was very pretty. And looking at you, Grace, I can believe it."

56

Francis was watching Anne as well. Paul set him down and got up, his eyes on the children. Francis went to stand on the other side of Anne.

"My mother was pretty as well. I've seen a portrait."

"I don't know what my mother looked like, I've never seen a portrait of her," Grace said wistfully.

"No there wasn't much opportunity going to India," Paul said lightly. "But if you want a fairly good idea, Grace, find a mirror. Your eyes are my colour but the shape of your face is Nell's and no mistake."

"Did you really know my mother?" Francis asked, and the wistful tone of his voice made Paul want to cry. He had not expected to see his children this week and he realised he had given no thought to how he would explain Rowena's death, his marriage to Anne and their complicated relationship. He realised abruptly that Anne had already thought about this and knew exactly what she wanted to say.

"I knew her very well, Francis," she said. "She was the best friend I ever had."

"And was she really pretty?"

"She was lovely."

"I look like my father," Francis said, and Anne studied him and laughed.

"You really do," she said. "But you have one little thing that reminds me so much of Rowena that I want to cry."

"What's that?" Francis said eagerly.

Anne reached out and ran her finger lightly over the bridge of his nose. "You have her freckles," she said softly. "Each one of them stamps her name all over you, Francis van Daan. And there are other things about her I'm hoping you have too."

"What?"

"Her goodness. Her kindness. Her sense of right and wrong. If you keep hold of those as well as your father's stubbornness you could be prime minister one day."

"I want to be a soldier one day," Francis said.

"Do you? Wherever did you get that idea from? Anyway, you can be a soldier and a politician, Lord Wellington has done both. Perhaps he'll be prime minister one day, who knows?"

Grace had reached out and was touching the silky strands of Anne's hair, which was coming loose without the tortoiseshell combs.

"Your hair is so beautiful."

"Thank you, Grace. Although I admit I always used to want fair hair like yours. I was envious of Rowena for that."

"I think you're prettier than my mother," Francis said quietly, and Anne reached out and caressed his face gently.

"No, you've just forgotten how lovely she was. You can't see it in a portrait. In the story books they gave me as a child, the prettiest princesses were always fair haired and blue eyed, like both of your mothers. What your father was thinking when he chose me as number three, we'll never know."

"I know," Francis said firmly. "I think you're beautiful. I think you're the most beautiful lady I have ever seen."

Anne was smiling. "There are an awful lot of beautiful ladies out there, Francis. But thank you."

"Number three?" Grace said, and there was an odd tone to her voice as though it had never occurred to her to place her long dead mother on the same footing as her two stepmothers. Paul felt guilt again and opened his mouth to speak then stopped as his wife reached out and put her arm around his daughter.

"Number three," she said firmly. "Your mother was the first, Grace, then Rowena and now me. I know I can't replace either of them with you, how could I? But I hope you'll get used to me. I've heard so much about you all. Now who is going to come up and see Will? He can't still be eating or he'll explode like a shell."

"And that one is going to haunt nursery teas for a while," Paul said, beginning to laugh. Anne smiled up at him.

"What is the point of nursery teas if you can't have unsuitable conversations? You should have heard some of the things my brothers used to say around the table, Nurse used to cover her ears."

"If your brothers were the most badly behaved at your nursery tea table, I would be very surprised, girl of my heart. Hand over my youngest daughter, you've had her long enough."

"Is that what he calls you?" Grace said, wide-eyed.

"He calls me a lot worse than that. Get those combs off her before she eats one of them, Paul, she can't be hungry it's not close to tea time."

Francis began to laugh. "Combs for tea!"

"Only if you don't behave, Master van Daan. Patience, I am so sorry, I've not even said how-do-you-do yet. And you as well, Joshua. Let me go and introduce Will, and when we've all driven him mad and he's howling through over-excitement I'll give him back to Gwen and come down for sherry and civilised conversation, I promise you. And I'll dump this lot off in the nursery on the way to wash themselves, Francis looks as though he's been through a battle on a wet day his face is so dirty."

"It is not! I do not!"

"You absolutely do, and don't argue with me, I've seen a lot of battles."

"Have you? I didn't know girls went near battles."

Paul was laughing so hard he could not stop. "They're not supposed to, Francis, but try telling your stepmother that, she hasn't the least sense of propriety."

His wife regarded him severely. "You're becoming as over-excited as the children, Colonel. Give me Rowena and put those combs on the table before you break them, I'm serving them to Francis for tea later. Don't come up, stay and be civil to your brother and Patience, I'm not sure you've even had a chance to speak to them yet. I'll see you later."

She left, and they could hear her progress with Francis and Grace suggesting a collection of bizarre items which could be served for tea. Paul crossed the room and kissed his sister-in-law.

"Come and sit down and have some wine. You look as though you've just been hit by an eight pounder. I do understand, my wife can have that effect on people. Josh, it's good to see you. Remind me again why I am holding a pair of tortoiseshell combs?"

He set them on the table and his family arranged themselves and accepted drinks. Paul sat down and smiled at his sister-in-law. "I'm sorry, lass, it's a bit of a shock, I know. But we weren't expecting the children."

"Good God, Paul, she's beautiful," Josh said. "When you wrote that you'd married a widow, I expected somebody older."

"I don't know why, but I didn't expect her to be so good with the children," Patience said, and Paul reached for her hand and held it. She laughed self-consciously. "And you're too acute. I should never have said that."

"Patience, this was never going to be easy for you, you're giving up your life to raise the alarming number of children I produce. Nobody is going to walk in and take over from that. And Nan understands it, I promise you."

"But one day she will," Patience said quietly. She smiled at his expression and shook her head. "Paul, it's all right. It is important that she develops a bond with them. I know they love me, I'm always there for them. And I don't forget that in a few weeks' time we'll all be back at Southwinds and it will be me who sees Will get his first tooth and take his first steps. She will miss all that. I arrived here prepared to give her whatever she needed to let her get to know the children because one day they'll be hers. I just expected her to find it more difficult. Has she much experience with children?"

"Only the camp brats. Although she is seldom without a few of those at her heels, now that I come to think of it. Nan doesn't really seem to treat children like children, it's odd."

"No, she speaks to them exactly the same way she speaks to adults," Joshua said. "You're looking very well, brother. Not much like a brigade commander, but perhaps your new dignity will become more obvious in time."

"It's hard to be dignified in the middle of a pack of children. Or anywhere near my wife."

"Paul, how the devil does she manage with regimental social events?" his father said, sounding fascinated. "I know it was hard for you with Rowena, but I can't imagine that girl doing the pretty with the generals' wives."

"Well, you will have the opportunity to find out, because I promised Wellington we'd host one or two parties the Portuguese grandees. If he thinks I'm being useful I can probably wring a few more days out of him. She's not like Rowena, sir. I used to ask her to keep an eye on Rowena at parties for me. She's a good hostess, she comes from a very wealthy Yorkshire family. Her father is a baronet, self-made through trade, and her stepmother who raised her, is related to the Dovercourts whom you know well. She wasn't brought up to be a hoyden and she can stop. Although only when she feels like it."

"Do you have any control over her at all, Paul?" Joshua said quietly. Paul was torn between amusement and irritation.

"A lot of my officers have spent more than a year carefully not saying that. Although they're all so used to her now, it hardly bothers them. I'm not trying to control her, Josh. You'll get accustomed to us, I promise."

Paul moved the conversation on, talking of the war and his fellow officers and the difficulties of his command and encouraging his father and Joshua to talk of the business. He enjoyed the normality of the conversation and the sheer happiness of being with his family again, but he was also aware that something had changed. Patience spoke little and Paul wondered at first if she was struggling with a little jealousy of Anne with the children. Halfway through the conversation he realised suddenly that there was nothing wrong with Patience at all.

He was the one who had changed. It seemed strange to him that she had so little to say, but he knew that if he began to talk about the children, or ask about the neighbours or Parish affairs, she would join in. Patience would have been horrified at the idea that she might even express an opinion about her family's business affairs and it would not have occurred to either Josh or his father to include her. There was nothing malicious about it and Paul realised that when he was last at home three years ago, he would not have thought it at all odd. Living with Anne had changed him in ways he had not known until now and he wondered how his conventional family were going to adjust to his lovely wife's eccentric personality.

They separated finally to dress for dinner, and Paul went in search of his wife, finding her curled up in the nursery. Will was feeding with his nurse and Rowena was sound asleep in her crib. The two older children were crammed onto one of the beds on either side of Anne, both in their night clothes as she told them stories.

Paul sat on the end of the bed listening until she had finished, then lifted up Francis who was drowsy and content and settled him into the other bed. Anne settled Grace and kissed her then went to kiss Francis.

"Behave the pair of you," Anne said. "I've barely spoken to the grown-ups yet; they'll think me a lunatic. Tomorrow we will continue the conversation about what it might be proper for you to call me, but you'll have to agree because I'm not being called five different names in a day, it will confuse me. Go to sleep. I love you all."

Anne went with him back to their room and Paul unbuttoned her dress and reached for the brush for her long hair. She sat in comfortable silence for a while, then smiled up at him. "Go and get changed, Jenson is waiting. Maria can help me dress."

"I'll be quick. I love you."

When he returned, his wife was ready, dressed elegantly in a white gown threaded through with gold and with a spangled scarf draped over her arms. Her hair was arranged in smooth braids low on her neck, a gold ribbon threaded through the coils, and a selection of gold pins like tiny flowers scattered throughout. Paul saw her studying her jewel case and smiled slightly as she selected the sedate pearls.

"Wear the diamonds, bonny lass."

"Too ostentatious," Anne said.

"No they're not, they're very tasteful. And there is no point in trying to play a part now, they all saw who you are earlier."

"I know," Anne said ruefully. "I had my script all prepared. It was the children. They're so lovely, Paul."

"I know. Don't worry about it, Nan, Patience understands. And they'll need to get used to us at some point. It may as well be now."

"I hope you're right. Shall we go down?"

Paul was amused to see his father's eyes on the diamond necklace as Anne greeted her in-laws. He watched with immense pride as she spoke for a while to his father then went to speak to Patience. Paul joined his father and Josh who were also watching the two women.

"I take your point, Paul," his father said quietly. "A remarkable transformation. Was this how you first saw her?"

"Oh – no. Not at all. I met her in a snowstorm in Yorkshire. We got stranded in a barn together in a blizzard for about fifteen hours or more. She was seventeen, out without any chaperone searching for the lost brat of one of their tenants, she'd no propriety, no shyness and no idea how much trouble she was in. One of the more difficult nights of my life."

Joshua was laughing. "I'll just bet it was, brother. Don't tell me you were a model of chivalry."

"It could have been worse, but not by much. I saw a lot of her after that. Carlyon was my quartermaster and trying to court her for her money. I don't think I'd ever wanted anything quite so much that I knew I couldn't have. By the end of six months, I knew she was the girl I never thought existed for me, but I couldn't have her. I went back to Rowena and off to Portugal and a year later found myself next to Anne on the deck of a ship coming back out here. She'd married Carlyon by then. She and Rowena became good friends."

"Wasn't that difficult?"

"Initially yes, but I became used to it. I loved the way she was with Rowena, and she brought my shy little wife out of herself in a way that surprised me. I learned things about Rowena through Nan that I'd never known; they were very close. Carlyon was a bastard, I know you've heard the story of how that ended. When he died…I suppose we could have waited, for propriety's sake. I was rather sick of propriety at that point, to be honest."

"She's managing my wife surprisingly well," Josh said, his eyes on the two women. "She's younger than I imagined, somehow. I suppose when you said a widow, I thought of someone closer to your age."

"She's nine years younger than me."

"She's lovely, Paul, I'm happy for you. But she's probably got some growing up to do before she's ready to settle down and take on your brood of children."

Paul glanced at his brother and smiled slightly. "She's not coming home with you, Josh, don't worry."

"God, Paul, I didn't mean…I'd understand if you wanted her to, and we'd be glad to have her. I think what I meant was that she's very free and easy with the children and they probably need a firmer hand at the moment, especially Francis."

"He needs a fair bit of discipline," Franz said. "Even Patience struggles at times."

"I thought him very well-mannered, earlier," Paul said mildly. "You've done a grand job with them, Josh."

"Oh he's a good lad. Although I thought Patience was going to sink into the ground when Grace was so outspoken about her situation. Your wife took it amazingly well."

"I'm happy you think so, Josh, but the truth is it wouldn't occur to Nan that Grace said a word out of place, she's in favour of plain speaking. I think Mario is ready to serve dinner, shall we go in?"

It was a week of surprises for Paul, watching his wife stepping into her new role as mistress of his house and stepmother to his children with more confidence than he had expected. He had known she would manage very well; she always did, but he was accustomed to her managing in a tent or a small billet and he enjoyed watching

61

her apply herself to her new responsibilities with the same determination that she brought to a difficult piece of surgery or a complicated financial problem. Despite her youth she seemed to experience no problems with the staff, all of whom had known her from her early days in Portugal when she and her first husband had been billeted at the villa.

His children had fallen under her spell within two days. Grace followed her about like an adoring puppy and blossomed under Anne's genuine interest in her. Francis clung more to Paul, but he was aware of his son's eyes following his lovely young stepmother and when they were together he peppered her with questions about her family, her home, her place in the regiment and her friendship with his dead mother. Rowena, too young to say more than a few words, was very shy but after three or four days Paul was aware that as soon as Anne entered the room she held out her arms to be lifted onto his wife's lap. Rowena was particularly fascinated with William, spending hours beside his nurse while she fed him, helping to bathe him and dress him and finding ways to make him laugh.

It had never occurred to Paul that in marrying Anne he had provided his children with a link to their dead mother, but it was clear to him very quickly that Anne had already thought it through. Another stepmother might have shied away from their constant questions about Rowena during the last year of her life in Portugal, but Anne did not hesitate, telling endless small stories about her, making up information if she did not know the answer. He remembered suddenly that Anne's mother had died when she was very young and that she had been presented with a young stepmother when she was the same age as Francis. He knew Anne was very close to Harriet Howard, and he wondered if she was modelling her behaviour with the children on her own upbringing. If she was, it explained a good deal about her own unconventional outlook on life. His children, motherless and raised by his rigidly conventional sister in law, opened up like flowers in the sunlight under Anne's laughing affection.

Anne's effect on the adults was more complicated. Both Franz and Joshua were clearly fascinated by her beauty and her charm and when they were in company with her, Paul noticed that like most men around Anne, their attention quickly focused on her. Paul was happy to sit back and let her do what she did best. She organised two dinner parties and a reception for the local dignitaries Wellington wanted to impress, letting Grace help her with the planning and organisation, much to his daughter's surprised delight. Paul used the opportunity to talk to some of the Portuguese and English diplomats about Wellington's plans and the difficulties he faced. He was cynically aware that he was disseminating only the information his chief wanted to share, and some of it false or misleading, since Wellington was cautious about his plans being leaked where they might be heard by the French, but he knew the part he needed to play.

When not in Anne's company, however, Franz and Joshua clearly had some reservations and Paul was fairly sure they were being fanned by his sister-in-law. He was not surprised that Patience was less enthusiastic about Anne. Two women could not have been more different. Patience was a pleasant-faced woman in her early thirties who had been a good and conformable wife to his brother. She had managed his household and worked hard to keep the peace with his difficult father and brother and as far as Paul knew, the marriage had worked well, the lack of children being their only grief. Patience had conceived several times but had miscarried. She had seemed genuinely happy to take on the responsibility for Paul's children and he knew she was very attached to them.

Patience had been kind to his gentle, shy first wife and Rowena had been very fond of her. She had been grateful for how generously Patience had accepted her into the family given that she had been pregnant when Paul married her and at the time, Paul had shared her gratitude. It was only now, looking back over the years, that he wondered if Patience had made rather too much of the younger woman's uncertainty and lack of social skills. Patience had constantly sympathised with how difficult it was for Paul to manage regimental life with a wife who could not support him socially.

When Paul had arrived in Portugal on the same transport as Anne and her first husband, it had not occurred to him that the girl he had fallen in love with could befriend his wife, but Anne had done so, seeming able to separate out her feelings for him from her genuine affection for Rowena. There was nothing shy or uncertain about Anne even at such a young age, but far from looking down on his wife for her awkwardness, Anne had taken her firmly under her wing and Paul had watched, with considerable surprise, as Rowena began to develop social confidence for the first time ever, as she never had when she was around Patience.

It was clear that Patience was finding her new sister-in-law a trial. She appeared friendly enough and very ready with advice about the children, about married life and about how to behave socially. Anne accepted her remarks with charming appreciation and went on to ignore all of them. Confident in her surroundings, and already known to local society, Anne had no need of her sister-in-law's patronage and although she freely admitted that Patience must know the children better than she did, she did not allow that fact to affect her own dealings with them at all. Within a week Patience had moved from gentle condescension in her dealings with Anne to a somewhat uncomfortable coolness which threatened to turn into active hostility as Anne continued to go her own way, despite all advice to the contrary from her sister-in-law.

"You have to remember that Patience is older by ten years, Paul, and she has a lot more experience than Anne," Joshua said one evening as the men sat in the courtyard drinking sherry before dinner. "She could be a little more conciliating."

Paul managed not to groan. "What's she done now, Josh?"

"It's no one thing, just a general attitude. She has overruled Patience again and again in matters of discipline, and this morning she took the children away from their lessons without a word of apology – simply laughed when Patience remonstrated with her and said that she would engage to take them somewhere educational and fill their heads with useful information."

Paul choked on his sherry. "And did she?"

"Apparently she took them on a picnic and let them fish in a stream. And when my wife demanded to know what was educational about that, she said that it was extremely useful to learn how to feed yourself at need, but that she had also taught them how to build a fire properly and given them a good deal of information about the local wildlife and flowers."

Unexpectedly Franz gave a crack of laughter. "Well that much is certainly true, Francis bored me senseless for twenty minutes earlier about the habits of scorpions. I didn't know he had it in him to absorb that much information, to be honest, she's a good teacher."

"All the same..."

Paul took a deep breath. "Josh, I am trying so hard not to engage with you over this because I'm well aware that time is running out on my visit here and God knows when we'll see each other again. I don't propose to waste the time arguing about my wife taking my children on a picnic. They've got a couple of weeks with us they don't need lessons during that time. And Patience doesn't think so either, she's just doing it to make Nan look young and irresponsible."

"Anne is young and irresponsible."

Paul looked at him for a long time then set down his glass. "I can see we're not going to be able to avoid this are we?" he said. "All right, Josh, I am going to be very frank with you here. With any luck you'll find a way to convey it to your wife, because if you don't, sooner or later I'm going to have to and I won't be as civil as you will. Nan is young. She isn't irresponsible. The responsibilities she's taken on since she came to Portugal would daunt a grown man, and she's damned good at it. She's my quartermaster in all but name and since she joined us, the accounts balance so well that I'm in funds most of the time which means I can buy tents and proper clothing for my men when other regiments are marching barefoot. She works with the surgeons, and she has the respect and support of Franck, the surgeon-general. She manages whole aspects of regimental life, so that I can get on with my job and she lives in appalling conditions while she's doing it. And when Lord Wellington wants to send somebody to charm the Portuguese while he's busy fighting a war, he sends her. I'm just here as window dressing. So don't sit there and tell me your wife is older and more experienced than her, because you have literally no idea what she's like or what she's capable of. And if Nan tells me that my children will benefit from a picnic instead of poring over books for the day, I'll listen to her. Now cut line and let's talk about something else because this constant whining about the girl I married is beginning to piss me off."

There was a silence in the room. Into it, his father said mildly:

"Do you know, Paul, in all the years you were with her I never once heard you speak up for Rowena like that."

Paul looked at him. "I didn't," he said. "But I should have. Nan taught me that."

Josh sighed. "Paul, you used to be very fond of Patience."

"I am, Josh. And I am grateful for all the work you're both doing raising my children. But they're still my children. And now they're Nan's; you need to get used to that."

Franz poured more sherry and passed the glass to his son. "Paul, your wife does take some getting used to. She's extraordinary."

"I know that sir. And I know she's a shock when you're not used to her. Look, I was going to leave this until it was time to leave. But since the subject has been raised, Nan and I have been talking and I realise that we need to have a conversation about the children's education. My memory is that there was a governess."

"There have been a number of governesses," Franz said drily. "The current one gave notice just before we came away. To be honest it was one of the things that affected our decision to bring them. Francis should be at school, he's running wild, he needs discipline."

"I'm sure he does, sir, but I've a feeling your ideas on that subject and mine still vary rather widely. In fact, I know they do because he's told me."

"Whatever he's said, Paul..."

"Look, I may only have another few days with you, sir, and after that it is conceivable that we might never see one another again, so we are not getting into a fight now about the mistakes of my upbringing."

Franz was silent for a moment. "Is it going to be bad?" he asked quietly.

"It's always bad. But we've another border fortress to storm, my least favourite part of war. It's so bloody unpredictable. My commander-in-chief is the best battlefield general I've ever come across, his eye for terrain and his ability to make quick decisions under pressure are unbelievable. But those things don't help as much when the only move you can make, is to throw men at breaches until either they're all dead or we're in and the city is taken. I lost my commander and friend last month in those breaches. I'd be stupid if I didn't acknowledge that this time it could be me."

Franz studied his son's face. "Are you afraid?"

"To some degree I'm always afraid, sir. We all are. The difference between a good soldier and a poor one is the effect it has on us. With me, it sharpens me up. I've no wish to die out there, and I absolutely hate seeing my men die. But a lot of them will, some of them might be my friends. I could lose Carl or Johnny or Michael or Danny Carter." Paul gave a slight grin. "In my case, I always have the extra frisson of knowing that my lass is up to her elbows in a hospital or dressing station and the French aren't always that accurate or that careful where they direct their cannon."

"She should not be doing that, Paul, she's a mother for Christ's sake."

"And I'm a father, sir. Four of them now, and we might well have more. So I need to sit down with you and Josh, and talk about the provision I've made for them and the provision I want to make."

"Everything that's yours will go to them, Paul. Money isn't a problem."

"I know. And there'll be an inheritance from Nan as well, her father made good provision for her when she married Carlyon and it's continued. They'll never lack for anything."

"Presumably that only applies to Will."

"No. She stipulated from the first that all the children were to be considered ours for legal purposes."

"And who administers all this, Paul? Who is their legal guardian?"

Paul shot his father a sideways glance. "Nan is," he said.

"Jesus Christ, Paul! Is that even legal? Do you realise they'll own a share in the company? And..."

"So will Nan, she inherits it from me."

"A woman on my Board? Are you out of your mind?"

Paul studied him in some amusement. "I'm really hoping it doesn't happen, sir. I want to come home at the end of this war and pick up my life and take care of my own children. But if that goes wrong, I need to know they'll be raised the way I want them to be. And they only person I can trust to do that is Nan."

"I can't believe you'd put a woman you've been married to less than two years in control..."

"Stop right there, before your temper causes you to say something that will piss me off. I've told you, I don't want to fight. It's all drawn up and it's legal..."

"More would have told me..."

"Mr More doesn't know. He will do soon, I've written to him. I've been using Wellington's man of business; he's used to dealing with the army. Sir, listen to me. If I die and she goes back home to England to raise my children, she'll bring them more than they could ever get from you and Josh and Patience. I realise that all you see is her youth and how she looks, but I'm telling you that if you ever end up with her on the Board of our company, I'm leaving you an asset you'd be mad not to make the most of, she'll triple your profits and you won't even know how it happened. As for the children, they already adore her."

Franz sighed and looked at Josh. "Paul, I'm not stupid; I can see how good she is with them. But this is going to cause ructions with Patience."

"Patience is jealous. She'll get over it. To be honest once things are in place, I'm going to leave it up to you and Josh what you tell her about this. I probably wouldn't mention it unless you have to, no need to upset her over something which might never happen. I don't want to interfere too much with the children just now. You're doing a good job with them. But I do want to choose a tutor for Francis and Grace. I don't want him going to school yet, we send them too young, there's no need. He's only seven and I remember to my cost, the joys of boarding school."

"He fights all the time, Paul."

"Find out why."

Franz looked at him. "Does it matter?"

"Of course it matters, don't be an arse, father! If he's bullying somebody that's one thing. If he's punching the Squire's son for calling his sister a bastard, my personal reaction would be to hold his coat and wish him well. Or deal with the Squire, the child hears it from somewhere."

"Paul, she is illegitimate."

"She's legally adopted and a considerable heiress. Put that about the neighbourhood and watch their attitude change. Look, the ladies will be joining us shortly, we can't talk this through now. We'll arrange a meeting tomorrow to go over this, I've a lad in mind for a tutor; he used to be one of my officers but he's selling out, he lost an arm at Fuentes. He's a Cambridge scholar, his father is a Don. You'll like him."

"Do you care if I don't?"

Paul studied him thoughtfully for a moment. "Not much," he admitted. "I want them to live with you, father. You're family and I know how much you love them. But if I hear one more story about you thrashing my seven-year-old because he needs discipline, I will take emergency furlough, come home without warning, take them out of your care and give them to Nan's parents to raise, stopping briefly on my way to throw you into the lake. You leave discipline to young Harcourt, he came through

66

the 110th and if he can discipline that lot without flogging them, he'll have no trouble with a seven-year-old, trust me."

"And Grace? She should have a governess."

"She can share Francis' lessons."

"There are other things she needs to learn, Paul," Joshua said.

Paul grinned. "Like what?"

His brother looked startled. "What? Oh lord, I don't know! What is it that they teach girls? Needlework and drawing and music…"

"If she wants to, then hire somebody. But I want her given the same education as Francis, she's bright enough."

"What the hell for?" Franz said. "She's a girl, for God's sake. What is she going to do with it?"

"Manage your board when she's old enough if that's what she wants. You won't be there to see it, don't worry, father."

Joshua took a deep breath. "And I suppose this is Anne's idea as well?" he said. "Do you know something, brother? Since you married that girl you seem to have gone completely mad. We've looked after your children for years without…"

"And I'm grateful. Do you want somebody else to do it, Josh? Because they've another set of grandparents as well, now, whom I understand would be very willing."

"No, of course I don't want that." Joshua sighed. "Honestly, Paul, I don't give a damn about who teaches Grace. Perhaps your tutor will do better than the endless stream of governesses she goes through. But Patience isn't going to like this."

"Patience will get used to it. Now enough of this, let's enjoy dinner."

He spoke to Anne later that night as she snuggled up against him in bed. "I'm sorry, lass. I didn't intend to raise it so soon."

"It's probably better that you do. We're doing very well here, but if you get much more than another week, I'll be surprised."

"So will I. Shall we do it tomorrow? No reason for Patience to be there."

"That will be up to Josh, Paul. If he wants her there you can't shut her out. Unless you're going to shut me out too."

"I'm not that brave," Paul said with a grin. "Nan, look – I'm sorry. I wanted this to be…"

"Hush. I'm not upset, Paul. To be honest I'd have been amazed if they'd accepted me immediately. I take a bit of getting used to."

"It didn't take me long."

"I meant for normal people, love. They'll come round. And if they don't, we'll manage it. Just at the moment as long as the children are all right while we're out here, and we have something in place if anything happens to you, that's all that matters."

Paul studied the beloved face on the pillow beside him. "Girl of my heart, I need you to tell me the truth right now. Are you happy leaving Will with them? Because if you're not, we'll arrange for your parents to take him."

"No, I want him to be with the others. They're a family. To be honest, I'm not at all worried about Will, he's still a baby. I'm more concerned about Grace and Francis. I think she's struggling a bit with being illegitimate and nobody will talk to her properly about it. But she can write to me now and that might help. And Francis will be all right if Mr Harcourt takes over as his tutor."

Paul kissed her. "I was hoping this would be easier, but I'm so glad they brought the children or we'd never have realised any of this." He smiled slightly. "I might not have realised anyway but they talk to you, don't they?"

"Yes."

Paul drew her closer into his arms. "Do you know, when I married you, I didn't give one single thought to my poor children," he said. "I wrote a four line scrawl informing my family and I left it to them to tell the children that their mother was dead and that I'd remarried. I wonder now how Francis and Grace felt about that. Rowena was the only mother Grace had ever known. I was so bloody selfish, all I thought about was myself and how much I wanted you."

Anne looked up at him, studying the lines of his face in the darkness. "Paul, I'm not sure you could have done much different."

"No, probably not, I could hardly have asked for leave at that point. But I didn't try." Paul gave a little laugh. "But do you know what? I've just realised that it doesn't matter. I've given them the best stepmother they could have had, completely by accident."

"Paul, don't hang a halo on me. I'm not sure I'm naturally that maternal."

"I'm not sure what that means, girl of my heart. I just know that they're going to learn more from you than my sister-in-law could have taught them in a lifetime."

Paul sensed her smile. "I hope so. Although none of them are going to be able to cook or sew, I'm afraid."

"That's all right, bonny lass. Luckily, they'll have the money to pay people to do that. Go to sleep."

Chapter Six

They met the following day in the dining room with Patience included. Her taut hostility told Anne that Joshua had shared Paul's conversation with her and she wished he had not. Seated around the long table Paul took his family through the arrangements he had put in place should he be killed. It was hard not to be sombre. He and Anne had talked it through months ago and then set it aside, refusing to let thoughts of potential disaster ruin the pleasure of their days together. They revisited it now.

When he had finished, Paul closed the file of documents. "I've sent copies of everything to More and also to Sir Matthew Howard's lawyers. A third copy will be held by the firm of Blundell and Merchison in London who represent Lord Wellington. They drew up the will and the trusts and they'll represent Nan if she needs anything. One of their junior partners is currently attached to Wellington's staff and knows her well."

Anne glanced covertly at her brother-in-law who was staring at his father. There was a veiled warning in Paul's words and she knew Joshua would have understood it. Franz was looking at Anne. "This is a huge amount of responsibility for a girl of your age," he said.

Anne studied him, weighing up her reply. "Sir, I know it seems that way to you. And I'd much rather not have to take it on, since that would mean the man I love is dead in some Spanish grave. But I'm capable of it. They send boys of my age out to lead men. Paul was younger than I am now, I believe, when he led his company at Assaye and nobody told him it was too much responsibility."

"That's different. He's a man."

"Why is it different?"

"Anne, I am aware that you are a very unusual young woman. And believe me, when I tell you that I have nothing but admiration for what you have done for my son. You've made him happier than I have ever seen him. But…"

"He's made me happy too, sir. But that's not our job. That's not what we do, that's just a consequence of two people in love being together. In addition to that we have other lives, other things that we do which matter. I…"

"My dear, while I think you are very noble to help with the nursing you can hardly equate that with what my brother-in-law does," Patience said with biting sarcasm. "Nor can I see how that is likely to help with managing four children, at least two of whom can be very difficult. Besides which, you are very young. Forgive me, but I would not wish to see Paul's children - or his fortune - fall into the hands of some ne'er-do-well whom you might decide to take up with after his death."

Anne shot a glance at her husband. He was keeping his temper surprisingly well, but she wished Patience would temper her remarks. "Well I would not wish to see that either, Patience, so let us not speak of it further," she said calmly. "I am hoping that none of this will ever be needed. We just want to be sure that if the worst did happen, my position with the children is very clear."

"My dear Anne, like you I hope it will never come to that," Patience said smoothly. "But if it did, I suspect in a court of law, the judge would consider everything, including moral character."

There was a frozen silence around the table. Josh said mildly:

"Patience, I know you're upset, but that was uncalled for."

"Uncalled for?" Paul said, and Anne looked quickly at his expression, seeing that his father was doing the same.

"No!" she said firmly. "Do not say any of the things you want to say just now, Paul, it will not help. And you can't hit her, she's a female."

"I'm rethinking my position on that one, girl of my heart. Patience, did I just hear you suggest that if I am killed in battle, my family would consider attacking my wife's good name in court in order to take my children from her?"

"I am simply pointing out…"

"We wouldn't, Paul," Franz said softly. "Christ, you must know that."

"I hope I do, sir, but it's an interesting light on the character of my sister-in-law. I am definitely beginning to think I want her influence on my children kept to a minimum if that's how her mind works."

He was visibly furious and Anne put her hand firmly on his arm. "Enough, love. We need to solve this." She looked at Patience. "For the sake of the children, who are genuinely attached to both of us, I am hoping we can put this to one side," she said quietly. "But please understand that if you were ever to impugn my virtue or attack my reputation in any way, the first person to stand up in court to defend me would be Lord Wellington. I would probably follow with Marshal Beresford and General Sir Charles Stewart. But I could choose any one of the senior staff. You would lose and you would look like a spiteful, vengeful female jealous of a younger sister-in-law. So let us put that idea away and focus on..."

There were sounds from the hallway and Paul looked around. Mario appeared in the doorway.

"My apologies for disturbing you, Colonel, but there is a messenger for you. It is apparently urgent."

Paul looked over at Anne and gave a rueful smile. Anne felt her heart sink. "Well you did better than you thought you'd do," she said gently.

"I know, girl of my heart. Who is it, Mario?"

"It's me, sir. Sorry."

Paul got up and Anne did the same. "It's good to see you, Sergeant, although I wish you'd managed to lose that on the way. Everything all right?"

Hammond came fully into the room and saluted. "Fine, sir. I've got letters from Colonel Wheeler and Major Swanson. And one for you, ma'am, from Keren."

"How is she, Jamie, I'm missing her?"

"She's missing you too, ma'am, we all are. Place isn't the same without you."

Paul observed with some amusement the consternation among his family at the sight of his wife embracing a sergeant. "At ease, Sergeant and hand it over. Is he yelling yet?"

"He's been pretty good, sir, but he had a letter from General Alten yesterday and it seems his return has been delayed. And he's ready to move out to Badajoz. All of a sudden he's marching in on Colonel Wheeler demanding to know where you are and why you're not back, as if he'd no idea how it had happened."

He handed Paul a letter in Wellington's familiar scrawl and Paul glanced at his father. "I'm sorry, I need to read this."

"Of course."

Paul opened it and skimmed it quickly, his lips quirking into a smile. "Grumpy," he said mildly. "He seems to have forgotten he gave me leave at all. He thinks we'll breach Badajoz before Alten gets here in which case he wants me in temporary command."

"Of the Light Division?" Franz said, shocked.

"Well, he's not going to put me in charge of the cavalry, that's for sure. Barnard and Vandeleur are going to yell at this one. Ah well, it won't be for long. But I am going to have to get back there and fast, girl of my heart, before he stamps all over their pride. He is not noted for his tact when he's in this mood."

"I know, love."

Paul came forward and lifted her hand to his lips. "I'm sorry. Look, why don't you stay a few days longer? I'll move faster on my own and you can come up with the supply column as we originally planned. It will give you a chance to say goodbye to the children properly, and you can make sure everything is in order with the column."

Anne smiled. "And it means you can ride through the night and sleep rough and not have to think about my delicate sensibilities along the way."

"You have none, bonny lass. It's up to you..."

"It's all right, Colonel, I know you need to get going. Stay tonight though and let Jamie get some rest since it's unlikely he'll get much for a few days."

71

Paul laughed and bent to kiss her very gently. Behind him, his brother said:

"Paul, are you mad? She can't do that journey without you or any respectable female to chaperone her."

Sergeant Hammond gave a splutter of laughter which he hastily turned into a cough and Paul grinned. "Bad cough that, Hammond. Josh, she'll be fine. There'll be an escort with the supply column, they'll probably pull together a few men returning from sick leave. And if they get lost, she'll tell them which way to go."

Anne glanced at Hammond. "Jamie, go with Mario and get something to eat. We need to finish here and then go and tell the children. Which I am going to find very hard."

When he had gone Anne turned back and looked at them. "I'm going to find the children," she said. "I don't need to be here. What you all need to do now is mend some bridges. He's going tomorrow and you don't need me to tell you…anyway, talk for a bit and then let's move on. I am sorry that you don't really approve of me yet. Perhaps you never will. But what is more important just now is that you make your peace, you don't need me here, I'm the outsider."

"No you're not," Paul said quickly and Anne smiled and went to kiss him.

"Not with you, idiot. But we're asking too much of them in a short time, Paul. I understand you had to tell them how we're arranging things, but they don't have to like it. Just talk to them."

She left and there was silence. Into it, Franz said:

"It's gone too quickly."

"I know." Paul turned and studied his family. "She's right," he said.

"According to you she's always right, Paul," Josh said.

"Josh, she's my wife and I love her. I also love you. But when it comes to the future of my children, I'm putting them first. I really hope you don't have to cope with this before you've had a chance to get used to the idea. Let's not fight any more."

Paul was exhausted by the time he was ready to set off the following morning, worn out by the tears of his children and the restrained unhappiness of his father and brother. Hammond waited impassively with Jenson and the horses and Paul knelt and kissed Grace, Francis and Rowena then took Will from Anne's arms and kissed his sleeping son very gently. He handed him to the nurse and turned back to his wife.

"Are you all right?"

"Yes. I'll be seeing you very soon, Colonel, don't worry."

"I won't, bonny lass." Paul turned to his father. "Father, it's been good to see you. Thank you for coming – you too, Josh. And for bringing the children. I can't tell you what it's meant to me. Will you tell Patience the same?"

His brother nodded and hugged him. Paul had the odd impression that they had never before really thought about the possibility of his death in battle and he supposed that talking through practical arrangements had made it real to them. He turned to embrace Franz and his father hugged him hard.

"Take care, Paul. Not that you will."

"I will. I always do as far as I can, sir."

"Listen to me, boy, because I know you've no time. You shouldn't have to go off without being sure. Whatever you want, whatever you've set up for her, I'll see it done. No question." Franz glanced over at his daughter-in-law with a slight smile.

72

"You're wrong to think I don't approve of her. I do, very much. It's just not what I'm used to. But I promise it will be done the way you want. And I'll take care of her."

"Thank you," Paul said softly. "It means so much…look I need to get out of here before I embarrass myself. I love you."

"I love you too, lad. Goodbye."

Paul turned to Anne and kissed her long and hard. "See you in a week or two, girl of my heart. I love you."

"I love you too."

With Paul gone, the villa suddenly felt empty to Anne. She concentrated her attention on the children, trying to cram in as much time with them as possible. At night, when the others slept, she would return to the nursery and sit with them, holding Will in her arms and crying silent tears over their imminent separation.

She was surprised there one night by Grace who woke unexpectedly. Anne rose, putting her finger to her lips, and lifted Will back into his crib. Smiling through her tears she beckoned to her stepdaughter to follow her back down to her bedroom.

"Come on, into bed if you want to talk, or you'll freeze. Tuck yourself in, there's plenty of space."

Grace complied, wide eyed with surprise and snuggled up to Anne who held her close. "Do you miss him? My father?"

"Yes. And in a few days I'm going to miss all of you. I can't have it all ways but it's very painful."

Grace tilted her face up to Anne's. "I don't want you to go," she said. "I don't want to go back to England."

"Why not, Grace?"

"It's not the same there. Here, with you, it's like I'm just one of the family. You talk about my mother."

Anne felt her heart twist in pain for the child. "Your aunt and uncle and your grandfather didn't know anything about her, Grace, that's the only reason they don't talk about her."

Steady blue eyes looked up at her. "No it isn't," Grace said, and Anne looked back at her and knew that a lie was not good enough.

"I know. I'm sorry, Grace."

"Sometimes I don't get invited to parties," Grace said in matter-of-fact tones. "Because my father and my mother weren't married. Once I heard my grandfather say that it was my father's fault for not keeping up the pretence that I was his ward. And my uncle said what was the point, I'm the living image of him."

"Well your uncle was right about that, you are. I wish I could help you with this right now, love. But this time my job is to go back to your father and help him to win this war."

"I know."

"But one day it will be over, and we'll be back in England. And at that point you shall point out to me these people who refuse to invite my beautiful step-daughter to their horrible homes, and I promise you, I will deal with them for you. And in the meantime, you shall write to me a lot and tell me all about it and I shall write back and tell you what I think of them."

"I don't think Aunt Patience would like me to be rude."

"Then don't be rude in front of Aunt Patience," Anne said calmly, and Grace began to laugh.

"You are not like any grown-up I have ever met," she said.

"No, I'm afraid I am not. But your father likes me this way, which is fortunate. How is Francis with all this?"

"He gets into fights about it with the other boys when they say things about me. My grandfather says he should be sent away to boarding school to have it knocked out of him."

"If he thinks he can knock that out of your father's son, he has learned nothing in all these years. Does Francis want to go to boarding school?"

"No, but he can't go on upsetting the neighbourhood."

"I'll bet he can, almost indefinitely. Why on earth did nobody tell us about all of this?"

"My Uncle Joshua said that father has enough to worry about with running a brigade and being married to you. And Aunt Patience said that you would be upset at leaving Will and can't be expected to take on responsibility for all his children at your age."

Her stepmother regarded her in some awe. "Grace, do you spend your entire life listening at doors?"

"How else would I ever find anything out?" the child said, reasonably. "Nobody ever tells us anything."

"No, I perfectly understand. I always felt the same way. All right, listen to me, my scary step-daughter. I am sorely tempted to go downstairs in the morning and do a good deal of shouting at my delightful but incredibly dense in-laws, but you know what would happen then, don't you?"

"They would know that I had been listening at doors and talking to you about it?"

"You are as intelligent as you are beautiful. That isn't going to help anything, especially since I can't be here to deal with them. They clearly think I am young and foolish and need to grow up a lot and understand how the world works. Whereas I could tell them that I am not at all foolish and understand very well how the world works, I just don't like it. I think your Aunt Patience needs a break from you all, you must drive her mad. How would you like to spend the summer in Yorkshire?"

"Yorkshire?"

"Yes, it's where my home is. I want my family to see Will, and I'd like them to meet you as well since you are all my children now. I'll talk to your father when I get back and we'll ask if you can go and spend some time at Helton Ridge. My stepmother will look after you and you'll love her. She raised me which is something of an achievement, you must admit. You can ride and walk and play in the fields and nobody will care two hoots about who your mother is, apart from the fact that I am now. It will be good for you all to meet your step-cousins, and it will give Rowena a chance to move more than two feet away from your aunt's skirts which is going to be necessary if the child isn't going to grow up into a mouse."

Grace was laughing. "Aunt Patience says it is enough to have one hoyden in the family, without letting Rowena grow up the same way."

74

"She should have thought of that before agreeing to take on your father's children. Wait until I have a girl, that will scare her into a fit. I'll see what I can do. In the meantime, love, next time somebody turns up their nose at you because of anything to do with your mother, you hold your head up high and you look at them right in the eye and you don't look down or look away. You make them look away first. Is that clear?"

Grace was staring at her in wonder. "Isn't that rude?"

"Sometimes rudeness is the best solution, Grace. Don't say anything, you're not old enough to get it right, yet. But don't you lower your eyes as if you've done something wrong; you haven't. And if anybody tells you off for that, you tell them that I gave you permission and they are to speak to me about it."

Unexpectedly Grace began to cry. Anne held her close, smoothing the fair hair. "I miss my mother."

"Rowena? I miss her too, Grace."

"I think I've decided. But I don't know what Francis will want."

"I've changed my mind about that. You call me what you want, and he can do the same even if it's different. I'll adapt, it's not as though I'm not used to it, your father calls me the strangest things at times."

"May I call you Mama?"

"You may, my love. In fact, I would love you to. We'll practice it in letters. Have you ever had your portrait painted?"

Grace looked at her in surprise. "No."

"I'll arrange it; my stepmother will know who is best. I'd like a miniature of you to show everybody how beautiful my eldest daughter is."

"And what will you tell them if they ask about my mother?" Grace asked.

"I shall tell them that her name was Nell and that she was very lovely and that your father knew her in India when they were both very young. And that he cared for her a great deal, which I know that he did. And if they are impertinent enough to ask any more – which they will not be, by the way, people seldom have the nerve – I shall tell them that she died very tragically, far too young and you are being raised by me, exactly as I shall raise my own daughter should I have one."

Grace looked up. "I wish I were your daughter," she said quietly.

"You are now. Don't ever forget it. And I am relying on you, as you are the eldest, to take care of Rowena and Will for me until I'm back with you all. Don't let Rowena be scared of everything, the world is not that frightening. Make sure you tell Will all about us when he is old enough to understand and read our letters to him. I want him to know who we are." Anne smiled slightly. "I wish I'd known your mother she must have been lovely."

The blue eyes clouded slightly. "I once heard Aunt Patience say that it was a relief that she was dead because nobody needed to know that I was the by-blow of a common soldier's wife."

Anne felt anger course through her. She bent and kissed Grace very gently. "You listen to me, Grace van Daan. Your father had a bit of a reputation with women before he married me, but I know him very well and if he chose to be with her, she was special. He was a lot more picky than you'd think. He really cared about her and he has often told me he wished you'd known her for longer. As for the rest, some of my best friends are common soldiers and their wives. Half of them aren't even properly married, and it doesn't matter."

Grace looked up, startled. "It's a sin…"

"God gives special dispensation to our lads, Grace, I'm convinced of it. In fact, I've never been completely convinced he needs a church wedding with the banns read to join a couple. People invented that later on. I think if two people love each other and want to be together and raise a family, what counts in his eyes is how they go about doing that. I understand that your Aunt Patience sees it differently, it's how she was raised. But don't you ever go through life feeling ashamed of who your mother was, love. Promise me?"

The child looked up and there were tears in the blue eyes which tugged unexpectedly at Anne's heart. "I'm so glad he married you," she whispered. "We were so worried when we heard…"

"Understandably so. Especially since I imagine it came soon after you heard about Rowena's death. She'd been your mother for years. You must have felt terrible. And I know how much she loved you, she talked about you both all the time."

"It doesn't matter so much now. But you mustn't die. I don't think I could bear that."

"I'll be fine, I'm very strong, Grace."

"You don't look it."

Anne laughed. "Looks can be deceptive, ask your father what I'm capable of."

Grace stirred in her arms. "I should go back to bed, my aunt will be cross if I'm not there in the morning."

"You can stay here if you want to, Grace."

The child shook her head. "No. Francis might wake up and be worried. Mama…I love you."

Anne felt her heart twist in pain. "I love you too, Grace. All of you."

The last few days were beset with problems as the supply column she was to travel with, struggled to find an escort. Anne wrote again to Paul explaining the delay, sent it off with a courier heading north and tried to contain her impatience. The Van Daans were due to sail for England the following week and she did not want to be alone in the villa, missing both her husband and the children.

Relations with her sister-in-law remained coolly civil. Anne had no wish to antagonise Patience any further, now that she had what she wanted and she did not want to make life difficult for Joshua whom she genuinely liked. She felt, in those final days, an unexpected sense of support from her irascible father-in-law who seemed to have taken his defeat over the contents of Paul's will surprisingly well. Anne was grateful and found an opportunity to tell him so on the evening before her departure when Patience had retired to bed early as she did most evenings and Joshua had followed her murmuring an apology. Franz reached for the port bottle and lifted his eyebrows at Anne and she laughed.

"I know very well that as a lady it's my place to murmur a polite no and retire, leaving you to drink in solitary splendour, sir. But I'm not going to, I'd love one. Thank you."

Franz smiled and poured. "I'm glad. We should be together as a family this evening, but I can see that's not going to happen. Anne – I am sorry. I'm really angry with my son and his wife over this, they're behaving like spoiled children. At least she is, and he isn't dealing with her."

"It's not as easy as that, sir, she's his wife and he loves her. Of course he supports her, even if he thinks she's being silly."

"Do you think Paul would support you in similar circumstances?" Franz asked curiously and Anne laughed.

"I think he would tell me I was being an idiot. But you can't take us as a model, we're not normal, even I know that."

"Perhaps if more people were like you two, the world would work more effectively."

"You've been lovely, sir. I'm so glad you came out."

Franz smiled. "So am I. I will be honest, Anne, when I first read my son's extremely brief note to say that he had remarried, I was not impressed, and the stories flying around Horse Guards did not help. I am not sure what I expected, but you are definitely not it."

"I didn't think you'd be so like him," Anne said. "But it should have been obvious, that will have been why you clashed so badly. I must say I'm looking forward to Paul with Francis as he grows up, it should be delightful. As for my Will…"

Her father-in-law smiled. "The difference is that we had nobody to intervene, so things simply got worse and worse. I doubt Paul would do it anyway, but I would like to see your reaction if he suggested sending one of your boys to sea at the age of fourteen."

Anne sipped her wine. "He's over it, sir."

"I know. So am I. I'm so proud of him it hurts. But I worry about him a lot. Meeting you, seeing how happy he is, will make that easier. Anne, don't worry about the children. I've taken on what you've both said and I'm going to trust that this new tutor will be able to manage them."

"He will, sir. Just keep an eye on Grace for me, will you? I didn't realise how much she has struggled with the stigma of being Paul's natural daughter."

"Nor did I, she's never said anything to any of us."

"It's sometimes easier with a stranger."

"Anne, I have known you for less than a month and I am already sure that you are the chosen confidante of half the regiment. I wish we'd had longer. Will you write to me?"

"I will, I promise. Thank you, sir. I should probably go up and make sure the children are settled, I've an early start tomorrow."

"How long will it take you?"

"Around seven or eight days allowing for mishaps. There always are mishaps with bullock wagons, believe me, and some of these are heavy."

Franz shook his head disapprovingly. "He should have waited and gone with you," he said. "I still don't like the idea of you travelling alone with a pack of common soldiers."

"He was needed," Anne said gently. "If Lord Wellington is ready to march on Badajoz and the new commander of his Light Division can't be there, he wants Paul. As a matter of fact, he'd want him anyway."

"He seems to place a high value on my son's abilities."

"He does, but it's more than that. They're friends. Lord Wellington struggles with his officers at times, sir. He's not good at delegating and he upsets people easily. The longer this war goes on, the more he is inclined to believe that nobody can be trusted to do anything without his personal supervision. But he trusts Paul, not only to be competent, but to tell him the truth. They argue – there have been times when the rest of the staff runs for cover when they get into an argument. But he trusts Paul. And now that he's lost poor General Craufurd he'll need him even more." Anne smiled. "As for a pack of common soldiers, you'd be surprised to hear they are often more respectful and well behaved than some of the officers. There will be an officer in command and it isn't going to offend my sensibilities travelling alone because I have none."

"Why didn't you bring your maid with you?"

"I don't really have one," Anne admitted. "At least, I had two but Teresa has married Sergeant-Major Carter and is expecting her first baby and Keren is…"

She broke off suddenly remembering that Franz was a close neighbour and patron to Carl's father, who was a parson. Anne was unsure what, if anything, Carl had told his elderly parents about his relationship with Keren Trenlow, but she did not want Franz to be the one to break the news. "Keren has found herself a man in the regiment and I didn't want to separate them," she temporised.

Franz rose and came forward to embrace her. "Well make sure he hires you a new one. It's not as though he cannot afford it. It seems to me that he treats you more like one of his officers than his wife; he needs to take better care of you. I hope he realises how lucky he is to have found you. I'll take care of the children and I'll keep a particular eye on Grace for you. Go to bed, you'll be tired tomorrow. Good night, Anne."

The column took the route east towards the Spanish border. The French were still in possession of Badajoz, but the supply train had been told to make for Campo Maior where they would receive further orders. Anne deduced from the deliberately vague nature of the orders that Wellington's army must be on the move south to invest Badajoz. His intention had been to keep his movements as secret as possible to avoid the French sending for reinforcements in time to raise his siege.

Anne cried unashamedly on the morning of her departure, hugging the children and holding Will in her arms for a long time, breathing in his baby smell and feeling the softness of his cheek against hers. There was a moment when she could not bear to let him go, and her sister-in-law stepped forward and unexpectedly put her arms about her.

"I will take care of him, Anne, I promise you."

Anne smiled at her through her tears. "I know you will, Patience. Thank you. And bless you for understanding. Will you take him from me? I need to mount up and go or I'm not going to be able to, this is killing me."

It took an hour or more before the tears finally stopped, and Anne was conscious of the young lieutenant in charge of the escort carefully giving her space to weep. She controlled it finally and dried her eyes then moved Bella up to join the officer.

"Thank you, Lieutenant, you can stop being tactful now, I'm over it. I am sorry, it's unlike me to be so emotional in public."

78

The young man glanced at her shyly. "It's all right, ma'am, I understand. I was told you've left your baby with family…"

"Along with my stepchildren whom I have just met and already adore. They'll be on their way back to England in a few days. I'm going to miss them dreadfully, but it's the best thing for them. I know we were introduced but I wasn't listening I was too busy pretending not to cry. I'm Anne van Daan."

"I know, ma'am. It's an honour. Lieutenant Harry Greene, ma'am, 52nd first battalion."

"Vandeleur's brigade?"

"Yes, ma'am. I was wounded at Fuentes de Oñoro and spent some time in England but I'm fit now. Looking forward to getting back."

"Well thank you for taking care of me, Mr Greene, my husband will be very grateful I promise you. Just to let you know, I'm used to long marches and army conditions so there's no need to coddle me. If I'm struggling, I'll tell you, but otherwise let's make good time if we can."

"Yes, ma'am."

Anne found him an easy companion once his initial shyness was breached. They rode eastwards, camping at night beside streams and watercourses. There were fourteen men in the escort, all returning to duty from convalescent hospitals in and around Lisbon, from a variety of regiments. Greene was visibly uncomfortable with Anne's easy familiarity with the men as they sat around the campfires during the evening. Sitting beside them she talked of their regiments and commanding officers and the battles they had fought and they responded cautiously at first, and then with genuine friendliness to her interest.

"Doesn't Colonel van Daan mind you being so friendly with the enlisted men, ma'am?" Greene asked her one evening as they stood watching the men lighting fires and drawing water. They had found a deserted farm, one of many scattered through the Portuguese countryside after the brutal years of occupation and war. One of the barns was almost intact although part of the roof was missing at one end, and Anne had directed the men to light their fires in that area.

Anne laughed. "He's worse than I am, Mr Greene. We're very informal in the 110th."

"I'd heard that," he admitted. "Not seen it first hand, mind. I think my Major would have a fit."

"We fight and die beside them, Lieutenant, I don't see any reason why we can't share a drink and a laugh with them."

Greene smiled. "I'm not sure that…"

There was a shout from one of the sentries and Greene turned. "Riders coming up, sir. Spanish, we think."

There were about twenty of them, materialising through the evening light, Spanish guerrillas mounted and armed. They were led by a slender dark man in his forties who bowed politely to Greene and with considerably more flourish to Anne.

"Captain Pablo Cuesta, Señora, I serve under Don Julian Sanchez."

Anne returned his bow. "I've met Don Julian several times, Captain – welcome. What brings you across the border into Portugal?"

"There was a French supply column, Señora, bound for Badajoz we think. They seem to have moved in this direction. I am not sure if they were lost."

"Well they must have been very lost if they've wandered this far into Portugal, Captain. We've not seen them, we're on our way up to Campo Maior."

"Is this your wife, Lieutenant?"

"No," Greene said hastily. "No, this lady is on her way to rejoin her husband – Colonel van Daan commands a brigade of the Light Division."

"The Light Division?" Cuesta looked faintly impressed. "A brave man, then. We met them often on the border a year or two ago. But if you have not seen these French…"

"Why don't you camp here with us?" Anne suggested. "We can share food and shelter for the night, you can search again tomorrow."

Cuesta glanced at Greene who flushed slightly. "Good idea, ma'am, if that's all right with Captain Cuesta."

"It would suit us well, thank you."

They roasted a goat which the Spanish had produced. Anne wondered if it had been paid for but did not ask. It was not her business to enquire into the foraging practices of the partisans although she had a suspicion that Paul would have been considerably more direct. She sat warm and fed by the fire and translated willingly between Cuesta and Greene as they talked of battles and campaigns and of the long harsh years of French occupation.

Tired out from long hours of riding, Anne settled finally in a corner of the barn, wrapped in her cloak listening drowsily to Cuesta and Green giving orders about sentries. She was amused by the fact that for the first time, Greene had given two of his men specific instructions to guard her and positioned himself between her and the Spanish. There was a moon and its pale light filtered through the broken roof tiles spilling silver across the floor where English and Spanish soldiers settled to sleep. Anne lay watching the shimmering light and thought of Paul wondering if he too were lying awake looking at the moonlight and thinking about her. Another five days, possibly, and she would be with him, wrapped warmly in his arms. The thought made her smile and she drifted into slumber dreaming of him.

Chapter Seven

The French attacked before dawn.

It was still full dark in the barn when the shocking sound of gunshots awoke Anne. She sat up quickly then scrambled to her feet, listening to the shouted orders of Cuesta and Greene as they tried to get their men to arms. Anne longed to run forward but controlled the urge, remaining in her dim corner, her back pressed to the wooden wall trying to make out what was happening. She could do no good running into the battle and might well hinder the men, or even be hit by a stray shot. Outside, the sounds of fighting intensified and she could hear the shouts of the French and an occasional scream of pain.

Anne had heard nothing from the sentries and guessed that the pickets had been cut down in the first attack. She was not surprised. Their numbers were woefully few and the men had only the most basic weapons and were not trained as a unit. The Spanish were guerrilla fighters, taught to melt away in the face of superior numbers and she was fairly sure they were outnumbered here.

Greene had taken his men outside to fight, but as Anne cautiously moved away from her dark refuge, he came running back into the barn. There were five men with him along with a few Spanish. Greene was calling to his men to conserve their ammunition and Anne realised that the French were about to overrun them.

It was not the first time Anne had stood in a barn and looked into the face of a French officer she could remember her terror. Usually, an officer's wife would treated with respect and returned to her husband but Anne knew that she was a long way from the army and nothing was certain. On the previous occasion she had been guarded by some of Paul's light company and accompanied by his wife who had just gone into labour. Most of the escort had been killed and for a short time Anne had thought that she was also going to die. Rescue had come, but there was nobody to help her here. She faced the knowledge and clamped down hard on her rising terror. It would not help any of them if she had hysterics now.

"Mr Greene, are these all that's left?"

"Yes, ma'am. They took us by surprise, must have shot the pickets first." Greene shot her a glance. His face was white. "Ma'am…"

"We're going to need to surrender," Anne said gently. She looked over at Cuesta. "Can you get to your horses?"

81

"Probably, Señora, they are just in the back there. But..."

"You need to go."

"Señora..."

"They'll slaughter you," Anne said quietly. "You know they will, you'll be taken under arms and out of uniform. Get out of here. Go straight to Lord Wellington and tell him about me. If this officer is a decent man he should release me straight away. But if he doesn't, Paul needs to know where I am and what happened. Please, Pablo. Do this for me."

"Señora." The dark eyes regarded her steadily. "When they get in here..."

"I'm English and the wife of a British officer. I don't think they'll kill me. But if they're going to, Captain, they'll do it whether you're here or not. If they catch you, they're going to shoot every one of you." Anne glanced across at the remains of his men. "Some of these boys are too young to die."

"You cannot hold them off, Señora."

"We're not trying to, Captain. Once you're away, we'll surrender. I'm hoping the worst that happens is a prison camp for these lads and an escort to the nearest British army camp for me. But in case I'm wrong, tell Colonel van Daan. Tell him where we are and which direction they go. He'll do the rest."

"Ma'am, you should go with them."

Anne turned to look at Greene and managed a smile. "My place is here with you, Mr Greene. My French is very fluent, I can speak for you if needed. And honestly, I don't think they'll hurt me. If I go with Captain Cuesta, I'll just slow him down. Besides, I'd like to be sure someone knows where I am, just in case."

"Are you sure, Señora?"

"Yes. Get going, Pablo."

"I will. Lieutenant Greene, I am sorry about your men."

"It wasn't your fault, Captain," Greene said stoically. "Nobody expected them to be here and they shouldn't be. But can you get a message to Lord Wellington and the Colonel about Mrs van Daan?"

"I can, sir."

"Go," Anne said. "I'm hoping they'll release me but if they want ransom, my husband will pay. Or an exchange of prisoners, I'm not much use to them, he'll arrange it."

"Yes, Señora."

Cuesta turned to go, shouting orders about the horses. At the door he turned. "Señora. It has been an honour; you are as brave as you are beautiful. I will make sure your husband knows where you are."

It was quiet after they had gone, apart from the regular sounds of pistol shots and rifle fire, as desultory shots were exchanged. Greene did not speak again although Anne could see him glancing at her occasionally and she understood the weight of responsibility that he felt and was sorry for him.

It seemed to take several minutes for the French to realise what was happening as the Spanish broke suddenly from the back of the barn and galloped towards the safety of the hills. Anne could hear their commanding officer screaming instructions, and shots were fired after the fleeing Spanish but there was little chance of bringing them down with a musket. Anne saw Greene lower his sword and look around at the remains of the escort. He seemed suddenly unsure.

"Stay where you are," Anne advised quietly. "Put down all your weapons where they can see them and raise your arms above your head as they come in. Don't move until they tell you to in case they think you're reaching for arms."

She saw them coming, around sixty French infantry. They had left the supply wagons well back, not wanting to risk what might well be ammunition and guns for Badajoz. Anne thought about Paul and hoped he would get the message quickly. Whatever happened to her now, she wanted him to know. She thought about her son, and Grace and the other children and prayed that she had not misjudged this. Staring out into the half light at the approaching men until her eyes hurt, she saw the barn door open and as they burst in, muskets and bayonets ready, Anne stood close to Greene and the others where they could easily be seen and held up her hands.

The French ran yelling through the barn then around the outside, but the Spanish had gone. Anne could hear several of them swearing colourfully as they poured back into the barn and she reflected that they must have hoped for a better prize than five soldiers, an officer and a girl in a blue riding habit.

Outside she could hear their Colonel bellowing orders in furious tones. The barn door banged as he kicked it open and entered. Anne studied him. He was a tall, broad man, probably in his thirties with bright ginger hair and a set of impressive moustaches. His eyes were dark, moving over the prisoners with cold fury.

"The Spaniards?"

"Gone, sir. On horseback." The speaker was a young captain. Another man came forward and saluted.

"Should we pursue, sir?"

The Captain shook his head. "It isn't worth it, Sergeant Cavel. They'd a good start and they're on horseback, they'll be high up and well ahead of us by now. If we go up there, they'll massacre us in those hills, that's their territory not ours."

Anne glanced at Greene and his men. Their blank expressions told her that none of them understood any French. She wondered if the Colonel spoke English, but as the thought entered her head the man stepped forward, his eyes on Greene.

"Name and regiment," he said in heavily accented English.

"Lieutenant Harry Greene, sir, 52nd. Escorting supplies to Lord Wellington."

"Is this all of you?"

"It is. The others are dead." Greene glanced over at Anne. "May I ask…"

"No, you may not." The Colonel's eyes shifted to Anne. Something about him made her skin crawl with discomfort at his regard. "Is she your wife?"

"No, sir. She is the wife of a colonel of the Light Division. Colonel Paul van Daan, commands the third brigade…"

The colonel spun around, staring at Greene, his expression so changed that Greene broke off and Anne felt her heart beating hard in sudden terror.

"Van Daan?"

"Yes, sir. We are escorting her back to him." Greene seemed to sense that something was badly wrong. "Colonel, Mrs van Daan needs an escort to return to her husband. I…"

The Colonel held up a hand to silence him. His eyes were fixed on Anne with frightening intensity. "Mrs van Daan," he said with mock courtesy. "I am charmed. I had the honour of facing your husband across the battlefield at Fuentes de Oñoro. More than once."

Anne found her voice. "You seem to have a good memory, Colonel."

"I will never forget, since he is the reason I am here - a ranking colonel of cavalry, wasting my time escorting supply wagons when I should be fighting for the glory of France and my Emperor."

Memory stirred. "Fuentes de Oñoro?" Anne said. "There was a cavalry colonel, as I remember, who led an attack on two companies of our wounded. Was that you?"

"I see he confides in you."

"I was there, up on the ridge with him. I saw it."

"My superior officers took exception to some of my actions during that campaign, madame, and I was removed from my command in disgrace. They felt that I took unnecessary risks."

"You did," Anne said. "More than once, I believe. Lord Wellington would have removed you just as fast."

"And so I am here acting as a delivery boy," the Colonel said. "Although it has its compensations, and you look likely to be one of them. Step forward."

Anne took one step forward. Her stomach was churning with fear, but she forced herself to sound calm. "It is Colonel Dupres, is it not? Colonel, if it's ransom you're after, my husband will pay," she said, switching to fluent French. "You don't need to kill me."

"What makes you think I intend to kill you, Mrs van Daan? That would be far too quick and easy. I would much rather keep you alive until he can see what I've done to you."

"Do you think that is going to help resurrect your career, sir?"

"I watched my career fall apart thanks to that arrogant bastard you married, Madame," Dupres said. "I doubt that anything I do to you will make that any worse."

Greene was looking between Anne and Dupres in bewilderment, not understanding the language, but he seemed to understand the sense of threat.

"Colonel, my men and I have surrendered and are your prisoners. But this lady should be released and sent back to her husband. You are an officer and a gentleman. I know you will do the right thing."

Dupres turned cold dark eyes onto him. "An officer and a gentleman. How very correct you are, Lieutenant. But of course, our army is different to yours and not all officers are gentlemen. As for prisoners, I now have a greatly increased wagon convoy to take up to Badajoz and a good deal of personal looting to do. You would be very much in the way so I think I will content myself with the one prisoner I have a use for."

Anne realised his intention before the young officer. "No!" she said. "No, you can't."

"I don't have any senior officers looking over my shoulder any more, Mrs van Daan, thanks to your husband. Out here, I am in command and I can do anything I damned well like. And before you nobly offer your favours to save his life, don't bother. I can take what I want from you anyway. Kill them."

Dupres lifted his sword and slashed once and Greene made a strange gurgling sound and fell forward, his hands clutching reflexively at his throat from which blood was gushing in a scarlet torrent down his coat. Around them the French infantrymen moved forward with raised bayonets and Anne put both hands over her mouth to stop herself screaming as the five remaining men of her escort died before her. On the ground Greene's body twitched and Anne ran forward and dropped to her knees beside him.

"Harry, no," she whispered, but he was already gone, his eyes wide and astonished looking up at the roof. The barn stank of blood and terror. Dupres bent to wipe his sword on one of the dead men's coats and turned to his officer and sergeant. Anne looked at the two men. Neither had taken part in the slaughter and she could tell by their expressions that both were disgusted that it had taken place.

"Don't look so squeamish, Bernard, you've killed enough Englishmen yourself."

"In battle, sir. These men had surrendered."

"Well I've no time for prisoners." Dupres looked at Anne. "Except for this one. I intend to spend a good deal of time with this particular prisoner."

Bernard shot an anguished glance at Anne. "Sir, she's an officer's wife. A brigade commander. You can't treat her like a Spanish peasant girl…"

"That's exactly how I intend to treat, her, Bernard, and if you'd an ounce of red male blood in your veins you'd look at her and want to do the same. Christ, I've dreamed of a way of making that arrogant bastard pay for my demotion, but I couldn't have asked for anything better. By the time he gets her back she'll be fit for nothing and he can go into battle next time imagining exactly what I did to her and how much I enjoyed doing it."

"Sir." Bernard sounded desperate. "I understand that you blame this Colonel for your misfortunes. But…"

"Misfortunes?" Dupres roared. "He ruined me, Bernard. Because of him I lost my command and my reputation and I was sent to rot out here. Well, I can't get to him, but I can damned well take payment off his wife."

Anne took a deep breath. She had a good understanding of her own nature and she knew that lowering her head and submitting was never the easy option for her, although she had schooled herself to do it during her first marriage. Robert Carlyon had been brutal to her, and with no means of avoiding him, she had made herself adapt, taught herself to lie quietly in his arms, to speak soothingly instead of scathingly, given him no reason to beat her. It had worked for at least some of the time and had kept her alive during the two years she had been married to him. It was not going to help her here.

"I'd take your Captain's advice if I were you, Colonel," she said. "Your superiors aren't going to be impressed if you abuse the wife of a senior English officer."

"I don't give a damn what my superiors think, cherie. And you are definitely worth a few risks, he did very nicely for himself didn't he? I do hope he won't mind sharing."

Anne felt sick. She looked steadily at him, refusing to give him the satisfaction of replying. Dupres looked her over with unsparing thoroughness. "How old are you?"

"I am twenty-two."

His hand reached out and cupped her face, scooping back the long dark hair. "Very nice age," he said. "Young enough to be fresh, old enough to have some experience. I am looking forward to the next few weeks, Mrs van Daan."

"If you bloody dare, and he finds out and you'll end up a screaming eunuch with your balls stuffed in your mouth, you piece of French shit!" Anne said distinctly, and Dupres hit her, hard.

"If you speak to me like that again, you foul mouthed English bitch, I'll take my riding whip to you. Learn some respect for your betters!"

"I don't see any of those here." Anne said.

He gave a grim smile. "I'd give a lot to know where you learned your French. You're very good at it, whatever else you are. You didn't learn that from the schoolroom."

"I picked up a good deal of it patching up your wounded when you run howling from the battlefield on a regular basis leaving them behind."

"Did you, by God? Well you're the one who has been left behind this time, Madame, and you had better think of a way to put me in a better mood with you. You're as arrogant as that husband of yours and with less cause. Learn to control that mouth or I'll send you back to your colonel in pieces. Sergeant, strip her, and take her shoes and stockings, she can manage in her shift. Let the rest of my men see what I'm intending to enjoy when I've brought her to heel, I don't think it will take long."

Anne could feel her heart hammering in her chest. "I'm not sure what that's going to achieve, Colonel. It certainly won't get you your ransom."

Dupres gave a small grim smile. "Death before dishonour – is that what you are saying? Well you may find that dishonour is sometimes the more comfortable option. We're marching up to the fort at Casa Braco in the morning. It's a three day march if we move quickly and I intend to. You will receive no food and you can walk barefoot in your shift. I give you three days and you'll be begging me for a ride on my horse." He laughed, looking her over. "Or you can get down on your knees and find something better to do with that lovely mouth than to call me names, and perhaps after a few hours of fun I'll send you back to him. Your choice."

"Sorry, Colonel, I'm picky what I put in my mouth."

"We'll see if you feel the same after a week without eating." Dupres looked at the Sergeant. "No food for her, water only. I don't like women who don't know their place."

"No, Colonel, you just don't like women," Anne said. Dupres looked at Sergeant Cavel and jerked his head. The Sergeant stepped forward, his face expressionless. Anne shook her head.

"I'll do it myself," she said, and she saw the relief in his eyes.

"Thank you, Madame."

Anne unbuttoned the riding dress with shaking fingers and dropped it to the ground, then bent and removed her riding boots and stockings. In silence Dupres looked her over, smiling slightly at the curves of her body revealed by the thin linen. "What is that on your arm. Remove it."

Anne unstrapped the small knife, which she wore in its leather sheath about her wrist and dropped it onto the pile. He looked at it and then back up at her.

"An interesting fashion item for a colonel's lady. I'm not sure you're that much of a lady at all. When I send you back to him finally with my handprints all over that very lovely body, I hope he beats you for losing your virtue to the enemy. If you've any left to lose, which I very much doubt."

"Colonel, I doubt you'll live long enough to find out."

Dupres laughed aloud. "The famous commander of the third brigade. Will he challenge me to a duel over your honour, Madame? I do hope so, I'd like to kill him in front of you."

"I doubt he would bother with a challenge," Anne said. "Enjoy yourself, Colonel Dupres because whatever you do to me, this will be the last time you do it."

"I shall make the most of it then. Did you want to say something, Captain Bernard?"

"The sentries are set, sir, and the wounded tended. There is only one serious. He has a bad leg wound."

"He can ride in one of the wagons. If he survives, there will be a surgeon in Badajoz. Take the woman up to the village and put her in my quarters. I'll deal with her later."

"Colonel – I want you to know that I protest at your treatment of this woman," the Captain said. Anne could sense his anger and frustration. "I want it recorded. She should be exchanged or freed or ransomed, not…"

"Oh don't be such a woman, Bernard. Look at her. Take a good long look and tell me you're not tempted. And if you've heard the mouth on her, she is not some innocent little bride. I'll bet she walks all over her besotted Colonel. I'm not going to kill her, but I am going to teach her a lesson she won't forget about how women should behave and what happens to them when they don't. She should be back at home with children and her needlework, not running around Portugal with a pack of Spanish guerrillas, she's asked for everything she gets. And if you want a turn when I've done with her, feel free, she's lucky I don't pass her around the entire company. That arrogant bastard made a fool out of me and she's no better. Well let's see how he enjoys her by the time I've finished with her. Now get her out of here and back to camp."

"Sir."

Outside the barn it was cold, with rain falling steadily. Sergeant Cavel looked at his captain. "I'll take her down," he said and Bernard nodded unhappily. Cavel watched him walk away then jerked his head at Anne. He began to walk along the rutted muddy track between the ruined farm buildings and Anne followed him.

After a moment Cavel looked at her. "We're camped in the remains of a village, about a mile away. He'll stay here today to rest the pack animals and then make his way up to Badajoz, taking your supplies with him. It's about a week to ten days march, depending on how fast we can move."

"I know," Anne said. She stumbled slightly as a stone dug into her bare foot and the man reached out to steady her. Anne looked up at him. He was a tall man, probably around Paul's age but more slimly built with steady grey eyes and curly dark hair.

87

"Your feet are going to hurt, I'm afraid."

"I'll get used to it."

"I am sorry," Cavel said soberly. "Look, Madame – I don't know what your husband did to him…"

"Nothing that wasn't part of his job, Sergeant. It was a battle and Paul was better at it than he was. He took it personally and made several attempts to get to Paul which put his own troop at risk. I imagine that's why his superior officers removed him from his command."

"I suppose so. He's not been in command here long and it's a strange posting for a ranking colonel so we all assumed that it was a punishment, that he was in disgrace. But that is no reason to take it out on a woman."

"I don't suppose I'm the first woman he's taken it out on, Sergeant."

Cavel shot her a sharp glance. "What makes you say that?" he asked.

"They're usually a type."

They were making their way through the ruined buildings of a Portuguese village. Ahead was the farmhouse, more solidly built and in better repair. At the open doorway Cavel stopped.

"His quarters are in here. He'll be busy for a while going through your baggage train. He's a thief, it's why we were in Portugal when we shouldn't have been. Looting churches. He won't want his superior officers to know that, so he'll buy the men off with a share of the loot."

"Was that why he slaughtered our men?"

"Probably."

"You don't like him much, do you, Sergeant?"

"No. He's a bastard. He tortures the peasants for fun. And you were right about the women. He's a rapist."

Anne felt very sick but she made herself meet his gaze. "Does he kill them afterwards?"

"No. He uses them and kicks them out. Might beat them a bit if they fight him too hard but most of them are too terrified."

"Perhaps I'll be that lucky," Anne said, attempting a light-hearted tone. He was not deceived and she could see the compassion in his eyes.

"Madame, I'll do what I can for you. When I am able, I will get some food to you."

Anne studied him. "Why would you risk getting into trouble for me, Sergeant?"

"I can't stop him from doing what he is going to do. None of us can. They talk about the brutality of our soldiers when we're trying to find food for our men, but I wonder how much better yours would be if they did not have their supply trains and commissariat. But Colonel Dupres is different. He does it because he wants to. I loathe him. If I could find a way to get you out of here I would, but I can't. I've seen him shoot a man for disobeying an order and my death won't help you. I wouldn't trust a lot of these men with you. So I'll feed you when I can and Captain Bernard will keep trying to persuade him to release you. It's the best we can do at the moment. I am sorry."

"I know it is. Thank you. And thank him for me as well, please."

He ushered her through into a musty hallway and from there into a small dark room. "I'm going to put you in here because there's a bar on the door. And because I am not delivering you to his room like a bloody…"

He stopped and despite her own distress Anne felt a stab of compassion for him. "It's all right, Sergeant. Go on, get going. I'll survive, you know. I'm very tough."

He gave a shadowed smile. "I can see that, Madame. Most girls would be sobbing by now."

"I don't cry that easily."

He moved away. Anne had a sudden thought.

"Sergeant?"

"Madame."

"What happened to the horses? They were in the barn."

"They are here. He'll take them with him, probably sell some of them, hand over the rest to the cavalry."

"The black mare is mine. Her name is Bella."

"I noticed her."

"She'd be worth something to him and he's greedy. If you have a chance to suggest a market for her that doesn't involve her going into battle…"

Cavel was staring at her in apparent astonishment. "You're worried about your horse?"

"I've had her for years, I love her."

"I'll speak to Captain Bernard. He'll see to it."

"Thank you."

He stared at her for a moment then nodded and moved away.

Inside the dark room Anne sat against the wall hugging her knees and tried hard not to think about the coming hours. She was under no illusions about Dupres intentions towards her and she was not naïve enough to think that any plea of hers could change his mind. She would have to endure it as best she could and think only of the promise of rescue.

When Paul knew where she was he would come for her. She knew that as surely as she knew that she would have given up her own life for him. Her only fear was that Cuesta might not reach Wellington's lines safely. She did not doubt that he would make the attempt. He seemed to be an intelligent man and he must know that a brigade commander of the Light Division was a good ally to have. She also suspected that he was an honourable man and he knew that she and Greene had saved the lives of his men.

Her mind touched on Greene and shied away. The memory of the slaughter in the barn haunted her. She had seen men die many times in battle and from wounds and illness but the shock of seeing six men she had known and liked cut down while they were unarmed and helpless was going to stay with her. She wondered if the French would have taken the trouble to bury them and hoped that Captain Bernard or Sergeant Cavel would see to it. They seemed like decent men.

The hours dragged on. Outside she heard voices, the sounds of horses and the rumble of cart wheels as the French brought up their captured wagons. Her own baggage would be in one of them and she wondered if Dupres had found her jewel case. If so he should be delighted. She owned little jewellery but one or two of the pieces were expensive and the diamonds Paul had given her the previous year were worth a small fortune. Oddly enough the thought bothered her less than the loss of her medical bag, and of the small, sheathed knife which she had discarded with her clothing. Paul had given that to her when she had first come to the Peninsula before they were ever married and made her promise to wear it. She wished she had it now.

It was dark when Anne heard the sound of the wooden bar being lifted and she got quickly to her feet trying to still the shivering of her body. A young private motioned for her to come out and ushered her into another room. It was large and warm, with a small brazier burning in the corner. Efforts had been made to make it comfortable with a mattress on the floor heaped with blankets and several pillows, and Dupres' possessions were scattered about the room. The Colonel was sitting writing at a folding table. He waved the soldier away and got up, coming forward.

"Mrs van Daan. I imagine it has been a long day for you waiting for this."

"I've had better days."

The thin lips curled in a slight smile. "You really are an extraordinarily beautiful woman. But I expect you hear that from a lot of men. I am more fortunate than they are. Take off your clothes and lie down on the bed."

Anne shook her head. "No," she said.

Dupres stepped forward. "Your choice, Madame," he said softly. "You can make this very easy for yourself. Or very unpleasant."

Anne shook her head. She felt sick and chilled. "No," she said again.

"As you wish."

He caught her wrist and pulled her hard against him and she fought furiously, kicking him with bare feet and trying to bite him. She heard him laugh and then he picked her up and carried her to the bed. He threw her down and she scrambled up and tried to move past him but he was quicker than she was and he was above her, holding her down as he freed himself from his clothing. He tore the flimsy shift from her and pushed her back, his mouth coming down on hers. She felt his body pressing into her and it sickened her. Twisting her wrist, she managed to free one hand and raked her nails hard across his face. He swore and pulled back and Anne scrambled off the bed and over to the far side of the room.

Dupres was holding a handkerchief to his bloodied cheek. Removing it he looked down at the bloodstains and then up at Anne. The scratches were very deep and bleeding badly.

"You bitch," he said softly. Anne could feel her heart pounding in her chest. She was terrified, beyond reason, no longer acting on anything other than pure instinct. Somewhere in her consciousness she knew that Paul would have told her to stop, to lie still, to do whatever it took to keep herself alive. She knew he would be right but at this moment she did not have it in her to think that rationally. She stood looking at Dupres.

"Do you know, I believe I am glad that you did that," Dupres said softly. "After all, I find that I did not want you to take the easy option."

He reached for a sheet and pulled it around his waist and then went to the door and shouted an order. After a moment there was a clattering on the stairs and two soldiers entered. Both of them stood to attention, saluting, their eyes on Anne.

90

"Get her and hold her still. Forward, over that table. Move her hair out of the way."

Anne struggled, pointlessly, their hands bruising her arms and shoulders. He stood behind her and she felt the tip of the riding whip moving very delicately down her spine. She could feel her whole body shaking, shivering with fear and cold. And then he struck and the whip cut into the skin of her back.

It went on forever. He could not have known that it was not the first time she had been beaten like this, but with her first husband it had never lasted this long or been this vicious. Anne gritted her teeth for as long as she could but eventually she could not hold back and she cried out, sobbing with the pain as he hit her again and again. She had stopped struggling and lay limply forward, the hard wood of the table digging into her thighs wondering if he was intending to beat her to death. Almost she wanted him to.

"All right," he said suddenly. "Get out, both of you. She won't give me any more trouble tonight."

They left and he pulled her upright, the pain cutting into her as he lifted her and carried her to the bed, positioning her as if she were a rag doll. The bloody stripes on her back were agony as they touched the mattress. He dropped the sheet, knelt, and lifted her legs, thrusting into her quickly. Anne gave a sob of pain and turned her head to one side, closing her eyes, trying not to think about what he was doing to her.

She had forgotten, in the two years since her first husband's death, the pain and the shame and the humiliation of a man's body invading hers against her will. She lay beneath him, hating him, trying to detach her mind from what he was doing to her body and from the pain of her back on the sheet. He finished finally with a groan of satisfaction and rolled away from her. Anne moved painfully, turning over so that her back was to him. She felt sick and dizzy and she could feel tears pouring down her cheeks.

Dupres' hand grasped her shoulder and forced her back. "Open your eyes and look at me or I'll use the whip again."

Anne opened her eyes. She hated doing so, hated the sight of his face, but common sense told her that she could not endure more tonight. She could feel blood soaking into the mattress beneath her injured back and buttocks.

"Stupid bitch," he said contemptuously. "What did you think was going to happen if you defied me? Not so full of yourself now, are you?"

Anne did not speak. She could suddenly remember vividly the horror of the previous rape, her first husband Robert Carlyon who had held her down in a stable to force her to marry him for her father's money. It had been four years ago and she had not thought about it for a long time. He had beaten her too, although never as badly as this. She had survived it.

"Can't you speak?"

"I don't want to," Anne said. "Not to you."

"We march tomorrow up to Casa Braco to await orders, then probably on to Badajoz. Three days if I march them fast and I intend to. By then you'll have started to heal. Now get up, you've got blood all over the bed."

He moved and Anne eased herself off the mattress. She was very cold, shivering violently with what her mind recognised detachedly as shock. He stripped

91

off the bloodstained sheet and tossed it to her and she wrapped it about herself to cover her battered body and stood silently. Dupres looked at her and gave a soft laugh.

"Was that what I needed to do to shut you up?"

Anne regarded him steadily. "I've nothing to say to you. You're not a man, let alone a soldier, you're a perverted piece of shit and you're going to die with my husband's sword in your throat. I just hope I live long enough to watch."

"I wouldn't rely on it, cherie. As for this, call it a lesson you needed to learn. Behave yourself and I won't beat you again. Now put on your shift. Guards! Get her out of here. Put her in the room over the stables. No food."

Anne reached for the garment and tried to pull it on without dropping the sheet. Dupres laughed again and came forward, pulling the sheet away from her. "No point in modesty, cherie, I've seen all that you've got to hide. It was very nice too – I'll do that again when you're less of a mess. Get out of here."

Anne moved to the door. She was conscious as she emerged of the eyes of every man in the camp upon her, of her bloody back and bruised arms. The two men who had held her down were grinning, whispering, and she heard their laughter and lifted her head high. Nothing would make her flinch away in shame no matter how bad she felt and she looked over at them, hoping that they could feel the contempt in her gaze. And then she heard a furious exclamation and Sergeant Cavel was there. He cuffed one of the two men hard around his head.

"You scum, keep your eyes down, you've done enough tonight. And that goes for the rest of you as well."

Anne felt the warmth of a thin, rough army blanket about her sore shoulders and she clutched it gratefully and felt him touch her arm gingerly. "It's all right, I won't touch you. This way, there's a house with a couple of rooms intact over here, it'll be more private for you."

Anne let him lead her down through the trees, her legs shaking, barely able to walk. He led her into a small stone building. There was a fire burning in the corner and two soldiers warming their hands at it. Cavel jerked his head.

"Out of here and give her some privacy!" he growled, and they moved away. Cavel helped her to sit down and she realised he had found her cloak, several blankets and a pillow which she suspected had come from his Captain. He knelt beside her and handed her his flask. Anne gulped the brandy, coughed violently, and then drank more.

"The Captain has gone for food and wine for you. Sit still for a moment."

Anne obeyed, trying to control her shaking body. "I'm sorry, I can't seem to help it."

"Of course you can't. Jesus Christ, I want to kill him."

Anne looked up. "He...he beat me. With a riding crop. And then he...oh God!"

She was crying suddenly and Cavel reached for her, careful not to touch her back, and let her rest on him, sobbing into his shoulder.

"I know, cherie. I know what he did. The whole camp knows, that bloody bastard, we could hear you crying in there. Christ, I hope your man catches up with him and cuts his fucking balls off, it's what I want to do."

92

Despite her anguish Anne was aware of a flicker of appreciation at his fury. She eased herself away from him trying to get her tears under control. "Sergeant, what is your first name?

"My name?" He seemed startled. "My name is Damien."

"Damien, thank you. You're being very kind."

"Don't thank me. He should be dead. I should go up there and blow his bloody head off."

"Please don't. You'd be shot for mutiny and what would happen to me then?"

"She is right, Cavel."

Anne turned and saw Captain Bernard approaching. He knelt beside her. "Here. Eat it. I know you feel sick but you will need your strength."

Anne took the bowl. It was some kind of stew, thick and strongly flavoured. She savoured the taste and realised that he was right. The heat flooded through her and she felt some of her shaking ease. She took the wine cup he offered and drank.

"Captain, thank you."

"Madame, I am so sorry."

"I know, Captain. But you are helping."

"Once we are at Casa Braco I hope for orders. We are supposed to go to Badajoz with the stores..."

"I rather imagine you're too late for that, Captain."

"That may be so. But I am guessing that your husband will be at Badajoz if they are investing the town. We could send a message. If this is about revenge, I think he has taken it. If I can persuade him to send you back, I will."

Anne finished the food and held the wine cup between her hands. "Does he...has he done this before? With local women?"

"Beaten them?" Cavel studied her and shook his head. "No. The occasional slap, a few punches maybe. No, this was bad even for him. I think this is aimed at your husband, Madame."

"My husband is going to kill him."

"Your husband might not get the chance, cherie. Look – I know this is bloody awful for you. You must be shocked and terrified...but you need to stop antagonising him. He's not used to a girl speaking to him the way you do. If you want to get back to your man..."

Anne saw the thought behind his eyes and managed a wan smile. "It's all right, Sergeant, no need to be tactful here. You're wondering what my husband will say to me when he discovers I've been raped by a French colonel."

"Madame, nobody could think this was your fault..."

"Some people probably will. Like Dupres they'll think I shouldn't be here in the first place. But Paul isn't one of them."

"I hope you are right, Madame. You need to rest. I've set two guards on your door, they're good men, been with me for years, they'll make sure nobody bothers you. Try to sleep, we've a long march tomorrow."

"Thank you, Sergeant. And you too, Captain. You've been very kind."

Cavel got up. "I'll see if I can find you something else to wear, you can't march in that. Get some rest."

When they had gone Anne settled herself as best she could, lying on her front. Thoughts whirled in her shocked brain at dizzying speed. Only twenty-four hours earlier she had lay in the barn thinking about Paul, expecting to be with him soon. She wondered despairingly if she would ever see him again, and then stopped the thought deliberately. Thinking that would drive her mad. Cuesta would reach him within a few days riding fast, and she knew he would come for her. It was her job now to endure, as she had endured the long two years with her first husband. Paul would find her, when he came, unbroken by whatever Dupres did to her.

She had not expected to sleep, but shock and pain had exhausted her and she fell quickly into a deep and surprisingly dreamless slumber.

Chapter Eight

Anne awoke to the sounds of the French breaking camp outside. It was barely dawn and she was cold, her back on fire with pain and a soreness inside her from the brutal assault. She sat up cautiously, drawing her cloak around her. Her torn shift had stuck to the wounds on her back and she spent agonising minutes carefully peeling it off them, wincing. She wished there was some way of washing herself and cleaning the wounds and wondered suddenly about the stream.

There was a sound outside and then two men appeared, Colonel Dupres and his Sergeant. Anne looked past Dupres and met Cavel's steady grey eyes. She sensed a strong ally in the Sergeant.

"Get up."

Anne got shakily to her feet. Dupres regarded her in silence and she lifted her head and looked back at him without speaking.

"Can you walk?"

She nodded. He moved forward and Anne concentrated on not flinching. Lifting a hand, he pushed her tangled hair back from her face and caressed her cheek. "Still defiant, cherie?"

Anne did not respond. She fixed her eyes on the wall behind him and tried not to think about the feeling of his hand on her face although her skin crawled. After a moment he moved closer. Anne stood rigid, flinching as his hand touched the raw skin of her back.

"Does it hurt?"

Anne did not reply. He pressed harder and Anne bit her lip to stop herself crying out. She felt his mouth close to her ear. "You'd better start talking, cherie, or I'll do it again. Does it hurt?"

"Yes."

"Learn from it. I don't want to have to beat you every day, it will kill you." Very gently Dupres ran his finger across her neck and then down to the deep neckline of her shift. "It will also scar something very lovely, and I dislike that idea. Do as you're told and it will get easier."

Anne did not reply. Dupres put his finger under her chin and tilted her head back to look at him. "And don't think you're going to get away with silence either."

"What do you want me to say?"

95

"I'll let you know," he said. "Trust me, by the time we get to Badajoz you'll be saying whatever I tell you to, cherie. We'll march in half an hour. You can give her some water, Sergeant but no food."

"Yes, sir," Cavel said woodenly. "Sir, her clothing – she can't march like that."

Dupres surveyed Anne and gave a slight smile. "Why not, Sergeant? I find it rather attractive, myself."

"Sir..."

"Are you questioning my orders, Cavel?"

"It's all right," Anne said quickly. "It doesn't make any difference to me, Sergeant, I don't give a damn what these men think of me, they're going to die anyway. But I would like ten minutes down at the stream to wash. I'm worried these wounds might get infected. They should be cleaned." Anne glanced at Dupres. "I'm not sure how much it would inconvenience your Colonel if I get blood poisoning, but..."

"If you get sick, cherie, I will simply tell them to shoot you in the head," Dupres said pleasantly. "But you can bathe. I might come down to watch."

Anne's stomach churned in distaste but she did not flinch. "That's up to you, Colonel, I don't have much interest in how you spend your time."

Anne was relieved when he left her alone. Cavel stood guard with his back turned and Anne stripped off the shift and waded into the freezing water. She washed carefully, feeling as best she could the raised weals on her back and buttocks and decided they were not too bad. The pain would ease after a day or two. There were bruises on her arms and shoulders where she had been held down and a dark bruise across the front of her thighs which puzzled her until she realised it must have been where the table had dug into her as she was held forward across it. She washed her lower body thoroughly, cleaning every trace of him from her.

Anne washed her hair and then her shift, and when she put it back on she wore it back to front. It had the double advantage of preserving a little of her modesty while leaving her back partly bare to give the stripes a chance to heal. While the shift dried she put on her dark cloak. It would be hot to march in but that could not be helped.

Climbing up from the river Anne found Captain Bernard. He handed her a piece of bread and a chunk of bacon in silence and Anne smiled up at him and turned her back on the camp eating quickly and silently and then accepting a few sips from his flask.

"Captain, I'm so grateful but don't get yourself into trouble over me."

"Madame, as soon as we are close enough to a French post, I am going to find a way to report this. I promise you our generals will be horrified; this is not how an officer's wife should be treated. Until then, we will do what we can for you. Today he has given orders for you to be tied to his saddle to march. This will be hard for you, you are a delicately bred lady, not used to..."

"You might be surprised, Captain, I'm a lot tougher than I look."

"I had already guessed that Madame. I must ride, but Cavel will walk close to you. If you fall, he'll cut the rope, so you're not dragged."

"Thank you."

Beyond him, Anne saw the figure of the Colonel, already mounted, riding forward.

"Time to march. Corporal, tie her to my horse. When you get tired, cherie, just ask and you can ride up with me."

It grew hot early and Anne found walking in the heavy cloak a trial. Dupres had been true to his word and Anne received no food other than the small amount from Bernard. She drank as much water as she was allowed. Thirst was the real danger out here. As they lined up for the march one of the guards approached her and motioned for her to hold out her hands. He bound her wrists together and then tied the end of the long rope to the saddle of Dupres' big black gelding. The company marched at a steady pace and by the middle of the day Anne's head was pounding and her feet were sore and bleeding.

They stopped briefly at noon and Anne drank from the water bottle Cavel brought to her. He was studying her in some concern. "Are you all right?"

"I'm fine but I can't keep walking in this cloak, it's weighing me down in this heat."

"I'll take it. Wait."

He moved away and came back shortly with a linen shirt. Untying her hands he helped her into it, doing up the buttons for her. Beyond him Anne saw Dupres watching with what looked like amusement. Cavel tied the rope again but more loosely. Already Anne's wrists were raw and chafed.

"Playing ladies maid, Sergeant?" Dupres enquired, moving closer.

"Just trying to keep the lady alive, sir."

Dupres turned to look down at her. "You look tired, Madame. Concentrate on keeping your feet, I'd hate to take the skin off that body dragging it along in the dirt. At least before I've had a chance to enjoy it again."

Anne heard one of the two lieutenants laugh. She said nothing. Eventually Dupres reached out with his riding crop and placed it beneath her chin. "Nothing to say, cherie?"

"I was just thinking, it's strange looking at a dead man sitting a horse."

Dupres flicked the crop and Anne felt a stinging pain across her arm but she bit back her cry. "You still look dead to me," she said and turned away.

They marched on. By mid-afternoon Anne was stumbling. Conscious of a presence beside her she looked around and saw Cavel. He did not speak but she was aware of his silent support and it helped.

Anne collapsed exhausted when they camped for the night. The smell of cooking over the fires made her feel light headed with hunger. As the men settled down to eat, Colonel Dupres disappeared into his tent. Anne saw Captain Bernard speaking quietly to Cavel and then Bernard disappeared into the Colonel's tent holding a bottle. After a moment Cavel appeared before Anne.

"Over here. I'm going to untie your hands but for God's sake don't try to run. The guards have orders to shoot to kill. Do you need a moment's privacy?"

Anne nodded silently. Cavel jerked his head and Anne preceded him into the trees. When they were out of earshot he said:

"I'll wait here. Don't try to run. You can't outrun the guards and..."

"I won't."

He waited while Anne relieved herself and as she returned, he led her a few feet away and then stopped. Reaching into his coat he withdrew a chunk of bread and a wrapped package which contained some cheese and a chunk of ham.

"You'll have to eat it here, I can't trust most of them."

Anne began to eat. "Thank you, Sergeant. This is very good of you, but I don't want you to risk getting into trouble."

"I won't. Captain Bernard is distracting him. Here."

He passed her a small flask and Anne drank the wine. She finished the food without further speech and he led her back and watched as she seated herself.

"Cavel, bring her up here."

Anne felt her stomach lurch in horror at the sound of Dupres' voice and she saw the flare of anger in Cavel's eyes. Quickly she said:

"It's all right. Don't say anything. If he thinks you're too sympathetic to me he'll make sure you don't get near me. And I am going to need your help to get through this, Sergeant."

She gave him a brief smile, reached out and touched his hand, then walked past him and up to the colonel's tent.

Dupres was seated in a camp chair with a cup and a wine bottle on the table before him. Captain Bernard was sitting in the other chair and she could sense his discomfort as she entered and stood silently before them.

"Mrs van Daan," Dupres said genially. "How's your back?"

Anne did not reply. She sensed that her lack of response irritated the Colonel. After a long time, Dupres got up and walked around the table towards her.

"Sit down," he said, and waved at a wooden chest. Anne hesitated and he gave her a little push. "Sit. Bernard, get another cup for our guest. It isn't often on this campaign that we'll get to share a drink with a woman this lovely."

Anne sat and Bernard poured wine and set the cup on the table before her. Anne did not touch the wine. Dupres sat down, smiling.

"You've had a day to think about this, cherie, and I'm damned sure it's been a long one," he said. "Are you ready to be more cooperative?"

Bernard shifted. "Sir, I should see to the sentries."

"That's Cavel's job. Are you trying to run away, Bernard? You shouldn't be frightened of a pretty woman. Especially one in her position."

"Sir, I am not comfortable with this. I have already told you…"

"Yes, yes. You protest. I ignored you. I took her into my bed and I…"

"Sir, please!"

"Don't you want the details, Bernard? You surprise me. Most of my men out there would love to know what she looks like without her clothes on. Not that she's wearing much at the moment. I wonder what your husband would think if he knew you were parading about an enemy camp in front of sixty randy Frenchmen in a transparent shift and a sergeant's shirt?"

Anne studied him, still not speaking. She had not touched the wine. After a long moment, Dupres leaned forward. He was smiling.

"You keep this up, cherie, and you'll find yourself with a second set of stripes to match the first, I don't mind doing that again, I quite enjoyed it. It gets me in the mood."

Anne lifted one eyebrow. "Can you not manage it otherwise, Colonel?" she said.

Captain Bernard choked on his wine and she saw Dupres flush with anger. "You must be mad!" he said softly. "To risk angering me..."

"This isn't about anything I say or do, Colonel, you'll do what you want anyway. Nothing I can do will change that."

Dupres looked at her and Anne felt her stomach twist in distaste at the expression in the dark eyes. "I will," he said. "I was going to wait, but looking at you, I've just changed my mind. Drink the wine."

"I'm not thirsty," Anne fought to keep the tremor from her voice.

Dupres picked up her cup and stood. "You're dismissed, Bernard. Make sure they know I'm not to be disturbed."

"Sir..."

"Get out," Dupres said softly, and Anne glanced at the Captain and shook her head slightly. He turned and left and Dupres walked forward.

"Are you going to drink this or am I going to make you?" he enquired.

Anne regarded him steadily, then took the cup and drank the wine down in one steady stream. She set the cup down on the table. "If I'm lucky that might make me pass out," she said, and he slapped her across the face.

"Bitch. Are you going to take those clothes off or do I tear them off you? I'm warning you, you don't get anything else to wear on the march tomorrow."

Anne fought a brief battle with herself. Eventually she stripped off the shirt and shift and dropped them onto the chest. He studied her for a long time and she felt herself cringe internally at the flare of desire in his eyes. After a moment he stepped forward and drew her to him.

"Don't fight me. I don't want to have to beat you again."

He leaned in to kiss her and Anne very deliberately turned her head to one side. Dupres caught her by the jaw and turned her face back to him, kissing her hard, his hands moving around her body. She flinched as he touched the fresh wounds on her back and his hands stopped and lingered there, testing her pain. Anne forced herself not to make a sound and he gave a soft laugh.

"You're surprising, cherie. I've tortured grown men in these villages and you're tougher than many of them. Come to bed. I'm not expecting enthusiasm but if you lie still and don't fight me I won't hurt you."

Anne felt a sudden flood of anger at how casual he made it sound. "Dear God, you can't think what you're about to do to me isn't going to hurt!"

"I think you can make it easier on yourself." He took her hand and pulled her to the bed, pushing her down. Anne clamped down hard on her urge to scratch the other side of his face. The marks she had made were still visible, three deep red scratches. He was regarding her with an expression which made her cringe inside. "Why don't you think about your husband? I've an idea I might enjoy that."

Anne felt again the rush of nausea. "Don't even mention him here."

He stretched out beside her, leaning over to kiss her. "It's not hard to find your weakness, cherie. I truly hope that he shares the same one. Because if he does, finding out I did this to you is probably going to kill him. No – don't try to hit me. You're not strong enough and you'll just get hurt. Lie still and close your eyes. If you're lucky you might get through tonight without a beating, I'm in a good mood."

Anne lay rigid, closing her eyes. She desperately wanted to fight him, to bite and kick and scratch, to mark the other side of his face. But she had his measure now and knew that he would not hesitate to beat her again and she was not strong enough to endure that every day. She had learned long ago during her first marriage how to survive, how to detach her mind from what was being done to her body, and she drew on the memories, trying not to cry out with the pain and discomfort. It was over finally and as soon as he moved away from her she sat up, moving to find her clothes.

"Turn around."

Anne obeyed, pulling the clothing on. He studied her. "You're crying."

"Yes."

"You'll get used to it."

"I'm never going to get used to it."

"You'll sleep here. In the bed if you wish."

"No."

"Then on the floor over there. I'll get Cavel to bring up your cloak. And you can take this blanket.   Do you want food?"

Anne shook her head. "I'd be sick," she said candidly. "And I'd rather sleep outside."

He was silent for a long moment, studying her as if he could not quite believe what he was hearing. Then he laughed suddenly with what sounded like genuine amusement.

"You're a stubborn bitch, Mrs van Daan. But you don't get to decide what you do or don't do any more. You'll sleep here." Dupres picked up a blanket and threw it to her then walked to the tent flap. "Sergeant Cavel!"

Cavel appeared so quickly that Anne knew he must have been close. She felt a rush of gratitude to this ordinary, taciturn Frenchman who seemed to have constituted himself her champion for no apparent reason. "Colonel?" His tone was barely civil but Dupres did not appear to notice.

"Get her cloak. She's sleeping in here from now on."

"Sir."

"Is there any food left?"

"Yes, sir."

"Bring her something. We've a long march tomorrow, I don't want the trouble of her collapsing."

Anne sat to eat and drank the wine he gave her in silence. She wanted to throw it in his face, but common sense told her she would need her strength. When she had done, Cavel removed the bowl and Anne gave him a reassuring smile as he left. She turned to find Dupres watching her.

"That's a pretty smile," he said. "For my Sergeant?"

"Your Sergeant hasn't raped or beaten me, Colonel. For him I can manage a smile."

Dupres studied her, then indicated the floor at the foot of his bed.   "There, if you're too stubborn to sleep in my bed."

"I'm surprised you'd let me sleep in here at all, Colonel. Is it safe?"

Dupres considered. "I don't think you're that stupid," he said. "If you kill me, you'll have to deal with the rest of my men. They might not care that much if I live or die, but I'm damned sure they'd be happy to share you around. Just now I'm the only thing standing between you and that. You might want to try being nicer to me."

"Or I might not."

"Get some sleep. We've an early start."

***

It had been a frustrating few weeks for the commander of the third brigade of the Light Division. Arriving back at Wellington's lines, Paul found his General in a foul mood, furious about delays in reinforcements arriving, problems with his supply lines and the slow progress of his siege train. Wellington was still in Freineda, leaving it to the last possible minute to move his headquarters towards Badajoz. He had spent weeks feeding disinformation to the French about his intentions and had been rewarded by a significant lack of troop movements towards the city, but he knew that once it became clear that he intended to invest the fortress, the French would move to try to relieve it. It was a delicately balanced strategy and Wellington found himself, not for the first time, short of men, money and equipment. He was also short of a commander for the Light Division as his choice, the Hanoverian General Charles Alten had been delayed.

Wellington's staff officers greeted Paul's return with evident relief, which told him all he needed to know about his commander's mood during the past weeks. Since the quick series of promotions which had led him to command a brigade at thirty, Paul had faced a good deal of resentment from some of the other officers. He had heard himself described as a wealthy, middle class upstart who had bought his way to success and initially the young aristocrats who made up the bulk of Wellington's headquarters regarded him with suspicion, unable to understand his close friendship with their difficult chief.

More recently, relations had improved and Paul was aware that Wellington's ADCs often relied on him to manage the Commander-in-Chief when he reached the point of addressing his generals with the biting sarcasm of a disgruntled Latin master speaking to a particularly dense first year. The tone of his note requesting Paul's return had been abrupt to the point of rudeness.

Paul was greeted with pleasure by his own officers. He bathed and changed and took himself up to Wellington's headquarters where his chief regarded him with a frosty eye.

"So you're back?" he said with heavy sarcasm. "I hope you're well rested, Colonel? I wouldn't want to think I've interrupted your holiday too soon."

"Well you did, sir," Paul said frankly. "My family brought my children out to see me, I could have done with another month to tell you the truth. But the tone of this charming missive informed me I'd done as well as I was going to. What's going on?"

He dropped Wellington's letter onto the table and stood waiting. His chief picked it up and looked at it for a moment. "Don't you want to hold onto this, Colonel? All my other officers are saving my briefing notes for their memoirs," he said.

"No thank you, sir, I've had enough rude letters from you over the years to be able to recreate a generic bollocking without an aide memoire. The only letters I hold on to are those from my wife. She's a better correspondent than you are, to be honest. What's the matter, siege train not arrived?"

"Nothing has arrived!" Wellington said. "Get yourself a drink, for God's sake and pour me one as well. I thought you'd be in a better mood."

"I was until I walked in here and you started yelling at me." Paul went to pour brandy and Wellington's servant grinned and effaced himself. "Do you want me to tell you about our lovely parties in Lisbon?"

"You don't need to; your wife wrote to me. Her description of the Regent's attempts at flirtation are the only thing that has made me laugh this month, she has a gift. I wonder if she would accept a post as my secretary?"

"She isn't going to accept any of the posts you're likely to offer her, sir, since they would all lead to the same thing and I do not trust you with her." Paul put the glass down on the table and sat down without being asked. "Tell me what's been going on."

***

Moving between his own brigade, Wellington's headquarters, and a cautious patrol of the border to seek out any signs of French activity, Paul had little time to write to his wife. He was expecting her to join him soon, so he wrote a brief note in carefully worded terms in case the message was intercepted and suggested that she return to their previous billet at Freineda and await further information. He was hoping that by the time she arrived the army would be ready to march on Badajoz and he could take her with him.

They encountered a French scouting party just to the east of Ciudad Rodrigo, clearly on a mission to discover what they could about the movements of the Allied army. The French were heavily outnumbered by the six companies of the 110th and 112th that Paul had with him and most of them surrendered quickly. Arriving back at the farm tired and muddy after sending Michael O'Reilly to escort the prisoners to headquarters, Paul's mood improved considerably at the sight of a letter from his wife awaiting him on his desk.

"Jenson, I am hot and tired and dirty. If my wife were here, there'd be a bath waiting for me."

"If your wife were here, you'd be in a better mood, sir. I'll get them to heat the water, but it might take a while. I think Mrs Bennett is still laid up with that sprained ankle, and Mrs Venables is going to make sure Captain Manson gets the first lot of water, she's got a thing about him."

"Which is manifestly unjust when I remember that I once saved her bloody husband from a hanging he richly deserved. It'll serve him right if she ends up in bed with Captain Manson. She might too, she's a pretty little thing and Manson has that diffident charm which fools them."

"Captain Manson has more sense than to go to bed with the wife of one of his NCOs, sir."

102

"Implying that I might not have at his age? I'd like to argue with that, but you know too much. All right, I know my place, I'm not going to try to compete with the charms of my light company captain. Do you think we can manage enough to wash in?"

"Easily, sir, I'll see to it. Why don't you sit down, have a drink and read Mrs van Daan's letter, it'll cheer you up?"

"Only if it tells me very specifically that I'm going to see her soon," Paul said with a grin, seating himself at his desk. He had barely unfolded the letter when Jenson reappeared.

"Sorry, sir. This just came for you."

Paul swore. "Jenson, can you not lose these bloody things when they turn up, I thought I'd trained you by now. I have been back all of five minutes, I am tired and hungry and in need of a wash and a drink and I was about to enjoy my wife's letter. He can piss off for half an hour."

"Apparently it's urgent, sir."

"He can still piss off for ten minutes, I'm reading this letter. Try and get some of the mud off those boots while you're waiting, will you? Who brought this?"

"Captain Graham, sir."

"Well ship him in and get him a drink while I read this. Good day, Richard. Does he have lookouts posted to see when I get back to my billet and sit down? How are you? Looking forward to another siege?"

"Too early to say yet, sir."

"Trust me you'll give a different answer in a week, this is not going to be as simple as Ciudad Rodrigo, and I didn't much enjoy that."

"No, sir, although you did cover yourself with glory."

"I covered myself with blood, some of it mine when I ran into a ditch lined with rusty swords, and most of it belonging to my friend and esteemed commander who did not survive the experience. I hate bloody sieges. Almost as much as I hate Lord Wellington just at this moment. Let me read this and I'll be with you. It's from Nan."

Her letter brought a smile to his face as he read. She wrote as she spoke, a gift few correspondents possessed in his experience and reading her words made him feel as though she were in the room with him.

"I believe I have finally organised the supply column to my satisfaction and hope to be with you within the fortnight, ready to enjoy your colourful views on Spanish military architecture. I cannot wait, as much as I love your children I am missing you desperately now and I know that I cannot trust you not to get yourself into trouble if I am not there. Give them all my love and take care of them and I look forward to seeing you very soon."

Paul smiled, folded the letter and tucked it inside his coat. "Those boots ready, Jenson? Well done, lad, how do you manage that in such a short time?"

"Practice, sir, you're such a messy bugger."

"Everybody says that about me. Along with a lot of other things."

"Most of which are true, sir. Are you going to see Lord Wellington in that shirt?"

"If Lord Wellington can spare me time to change it then I will. I'll be with you in five minutes, Richard, Jenson is worse than my wife."

Paul rode over to the village beside Graham, chatting easily about his recent mission and his time in Lisbon and found Wellington seated in his office. He was accompanied by two Spaniards, one of whom Paul recognised as Don Julian Sanchez who commanded the Spanish irregular forces. Wellington's relations with the Spanish had not been good in the past, but he had developed a good rapport with the dark haired, intense Sanchez. Paul smiled and nodded to him, saluted his chief and glanced curiously at the third man.

"Good afternoon, sir. This is quicker than usual, I've only been back five minutes. What have I missed?"

"Come and sit down, Paul."

Paul moved to one of the chairs and then stopped, noticing the expression on Lord Wellington's face. His chief looked pale and tired and there was something in his eyes which suddenly froze Paul.

"What's happened?" he asked.

"Paul, sit down."

Paul lowered himself into a chair his eyes still on Wellington's face. "What's happened?" he asked again.

Wellington nodded to Graham to sit and indicated the two Spaniards. "You know Don Julian, Paul. I'm not sure if you've met Pablo Cuesta. He was with Don Julian at Fuentes de Oñoro."

"I'm not sure we were introduced. Sir, what is this about?"

Wellington took a deep breath. "There isn't an easy way to tell you this, Paul, it's about your wife."

Paul felt the shock hit him hard, winding him. He sat very still for a moment, trying to marshal his thoughts. "Nan? What...she's not..."

Wellington's eyes met his. "She's not dead, Paul, she's a prisoner. Of the French."

Paul remained still and quiet, letting himself absorb the information. Nobody spoke but he saw his orderly come in through the tent flap and position himself just inside without bothering to ask for permission. Jenson was the most accomplished eavesdropper Paul had ever known but he was grateful for his presence. Eventually he had himself under control and looked up again.

"What happened? I've just read the letter she wrote from Lisbon telling me she was about to set off with the supply column. How the hell...?"

"Captain Cuesta was leading his men in pursuit of a French supply train on their way with ammunition and guns to Badajoz. It appears that their Colonel had taken a detour into Portugal. Cuesta's sources say that the man is making himself rich looting Spanish and Portuguese treasures. A lot of churches and abbeys were stripped and burned during the war but a fair few hid their treasures, and I am afraid that despite my advice, some of them have now brought them out of hiding to decorate the churches again. They see that the French have gone and many people are returning to their farms and villages. I think it is too soon but my warnings are sometimes unheeded."

"So this Colonel wanders with his troop over the border to scoop up a nice selection of gold crosses and plate and Captain Cuesta follows him. I'm with you so far."

"They came across a small group of English soldiers under a very young lieutenant. Men returning to their regiments from the hospital in Lisbon, escorting a supply train."

"And Nan."

"Yes. Food, medical supplies and some ammunition. They camped together in a deserted barn, ate together and settled down to sleep. The French ambushed them, a night attack. They put up a good fight but the French were too strong."

Paul looked over at Cuesta. "You got away."

"I lost half my men, Colonel. And most of the escort were killed. We had moved back into the barn but ammunition was running low. Your wife…it was her idea that we take our horses and run for it. She said that they would take the English prisoner but that they would slaughter us and probably torture us first."

Paul nodded. He was feeling very sick and wondered if he would need to go outside.

"Why didn't she go with you?" Graham asked. "She must have had a horse."

"The young lieutenant stayed with his men," Cuesta said. "She would not leave them. She said she spoke good French, could speak up for them. She asked me to bring the news here, to you."

Paul understood. "She wouldn't have left our lads there," he admitted. "Nan doesn't have it in her to run. But why the hell haven't they released her or sent a message? It's what we all do if we pick up officers' wives or women. I don't understand."

"Nor did I, Paul," Wellington said gently. "But Captain Cuesta did not leave the scene immediately. He wanted to see what happened and which way the French marched so that he could bring the information back to me."

"So do we know what happened to her? Do we even know if she's still alive?"

"Colonel, I sent my men to safety, but two of us remained close to see what happened so that I could report to you. They did not kill her but they did kill every man of her escort. The Colonel commanding them killed the young lieutenant himself with his sword. The others were bayonetted in front of her. I am sorry."

For a moment Paul was unable to trust his voice. Wellington reached across and put a comforting hand on his shoulder. "They didn't kill her, Paul."

"Not then. But this is not bloody normal, sir, we both know that. What the hell is going on?"

Sanchez leaned forward. "You are right, Colonel. As soon as his Lordship told me I have had my people out, seeking intelligence. One of my bands had news, they had picked up some French wounded on the border, left behind when the company fled from Captain Cuesta's men."

"And?"

Wellington met his eyes. "Colonel, the company is commanded by Colonel Dupres – the same Colonel Dupres who was removed from his command in disgrace after his conduct at Fuentes de Oñoro and sent to a posting escorting supplies."

Paul knew that the last of the colour must have drained from his face. "Oh sweet Jesus, he's going to kill her."

"We don't know that for sure, Paul…"

"Yes we fucking do, sir, I've seen this bastard in action and he hates my guts. If he lost his command because of Fuentes de Oñoro, I'll guarantee he blames me. I need to find him. Because if we don't do it soon there won't be anything left of her to find."

Lord Wellington's face was very pale. "I've spoken to Don Julian," he said quietly. "And I've sent out messages to every exploring officer and scouting party we can reach. They've instructions to hunt for this man and as soon as he's found, they'll send a message and you can take the 110th and get her back, Colonel. I don't care where we are in this siege, she comes first."

Paul studied his chief. "You wanted me to take charge until General Alten gets here," he said.

"I still do, but not ahead of your wife's safety. We have weeks, I'm hoping to God she'll be back before we breach. If she's not and you need to go, Vandeleur or Barnard can take over instead, and Colonel Wheeler can command your brigade. We'll get her back, Colonel, but you are not to go haring off on your own. Wait for information; it will come."

"I know. And I won't. I might go completely in the wrong direction and then not be available when the news comes in."

"I'm glad to see you're still capable of thought," Wellington said quietly. "In the meantime, I've news of my siege train finally. Once it's close enough I intend to march my remaining troops to Badajoz."

Paul looked over at Cuesta. "Was this supply train heading for Badajoz?" he asked.

"Our sources suggest that they are escorting supplies for the town. Your army will be there ahead of them but they may not realise that for some days. I imagine once they find out, they will divert up to Salamanca to join Soult's army there."

"When did it happen, Captain? How long has that bastard had my wife?"

Cuesta hesitated. "Eight days," he said quietly. "Colonel, I am sorry. If I had known, I would have taken her with us. But none of us thought…"

"No, it's all right, you can't have known any more than she did. God help her, she'll have told them who she was straight away. It ought to have guaranteed her safety and a quick release. Sir, will you excuse me? I need some time alone."

"Of course, Colonel, take whatever you need. She is your priority just now. As soon as I hear anything…"

"She should have been my priority a few weeks ago, sir, and then she'd be here with me instead of out there enduring God knows what." Paul got up. "I need to get out of here."

Outside he mounted and watched as Jenson did the same. "Freddie, I need to be alone for a bit. Will you get back and tell the others? They'll need to know, but just at the moment…"

"I'll see to it, sir." Jenson studied him. "Are you all right? I thought you were going to throw up in there."

106

"So did I. My bloody imagination is working overtime right now, but the worst of it is that I'm probably not wrong. He's a nasty bastard at the best of times. And Nan…"

"Don't, sir. It won't help."

"I can't help it," Paul said. "I'll see you later, Freddie."

He rode until it was too dark for Rufus to see properly and then walked his horse slowly back to the quinta. Part of him did not want to go back to his friends, to see his own fears reflected in their eyes. She was loved throughout his brigade and they would all be anxious for her. He was aware, agonisingly, that they would all have some idea of what would probably be happening to her and he dreaded their helpless sympathy. At the same time, he knew it was foolish to isolate himself. This was a shared ordeal so he made himself ride back into the wide square outside the house, and dismount, standing still as his friends came running to meet him.

Carl reached him first and the expression in the green eyes almost overset him. "Paul – dear God. Look, come inside. You're probably not wanting food although there is some. George isn't used to his roast pork not being eaten, but I can't say most of us had much appetite. But come and get a drink. You look like hell."

"I feel empty," Paul said. "As if it can't really be true. I'd just read her letter telling me she was on her way…Carl, what if he kills her? What if I get there and find her dead? Or what if I never find her at all – if I never know…"

"Paul, we'll find her. Sanchez has every single one of his men out looking for them, and we know roughly where they ought to be. Once he's found them, he's given instructions to send runners back but to keep tracking them. He likes your wife."

"I know he does. Poor Wellington…he looked fairly much the way I feel. I know we'll find them, Carl. I'm just terrified we won't find them in time."

He sat down at the table in the dining room and shook his head as George Kelly set food before him. "Not now, George – I can't."

"You'll need to eat, sir."

"I will. I'm not going to starve myself, I'm not that stupid. But I can't eat just now."

Wheeler set a glass of wine before him. "You're worried he'll kill her?" he asked gently.

"Yes."

There was a silence. Into it, Michael O'Reilly said flatly:

"He isn't going to kill her, Paul."

Paul looked up, conscious of the faint frisson of shock running through his officers which told him they had all been thinking the same thing although none of them could have said it to him.

"You think he'll find another use for her?"

"I'm bloody sure he will," O'Reilly said, and Paul could sense rage bubbling beneath the surface. Strangely it made him feel better than the agonised sympathy of the others.

"Michael, I'm sure you're right. But if he decides to pass her round the entire company that might be a death sentence in itself."

"He might, but I doubt it. If this is about revenge, he'll want her alive until you can see what he's done to her. And also…"

"Also?"

"Paul, the world is not full of women like Anne. He's not going to hand her over to his men. I'm sorry, it must kill you to hear it, but he isn't."

"I know, Michael. But what frightens the hell out of me is how she'll react. This is an officer who started a one-man feud which put his whole troop at risk just because I pissed him off in a skirmish, it's not normal. And you need to trust me when I tell you that if he puts a hand on my wife she is going to fight back. She's going to get hurt."

"Sir, I can't tell you she won't. But she's a very clever woman - smarter than most men. She'll work out how to keep herself alive because she knows we'll come for her. Don't worry about him killing her, although the thought of whatever the hell else he's been doing to her is probably making you want to vomit just now. But she's a survivor. All we need to do is find her."

For the first time Paul felt himself relax a little. He nodded, his eyes on Michael's face. "Is that actually what you think, Michael, or are you just trying to make me feel better?"

The Irishman pushed the glass towards him. "Drink the wine. I think if he'd been going to kill her, he would have cut her throat along with the escort, poor bastards. And once he's had her round him for a few days it's going to get harder and harder to do. She's a lot more than a pretty face and you know it."

"I do." Paul drank deeply. "Thank you – all of you. Look, I'm going to bed. Not sure I'll sleep much, but I need to be on my own for a bit. But I'm grateful. I know I'm not going to be the only one worrying about her. It feels better somehow. I'll make sure you know everything I do. Goodnight."

They watched him leave in silence. Johnny reached for the wine and poured a glass. "I honestly don't know what to say to him."

Michael shook his head. "Poor bastard. I doubt he'll sleep properly until she's safe back."

"And did you mean what you just said?"

"Yes, although I was trying not to be too specific. That bastard will have taken one look at Nan and thought it was Christmas. She's young, she's beautiful and she's the wife of a man he hates, and we all know how keen he is on revenge, we've seen him in action. I'm damned sure he's enjoying himself very much and that thought must be driving Paul completely mad. No point in dwelling on it. We just have to find her and get her back."

"And what then, Michael?" Johnny said soberly. "Christ – what is that going to do to her? And to Paul?"

"God knows," Michael said. "At that point it'll be up to them to work that out. But I very much doubt Colonel Dupres is going to survive the experience."

Chapter Nine

After ten days of captivity Anne was used to the routine of the French company. In many ways it was as familiar to her as the routine of the English army, an early start and marching until late afternoon with stops for water and food, followed by making camp, a meal and time spent around the campfires. There were foraging expeditions into the countryside and when the men returned with food and provisions, Anne felt herself flinching internally wondering what the Portuguese villagers had suffered in the loss of the supplies, since she knew that the French were told to live off the land and would not consider paying for what they took.

They reached Caso Braco, a small star-shaped fortress just over the Spanish border, held by a skeleton garrison under a very young captain who seemed wholly intimidated by Colonel Dupres. Anne was taken to a chamber in one of the towers where she waited in furious rebellion while Dupres ate and drank with his host and received new orders. When he came to the room he had been drinking and was unusually mellow. He had brought food for her and she ate it in her usual silence. The temptation to throw it in his face was strong but Anne was a practical girl and the long days of marching made her hungry.

Anne had been sick several times during the past days and she suspected a combination of fear and exhaustion was causing it, but she knew she needed to maintain her strength until Paul found her. Dupres watched her eat and poured her a glass of wine. Anne sipped it slowly, still not looking at him or speaking. She was aware that her silence infuriated him, but she broke it only when his threats looked likely to be carried out. He had beaten her three times now and it was taking longer to heal.

When she was finished she got up and went to wash the bowl. He stopped her, his hand on her arm. "Not now. I've orders. It seems the English are investing Badajoz."

Anne did not move or speak. The hand tightened on her arm until it hurt. "I'm in the mood for conversation, so unless you want another beating, cherie, I would open your mouth and speak."

"I've nothing to say."

"What it means for you is either I send you back to Wellington's army outside the walls, which is only a day's march or so, or I take you on to Salamanca with me. Which is it to be, ma petite? Am I ready to let you go yet?"

"What point in keeping me here? Unless you plan on cutting my throat, in which case it would be a favour to do it now. I'm tired of this."

He gave a soft laugh and drew her close to him. Anne pulled back and he tightened his grip. "Stand still. I like this. I come back to my room and find you here, and you eat, and we drink, and I can look at you and pretend for a while that you want to be here. And then I take you to bed."

"That part is called rape, Colonel. Is it worth dying for?"

"I'm not going to die. He hasn't come for you yet."

"He will."

"Wellington won't let him. There's a war on and he needs to do his duty."

Anne turned her head to look at him. She seldom looked directly at him, preferring to avert her eyes whenever he touched her. "Lord Wellington will tell him to come as soon as he knows where you are, Colonel. But if he didn't, Paul would come anyway. Don't forget he's not a conscript, he can just sell out."

"His men can't."

"His men would die for him. And for me."

The hand closed hard on her arm, bruising it. "If they come after me they will need to," Dupres said. "Get into bed."

Anne remained still. Eventually Dupres lifted his hand and slapped her, not particularly hard. Anne raised a supercilious eyebrow then moved towards the bed. She stripped off her shabby garments and lay back, her face averted and her eyes closed, and flinched as she felt the weight of him settle beside her.

"I might need more than this tonight, cherie," he said softly, against her hair. Anne did not move or speak. Finally she felt his hand on her face, forcing her to look at him. "But I can see that you are not of my mind. I wonder how long it will take before you realise your life would get easier if you pleased me?"

Anne jerked her head free. "You don't have that much time, Colonel."

"I have tonight," Dupres said, and Anne felt his weight shift. She lay rigid, trying not to cry, and wondered despairingly how much more of it she could endure.

***

The officers and men of the 110th watched their commander through the next few days in agonised sympathy. As far as Carl could see he barely slept at all. Carl knew that Wellington had effectively excused him from duty, but Paul continued to observe his daily routine in white faced misery. He spoke very little, ate without savouring the food to keep himself going and flinched every time a rider approached which might have come from Wellington. The army moved out towards Badajoz and set up camp within sight of the walls and Paul joined the work parties down in the trenches on most days. Riding down to inspect the fifth company who were on night duty, Carl was surprised when he realised that the tall figure in the ditch, wielding a spade with grim efficiency alongside the men, was the commander of the third brigade of the light division. He dismounted, handing the reins to Jenson, who stood watching with Rufus.

"Jenson, how long has he been down here?"

"Four hours with the night shift. But he did about three hours this afternoon as well." Jenson looked at Carl. "See if you can do better than I have, sir. He needs to rest a bit at least."

"Is he sleeping at all?"

"An hour or so here or there. I'm trying to pour brandy into him at night. Sometimes he dozes off, but I think he's dreaming."

"Poor bastard," Carl said softly, his eyes on his friend. "All we keep telling him is that she's still alive, that he'll get her back. But I am wondering what he'll be like if he doesn't."

"What do you think, sir? Is she still alive?"

"Well we know she was, and she's very strong. But every day that goes by…" Carl glanced at Paul's orderly. "Honestly, Jenson, what worries me is that if Dupres has raped or abused a colonel's wife over some imagined insult which has already got him into trouble, his superiors are going to bloody shoot him this time. They might be bastards with the local women when they think it doesn't matter but a French officer doesn't treat a captured officer's wife this way."

"What makes you so sure he has this time, sir?"

"Because he slaughtered the escort in front of her. That is not normal behaviour. And also because we'd have had a message by now if he wanted ransom or an exchange of prisoners. Wellington has sent messages to all the French commanders and it's not like Soult doesn't know where we are. And that's what bothers me. Most of them are honourable men. They're going to be appalled at what he's done. Bad enough that he's been looting without sharing it out, but this? If he arrives back at headquarters with her, they'll release her immediately and send her back and they'll send him for trial. They don't want to be seen as brute beasts. And no matter how crazy Dupres is, sooner or later he's going to realise it. At which point he may well want to get rid of the evidence."

"Christ." Jenson jerked his head towards the ditch. "Do you think he realises that?"

"Well he's at least as bright as I am, lad, probably a lot more so."

"No wonder he's down here digging his way to hell every night. Still, we need to get him out of there before he…"

"Colonel van Daan!" A voice cut through the darkness and Carl and Jenson both turned. A horseman was approaching, his way lit by a soldier holding a lantern. "They said he was down here. Anybody seen…"

"I'm here," Paul called, and dropped his spade, reaching up to climb out of the ditch. Hands on all sides reached to help him.

"Sir, let us know," a voice called from the ditch. "We're all waiting."

Carl watched his commander turn. "Who's that, I can't see?" he demanded.

"Pryce, sir."

"Corporal Pryce, don't think I don't know you spend half your time hanging around the hospital offering to help, just to spend time with my wife," Paul said. His voice was remarkably steady, Carl thought, considering that there was clearly news

111

and he had no idea what it was. "I am on to you, Pryce, you're smitten. But I will send a message down if there's news, providing you get your backs into it and keep your heads down." Paul indicated the citadel. "They're very quiet up there tonight, but it doesn't mean they won't start up soon, and if she gets back to find she's got to dig shot out of your backsides because you got careless, she is going to be pissed-off like you've never seen."

Carl heard their laughter, muted to avoid attracting too much attention from the French. Jenson moved forward with Paul's coat and Paul shook his head. "Don't bother, Jenson, I'm filthy anyway. What's going on, Mr Beaumaris?"

Wellington's youngest aide saluted as Paul swung himself into the saddle. "Sir, all I know is that he wants you up there now."

***

Paul rode as fast as he dared in the darkness over the uneven ground. Lights shone from the commander in chief's tent and as Paul dismounted, Captain Richard Graham emerged.

"Colonel, come in."

"Is there news?" Paul was suddenly very aware of his muddy clothing. "I should have changed...."

"Come in, sir, nobody is going to give a damn."

Paul ducked into the tent. Wellington was sitting in his usual camp chair, but he stood up as Paul entered and Paul saw the news in his face.

"You've found her."

"We know where she is. She's still with Dupres, Colonel. But she was definitely alive yesterday morning."

Paul felt light-headed with relief. His commander moved forward, pulled out a chair and shoved him into it. "Graham, get him a brandy."

"None left, sir, but we've wine."

"I doubt he'll care. Paul, I don't have to introduce you to Captain Fenwick from the Corps of Guides. He rode in about half an hour ago with news."

Paul looked at Fenwick, feeling slightly dazed. "Giles? Dear God, tell me she's alive."

His former officer studied him with sympathetic blue eyes. "She is, sir. I came across them early yesterday morning, they'd just started their march. From the direction, I'd say they were heading up towards Salamanca, bypassing Badajoz – they've probably had new orders now that it's invested and they won't get their supplies through. Between sixty and seventy men, I'd say, led by Colonel Dupres along with a captain two or three junior officers. A lot of wagons and carts, it a big convoy."

"Some of those will be ours," Wellington said grimly.

"And my wife?" Paul said, trying to keep his voice steady.

"She's there, sir. Marching with them."

"Marching?"

Fenwick glanced over at Wellington and Paul picked up the expression quickly. "No," he said. "No, you don't have the right to edit what you tell me here.

112

Not just because I'm her husband and I should know, but because if I'm going in to get her out I need to know everything. And I'm going to find out anyway, there's nothing she can't tell me."

"Tell him, Captain," Wellington said quietly.

"Yes, my Lord." Fenwick's discomfort was obvious. "Sir, she's on foot, although there's a fair few extra horses, one of them might be hers. She was walking barefoot and she's in her petticoats. I'm sorry, sir."

Paul absorbed the information and found, to his surprise, that it upset him less than he had expected. "Is she hurt?"

"I couldn't tell, sir. She's walking, moving very easily. Her hair was down. I could see her through my glass. She's upright and she's mobile. It's definitely your wife, sir, I'd know her anywhere. And if I'd had more men with me, I'd have gone down there myself, the bastards…"

Paul smiled. It was not much, but he realised it was the first natural smile he had given in a week. "I know you would, Giles, you've no need to tell me how fond you are of Nan. Thank you. How far away?"

"Surprisingly close, sir. Less than a day's march - you could do it in four hours marching quickly, they're heading this way."

"Can you help me find them?"

"Ready when you are, sir. I've left my Portuguese guide tracking them in case they suddenly change direction."

"We'll be there before they have a chance." Paul looked at Wellington, who nodded.

"Go with Colonel van Daan, Fenwick. Tell him everything he needs to know. Colonel, when you have your plan come back and tell me what it is."

"I will, sir. Thank you."

"Get her back," Wellington said. "I don't give a damn how you do it."

***

Colonel Dupres marched his men north-east over the Spanish border and up towards Salamanca. Anne suffered in grim silence the pain of bruised and bloodied feet on the rocky paths and the sun beat down on her through the march while the nights she slept on the floor of Dupres' tent were cold. She learned to value the unwavering support of both Cavel and Bernard. Dupres had relented on the matter of food and she ate when the men did. Nausea came and went and she endured it, understanding that her body was rebelling against its ill treatment. He had not beaten her again but every few nights he took her to his bed. He had stopped gloating and trying to bait her, he simply held her down, ignoring her struggles and her distress and it took all of Anne's strength of will not to beg him to leave her alone. Sometimes she wondered if that was what he was waiting for.

On the thirteenth day of Anne's captivity a forage party returned with a feast of fresh bread and cheese and wine and a sheep to roast. Dupres called her to sit by the fire with his officers and she sat in silence as they laughed and drank and wished passionately that she was sitting with Paul and her friends. The scene was so familiar and the company so alien that it upset her and she struggled to keep back her tears.

113

Cavel, who was always sensitive to her moods, moved closer to her under cover of their laughter.

"Are you all right, Madame?"

Anne shook her head. "No. I miss my husband and my friends. And I am afraid, all the time."

"I'm sorry, it was a stupid question. Perhaps you could feign illness. He is drinking, he might…"

"Cavel!" Dupres voice boomed out. "What are you whispering to my woman?"

Anne turned her head. The words sent rage flood through her body, temporarily blocking out fear and caution. She lifted her eyes to the florid face. "Your woman?"

Dupres looked back at her mockingly. "Since you share my bed most nights, what else are you? Nobody else gets to enjoy you. And you are getting more co-operative."

"Your English isn't very good, Colonel, but luckily my French is excellent. And in either language I can distinguish clearly between co-operation and coercion."

Dupres dropped to sit beside her, took hold of her and kissed her long and hard. "And what do I need to do to engage your enthusiasm, cherie?" he asked. Anne could hear the laughter of some of his officers and many of his men. Unexpectedly she lost her temper.

Pulling back, she regarded Dupres thoughtfully and then made herself laugh, a low warm sound, and leaned forward kissing him fully on the mouth. She felt the shock run through him, a shiver of surprise and then desire. He opened his mouth and Anne leaned into him, kissing him as if she wanted him. She had learned during her two years with Robert how to dissemble in order to stop him from hitting her and she was not sure her husband had ever known how much she hated sharing his bed. It was a skill she had not forgotten. Dupres hand lifted to her breast and instead of flinching away as she always had, she laughed against his mouth and moved closer, reached out and slid her hand down his body, feeling him harden against her caressing hand. The men around them fell silent, shocked by her sudden responsiveness. Finally, Anne drew back slightly and regarded him and saw his dark eyes, wide and startled and full of desire on hers.

"You're lucky to get co-operation, Colonel," she said, loudly and clearly, in idiomatic French. "If you want enthusiasm, you're going to have to improve your performance. After the first shock, frankly I have trouble staying awake in there."

There was a ripple of appalled shock and amusement through officers and men. Anne heard Cavel make a faint protest, knowing what she had done, but she kept her eyes on Dupres and saw his expression change, saw the fury and humiliation flooding through him. He pulled away from her and got up, his face scarlet and Anne rose too and stood looking at him mockingly. She knew that he was going to hit her but the expression on his face was worth it.

Stepping forward, Dupres punched her hard in the stomach. Anne folded up in agony and he followed it up with two more blows. She was on the ground, winded and in pain, and he kicked her several times in the ribs and back, very hard. Another kick hit her arm and she felt pain radiate up into her shoulder and neck. The foot went back again and then she heard a furious protest and arms went about her.

114

"Colonel, no! You will kill her. You cannot do this!"

She realised that Captain Bernard had placed his body between her and his Colonel and she lay still, not wanting to antagonise Dupres into attacking his Captain.

"Out of the way, Bernard. The bitch needs to learn her place!"

"She has learned it, sir. It is enough. Cavel, get her out of here and see to her."

After a moment Anne's vision cleared and she felt herself scooped up into strong arms. The Sergeant carried her away from the fire and into the darkness. He lay her down on cool grass and she rolled over and retched distressingly. When she had finished, he brought a cool cloth and bathed her face then supported her and gave her water.

"Lie still, you're hurt."

Anne lay still, winded, trying to breathe through the pain. She felt the Sergeant's hand resting on her ribs

"You're hurt and I've no way of knowing how badly. Mary Mother of God, cherie, why did you do that?"

Anne lifted her eyes to his. "Because he's a bastard, and a rapist, and I'm tired of lying still and taking it," she said, and she saw him flinch.

"Oh cherie, I know," he breathed. "But I can't think of a way to get you away from here without getting both of us killed…"

"Sergeant, this is not your problem."

"It is," Cavel said savagely. "It is the problem of any decent man among us. But you cannot antagonise him like this, ma petite. This has gone well beyond revenge against your husband now, he's obsessed with you. I am afraid he will kill you."

Anne lay back and closed her eyes, feeling exhaustion flood through her, joining with the pain. "Sergeant, you're very kind. But tonight, I'm not sure I care all that much," she said softly.

The following two days were almost more than Anne could bear. Constantly in pain she endured the nights as silently as she could, but he was brutal in his use of her body, uncaring how much he hurt her and she lay crying on the tent floor afterwards and wondered despairingly if she would survive until Paul reached her. She refused to remain in the bed beside him although she spent her nights cold and shivering under her cloak and a thin blanket.

On the third day Anne stumbled along behind his horse on the march, too exhausted and in too much pain to even lift her eyes. He had tied her to his saddle again, after several days of allowing her to walk freely. Her world at this moment was reduced to an ache in her abdomen and ribs, and a worse ache in her lower back. She was bruised and battered, feeling weak and light-headed and moving her arm hurt so much she wondered if he had broken something. Beside her, Cavel was quiet and anxious, reaching out to steady her every time she faltered.

Dupres called a halt earlier than usual and Anne stood passively waiting to be untied. As Cavel approached her, the Colonel stepped in and waved him back. He reached for the rope and unfastened it as the men around him began to unload their kit and lift the officers' tents down from the wagon.

"Your wrists are bad," Dupres said suddenly.

Anne looked up, startled, and then down at the chafed skin of her wrists which were bleeding. By now her whole body ached so much she had not really noticed the discomfort. She nodded without speaking and suddenly he took her hand and turned it over, examining the wounds.

"Are you still in pain?"

Anne nodded again, not looking at him. Quietly he said:

"I do not think I have heard you speak for two days."

"I've nothing to say," Anne said.

"Look at me!" Dupres said sharply and she did so, surprised to see something like concern in his eyes.

"You need to rest, you're not well. When the tent is up I want you to lie down on the bed. I will..."

"No."

"I will remain outside. You are not sleeping, are you? I hear you during the night."

Anne shook her head.

"It must be cold on the ground. You should sleep in the bed."

"No."

"You need to rest; we still have a long way to go."

Anne shook her head silently. Dupres reached out and cupped her face in his hand. The gesture appalled her. It was one Paul often made and she felt a rush of longing for him. Despite her efforts something must have shown in her face.

"Stop fighting me," Dupres said quietly. "You cannot win and you are making yourself ill with this pointless stubbornness."

"If I can't make it, Colonel, I understood your intention was to shoot me in the head."

"I would not kill you," Dupres said softly.

Anne looked at him steadily. "Colonel, I'm beginning to wish you would," she said.

There was a distant shout and Anne jumped. Dupres spun around. "That was the pickets. Cavel, what...?"

"Partisans!" Bernard yelled. "To the wagons, load weapons!"

The French scrambled to the wagons as the horsemen rode in. They came from all directions and Anne felt a spurt of terror. They were Spanish guerrillas, fast and lethal, and she did not trust that they would give quarter to any woman marching with the French or stop to wonder if she was a prisoner. Dupres was shouting orders. He put his hand on Anne's shoulder and pointed.

"Over there by the wagons. Keep low."

Anne ran and ducked down, careful to keep as far as she could from the powder wagons. She flinched as two of the Spanish rode past, close to her. One of them fell from his horse shot down, the other galloped away.

It was a raid, not a battle. There were not enough of them to take the column, but they were mounted and fast and their aim was to kill as many of the French as possible before Dupres got his men into good order. It took him a long time and Anne was conscious of her own sense of impatience. Any company of the Light Division would have been at arms and fully functional in five minutes. Paul's men could do it in two.

As the French muskets began to do some damage, the Spanish pulled back, wheeling their mounts further out, firing pistols to try to take down one or two men before fleeing. Anne had thought them gone until hooves sounded close to her and suddenly a hand caught at her shoulder. It was the arm where Dupres had kicked her and she cried out in pain.

"Hush!" the Spaniard said, leaning from his horse.

Anne looked up at him, blinking away tears of pain then her eyes widened. She was looking up into the dark eyes of Pablo Cuesta.

"Pablo," she whispered.

He was scanning her face and body and she saw horror and pity. "Señora…"

"Is he here?"

"Yes. We are just making sure you were."

"Go. Don't tell him what you've seen, just that I'm alive. It might make him careless."

He looked at her with quick comprehension. "Tonight or tomorrow," he said, then he released her and Anne fell back to the ground.

Cuesta wheeled his mount with superb control and galloped off, yelling for his men to follow. Anne watched him, her heart in her mouth, terrified that he would be shot down before he could escape with the message. He was not and the dust thrown up by his horsemen floated into the air as the French lowered weapons, drew breath and assessed their losses.

There were six men on the ground. Anne pushed herself cautiously to her feet and watched dispassionately as their comrades ran to their aid. Four were undoubtedly dead. Sergeant Cavel, who sported a bloody arm where a ball had grazed it, knelt beside the fifth, felt for a pulse and looked up.

"He is alive, sir," he said to Dupres. "But look at his arm."

Bernard was beside him. "With a surgeon he might make it, but what chance out here? How is Peron, Corporal?"

"Bleeding, sir. More blood than I've ever seen; I can't seem to stop it. I don't think…"

Instinct cut in. "Let me look!" Anne said sharply.

They turned to stare at her in mute astonishment, having become so accustomed to her self-imposed silence except when she was obliged to speak that her raised voice shocked them. Bernard took a step forward, glancing uncertainly at his Colonel.

"Madame?"

"You have minutes only," Anne said shortly. "Let me look and find the black medical bag with my baggage. Or let them die. It's up to you."

Nobody spoke. Anne saw Cavel look around then suddenly he swore and beckoned to her. "I'll find the bag."

Anne ran barefooted over to where two men, both slightly wounded, bent over a third who was soaked in blood from a wound high in his chest. Anne pushed past them, ignoring them, reached for the man's coat and pulled it open. She ripped open the soaked shirt.

"Get me some water, I can't see what I'm doing," she said, and a water bottle was pushed into her hands. Anne tore a piece off the shirt, soaked the wound and swabbed the blood and water away so that she could see.

As she worked, she was vaguely conscious of the column around her beginning to stir into life. Dupres gave orders for graves to be dug and yelled at his pickets for not being fast enough to spot the approaching Spaniards. Cavel appeared beside her and set down her black leather bag.

"Do you need anything else?"

"Something to use for dressings and bandages. I'd cut up a petticoat if I had one but if I tear anything more off this I'll be marching naked. And if you've some brandy or rum or something I can give him to help him relax…I'm going to take the ball out."

"Here?" Cavel asked startled. "Can you even do that?"

"I'm very good at it, actually, Sergeant. It's not ideal. If it were his leg or arm I would dress it and leave it until we've better facilities, but I can't leave this. You'll have to move him and given where it is, it must be close to lungs or heart. I don't think his lungs are hit, the blood doesn't look right for that, but if I don't remove it the ball could shift with movement and he'll be dead."

Anne reached for her bag and saw him run off shouting orders. He returned quickly with several thin towels which he ripped up using his knife while she took the brandy bottle from him and managed to get some of the spirit into the injured man. He was conscious now, his eyes huge on her face and she recognised him suddenly as one of the two men who had held her down in Dupres' chamber on the first night he had beaten and raped her. The thought made Anne hesitate for a moment and she saw the expression in his eyes shift and knew that he had understood her pause. Then she shook her head, deliberately cleared her mind and focused on the job.

Cavel and another man held him still as she cut and dug. He screamed at the first cut and Anne closed her mind to his pain, knowing that it was a distraction. When the ball was out she tied off the blood vessels with catgut sutures and then closed and dressed the wound. When she was finished she looked up at the Sergeant.

"He needs rest and plenty of water now. I've no laudanum here for the pain but you can give him more brandy, it might help. I don't know what your Colonel will say but he shouldn't really be moved for a day or two. After that you can put him in one of the baggage wagons and get him to a hospital. He might make it."

"We will camp here for two nights. There is water and the visibility is good."

She looked around, startled at the voice, and realised that Dupres had been standing watching her. There was a curious expression on his face. Anne got up stiffly, wincing at the pain in her ribs. Ignoring Dupres she looked at Cavel who was calling orders for the man to be removed to the shelter of a small copse of trees.

"Are there any others?"

"De Castre. But he's had half an arm blown away, there's nothing…"

"Let me look."

Cavel studied her. "Madame, you cannot…"

"Let her see," Dupres said. He was still staring at Anne. Cavel shrugged and led her over to the other badly injured man. One look at his arm told Anne that he was right.

"The arm needs to come off. I can do it, but I'll need something firm to rest it on – a chest or a box...? And I'll need three of you to hold him still."

She saw, this time, genuine shock in Cavel's face. "You cannot amputate a man's arm, Madame."

"Yes I can, Sergeant, I've done it many times. To be honest it is one of the things I try to leave to the men, they're stronger than I am so they do it quicker. But in battle there aren't enough surgeons, so I do my share. Do you want me to try?"

Cavel looked uncertainly at Dupres and the colonel nodded. Around Anne, the men were making camp, lighting fires and drawing water and she waited as a sturdy chest was set up and then instructed her assistants.

In the end it was a quick and easy amputation, with so much damage done that it was more a matter of tidying up. Anne closed and dressed the stump with the man mercifully unconscious with pain and gave instructions about his care then straightened wearily and looked at Cavel.

"Let me look at that arm."

"It isn't serious."

"No, but if it isn't kept clean it could get serious very quickly. Take off your coat."

Cavel obeyed in silence. When she had finished, he called out several names and men came over to have their wounds cleaned and dressed. Fires had been lit and there was the smell of food cooking. Normally by this time the men who were not on sentry duty would be talking and laughing and sharing their wine rations, but there was something quiet about them tonight. The graves were completed and the men gathered around as their comrades were lowered into them. There was no prayer and no sharing of memories as Anne was used to and she used the time to go to the stream to wash and clean her instruments before neatly packing them into her bag again. She drank thirstily from the stream, washed her hands and splashed water onto her face. As she rose to go back to the camp a man's form moved out of the shadows and Anne jumped. Dupres came forward.

"Give the bag to Cavel, he will put it back with the luggage. If you need it again it can be brought to you."

Through her exhaustion Anne was faintly amused. "Yes, I can understand you'd not want me sleeping in your tent with a bone saw within reach."

His eyes were on her face. "Why did you offer to help?"

"I've treated French wounded for years, Colonel. This is no different. Although honestly, I'm not sure what I'd have done if it had been you lying there bleeding to death."

"I can understand that. But you still need rest. You have barely eaten in three days and I have seen you being sick again."

"Why would you care?" Anne said shortly, turning away. He took hold of her arm.

"I told you, I want you alive. And this silence...I am beginning to miss the bad-tempered bitch I picked up in Portugal. Go over to the fire and sit. When you have eaten you can sleep. I will not trouble you tonight. You need some time to heal."

Anne stared at him uncomprehendingly. "God in heaven, you can't pretend you care how I feel," she said, appalled. "After what you've done..."

119

"I don't," Dupres said quickly, a slight flush staining his cheeks. "You're the wife of a man I despise. A means of taking revenge. Nothing more."

"Good. If you don't require me to be in your tent I'd like to remain with the wounded," Anne said. She was deliberately trying to keep her voice flat. He must see no difference in her demeanour, although inside she had gone from flat despair to soaring joy and hope within an hour. Somewhere close by was Paul and she suspected that once he heard from Cuesta that she was definitely here he would attack that night. He would not leave her here an hour longer than he needed to. If she could remain with the wounded, she could keep herself away from the fighting. Anne was afraid that if Dupres realised what was happening he would kill her before Paul could reach her.

"You'll need a guard."

"Sergeant Cavel will probably do it," Anne said.

He nodded and did not speak again. Anne moved to the fireside and accepted food although she ate very little. Her whole body was tense with anticipation. She was terrified that something would go wrong, that Paul would be injured or killed through some fluke shot during the attack, although common sense told her that he would have superior numbers and would have scouted the camp thoroughly. Having seen Dupres' men struggling earlier to cope with the surprise attack of the Spaniards she was fairly sure that the 110th would cut through them in minutes, but she had suffered so much that she was afraid to let herself hope.

When the camp began to settle for the night Anne took herself to the baggage wagon where several of the men had rigged up a makeshift shelter for the two badly wounded men. Cavel followed her and handed her a blanket.

"Do you need your cloak, cherie? I can look for it."

"No, I'm all right. Not sure I'll sleep much tonight."

He studied her. "Are you still in a lot of pain?"

"Some," Anne admitted.

"I'm worried he's done some damage. I've never seen you look as bad as you have the past couple of days."

"I thought he might have broken some ribs, but it feels easier today so it's probably just badly bruised. Look, do you mind staying with me tonight? He wants a guard on me and I'd rather it was you or Captain Bernard. I don't wholly trust any of the others. If you'll do it, he'll let me stay here…"

"Of course, I'll do it. At least I can see you're safe."

Anne nodded and went to check on the two men, then moved to sit with her back to the wagon. All her senses were on the alert. He was watching her curiously, and she realised that she needed at least to feign sleep, so she lay down. She wished she had brought her cloak, but she was not prepared to go to Dupres tent to find it. He might change his mind. Cavel lay a few feet away from her and after a while she heard his breathing change and knew that he slept. She had thought that tension and expectation would keep her awake but her exhausted body needed rest and she drifted finally into slumber.

***

120

Paul had brought six companies, five from the 110th and the light company of the 112th under Michael O'Reilly. He had a suspicion if he had not included Michael he would simply have followed. Led by Giles Fenwick and Antonio, his Portuguese guide, they met Cuesta with his men about three miles from the camp.

"Colonel van Daan."

"Pablo, any news?"

"We attacked earlier. A short raid."

"You did what?" Paul said, his voice rising. "You launched an unplanned attack on a French camp where we think my wife is a prisoner..."

"She is there and she is alive, Colonel. I spoke a few words to her. She knows you are coming."

Paul took a very long breath. He could feel relief flooding through him. "They didn't realise...?"

"No. They were not well prepared, Colonel."

"They might be more so tonight, now that they've been attacked once today," Paul said shortly. He was trying not to lose his temper with the Spaniard although the thought of what might have happened chilled him. Urgently he needed to attack, to find her and know for sure that she was safe.

Leo Manson put his hand on his Colonel's shoulder. "Sir, at least we know we're attacking the right troop," he said. "Only another few hours."

Paul nodded and looked back at Cuesta. "Did you lose any?"

"Two. But we killed several of theirs so I do not regret it. We will accompany you..."

"No," Paul said forcefully, and then forced himself to moderate his tone. "Thank you, Captain, but you've done your share. I want my own men to do this. I'm sorry, but I can't risk her." He looked at Carl, who had joined them. "Major Swanson, get the details, will you? I need a minute."

Paul walked away into the darkness, then stopped once he knew he could not be seen. He did not want Cuesta to see that he was crying. He did not really mind if Carl and Leo saw him. Behind him he heard Carl say:

"Is she all right, Captain Cuesta?"

Paul froze, waiting. He knew that Carl had asked the question deliberately, knowing how good his hearing was and he wondered why. For a moment he considered moving quickly out of earshot, but he remained where he was, listening.

"No, Major, she is not," Cuesta said softly. "But he does not need to know that just now. She asked me to tell him nothing before the fight."

"What have they done to her?"

"Very much what one might have expected a troop of French animals to do to a young, unprotected girl, Major, they do it to our women every time they enter a village or town. She is dressed in nothing but a shift, she is barefooted and even a brief look at her tells me that she is covered in bruises. I'm sure you can work it out."

Paul felt himself flinch. It was what he had expected but faced with the reality he found it hard to bear. For a moment he was angry with Carl for making sure that he heard it.

"The Colonel is going to go completely mad," Manson said softly.

"That is why he should not hear it before a battle," Cuesta said soberly.

121

"Oh, I don't know about that, Captain," Carl said evenly. "In my experience the Colonel is pretty good in a fight when he's angry. And it occurs to me that if it was my wife, I'd want to know before I came face to face with her. Just to be sure I said the right thing at the right time."

Paul closed his eyes. He found that he was smiling through his tears. He should have known he could trust Carl.

"I hope he slaughters them to a man." Cuesta said. "I do not know her well, I only spent a short time with her. But I liked her and after this, she may never be the same."

"You might find she surprises you, Captain," another voice said, and Paul recognised Michael's distinctive tone. "I've know her for four years and she surprises the hell out of me all the time. Let's have details of numbers and weapons, shall we, so we know what we're dealing with?"

Paul stood quietly for a moment absorbing the news. She was alive and she knew that he was close. She would tell him the rest when he reached her. All the same he was passionately grateful to Carl for giving him a chance to hear something of her condition, so that he had time to get used to it.

Paul knew that his friends had been worrying over the details of Anne's ordeal and he had spent every night since he had heard what had happened lying awake for hours trying not to imagine what she might be going through, but now that he knew she was alive, he was suddenly no longer afraid. He knew Anne in a way that none of them did. She was a slender woman with an almost delicate appearance, but he was not deceived. Over the past four years he had learned with considerable pride never to underestimate his wife. She had powers of endurance which one of his veteran soldiers might have envied and no matter what he had done, Paul did not believe Dupres had broken her.

Paul waited until it was full dark and the camp had settled for the night. By then he knew by heart the position of every sentry, and he called the men of his two light companies round him and gave them their orders in low tones. This would not be a traditional battle with drummers and buglers calling. He needed his men to go in quick and fast and to show no mercy, and he had chosen these men specifically to lead the way, partly because they were the best fighting men in the army and partly because each man knew Anne personally and would risk their lives without hesitation to ensure her safety. He had told them to take no prisoners until she had been found and was safe. After that he would allow the French to surrender. He did not bother to mention Colonel Dupres, and nobody asked.

When he gave the order, his men set off at a cautious run down the slope towards the camp. Twenty selected men went on ahead armed with knives, bayonets or swords, and the sentries died in bloody silence, their throats cut. Through the darkness the men of the 110th and 112th light companies made their way into the camp where the French slept peacefully and as the first man awakened with a scream there was a crack of rifle fire and cries of pain. Paul's troops ruthlessly bayoneted men trying to scramble out of their bedrolls as they went through the camp searching for Anne.

Chapter Ten

Anne awoke abruptly to the sound of gunfire. It was shocking in the silence of the night, and it sounded very close. She sat up, her heart racing in panic. For a moment, she imagined she was back in the barn in Portugal with the French attacking and she was terrified and disoriented. Then she remembered and her heart leaped again with a combination of hope and fear. Somewhere in the darkness, in the confusion of battle and death, was Paul.

Anne got to her feet, seeing Sergeant Cavel scrambling up, reaching for arms. She moved quickly and took his arm.

"Damien, no."

Cavel looked over at her through the darkness and although he could not have clearly seen her face, something in her voice seemed to alert him. "What do you mean, no?"

"Put the bayonet down and come over here, stay close to me. Where is Captain Bernard?"

"Out there fighting for his Emperor," Cavel said shortly. "Where I should be. Get back there with the wounded, we don't know who this is. I'll…"

"I do know who this is, Sergeant and you need to stay close to me. Please."

Cavel stared at her for a long time as the crack of rifles and muskets exploded around them and the sounds of battle drew closer. Anne could locate the English by the flash of fire in the night. One of the officers' tents was still lit by lamps and she could see running men silhouetted against it and knew they were not French.

"The Spaniards," Cavel said finally, understanding. "You knew them?"

"Yes. They were from the same company that you attacked two weeks ago. But this is not the Spanish, Damien, it's my husband."

"Dear God, how did you keep that to yourself, cherie? I'd no idea."

"You would be surprised at what one can do when you're as desperate as I am. Just wait, it's almost over."

Anne could feel the tension of his arm under her hand. "I cannot remain here while my men…"

"Do you want to go out there and fight in support of what he has done to me? Of what he did to Harry Greene and his men?"

Cavel turned to look down at her and even in the darkness she recognised his unhappiness. He did not reply, but to her relief, neither did he move. They stood side by side, listening to the sounds of battle as the English troops drew closer.

**

Paul fought his way into the camp with single minded ferocity. Some of the French had managed to reach for their bayonets but those who ran forward to face his troops were cut down. Most of them were sleepy and bewildered and unprepared and after the first bloody rush of the British attack, were holding up their hands in surrender.

A small contingent of half a dozen French infantry had formed a defensive group on the banks of the small stream. Paul turned to shout an order and found Michael O'Reilly beside him.

"Get going, sir, we'll deal with these. Find her."

The ragged fear in the Irishman's voice was an echo of Paul's own. He had been confident as they attacked, but suddenly he was terrified that something had gone wrong. What if somebody had seen Cuesta speak to her and realised that rescue was imminent? What might they have done to her?

His logical brain told him that if the French had been expecting the attack, they would have been better prepared but now that he was so close to finding her, he was beyond logic and beyond common sense. All he could feel was sheer terror that he might find her dead or dying. It would be a fitting last act of revenge for Dupres.

As Paul ran towards the tents and wagons a figure moved out of the darkness towards him, holding up his hands. He was an officer, young and dark, his features indistinct in the dim light. Paul raised his sword and put the tip against the man's throat. It was not Dupres but at this point his fear was so great that he did not care who he killed.

"Where is she?" he snarled.

"The girl? Your wife?"

Something about the young officer's manner stilled Paul's hand. "Where is she?" he asked again and the man pointed.

"Over there, by the wagons with the wounded men. She is safe, my Sergeant is guarding her."

Paul lowered his sword and paused, looking into the darkness. There were three tents, one larger than the others, and over by the wagons he could make out some kind of makeshift shelter. He moved forward.

"Nan? Where are you?"

"Paul."

Her voice was closer than he had expected. He took several steps towards the wagons and saw a figure break away and begin to run. Just as she reached him she seemed to stumble and he dropped his sword, caught her and swept her up against him, his mouth coming down on hers. For a long moment they kissed and then he raised his head.

"Nan. Oh Christ, love, I thought I'd lost you."

124

Anne gave a shaky smile, reaching up to caress his face. "So did I," she said. "Paul – thank God you found me. I'm not sure I could have gone on for much longer."

Paul moved his hand to her face, caressing her, pushing back the tangled mass of her dark hair. His throat was so tight with emotion it was difficult to speak. "Nan. Oh, love…"

Already he was assimilating her condition. She was shivering in his arms and he realised that she was wearing only a shift, badly ripped at the back where his hands rested. He moved his hands over the bare skin very gently and could feel raised weals, some of them with scabs on them where they had bled. Paul felt his stomach clench in horror as he realised she had been beaten.

"Girl of my heart, what have they done to you?" It came out a whisper and in response she clung closer to him as if she could not bear to move away.

A man's figure came forward and Paul scooped her close to him with one arm and stooped to pick up his sword in one movement. Anne caught his arm quickly.

"Paul, no. Not him. This is Sergeant Cavel and he has been a very good friend to me. Along with his Captain, whom I'm hoping has survived this."

"I'm here," a voice said, and Paul turned to see the young officer approaching cautiously, his hands raised. His eyes were on Anne's shivering form.

"Colonel, why don't you take your wife into my tent. The lamps are still lit; I was not sleeping."

Paul looked down at Anne and sheathed his sword. "Thank you. I'll speak to you afterwards. Are these the wounded men? You can both remain with them providing I can trust your parole."

"You can," Bernard said quickly. "Or we can join the prisoners…"

"No, stay here. Come on, lass, let's get you inside and warm. Michael…"

"Major Swanson is seeing to sentries, sir, and I'll get them to build up these fires and light the lanterns. It'll be light in an hour or so anyway. Take care of her. It's good to see you, ma'am. We've been so worried about you."

Paul led her to where he could see the well-lit tent and drew her inside. She turned into him immediately and he held her close, kissing the top of her dark head, warming her with his body. Finally, her shivering eased a little and he set her away from him and studied her.

The signs of some of what had been done to her was plain on her body. The shift she wore was torn and ruined and beneath it the pale perfection of her skin was covered in dark, angry bruising. He could see the damage done to her feet through marching barefoot, and there were rope marks on both wrists. Paul was conscious of anger burning within him, a fury he could not remember feeling since he had realised that her first husband had been beating her.

"Oh love, what have they done to you? I am going to kill every single one of them," he breathed.

He saw her flinch then she took a deep breath. "You can't see everything that's been done to me, Paul," she said quietly.

"Yes, I can," Paul said gently. Her expression broke his heart. "I can see it in your eyes."

His wife made brave attempt at a smile. "Thank you. I can't seem to say it aloud."

125

"Oh love, I wasn't going to ask you to make a speech about it. Don't look at me like that, you look as though you're expecting me to yell at you."

"I don't normally care if you yell at me, Paul, but telling you this is proving harder than I thought it would be."

"You don't need to tell me anything just now, girl of my heart."

"Yes, I do. I need to get it out of the way." There were tears coursing down her cheeks. "Paul, he raped me. He beat me and he punched me and he raped me. More than once. I'm so sorry."

The apology cut into Paul. He held her close, letting her cry on his shoulder and absorbed what she had told him. He was not shocked, having known from the start what was likely to happen to her. His fear had been that Dupres would kill her when he grew tired of her or send her back to him maimed beyond recovery. Paul wondered briefly what she had needed to do to keep herself alive and his mind shied away from the thought. It did not matter now. She was safe and despite everything she appeared whole.

"Sorry? Nan, you've nothing to apologise for. Christ, this is my fault, I should never have left you to travel without me. Come here."

Paul kissed the top of her head, feeling his own cheeks wet with tears. He waited a few minutes and then put his hand under her chin and turned her face up to look at him very gently.

"Nan, I love you. There is absolutely nothing you could tell me that will change anything about how I feel about you, other than it's made me realise that if I lost you, part of me would never get over it. So tell me everything, or tell me nothing – in your own time. All you need to know is that if you stood there and told me you'd slept with half the French army to keep yourself alive until I found you I wouldn't give a damn. I've got you back. Nothing else matters to me."

She was looking up at him with wide, tear-drenched eyes. "You really mean that, don't you?"

"Yes. Always and forever."

It seemed to break the damn of her self-control and suddenly she was sobbing. She clung to him and Paul put his arms around her. He could not understand everything she said and was not sure that he needed to just at this moment. He held her, murmuring soothing nonsense, until she was a little calmer and he was able to grasp the sense of her words.

"What did you just say, Nan?"

She looked up apprehensively. "I was afraid you'd be angry."

"You can't possibly have thought that. You know me better than anybody in the world. What put that into your head?"

She did not reply for a long moment and Paul felt another rush of fury. "He did, didn't he?"

He saw her flinch at the mention of Dupres, then she took a deep breath and straightened her spine in an unconscious gesture.

"Yes," she said. "But I knew it was nonsense. I'm sorry, Paul, I'm just exhausted."

Paul kissed her very gently. "Come and lie down for a bit," he said. "I need to hold you, to convince myself you're real."

126

Paul drew Anne to Bernard's camp bed. Lying her down very gently he stretched out beside her and drew the blankets over both of them, holding her close. Anne lay in his arms, still crying, letting herself admit finally the sheer horror of the past two weeks. He was warm and solid against her and Anne realised that this was what she had dreamed of when she had wanted him so badly; not the fierce pleasure of his lovemaking but the joy of lying in his arms knowing herself loved. For a time, she felt no need to speak or to explain and he asked nothing of her.

It was beginning to grow light when she stirred finally, aware of movement in the camp outside the tent. "Paul, can I tell you?"

"Are you ready to? We've plenty of time, Nan."

"I think I do want to. I'd like to get it over with, though you probably know some of it."

"Tell me anyway."

Anne did, her voice halting and choked with tears at times as she related the events since the French attack more than two weeks ago. Telling him was easier than she had expected. Somehow, she had allowed herself to imagine that his shock and distress would overwhelm both of them, but he was quiet and calm, stroking her hair gently and kissing her occasionally when she broke off, unable to continue. By the time she had done, pale daylight was creeping into the tent and she was exhausted but better, her tears over.

"Paul?" she said finally.

"Yes, love?"

"Are you all right?"

Paul stared at her, looking surprised, then laughed aloud. "That is so typical of you, love. No, I'm not. I'm not sure I've ever been this angry. Or this proud of you. How the hell you've survived this I don't know. Girl of my heart, I've been dying inside every day since this happened, worrying about you."

"Are we going to be all right?"

"Of course we are, this is us! Christ, Nan, you survived two years with Robert Carlyon and still came into my arms without flinching, I don't think a few nights of being held down by that lump of French lard is going to damage what we have. But I am going to need ten minutes just now, because I am going out there to cut his fucking throat if he's still alive. After that, it's over and he's gone and I can concentrate on you. Stay here, Carter and Hammond are outside. I'll be back."

He kissed her long and hard and Anne clung to him. To her immense relief she felt a familiar surge of longing running through her exhausted, abused body and when he finally lifted his head she was smiling through her tears. "Oh God, I've missed you," she whispered.

"Oh love, I've missed you too. Just wait here and rest, will you, you look exhausted?"

Anne watched as he moved from the bed, picking up his sword on his way to the flap. Outside the tent she heard him say to Sergeant-Major Carter:

"Keep an eye on her, I've something to do, I'll be back."

Suddenly, panic flooded through Anne's body at the thought of him leaving her. She scrambled up and ran to the tent flap and saw his tall figure striding through the camp. In the pale light of dawn, the men of the 110th and 112th were in control, keeping the French prisoners together under guard. Some of them were going through the pockets of the dead, others were examining the supply wagons under the supervision of several of Paul's officers.

"It's good to see you, ma'am. Thank God you're safe."

Anne turned to find Carl Swanson regarding her with steady green eyes. "He's going after Dupres. Is he still alive?"

"I think so. Although probably not for much longer. Wait here, ma'am, I'll stay with you."

"No, I have to go over there. I can't stay here."

Anne saw his eyes move down her body, taking in her skimpy attire. "Ma'am, half the regiment is out there, you can't go out like that. Why don't you…?"

"No! I need to be there."

Carl put his hands gently on her shoulders. "Oh Nan, I know you're upset. I'm so angry myself, I'd like to do it for him. But you need to stay here until we find your bags and…"

"No!" Anne shouted, suddenly furious. "Get your hands off me, Carl, or I swear to God I'll hit you! I need to be there."

"Take my coat," a voice said, and she turned, desperate and found Sergeant-Major Carter stripping off his red coat. "Come on, lass, let's get you decent and over there, I'll come with you."

"Carter, she can't," Carl said. "He wants her to stay here, and she can't walk over there like this. Every man is going to…"

"She's been raped!" Carter said, his voice suddenly harsh. He made no attempt to lower it or conceal his fury. "Look at her, sir. She's been held down by that French bastard and raped, just like the girls in those villages we've marched through these past years. Just like my wife was, during the first invasion. You think every man of this regiment isn't going to know what he did to her? She needs to get over there and watch her man kill that bastard just as badly as he needs to do it. It gives you a good incentive on the battlefield, by the way. I often wonder when I'm taking aim at some tirailleur, if he was one of the vicious shits who invaded that convent all those years back and held my wife down."

"Carter, I know. But…"

"No, you don't know, sir. She's got nothing to be ashamed of, and she's got no reason to be cowering in a tent, she's the Colonel's lady and she's a member of this regiment. You let her walk over there with her head held high and watch him die and she'll be all right. And not one man of this regiment will feel anything other than respect and admiration for her. They'd die for her. Let her go, sir."

Carl hesitated. Then he stepped back and Carter helped Anne into his coat. It was warm from his body and Anne looked up into his concerned dark eyes with gratitude.

"Danny, thank you. I forgot how well you'd understand."

"We all understand, ma'am. Normally it's our women they get hold of, the officers' wives are mostly safe. And if Major Swanson gives it some thought and imagines how he'd feel if some Frenchman got hold of his girl and..."

"All right, Carter!" Carl said sharply. Then he gave a faint smile. "I get the point. Get going."

"Thank you, sir."

Anne was running, barefooted through the remains of the camp. Vaguely she was conscious of the men around her turning to stare but she did not stop, heading towards the open ground where the prisoners had been herded. Paul was already there, scanning their ranks. His men were beginning to gather, their ranks quiet and menacing, and she could sense the growing unease of the French. At the front of their ranks Paul stopped, lifted his sword, and placed it at the throat of the only visible officer.

"Where is he?" he asked quietly.

"Sir..."

"This is not a conversation, Lieutenant. Don't think I won't start with you, just at the moment I am not that fussy whose throat I slit."

Anne came forward. She could see Dupres standing in a group of prisoners. He had removed his coat and she wondered if he had hoped not to be identified.

"Over there, Paul," she said, and her husband turned and surveyed the Colonel. He did not appear to flinch at her appearance in front of his regiment and the French prisoners wearing her shift and his Sergeant-Major's coat.

"Ah yes. Cowering behind his men. I should have looked there first. Thank you, bonny lass. Danny, Leo, take care of her for me. This won't take long."

Paul surveyed Dupres. There was a very long silence. Finally, he spoke.

"Colonel Dupres, step forward."

Dupres complied. "There are rules about how prisoners are treated, Colonel," he said. "Your Lord Wellington will expect you to follow them."

"Lord Wellington would be astonished if I followed them, Colonel, he's known me for years. If you were a man of mine, you'd be up on a charge and I'd make sure you hanged, but we don't have any mechanism for trying an enemy officer for how he behaves in wartime."

Dupres studied Paul for a long moment and his lips curved in a smile which made Anne feel slightly sick. "On what charge, Colonel?" he asked, and Anne saw the expression on her husband's face. She stepped forward again and took his arm, her eyes on Dupres. The Frenchman looked her over.

"Did you tell, him, cherie?" he asked mockingly. "I make you my compliments, very few women would have, but I've reason to know there's not much you wouldn't dare. By the look on his face, I'd say he knows exactly what I've spent the past two weeks doing to you. Is that the charge you'd hang me for if you could, Colonel? Rape? Do you need to know how many times I did it and what she felt like in my arms and how much she cried when I held her down? It might please you to know I had to hold her down; she's a fighter this one."

Dupres voice was deliberately raised, made to carry through the ranks. Anne felt the shock and horror ripple through the assembled men of the 110th and 112th. She could feel her face burning with embarrassment, but she did not move or look away.

She understood what Dupres was trying to do, and she looked at Paul's expression. She thought abstractedly that she had never seen him look so merciless.

Sergeant-Major Carter broke the shocked silence. "You want me just to shoot him in the head, sir? Very happy to. In fact, I think you'll find a few volunteers."

"It's tempting, Carter, but I'd rather kill him myself. Give him his sword back, Michael."

Anne looked at his face and was suddenly afraid.

"Love, no. Don't put yourself at risk over his foul mouth, it means nothing to me."

"It means something to me," Paul said quietly. "Give him a sword, Michael and move back."

"Sir." Carter turned to the men and raised his voice. "Form square. Leave a nice big space, lads, you don't want to get in the way of this."

Paul began to unbutton his coat. Anne stepped forward. "Here," she said quietly, and helped him off with it, handing it to Jenson who had come up to take it. She turned to see him in shirt sleeves, his sword in his hand, loosening up his arm. It reminded her suddenly of the scene in the square in Ciudad Rodrigo when he had been about to fight Major Brodie. Paul met her eyes and his expression softened slightly.

"It's all right, girl of my heart, I'll be careful. Trust me, it's a lesson learned, if this one trips up he'll be dead in a heartbeat, I promise you."

Anne felt sudden a lightening of spirit at the shared recollection, and she smiled. "Good. I do not want to be sewing you back together again today, I'm tired."

Carl had retrieved Colonel Dupres' sword and handed it to him without a word. "Thank you, Major."

Carl did not respond, merely moved to where Anne was standing, her heart in her mouth. "Come over here, ma'am and stand with me. Don't worry, it will only take a few minutes."

Anne nodded and stepped forward suddenly, reaching up to kiss her husband. Paul put his free arm about her and drew her close, kissing her hard. Anne was conscious that Dupres had stopped to watch them, and she stepped back and looked at the French Colonel. It was the first time in a long time she had allowed herself to look at him properly. In order to endure what he had done to her she had found it easier to look away, not to see him at all. Now she studied him and let herself remember him beating her, remembered his body forcing its way into hers. She could feel the warmth of Paul's arm about her shoulders, and unexpectedly she felt confidence and strength coming back to her.

"If I could," she said clearly, "I'd kill you myself. Not just for me, but for Harry Greene and his men whom you murdered in front of me. You're going to die right now, and I'm going to watch. And then I'm going to walk away and forget about you, which is what you deserve, you piece of scum."

She looked up at Paul. "Take care. Don't let him goad you."

"He's already done that, girl of my heart, by abusing my wife. Anything he says is superfluous. But I won't let it make me clumsy, don't worry."

"I'm not worried. I love you, Paul."

Paul turned to look down at her, and the expression in his eyes melted the ice from around her heart. He smiled at her and reached for her hand. His eyes on hers he lifted it to his lips in a formal salute worthy of a London drawing room.

"I love you too, lady mine. Go with Carl and Danny."

Anne nodded and stepped back. Beside her, Sergeant-Major Carter said softly:

"Ma'am. Just in case you were wondering if I'd mislaid Sergeant Hammond, he's over there by the wagons where the light is good, and his rifle is trained on that bastard the entire time. Something happens he doesn't like the look of, he'll shoot, and he won't miss."

Anne looked up at him with quick appreciation. "Thank you, Danny. I don't doubt Paul's skill, but I don't trust this man."

"Why would you? But he's getting no chance to do anything here, he's going to be dead in less than five minutes."

Paul turned and faced Dupres, raising his sword in a formal salute. Dupres returned the gesture and then stepped back, his eyes on Paul. His lips curved in a mocking smile.

"A pointless gesture, Colonel, since we both know I'm going to die today, either by your hand or by one of your men. You ruined my career with your arrogance. I'd a right to take vengeance."

"On a helpless woman? If you wanted revenge, Colonel, you should have come after me."

Dupres glanced over at Anne again. "I enjoyed her," he said. "I wonder how long it will be before she'll let you do the same."

Anne felt her stomach clench but to her relief, Paul did not flinch. "The fact that you can even compare the two things, Dupres, tells me all I need to know about you. Are you going to fight, or do you plan on boring me to death?"

Watching her husband's face, Anne thought that she had never seen him look so remote. She thought about him in the tent only fifteen minutes earlier, holding her as she cried and wondered how he was able to make the shift between the gentle man she loved and this hard-eyed killer. Anne supposed that his ability to do so was what made him so effective in battle, but she had seldom seen it illustrated so clearly. He looked like a different man.

The two men circled each other, trying a few passes, testing each other's range and strength. Paul was the taller of the two and Anne suspected the lighter of foot. Despite the height and strength of the Frenchman, he had a roll of fat around his middle, and she did not believe he spent the long hours of physical training with his men that her husband still did. He clearly had some skill with a blade, and Anne's heart skipped a beat as he suddenly went on the attack, causing Paul to fall back, parrying quickly. She felt an arm go about her shoulders and looked up to see Leo Manson beside her, his eyes on the fight.

"He'll be all right, ma'am. He knows what he's doing."

"I know. But I didn't want him to risk himself."

"No risk," Manson said quietly, watching as Paul moved forward suddenly at speed, the French Colonel stumbling backwards under the ferocity of his attack. He managed to parry, and Paul stepped back, his eyes on the other man's face. "I can't

131

imagine how this must feel for either of you, ma'am. I only know how he's been these past weeks. It's driven him mad."

"I know. And what he found when he got here has made it worse."

Manson glanced down at her. "If there is anything I can do," he said softly, and Anne leaned into him.

"Leo, you help me just by being here."

"Good." Manson's eyes were on the two swordsmen again. Dupres looked as though he was beginning to tire, his movements slower and heavier. Paul circled, watching him. Then suddenly he moved, faster than Anne could have believed possible, and Dupres sprang back, shocked by the force of the onslaught. He parried desperately, but he had neither the speed nor the strength to hold off the attack and there was a ringing clatter and a scream of agony, and Anne saw his sword fall to the ground and Dupres dropped to his knees, clutching at his abdomen. He looked up at Paul with wide astonished eyes. Blood was welling between his fingers. Nobody moved or spoke.

The Frenchman did not move for a long moment. Paul stood looking down at him. There was no expression on his face, it was hard and set. After a moment, Dupres turned his head slightly and looked over at Anne. His eyes were pools of agony. Anne did not look away although she felt suddenly very sick and slightly dizzy. Dupres looked back at Paul.

"I meant to kill her," he said, and his voice was hoarse. "I meant you to find her dead. But I could not."

"Don't you dare waste your last breath telling me you gave a damn about my wife, you spiteful bastard. You deserve that I let you take your time dying of that, but unlike you I'm a man, not an animal, so I'll make it quick."

He slashed once, stepping back to avoid the spurt of red blood from the Frenchman's throat as he died. Paul stood looking down at him for a moment, then bent and wiped his sword on the blue coat, sheathed it and stepped back.

"Add him to the pile for burial, he doesn't deserve a separate grave," he said dispassionately. "Go through the wagons, Major Swanson, see what we have. The lads can take what they want from the dead men."

Paul bent over Dupres and went through his pockets, removing a silver flask and a purse. He opened the purse and checked the contents then handed it to Carl. "Share it out between the officers," he said. "Carter, do you want this, yours is very battered?"

He held out the flask and his Sergeant-Major shook his head. "No thank you, sir. I'd choke on it."

Paul smiled slightly. "So would I," he said. "But take it anyway, Danny, and sell it." He looked at Anne and seemed suddenly to realise her condition. "Nan, are you all right, you're as white as a sheet?"

"I'm fine, Paul."

"No you're not. Come back to the tent…"

"Just a minute, sir," Carter said quietly. He turned and raised his voice to a bellow. "110th, 112th form up, parade in companies! Move your sorry arses!"

***

132

The bugler sprang to attention and made the call and the troops moved, falling quickly into parade ground order, abandoning their looting. Paul stood watching them, not understanding, but trusting his Sergeant-Major. He was aware of the bewildered gaze of the French prisoners.

With the men formed up, Carter turned. "Men of the third brigade, present arms! Salute to the Colonel's lady!"

The men snapped to attention and Paul looked down at his wife. Anne's eyes were on the ranks of men and he could see that they were bright with unshed tears. She looked up at him, smiling, and then she looked back at the men, and returned the salute with considerable panache. There was a cheer from one of the light companies, and it was taken up by the others until the ranks were yelling to a man. Anne was laughing, colour coming back to her cheeks again and she moved forward to the front rows, holding out her hands to them. They broke ranks and converged on her, a slender girl in a ruined shift and a Sergeant-Major's red coat, letting them shake her hand, moving through the ranks to accept their greetings and their congratulations on her return. Paul stayed back, watching her, his throat tight.

"Are you all right, sir?"

Paul looked around at Michael. "I am now, Michael. Thank you."

"Just doing my job, sir."

"I didn't mean for this, although your lads were amazing, as always. I meant for the past two weeks. You, Carl, Johnny and Leo…I wouldn't have got through this without you."

His friend looked up at him, smiling slightly. "Christ, Paul, you're not the only one been going through hell about her. I'm not sure any of us have slept that well. Thank God it's over."

Paul nodded, his eyes on his wife. She was talking to Private Cooper and something he said made her laugh, a familiar sound which tugged unexpectedly at his heart strings. He turned and looked around for his orderly.

"Jenson, can you find my wife's bags so that she can change? I want a word with a couple of the prisoners, and we'll need to find space for the wounded men, since I rather suspect she's been taking care of them. I want to get her away from here as soon as possible."

Paul walked over to Captain Bernard. The Frenchman was looking at him steadily. He was very pale but composed. Paul jerked his head. "I want to speak to you. And you, Sergeant Cavel. Let's go into your tent."

Bernard ducked into the tent followed by Cavel. Paul reached for a folding chair and lowered his tall frame into it.

"My wife has told me that I owe you both thanks."

"We tried," Bernard said. "It was not enough."

"You did what you could. And particularly when he last beat her, she says that you probably saved her life."

"She told you everything?"

"Yes."

Cavel shook his head. "I still can't believe she said what she did to him. It was madness."

"It was Nan. No surprise to me. But thank you both, from the bottom of my heart. She means the world to me and you helped her through this. The prisoners will be taken up to headquarters and then sent to a prison camp. I'm not sending you with them. I'll need to speak to Lord Wellington, but I know he'll agree. You'll both be given free passage to go back and join the French army at Salamanca and we'll make sure you have horses and provisions along with a letter of commendation from Lord Wellington and myself."

Cavel said quietly:

"That's generous beyond belief, sir."

"You've earned it. Taking care of my lass is not easy. Thank you."

Paul found Anne with the horses and stood watching her as she fussed Bella. She seemed to sense his presence and turned. Paul smiled and came forward.

"Jenson has found your bags. He's taking them to Bernard's tent. Come on, bonny lass."

Paul seated himself on the bed and took her into his arms, kissing her very gently. "How are you? You must be in so much pain, Nan."

He realised that she was crying, silently as she always did. "I ache all over," she said. "But the beatings weren't the worst of it."

"I know, girl of my heart."

"It was horrible; I feel as though I'm never going to get clean again. Paul...what if I'm pregnant?"

Paul reached down and smoothed the tangled dark hair back from her face lovingly. "Then you'll have a child, bonny lass, no question about it. And boy or girl, it'll be ours. Love – if you're pregnant it's more likely to be mine than his, we both know that. So we'll assume it is and love it just like all the others. And if you struggle with that for a while, I'll love it twice as much to make up for it. Because whoever fathered it, you'll be its mother and that's enough for me."

Anne smiled through her tears. "You're so soft, Colonel."

"I really am. Look, Nan, I'm taking my cue from you with all this. It's nobody's bloody business what was done to you, although we all know some of them are going to get off on imagining it."

"Your regiment don't seem to feel that way. After that display earlier I can face the headquarters busybodies. Nobody who matters to me will care, Paul."

"That's so true. As for you and I, you'll have to tell me what you need, there's no rush for anything. I love you, bonny lass, and I'm so proud of you."

For the first time since their reunion, Paul saw a spark of genuine amusement in the black eyes. "What I need, Paul, is a hot bath, a good meal, and about twenty-four hours in bed with you to make sure I don't remember a bloody thing about him. Do you think we can manage that?"

Paul grinned. "Is that a serious question?" he asked. "Girl of my heart, when have you ever known me to say no to an offer like that? Come on, let's get you changed, Carter needs his coat back. Although it does look good on you."

"I'm glad you think so. It isn't going to affect us, Paul, I promise."

Paul looked down at her, his heart warmed by the expression in her eyes. "Nan, what will be, will be. If there's a problem, we'll sort it out. We're together; just now that's enough for me." Paul raised his head, listening. "Is that you, Jenson?"

134

"Yes, sir. Got your lady's bags here. Shall I bring them in?"

"Yes, please," Paul said. "Have they started burying the dead?"

"Yes, sir. I thought you might not want to attend this one."

"The only prayers I have for him is that he goes straight to hell where he belongs."

"Did we lose anybody?" Anne asked.

"No, ma'am, nothing more than a few scratches. They didn't see us coming, their sentries were asleep and their reactions were crap. If the rest of the French army are as dopey as this lot, Badajoz should be a cinch."

Paul grinned. "No such luck," he said.

Jenson brought Anne's bags and left and Paul knelt to open one. She joined him, glancing at him in apparent amusement. "Paul, I can manage. Go outside, I'll join you."

"No. I'm using this as an excuse to see exactly how bad it is."

Anne pulled out a chemise and one of her velvet robes in dark green and rummaged again for the soft slippers she wore in camp.

"Not exactly riding clothes I know, but it might be a week or two before I can get my feet into boots. And I just want to be comfortable," she said, and rose. Paul looked at her and she dropped the ruined shift to the ground and stood before him naked. He got up and studied her, appalled.

The ivory of her back was striped with marks from the riding crop, and Dupres had beaten her until some of them bled. She was bruised all over, as if she had been repeatedly punched. The marks around her wrists were made by ropes but he could see bruises on her arms the shape of a man's fingers and he reached out and touched them very gently.

"He held me down," Anne said. "And he punched and kicked me. It looks awful, I know…"

"Nan, you always look beautiful to me. But this is worse than I thought. I'm frightened to touch you."

"Don't be. That would upset me more than anything else." Anne reached for her chemise and drew it on and Paul saw her smile at the relief of clean clothing. He came forward and helped her to dress, his hands gentle on her bruised body. When she was ready he kissed her lightly and she pulled him closer.

"Paul, this is going to be hard for both of us. Half the army is going to speculate on what happened to me these past weeks. If they can't find out, they'll make it up. If I let it, it will be worse than what he did to me. Our friends will be lovely to me, and Lord Wellington will defend me to the hilt, we know that. But some of the ladies and a few of the officers from other regiments are going to be sniggering behind their hands at Colonel van Daan's uppity wife being used for a few weeks' entertainment by the French. They'll say I had it coming because I don't behave and don't conform and don't do what I'm supposed to do."

Paul nodded, his eyes on her face. He knew she was right although he would not have raised it this soon. It was typical of his direct, uncompromising wife to refuse to avoid unpleasant issues.

Anne kissed him again. "Well I'm not changing," she said. "I'm riding back into camp with my head high and I am not going to give a damn, because if I start

135

caring now it will break me. And I'm not letting that happen, for your sake and for mine. I'm just not."

Paul struggled for a moment to find the words he wanted and failed. Eventually he shook his head:

"Christ, Nan, I am so proud of you. Come on, let's see if they're ready to march yet."

Anne emerged into the cold grey light to see the men brewing tea. Paul was holding her hand and drew her to join his officers. As they approached, Carl Swanson detached himself and came forward.

"Better?"

"Much. I'm sorry about earlier, Carl. I just…"

"Don't be, I was being over-protective. We're all going to struggle with that for a while, ma'am. He's not the only one who has been in a state about you. Just let me know what you need."

Anne reached up to kiss him lightly. "I need Keren and Teresa," she said ruefully.

"Those you can have as soon as we get back. They'll be so relieved; I don't think my girl has slept for two weeks. Have some tea, it'll warm you up."

"Thank you, Carl."

Paul took her hand. "You look better already," he said, studying her.

"I am, Paul."

"All right, girl of my heart, we'll get going. I'm just going to have a word with Carter, and we'll get these tents down. We may as well keep them, we're always short. I…"

"Not that one," Anne said.

Paul caught her tone and flinched internally at the meaning behind it. "No, you're right. I'll go through it, see if there's anything we ought to take back to Wellington and as we march out, we'll set fire to it."

Anne looked up at him with quick appreciation. "Thank you," she said softly. Paul bent to kiss her then looked up at Carl.

"Look after my lady for a bit, will you, Major? I'll be back."

Paul went to find Carter. His men were still lowering the French dead into graves. Many of the bodies were barefooted. Footwear was a constant problem, and most of his men usually ended up wearing the boots or shoes of a dead Frenchman, which were far better quality than the shoes the British army provided. Paul was trying to get his men's footwear replaced by the sturdy boots that most of his officers wore but it was an uphill struggle.

A voice hailed him.

"Sir – over here. You need to see this." Carter's voice was quiet. Paul glanced at him, nodded, and followed. His Sergeant-Major led him into Colonel Dupres tent. He had obviously brought some of the loot inside to be opened and Hammond was guarding the entrance.

"Found your lady's saddle and tack, sir, we'll get Bella saddled up for her. There are a couple of nice animals back there, you might want to take a look, we could do with a couple of good spare mounts."

"I will, thanks, Carter. What's this?"

"The Colonel's personal luggage, sir. Thought we should have a look before the lads get to it. We found this."

He passed a slim black box to Paul who smiled. "Nan's jewel case. Thank you, Danny, she'll be pleased. Although I doubt any of the lads would have tried to lift these."

"That's not what I wanted you to see, sir." Carter indicated two stout wooden boxes. Paul pocketed the case and moved forward to look.

"Bloody hell," he said softly.

"Yes, sir. Can't let the lads see this."

"No." Paul stared down at the gleam of gold, the sparkle of jewels. He bent and picked up the top item, a gold church plate. "There's a fortune in here. At least we know what Dupres has been doing in his spare time other than abusing my wife."

"Yes, sir. Explains why he was in Portugal when he should have been halfway to Badajoz with supplies. Greedy bastard has been looting every church and monastery he finds. Is Mrs van Daan all right, sir?"

"She will be, Danny." Paul looked up at his Sergeant-Major. "Thank you for what you did earlier. There aren't words to tell you what that meant to her."

"I meant what I said, sir, I'd have liked to have blown his fucking head off myself. But I'm glad you did what you did, he had it coming. Waste of ammunition shooting that bastard. What are we going to do about this, sir?"

"Close the boxes and take them back to Wellington. You'll all get a share of the prize money." Paul smiled. "If the late and much missed General Robert Craufurd were here, he'd probably sell it to buy supplies, but that tends to upset the authorities. Although..."

Paul bent over the second box, picked up a leather bag, weighed it in his hand and then opened it, checking the contents. Closing it again he tossed it to Carter. "Share it out," he said. "Usual distribution between NCOs and men. Don't worry about the officers, Dupres' purse was nice and full. The rest goes back to Wellington."

Carter saluted. "Thank you, sir. You'd never know you were born into the officer class, you know that, don't you? You're a born pirate."

"I realised it fairly early, Danny. Just don't tell them I gave it to you, Wellington will shoot me if he finds out I've been looting. Get this lot loaded back up, I want to get going. I'm going to go through the rest of this tent. Get the lads to take the other tents down, we'll find a use for them. When we march out, I'm setting fire to this one. And don't worry about saddling Bella, Nan is going to ride with me on Rufus, at least to start with."

Carter left and Paul surveyed Dupres' possessions. A pair of leather saddle bags were slung over a folding chair and there were a number of boxes and chests. Over one of them was a garment and Paul recognised it suddenly and went forward, his stomach churning, realising that it was Anne's cloak. The sight of it in Dupres' tent made him feel sick, but he picked it up and laid it over the folding chair to be given back to her.

Paul went through the boxes finding little but spare clothes and personal effects. He left those for his men to find. Having ample private means of his own, he did not need to claim prizes of war. There was another heavy purse, which he pocketed to share between his officers, and a stack of letters and papers. Paul piled them up to take back to Wellington's intelligence officers and code breakers. There might be some useful information in them.

He turned to the saddle bags and extracted a pair of duelling pistols in an elaborate case, a bottle of good brandy and more letters which he added to his pile. In the second one he found a spare shirt, a riding crop and small, elegant knife in a leather worked sheath which was designed to be worn around the arm and concealed by a sleeve. Paul held it for a long moment, looking down at it. The knife had the distinction of being the first gift he had ever given to his wife. During her first months in Portugal when Anne had still been married to Carlyon, he had been appalled when she had told him of her intention to accompany her husband with the army marching into Spain. He had given her the knife which had been a gift from an Italian guerrilla fighter and told her to carry it with her at all times and she had done so ever since. It had saved her life, and that of Carter and O'Reilly several years ago in a barn in Portugal, and he knew she valued it above any jewels or silks he could have bought for her.

Paul had ample means to shower Anne with expensive trinkets. He had always been generous with the women in his life, and the jewellery, which he had given to his first wife was in the care of his sister-in-law, for when his daughters were older. Anne wore the intricate gold band he had given her for a wedding ring, and a simple pair of pearl earrings, which he had bought in Lisbon last year. The contents of her jewel case were few but worth a small fortune, but she seldom wore the jewellery except on those occasions when she went to parties or dinner at headquarters. Paul looked at the knife in his hand and thought that it was a symbol of his relationship with the extraordinary young woman that he had married that this first, practical gift meant so much to her.

Paul collected together the items he wanted to take and put them into the fine leather saddle bags, then went outside. Private Jenson was there with a black gelding, sweating and terrified but beginning to calm under Jenson's soothing hands. Paul went to join him. There was a long graze down the horse's flank which looked as though it had come from a stray shot. Saddle and tack were of good quality.

"We've roped up the officers' horses to take back with us, sir. Good cavalry stock mostly. But I wanted you to see this lad."

Paul ran his hand down the horse's neck. "I can see why," he said. "Was this Dupres' horse? He got hit."

"Just a scratch, sir, shot must have gone astray in the dark, just winged him."

"I'm glad about that, I hate killing animals." The horse turned his head and nuzzled Paul's shoulder and he laughed. "No, I've nothing for you, boy."

"I was wondering if he might suit your lady, sir. She's in need of a good second mount. If Bella throws a shoe, we always find her something from the lines, but she should have her own. There's not much wrong with him saving that cut from the bullet and that will heal. He's a big horse for a woman, but she can handle him."

Paul stroked the horse again. "Yes, I think she's earned her share of this particular prize, Jenson. Unless he brings back bad memories."

"Ask her, sir."

Carl approached. "Find what you were looking for?"

Paul nodded. "I'm going to keep this lad for Nan, and I've taken what I came for. There's some paperwork in the saddle bags for Wellington, and a pair of pistols that we can find a use for. The men can take whatever else they like." He removed the purse from his pocket and tossed it to Carl. "Share it out how you like. Looting was a profitable business for Dupres."

"Thank you." Carl glanced around. "I've let Bernard and Cavel take their personal possessions."

"Good. They can take a couple of horses if Wellington agrees to release them but they can march with the prisoners for now. Let's get out of here."

His wife stood beside Rufus as Paul set fire to Dupres' tent using one of the oil lamps. As the flames leaped into the air he turned to her and Anne smiled at him and let him lift her up before him. She rode wrapped in her long cloak, the dark hair loose about her shoulders and he held her close, walking Rufus through the damp morning at an easy pace. Occasionally she turned her head and he bent to kiss her. The others left them alone, seeming to understand his need to hold her, to savour the sense of being with her again after coming so close to losing her.

***

When the sun was fully up, they stopped to eat breakfast and water the horses. Anne could feel Paul watching her and she smiled at him reassuringly. He smiled back. "Your hair needs washing. Want to come and bathe while they get breakfast going?"

Anne laughed. "Jesus, Paul, how do you read me so well?"

"I've known you for a while now. Come on, where's your soap?"

Anne collected the portmanteau and he carried it down to the river for her and watched as she undressed and slid into the cold water, diving under to soak her long hair. She came up, sleek as a mermaid and Paul smiled and set the soap jar down on a stone by the edge of the water. Anne looked up at him.

"Better?"

Anne nodded. "Yes. I needed to wash him away. Thank you for understanding, Paul."

"It's my job, bonny lass."

"Why don't you come and help me?" Anne said softly and she saw him blink and then laugh.

"Girl of my heart if I get into that water with you this is not going to stop at a bath, I'm telling you, and it might be a bit soon for that."

"Isn't that rather up to me to say?"

Paul looked at her for a long time. Then he got up and began to unbutton his coat. Anne waited, aware of a fluttering of nerves in her tummy that she had not felt with him since the first time they had shared a bed. It was absurd, but she realised that she was terrified. His eyes were on her face, and she knew that he would know so she said:

"I'm scared."

139

"I can see that, bonny lass. If your eyes get any wider they'll take over the rest of your face. You look exactly like that nervous seventeen-year-old I kissed in a barn in Yorkshire a few years back."

Paul slid into the water, gasping at the cold, and reached for the soap scooping out a handful and running it over her hair. "Let's get you clean first. We'll decide what else happens as we go along, shall we?"

There was a blissful familiarity about the routine. They had bathed together in rivers and lakes through Portugal, and Anne appreciated his calm practicality as he washed and rinsed her hair and then soaped her body, sliding his hands over her. At the same time, she was aware of his increasing arousal. Normally by now she would be in his arms and Anne knew that he was holding back. Desperately she tried to feel what she wanted to feel and knew that it was not happening. The sheer disappointment brought tears to her eyes. She turned into him, burying her face into his shoulder.

"Paul, can we just do it?"

"No, love, we can't just do it. When in the whole of our time together have I expected you to do this just because I wanted to, regardless of how you feel? Does that sound like me?"

"No. But what if I can't? What if this feeling doesn't come back? What if…"

"Stop panicking, Nan, it's been less than a day. We've got the rest of our lives to sort this out." Paul held her at arms-length, looking down into her eyes. "I'm going to get you dry and dressed and we're going back to camp. And we will take this as slowly as we need to. I do understand that you're worried. But I am not going to make love to you until you're ready for it. All that will happen is you'll feel disappointed, and I'll feel like I'm using you. And you've had enough of that recently."

Anne kept her eyes on his face. "Colonel, you are so bloody stubborn."

"I am, girl of my heart, when it comes to you. You're the most important thing in my world. I lost you and I've got you back. Everything else will fall into place in time."

Paul turned her around and bent and Anne felt his lips on her back, very gently kissing the healing scars of Dupres' riding crop. She stood very still, conscious of his tenderness, and slowly she began to relax, letting herself feel. Suddenly the tears came, and she was crying properly. Paul turned her towards him and took her into his arms and she was sobbing into his shoulder.

"Oh God, Paul, it was so awful. By the end, I just lay there and let him do it so that he didn't keep hitting me. I tried not to think about you and I hated that, but I couldn't bear thinking of you and what we do and what we have while he was…."

Paul was stroking her wet hair. "I understand, love. Christ, I don't know how you survived it at all. He was a bloody animal and I shouldn't have killed him so quickly. How any man could choose to hurt you is beyond me."

Anne looked up from tear drenched eyes, trying to smile and her gallantry broke his heart anew. "Perhaps it's me. First Robert, now this. And there was that French officer in Portugal. Perhaps something about me…"

"It's not you, Nan. It's men and war and what some of them think is acceptable to do to women. Look around you. Teresa was raped by half a dozen Frenchmen in the convent. Keren endured eight months being battered by that bastard Simpson. War is hard on men but it's worse on women. This would never have happened to you, if you'd stayed home in Yorkshire and married Julian Carew."

Anne reached up to caress his face. "No. But then I wouldn't have had you. And God help me, that's worth all the pain and misery I've had to go through to get here. Kiss me."

Paul did so and felt her body arch into his, cold and slippery but suddenly fiercely aroused under his hands. He lifted her up and she wrapped her long legs around him and pulled him into her, all fear seeming to have gone. He whispered her name against her hair and she moved urgently against him. When she reached her climax she cried out and Paul realised with some amusement that in the still warm spring air, her voice was going to be clearly audible up at the camp.

"You done, Colonel?" she whispered, her voice husky against his ear and Paul laughed softly.

"Not yet. Come here."

He picked her up and carried her to the bank, laid her down in the springy grass and stretched out beside her, leaning over her. Anne was laughing, all hesitation seemingly gone.

"Don't you have somewhere to be, Colonel?"

"I do and it's right here doing what I'm doing. If they get bored, they can piss off back to Badajoz without me. There's nothing to do there anyway, I hate sieges. Wellington can do without me for an hour or two. Although by the time I've finished with you you're probably going to need another bath."

Anne gave a gurgle of laughter, a particular sound which Paul always associated with making love to her. "That's all right, there's plenty of water. Do you know what I've missed?"

"Apart from hot baths and bossing my regiment around?"

"Apart from those." Anne ran her hand down over his chest. "I've missed how you feel. Look at you, there isn't an inch of spare fat on you. And your skin has a particular smell and taste – like fresh air and sunlight."

Paul was laughing, lowering his mouth to her, nuzzling her body. "I'm getting the distinct flavour of strawberries. And you're the colour of honey...beautiful."

"Unsuitably tanned for a lady," Anne said teasingly.

"It's gorgeous. Although perhaps I should be worried about why it affects so much of you that ought to be covered up."

"Too many hours lying naked on river banks with you, Colonel," Anne said laughing.

"Time well spent in my opinion. You do realise by the way, that every single one of those bastards knows exactly what we're doing down here?"

"I don't care."

"Nor do I," Paul said, and eased himself onto her. "Welcome back, bonny lass. I've missed you."

***

141

Manson watched them walk back up from the river hand in hand an hour later and their unselfconsciousness amused him. He looked at Carl and saw that he was smiling too.

"Do you think she's all right?"

"She will be."

Manson was watching Paul. "I'm not sure I've ever seen him that angry."

"I probably have, but it's been a while. The last time would have been with her first husband, for much the same reasons."

"She's been through a lot."

"She has. I used to wonder why he didn't just send her home and keep her safe. But I think I understand now."

Manson studied his commanding officer. "I rather imagine you do, sir, I'd like to see your face if anybody suggested putting Keren on a transport home."

Carl shot him a startled glance and then burst out laughing. "You cheeky bastard, Captain Manson!"

"Yes, sir. Although I notice you're not denying it."

Carl moved to find cups for Paul and Anne. "No. I was trying to imagine earlier when that bastard started spouting poison, how I'd feel if that were Keren, and I really understand why the Colonel did what he did. I think I'd have needed to do that personally as well."

"So would I," Manson said.

He took tea to Paul and Anne and watched as his Colonel spread a blanket for her to sit on. It seemed to him that Paul could not take his eyes from his wife's face. She had found her hairbrush and when she had eaten and the men were packing up and dousing the fires she stood brushing out the long damp black hair with an unselfconsciousness which made Manson smile. She was as much at ease here under the gaze of several hundred enlisted men as she was at a headquarters party dancing with Lord Wellington and it occurred to Manson suddenly that his association with Anne van Daan from an early age had probably coloured his view of women for life. He could not imagine settling down with any girl with no opinions or interests of her own and he wondered how many of the young officers who came through the 110th or 112th would have the same difficulty.

As Manson moved to supervise the men lining up the prisoners, he noticed one of the officers, a young dark lieutenant, looking at Anne as she shook back her damp hair. Manson moved forward.

"Eyes down," he said shortly.

The man turned to look at Manson. "Sir, you mistake me. I was not..."

"You'd better not be, Lieutenant. You're lucky to be alive here, but I hope they send you to the shittiest prison hulk in the Medway."

"I wanted to protest," the man said. His voice was low. "I knew it was wrong. But he was my commanding officer, I could not..."

Anne spun around suddenly and Manson realised in horror that she had heard. He looked at her face and saw that her black eyes were blazing with fury. She strode forward with the grace of a young lioness and when she reached the French officer she hit him very hard across the face. The sound made every man turn to stare.

"You bloody liar!" she spat. "You laughed. I remember walking out of his room the first time he beat me and raped me and I could hear you laughing. You laughed and you spoke to your friend there and you asked if he thought the Colonel would be willing to share me around when he got bored."

The Frenchman's eyes were wide and shocked. "Madame…"

"Don't speak to me. Captain Bernard and Sergeant Cavel tried to help. And a few of the men were very kind to me. But you thought it was funny."

Manson looked at her furious face and then back at the Frenchman. His face was scarlet and he seemed unable to speak. Manson took a deep breath. The picture she had conjured up for him was appallingly clear and he could almost see her, bleeding and in agony and trying not to show it, hearing them laughing about it. Manson stepped forward and swung his fist. He had taken boxing lessons as a boy and was considered very good. The Frenchman went down and lay still, dazed. Manson stood over him looking down at him.

"You'd better get yourself up and walking by the time we march you cowardly piece of shit or I'm going to tie your hands to my saddle and drag you all the way, see how you bloody like it."

He turned and saw his Colonel putting his arm about his wife's shoulders. She was shaking with anger. Paul bent and kissed her very gently, his eyes on Manson's face.

"Thank you, Captain Manson," he said quietly. "Come on, girl of my heart, let's get going."

When they were ready, Anne mounted this time on Bella, her black mare, managing the skirts of the velvet robe admirably to preserve her modesty. She looked to Manson's appreciative eyes like some medieval painting of a mythical queen. She seemed to sense his regard and looked over at him, laughing.

"Not traditional riding gear I know, but perhaps I'll set a fashion."

"You ought to, ma'am, looking like that," Manson said, and Anne smiled.

"Thank you. I feel a complete mess, but the fact that I'm conscious of it is probably a good sign. I wasn't sure how I'd be, riding with this arm, but it feels fine, I think it's healing."

"What happened?"

"Colonel Dupres kicked me. To be fair I was extremely rude to him." Anne met his eyes. "Leo, thank you."

"You're very welcome, ma'am. Frankly I'd be happy to punch him again."

Anne smiled and wheeled her horse trotting to the front of the regiment where Paul was waiting, taking her place beside him. Manson watched them move ahead with a slight smile. He felt a deep affection for his commander and his wife which meant rather more to him than the somewhat tepid regard he had always felt for his own parents. Any emotion he had left for his father had long since hardened into dislike and he no longer felt more than pity for his mother who had allowed he and his cousins to be bullied all their lives and continued to put up with bullying herself rather than confront his father and move away. Coming to the regiment at nineteen, Manson knew that Paul van Daan was both his mentor and father figure, despite the fact that there was only ten years between them.

143

He had watched in agony as his Colonel suffered through the past two weeks, and had been relieved beyond measure at recovering Anne and appalled at the condition they had found her in. It was not the first time Manson had come across a woman who had been raped by French troops, it was common in the towns and villages he had marched through, but it was different with a woman that he knew and cared about.

Watching Anne laughing over at her husband, Manson felt a rush of pride in her resilience. Whatever had been done to her she was still herself, still the woman he adored and admired so much. He thought, falling in at the head of the light company, that it would take more than a misogynistic French colonel to break a spirit as indomitable as hers. Looking around, he could see many of his men watching her, probably sharing some of his emotions. They had suffered with their Colonel these past weeks, missing her warmth and laughter and the practical good sense which helped to make the 110th what it was. The sight of Anne van Daan back where she should be, filled Manson, and he suspected most of the regiment, with relief and pride and confidence again.

Chapter Eleven

They took the march at an easy pace, having no reason to hurry, and arrived within sight of Badajoz towards midday. On the journey, Paul spent the time explaining to Anne the progress of the siege and how the engineering works were laid out. She listened with interest, asking an occasional question, and the normality of their conversation eased the tension in him. It was going to take a while, he knew, before he could take her loving presence at his side for granted again, but she seemed determined to set aside the nightmare of her ordeal and focus on the present.

They reined in, to look out over the town and the sprawling lines of the Allied camp. Paul glanced at his wife.

"Let's get you back to the tent, bonny lass. Carl can get this lot up to headquarters and the quartermasters can have the headache of sorting it all out. I'll leave you with Teresa and Keren and go up to let Wellington know you're all right, he's been frantic. He doesn't need details."

"Tell him," Anne said quietly. Paul studied her.

"Are you sure?"

"Paul, in most cases I'd say no, but I'd trust him with my life and so would you. When the ladies are sniggering behind their hands in winter quarters, he'll defend me against anything, and you know he will. It's not fair that he doesn't know exactly what he's defending me against."

"That's a fair point, bonny lass. I hope it's not that bad, mind, or I'll spend all winter punching people."

Anne laughed aloud. "It usually passes fairly quickly and I'm very good at ignoring it."

"I'm not. Which is why…"

Paul stopped abruptly at the sound of gunfire, a frantic exchange of shots which cut across the plain from the earthworks. Paul reached for his telescope, put it to his eye and surveyed the trenches.

"Jesus Christ, it's the French, they've sent a sortie against our lines." Paul wheeled his horse. "Sergeant-Major Carter!"

"Yes, sir. Buglers, sound the alert! And make it bloody loud, they need to hear it in our lines. 110th, 112th skirmish line. We're going in, dump your packs here."

"Major Swanson, the wagons…"

Anne walked her horse up to join him. "Leave me Jenson and ten men, Paul, I'll get them up to the lines."

Paul looked at her with anguished indecision. Anne understood. The thought of leaving her to manage the supply train and French prisoners in her fragile state appalled him but the men in the trenches were being slaughtered and Paul's troops were the closest and could make an immediate difference. Anne met his eyes steadily.

"Paul, go. They need you."

After a moment, he gave a nod and swung himself down, relinquishing his reins to Jenson.

"Look after her, Jenson."

"You know I will, sir."

Paul scanned the ranks and shouted ten names, then moved to the head of his men looking over at Anne. She gave him what she hoped was a reassuring smile and watched as the companies moved forward in skirmish formation, fast and lethal across the ground. As they disappeared into the smoke which was rising from the trenches she heard Paul's voice, bellowing above the crackle of musket fire.

"Move your arses, they're slaughtering our lads down there. They don't know we're here, let's give them the fright of their bloody lives."

Anne could not help smiling. She turned her horse to see Jenson roping together the officers' mounts behind his own. He grinned at her.

"I'm not sure you really need looking after, ma'am, but he's going to be a bit edgy for a while."

"I know," Anne said. "Thank you, Freddie."

She turned to survey the ten men Paul had left. "Private Cretney, Private Kane, take two men and guard the prisoners, we're taking them back up to the lines. Barrett, will three of you collect up these packs and dump them on one of the wagons, we'll take them up with us. I'm not having our lads robbed while they're down there fighting."

Barrett saluted. "Yes, ma'am."

Anne rode forward, looking down over the Frenchmen. The three officers were at the front of the line, and Cavel just behind them. Anne observed with grim amusement that neither of the lieutenants seemed able to look at her. Bernard was studying her with considerable interest.

"Captain Bernard, did I hear you give my husband your parole earlier?" she said, reverting to French.

"I did, madame. And I will hold to it."

"See that you do, Captain. I consider you a friend, I'd hate to have you shot. Sergeant Cavel, I'm trusting you too. Lieutenant Sevigny?"

"Yes, Madame?"

"We're marching up to the lines with the supply wagons and I'll hand you over to Lord Wellington's staff there. In the meantime, I don't expect you to give me or my men any trouble. If you do, I will not hesitate to give the order to shoot you. I suspect that these men would be only too happy to oblige. I'm sure you understand."

"I do, Madame."

"Good. Get moving." Anne caught Cavel's eye and smiled. "Are you all right, Sergeant?"

"I am," the Frenchman said. "It is interesting watching you here, doing this. Now I am less surprised at what you did back there. You have my respect, Madame."

Anne laughed. "Sergeant, if it hadn't been for you and Captain Bernard I would not have got through that. Stop being so formal, we're friends."

Cavel gave his sardonic smile. "I am being careful, cherie, I do not want your young champion to punch me also. It looked as though he was very good at it."

Anne grinned and turned to survey the wagon train as it moved up towards the lines and then looked back towards the trenches. The sounds of battle were louder now as more of the British troops were streaming down to the works to aid their beleaguered comrades. It was hard to see much, as the smoke of rifle and musket had completely obscured the trenches, but Anne could see French cavalry wheeling about and she hoped Paul's men were prepared. An enormous crash of artillery told her that the French had brought their field guns into action. The sound was alarming but it reassured Anne. The garrison would not be firing on their own men, which probably meant the French troops were preparing to withdraw and the artillery was being employed to cover the retreat.

"Are those packs all loaded, Jenson?"

"Yes, ma'am. The lads will be grateful, a lot of them will have their prize money in there."

"Along with whatever else they managed to loot without the Colonel seeing."

"Very likely, ma'am."

Anne laughed. "Come on, let's get them up. I want to get my medical bag, there'll be casualties."

"Yes, ma'am. We're camped up this way." Jenson looked back down the column as it began to move again, to where Cretney and the others were walking beside the prisoners. "If I were those Frenchmen I don't think I'd move a muscle out of place. Our lads look as though they'd quite like to shoot somebody."

As they arrived at the edge of the lines of the 110th and 112th there was a cry of joy and Anne slid from her horse and into the arms of Teresa Carter. She hugged her close as the other women erupted from tents, running up the lines to greet her, their cries and exclamations almost drowning out the sounds of battle.

"Keren, Teresa. It's so good to be back." Anne surveyed her friends and broke into a smile. "Teresa you look as though you are about to give birth."

Teresa laughed. "Another two months we think and I am very well. But ma'am, are you all right? And what's happening below? To come back into this!"

"The Colonel led his companies in, we had just arrived and saw the attack. Have the rest of the brigade gone to join them?"

"Colonel Wheeler led them down."

"Good. Jenson, will you get the wagons and the prisoners…"

"No need, ma'am," Jenson said quietly, and Anne turned to see the tall lean form of the Commander-in-Chief approaching, closely followed by Captain Graham and Major Scovell.

Wellington stopped at the sight of her. Anne hoped that most of her bruises were concealed by the long sleeved robe but his shocked expression told her that something of her ordeal was visible.

"Nan," he said softly, and Anne moved forward holding out her hands. Lord Wellington was always circumspect with her and she had almost never heard him use her given name although she had long ago given him permission. It was a reflection of his anxiety for her that he had forgotten his self-imposed rule. He took her hands and lifted first one and then the other hand to his lips.

"I'm all right," she said quickly, striving to sound reassuring. "A bit battered, but nothing that time won't heal. Thank you, my Lord, for letting him come for me."

"If it had been necessary, I would have come myself," Wellington said, the blue eyes scanning her face. "But I knew your husband was more than capable once we found you. You look so tired, ma'am. I still cannot believe you were treated that way."

"I'm safe and that's all that matters. Paul will tell you the details later, it's a bit soon for me to talk about it. But, sir, I want to get my medical bag. Do you know where we're set up?"

"The nearest hospital is in Elvas, ma'am." Wellington raised Anne's hand to his lips again then released her. "There is a large dressing station set up in the quarry across to the east which is where we have been sending those wounded in the works. But you should not attempt to work today, ma'am. No matter how redoubtable you are, you need to rest and recover."

"I'll do that afterwards." Anne looked at Scovell. "Major, as you're here, I've prisoners and supplies – some of them were ours from the column I was coming north with, some are from the French. Jenson, will you get our men's gear unloaded and set a guard until they get back up and sort it out. Major, would you…"

"We'll see to everything," Richard Graham said. "It is very good to have you back, ma'am, you've been sorely missed."

"It's good to be back, but I've work to do. Teresa…oh thank you."

Her maid was holding out the black bag. As Anne took it, she saw a rider approaching Lord Wellington. He dismounted and saluted; a young Ensign from the second division. His appearance made it clear that he had just come from the battle. His face was black with powder and there was blood staining one arm. Lord Wellington stepped forward.

"What news, Ensign?"

"The enemy is being driven back, my Lord, and our men are inflicting some losses. We've taken heavy casualties in the trenches, though. Our men had no idea they were coming until they were on top of us, but there were six companies of the 110th close by. I don't know how they came to be there, but they hit the enemy hard on their left. They came out of nowhere, it shocked the life out of the French, my Lord. Surprised us too."

Wellington glanced at Anne. "Colonel van Daan was returning to camp, Ensign. A lucky coincidence. You're wounded, get yourself over to the surgeon's tent."

"I'd prefer not to, my Lord, with your permission. The medical tents are taking heavy fire from the town, they're within musket range…"

"Oh whose brilliant idea was that?" Anne said, furiously. "How can we be expected to treat men who are frightened of being shot in the medical tent? Browning, where are you? There are several tents in that wagon, bring it down along with the medical supplies in the third one and we'll get set up out of range. Jenson…"

"On my way, ma'am." Paul's orderly was barely managing to hide his amusement. He saluted to Wellington and moved away, shouting orders. Captain Graham smiled at Anne.

"I'll see to the prisoners and the rest of the supplies. But please don't put yourself in danger, ma'am, he's been frantic these past weeks."

"The only person in danger right now, Captain, is the imbecile who ordered those tents set up within musket range." Anne looked at the Commander-in-Chief. It was obvious that his attention was still divided between the battle in the trenches and her own safe return. Anne decided that it was an excellent moment to ask a favour.

"My Lord, when there's time, Paul wants to speak to you about two of the prisoners. Captain Bernard and Sergeant Cavel were good to me in very difficult circumstances and as a favour to me, I wonder if they might be given special consideration? They deserve it, I probably owe them my life."

Wellington frowned. "I shall not trouble you now ma'am, but I intend to find out from your husband what happened during your captivity and I shall not hesitate to make very strong representations to the French command about your appalling treatment at the hands of their officers. I am pleased to hear it was not all of them. Ensure that Captain Graham has their names, and their freedom shall be in your gift. At this point I am willing to give you anything in my power, I am so glad to see you safe."

"Thank you, sir. If you will excuse me now, I think the worst of it is over. I may be needed."

The noise of battle was dying away as Anne chose her spot and organised for the setting up of the two large tents they had taken from the French camp, ruthlessly commandeering a dozen riflemen who were making their way up to the lines to help her. They obeyed with cheerful goodwill and she observed their young Captain, Harry Smith, watching the proceedings with considerable amusement.

"Sorry, Captain, but I needed help."

"That's all right ma'am, glad to be useful. I didn't know you were back. Was that the Colonel I heard when we got down there earlier, bellowing like a mad bull?"

"It was. We were on our way back in when the French hit so he took our six companies straight in. I think it surprised them."

"I should think it scared the life out of them, ma'am. Are you all right? We've all been worried."

"I'm fine, Harry, thank you. You're looking very well yourself – is that a permanent captain's bar I see?"

"It is, ma'am. Just a few days ago so I'm still getting used to it. Keep these fellows as long as you need them, I need to go and report to Colonel Barnard. He'll be delighted to know that you're safe."

"Thank you, Harry. And congratulations. May I send one of your lads over to the quarry to suggest that Norris and Daniels move over here to work?"

"I'll see to it, ma'am, and I'll get them to lend a hand carrying the wounded up for you."

149

Anne went into the tent. Three tables had been set up, strong boards laid across wooden barrels, and she went from one to the other testing to make sure that they were stable and strong enough. Teresa was bringing water and glancing outside, Anne saw that she had already built a fire to heat more. Anne was at odds with most of the medical establishment in her insistence in making sure that wounds were thoroughly clean before they were dressed. It had begun in her early days working with Adam Norris when she had felt an instinctive distaste for dirt around open wounds. Since then, she had written endless notes from her observations of the hundreds of men she had treated, and she had become completely convinced that cleanliness led to fewer deaths from infection although she had no idea why.

A groan made her turn and two of Smith's riflemen were coming into the tent with a man carried between them on a makeshift stretcher. Behind them came Dr Adam Norris and Dr Oliver Daniels along with half a dozen orderlies and assistants. Anne indicated that the man should be lifted onto one of the tables. Norris came towards her.

"Thank God you're safe, ma'am."

"Thank you, Adam. I hope you didn't mind me doing this, I was told that the dressing station is within musket range."

"It is. Bloody stupid place to put it." Daniels moved forward, took her hand and kissed it. "I've been worried sick about you," he said. "I'm so glad you're back. But are you sure you're well enough to do this?"

Anne met his eyes. "Do I look that bad?" she asked.

Daniels looked back steadily. "You look like you've been through hell," he said candidly. "When did you last sleep, ma'am?"

"A while ago. But I'll be all right, Oliver. Once this is over, I'll rest, I promise you. It's just that I think working might help me to feel normal again. It's been…it's been bad."

Daniels regarded her with sympathetic eyes. "When you're ready, ma'am, tell me what you want me to know," he said simply. "I'm not going to ask." Looking over, he eyed the man on the table whose leg had been shattered by round shot. "That needs to come off."

"Yes. Do you want to do it, Oliver? And thank you, it's good to be back."

Daniels nodded and moved forward to the table, motioning to two of the orderlies to come and hold the man. More wounded men were being carried in and Anne went to her table where a young soldier from the 43rd was being lifted on, bleeding heavily from shot which had penetrated his face and neck. Teresa came forward with a bowl and Anne reached for a cloth and began to wipe blood and black powder residue from around the wounds.

"You're going to have an impressive scar to show the ladies, Private. Keep still, I think there's something in there. Although you were lucky, it doesn't seem to have broken your jaw."

"Hurts, ma'am."

"It would. Take a swig of this and grit your teeth, I'll get this out for you and put a few stitches in. Teresa…"

Anne worked steadily, finding it easier than she had expected to get back to what she knew so well. The memory of her weeks of captivity faded quickly before

150

the need to cut and stitch and clean and dress wounds. In a brief moment between patients, she felt a flicker of surprise to realise how quickly Colonel Dupres had faded from her consciousness. Forty-eight hours ago, she had wondered if she would ever get over what he had done to her but now he seemed very unimportant in the scale of pain and loss before her. Her body still ached, but she felt like herself again. Despite her concern for Paul and his men fighting in the trenches, she felt better than she had done for weeks. She was herself again, Dupres had touched nothing of her that mattered.

Anne glanced over at Daniels who was working at the next table. His blunt remarks about her exhausted and battered appearance were very typical of Daniels, who had joined the 110th in 1810 before she had been married to Paul. She had been helping to set up a regimental hospital and the newly qualified junior surgeon who had arrived from England had been doubtful and somewhat annoyed at being asked to take orders from the unqualified wife of one of the quartermasters. Paul had needed to intervene to instruct Daniels to listen to her and Anne had wondered at the time if she would ever be able to develop a good working relationship with the aggrieved young surgeon. He had come round faster than she had believed possible, and these days she could not imagine working without him.

Most of the injuries were from musket shot and bayonet, although the cannons had done some damage to men scrabbling away from the carnage in the trenches. Limbs smashed by cannon balls or close range musket fire were usually lost to amputation, but Anne was cautious in her choice to remove a limb. In less obvious cases she often chose to remove the shot and sew up wounds. She was aware that she had the reputation of unusually high levels of survival, and although many of the qualified surgeons sneered at her ideas, the ordinary soldiers who had encountered her before, would often beg to be taken to her table if they knew she was operating there.

"Ma'am! Mrs van Daan!"

The voice was urgent. Anne was in the process of sewing up a cavalry sabre wound. "Over here," she yelled. "I'm busy."

Anne continued to sew, her heart beating faster as Sergeant-Major Carter threaded his way through men lying on the floor of the tent. The last time a man had come calling for her like this in a dressing station, it had been Michael O'Reilly at Talavera to tell her that Paul had been shot and might be dying. She concentrated on finishing her task as quickly and neatly as possible and looked up as Carter appeared beside her.

"Danny?"

Carter read her anxiety immediately. "It's not the Colonel, ma'am. It's Captain O'Reilly He's been shot through the thigh and it's bleeding badly, we can't stop it. I'm scared to move him…"

Anne spun around. "Teresa, finish dressing this," she said, and turned to Carter, picking up her skirts. "Show me," she said, and he nodded and began to run.

They sped down to the trenches against the tide of wounded men making their way up to the lines. Arriving at the edge of the large trench Anne looked down into the mud and filth and saw several men crowding around Michael who was lying on the ground. Kneeling beside him, Manson had his hands clamped over Michael's leg hard, but she could see the blood still pumping out.

A shell fell close by, making her jump and spraying earth and stones all over her. Anne held out her hand to Carter. "Help me down, I'm not dressed for this and I don't want to fall on top of him."

Anne arrived breathless and dropped beside Manson. He glanced at her. "Ma'am – you shouldn't..."

"Shut up. Right, when I say go, move your hands out of the way. I need to take a look."

"All right."

Anne took a deep breath and ripped Michael's trouser leg open to bare the thigh. "Go, Leo."

Manson removed his hands and blood spurted high giving Anne all the information she needed. She reached through the blood, parting the flesh with her fingers, concentrating on searching for what she knew was causing the problem. Her fingers were slippery with blood, and it was splashing down the front of her robe but she ignored it as she ignored the pain of her damaged arm. The stripes on her back ached dully and there was an irritating pain in her lower back.

There was a round of shot, frighteningly close by, and Manson rose, yelling an order. Hammond, Dawson, Cooper and Carter broke away, lifting rifles and the musket fire stopped immediately as the accuracy of the rifle fire caused the French to pull back quickly. A shell fell so close that debris rained down around Anne again and she heard Carter swear as flying shrapnel embedded itself in his arm.

"Bastards! They must be able to see we're trying to get the wounded out, what the bloody hell is wrong with them? Dawson, give me cover, I'm going up there and I'm going to take out those bloody gunners, it'll teach them to fire at medical staff. Hammond..."

"With you."

Anne's probing fingers found, suddenly, what she had been seeking and she squeezed hard, cutting off the blood flow. "Got it," she said. "One of you needs to get my bag, I need to clamp this and then we can get him up..."

"What the bloody hell are you doing down here?"

The bellow was so loud that Anne jumped and almost lost the artery. "Stop yelling like that, you almost made me lose this!" she snapped.

"Jesus bloody Christ, I thought I was seeing things. There are shells falling all over the fucking place, you need to get yourself out of here right now or I am going to pick you up and carry you out! Who brought you down here?"

Anne looked up at her husband. His face was black with powder and there was blood on his coat which did not appear to be his own. The blue eyes were blazing with anger. She had almost never heard him use that tone of voice to her and she could sense the frozen shock of the men around her.

"It's Michael, sir, we couldn't stop the bleeding," Manson said quickly. "I'm sorry, my responsibility."

"Which is your way of saying somebody else did and you're shouldering the blame. Get her out of here, Captain, before I shoot somebody."

152

"Don't you dare touch me, Leo, I am not moving from here until I've got a clamp on this. Where's my bag?"

"Terry has gone for it, ma'am, he'll be back in a minute. But the Colonel is right…"

"No he isn't, Leo, and you don't have to say he is just because he's a colonel and he yells a lot." Anne glared up at Paul. "You touch me and I swear to God you'll regret it. This is Michael, and he's dying and I am not leaving him when I think there's a chance I can save him. Do something useful or go away."

There was a flurry of rifle shots from up the bank and Cooper peered up through the smoke. "Well, they're not going to be shelling any more," he said. "Me and Dawson'll keep the muskets off you, ma'am."

Paul took a deep steadying breath. "They've pulled back into the fort," he said with an assumption of calm. "There are still a few cavalry milling about, but I've just put the rest of the 110th into square over there, so they're not going to hang around. Dawson, Cooper, get up there and put them off shooting my wife, will you? I realise that stopping her from getting herself killed has become a full time occupation for most of my regiment, but I'd appreciate it."

"On our way, sir," Cooper said.

"Thank you. Ah, Private Terry. Lose your way, did you?"

"Sorry, sir."

Anne glanced up and saw to her relief that Gibson, one of the hospital mates, had accompanied Terry. "Gibson, thank God. Get me a clamp, I'm holding on to the artery and my fingers are going numb."

He complied with quick efficiency. There was a spurt of blood as Anne moved her hand and then she tightened the clamp and the bleeding stopped. Anne reached for Michael's neck and checked his pulse.

"It's weak but steady. We need to get him up to the tents very gently, then we can tie that off properly."

"Got a stretcher here, ma'am," Terry said.

"Thank you, Private. What are they doing with the wounded?"

"Loading them up onto the wagons to go to the hospital on the edge of Elvas."

"Do we have many?"

"A few," her husband said. He sounded as though he was restraining himself with an effort. "We shall continue this conversation back up at the lines, I think. Ah, Carter – good shooting, thank you. Was it you who brought my wife down here?"

"Yes, sir."

Paul turned and Anne gave a cry of anger as he swung his fist and hit Carter hard across the jaw. The Sergeant-Major staggered back and then righted himself. Anne moved forward and inserted herself between Paul and his NCO.

"You do that again and you'll have to hit me first."

"And don't think I'm not tempted." Paul glanced at Michael who was being loaded onto the stretcher. "I'll take one end. Get yourselves back up to the lines. Carter, do a roll call, it was bloody chaos down there, I've literally no idea of losses."

"Yes, sir." His Sergeant-Major turned away. Paul put his hands on his wife's shoulders and moved her gently out of his way. He put his hand on Carter's shoulder, turning him back.

"I'm sorry," he said quietly. "That was completely out of order."

"That's all right, sir, I thought I might get a punch when I decided to go and get her to save my friend's life. It was worth it. I'll take the other end."

Anne walked beside Michael as they carried him up to the tent. Inside she instructed them to lift him onto the board. The tent was clearing now as men were removed to the wagons waiting to transport them to Elvas. Anne bent over her patient, concentrating on the wound, blotting out what was going on around her. She was carefully dressing it when she felt him stir beneath her hands.

"Michael?"

The dark eyes opened and studied her, wide and confused. "Ma'am. I was hit…"

"In the thigh." Anne placed a hand on his forehead. "Lie still. It missed the bone completely but nicked the blood vessel, you've lost an awful lot of blood, you'll be very weak for a while."

"Feels strange."

"It will. I'm not sending you up to the hospital, some imbecile will try to bleed you and with the amount you've already lost it could kill you."

Michael closed his eyes. His face was black with powder but Anne could still see how pale he was. Even his lips seemed colourless.

"I think they're supposed to bleed me, ma'am. It says so in a book somewhere."

"I've read more medical books than you have, Captain."

"And they all say the same thing."

"They're wrong," Anne said flatly. "I've watched men bleed to death. You would be one of them if I'd not got to you in time. How does it make sense to sew up this wound and then take more blood from somewhere else?"

"Why are you the only person who…no, never mind. I hate being bled anyway. Do it your way, ma'am."

Anne finished dressing the wound, reached for a cloth and began to bathe his face. "Thank you, Captain. You know that I had no intention of listening to you, don't you?"

"Yes, ma'am."

"We'll find you a billet somewhere, I want to keep an eye on you for a few days. You need complete rest. Don't do anything stupid, you almost died."

"Thank you, ma'am. I feel really confused, I thought I heard the Colonel yelling…"

"You did."

Anne turned, startled. Paul was standing watching her. He came forward and took Michael's hand. "She came down to the ditch to treat you with shells and musket shot falling everywhere. I got a bit over-excited."

"Jesus Christ, sir, I'm surprised you didn't expire after what you've just been through."

"So am I. I must be tougher than I thought. Two of the lads are here with a stretcher. I've commandeered a shepherd's cottage for our wounded, we've not done that badly, about ten wounded and only two dead. Almost all of those were from the work party, Giles Heron was down there with the third company. Carter has a wound in his arm, but it's not serious."

"And a bruise on his jaw," Anne said.

Paul met her gaze. "Probably. My fist hurts as well. Stop laughing, Michael, you'll kill yourself."

"Honestly, sir, you really are…is he all right?"

"He's fine. He might well have done the same to me if I'd taken Teresa down there, he understands. It didn't bloody stop him, mind, for which I'm eternally grateful, sometimes I am not the best person to make decisions."

"Is Heron all right?"

"Yes, apart from being bloody furious. Who wouldn't be, they bloody slaughtered the men in the first trench. Our lads did better because they were quicker, and didn't hang around waiting for orders. And the 95th were useful although we should have had more men guarding the works, I'll see to it from now on. Bloody infuriating mind, they'd orders to lift as many of our tools as they could, we've lost most of our spades."

"Good, they were bloody useless anyway, they kept breaking," Michael said tiredly. "Should see if we can buy some locally, they might be better."

"I'll get my quartermaster onto it," Paul said, glancing at Anne warily. "Get some rest, Michael, I'll be up to see you later." He looked at Anne. "Are you ready to come up to the tents?" he asked quietly. "We need to talk, bonny lass and Daniels can get the wounded settled."

Anne nodded. She bent to kiss Michael's forehead. "Do as I've told you. I'll be up tomorrow to check on you. Sooner if there's a problem, they'll call me."

"Tell them to call Daniels instead," Michael said. "You've done enough today, ma'am."

Anne watched as he was carried out and then went to the basin to wash her blood-stained hands. Ruefully she looked down at the green velvet robe.

"I don't think this is going to wash out."

"There's a very good dressmaker in Elvas, I'm told. You need a new riding habit as well. I think I'd rather like to see you in crimson, but it's your choice."

Anne glanced up. His voice was quiet again and she saw him studying her, the anger gone. She moved forward and he put his arm about her. Suddenly she was more tired than she could ever remember being in her life. There was a nagging ache in her lower back and her injured arm was throbbing. Glancing over she saw Teresa cleaning her instruments.

"Go, ma'am, I'll see to things here."

"Thank you, Teresa, but get Gibson to do it and rest, you must be exhausted."

They walked up through the lines in silence. At their tent Anne ducked inside and turned to see Paul lacing the flap. It was an accepted sign in the regiment that he wanted some privacy. It had become a standing joke over the years that his officers and men used his tent or billet as an informal meeting place, but Anne knew that he genuinely liked to feel that his door was open to them.

Turning, Paul walked to the folding table where a bottle and cups were set out. He picked it up and studied the label. "Jenson is clearly expecting us to celebrate," he commented and poured the wine, bringing a cup over to her. Anne sat down in one of the camp chairs. She felt almost as though she was too tired to stand. She took the wine and sipped it gratefully. Paul stood looking at her.

"This is not how I wanted your return to be," he said softly.

"Or I, Paul. I've been yelled at a fair bit recently. I could do with a break to be honest."

"Oh love, I'm sorry. I couldn't believe you were down there with people shooting at you, not twenty-four hours after you'd been rescued from the French."

Anne smiled tiredly. "Did I give you a fright?"

"That's the understatement of the year. Will he be all right?"

"I think so. He lost a lot of blood, but as long as he rests and drinks plenty and does as he's told I think he'll mend. But it was close. If I'd not gone down there..."

"Love, I know. You did the right thing, so did Carter. I am sorry, I just lost it."

Anne put down her cup and got up. "Paul, just hold me, please?"

He came forward, picked her up and carried her to the bed. Setting her down very gently he slid the robe from her shoulders and then laughed aloud. "I love you very much, girl of my heart, but I am not getting into bed with you like that. Come here."

Paul drew her to where Jenson had left hot water. It was still warm and he poured some into the basin and reached for the cloth, washing the sticky residue of Michael's blood from her. Anne stood unresisting, and let him finish, then he dried her off and drew her to the bed, tucking her in under the covers. Paul stripped and washed himself and joined her under the blankets, reaching for her to draw her close, her head pillowed on his shoulder. Anne was crying and he lay still, stroking her hair, murmuring endearments to her until the storm passed and she was quiet again.

For a while it was enough to lie there in their own tent, knowing herself safe and loved and home again. So much seemed to have happened that Anne's tired brain struggled to process it and she gave up the pointless struggle and did what she wanted to do which was to kiss him. Paul shifted to make it easier to reach her and returned her kiss, and there was something about the quiet desperation of it that brought home to Anne finally what he had been through.

"Oh love, I'm sorry," she whispered.

"For what? Saving my friend's life? Don't be daft, love, you're just being you."

"I know, but you've been completely frantic about me. You'd just got me back and then I went and did that. I honestly didn't think about it, but..."

"Nan, if I'd been there and you'd asked me I would have taken you down there. It's Michael, you know what he means to me. I'm sorry I yelled at you, I wasn't myself."

"I suspect you were very much yourself, Paul, I just don't usually encounter you on the battlefield."

Paul laughed. "Or I you, and I'm telling you it's a formidable sight. If you'd not had your hand inside Michael's leg, I suspect you'd have hit me."

"I might," Anne admitted. "But I am sorry, Paul. All I've thought about is myself, about what happened to me. But it occurs to me now that if I'd known you were out there with somebody hurting you I'd have gone crazy."

"And don't you? When I'm on the field?"

156

Anne considered. She felt, amidst her exhaustion, a sense of sheer relief at the conversation. Somehow, during those weeks, she had begun to feel less than human, less than herself. Despite her tiredness, Paul's curiosity about her feelings made her feel normal again.

"Yes. But having something to do helps. When I'm working, I don't have time to wonder if you're alive or dead all the time. Let's just say that you and I are better together than apart."

"For us and all those around us. It's awfully quiet out there, do you think they're all walking past on tiptoe?"

Anne laughed aloud. "Probably. Is Danny all right?"

"He is. I've apologised properly. He just laughed. I think he was speaking the truth when he said he'd expected it; it was worth the risk to him. Thank you, Nan, for doing the right thing. I love you, darling girl. At some point we'll need to talk to Wellington but not now. Are you too tired…?"

"No," Anne admitted, laughing softly. "Although I'd have sworn I was when I walked in here. Now that I'm in your bed I'm reconsidering."

Paul kissed her again. "Our bed. This is a partnership, girl of my heart, no matter what the rest of the army thinks. I couldn't do any of this without you. Come here. I'm feeling particularly tender towards you at the moment – let's see if I can show you how I feel."

Anne lay quietly afterwards in his arms, warm and secure and felt tears of happiness on her cheeks. His eyes were closed and she could feel his body relaxed against hers.

"This feels so good," he said.

"We forgot about supper."

"So we did. I've probably had all I need just now, bonny lass, but if you're hungry…"

"No. Let's stay here. I don't feel like being social."

Anne lay awake and quiet, loving the feeling of his arms about her. She thought he was sleeping until she heard a soft voice calling through the tent flap. Paul groaned.

"I thought it was too good to be true. Hold on a minute, it sounds like Manson, I'll get rid of him."

Paul rose, wrapping a blanket around his hips and padded to the tent flap. Anne peered through the darkness. She heard Paul laugh softly. He held back the flap and Manson entered with a tin tray holding two steaming bowls and a bottle with two cups.

"Don't come out tonight," he said quietly. "Everything is in hand, I've checked on the wounded and they're all fine, Daniels is keeping an eye on them. The work parties are back in the trenches. There's nothing else for you to do, sir. Have some time to yourselves, you shouldn't have had to walk back into that today, not after everything you've been through. And ma'am, thank you for what you did for Michael. He's my friend, I can't tell you how much it meant to me."

Manson saluted and left and Paul looked over at Anne, smiling broadly. "Supper is served, lady mine – let me get your robe and put something on and we can eat. Bless Leo Manson, he has to be one of the most tactful people I have ever met in my life."

157

Anne slid from the bed. "I might be hungry after all, if that is George Kelly's Irish stew."

"It is." Paul was rummaging through the chest. He drew out her other robe and passed it to her. "We definitely need to do something about your clothes, girl of my heart. Come and sit down. This is starting to feel like a holiday."

Chapter Twelve

Anne slept finally and deeply in the darkness, through the sounds of the work parties changing over and the sporadic firing from the walls of Badajoz. Waking early in the cold grey light before dawn she slid from the bed to relieve herself. There was a nagging discomfort which she had been vaguely aware of the previous evening. Returning to bed she went via the water jug to get herself a drink, and felt a twinge of pain, and then suddenly a knifing agony which cramped her whole body, leaving her helpless and curled up on the floor of the tent.

"Nan!"

Paul's voice seemed to come from a long way off, and she tried to speak but had no breath as the pain stabbed into her again. He was there, on his knees beside her, saying her name. Anne wanted to speak, to reassure him, but she could not form the words. His arms went about her and he scooped her up and returned her to the blissful warmth of the bed.

"Paul – it hurts…"

"I know, bonny lass, it's all right, I'm here. Just wait a minute while I call for help."

He left her and she heard him scrambling into his clothes and then yelling for Jenson. In a moment he was back, holding her close as she sobbed through waves of pain. She heard his voice giving orders as if through a veil and then Teresa was with her, kneeling awkwardly beside the mattress, taking her hand.

"Nan, Dr Norris is on his way up. Just hold on."

"Teresa, I think I'm bleeding."

Her friend drew back the covers and looked at Paul. "I think she is miscarrying, Colonel. I will get some towels, this is very heavy…"

"I'll go, stay with her."

"No!" Anne sobbed. "Paul, please, don't go…"

Paul dropped beside her again and took her hand, as Teresa moved away. "All right, girl of my heart, I'm here. I won't leave you, I promise."

Anne was aware of him there, through waves of shattering pain. When it eased slightly, he lifted her so that Teresa and Keren could remove the bloody towels. He held a wine cup for her to drink, stroked her face and hair which were damp with sweat, murmured endearments and held her as she sobbed into his shoulder.

It was four hours or more before the pain finally eased. Adam Norris, who had left for a time to tend to some of the wounded, returned and examined her, felt her sore abdomen gently, and looked at Paul.

"I think that's it. It was particularly bad, I suspect she was four or five months along, but I think it's done now. She'll be sore for a while and very tired, she's lost some blood with the child. I don't know…did she suffer some injury…"

"He punched me in the stomach," Anne said. Her voice sounded strange and distant in her own ears. "I didn't know. That I was pregnant again. Paul, I'm so sorry, I didn't know."

She was crying, and Paul bent to kiss her. "Don't you dare apologise, Nan, this was not your doing."

"No. But I did antagonise him." Anne closed her eyes. "He killed our baby. Paul, what if he did more damage? I might not be able to have another child."

"Oh love, don't think of that now, I just need you to get well. Walking back into that chaos yesterday won't have helped. I feel so useless, it just keeps getting worse for you."

"No." Anne squeezed his hand hard. "No it doesn't, I'm back with you and that's all that matters. I'll be all right, Paul, it's just a shock."

"I know. You need to sleep, girl of my heart. Stop trying to explain and apologise. I'm here. The only thing I need you to do just now is rest."

Anne obeyed. She was not sure she was going to be able to sleep but she was too exhausted to carry on talking. Her mind whirled with a jumble of thoughts. Memories of the long days of her ordeal were mixed up with thoughts of the children, who were probably home by now and would be waiting for a letter. She thought about William and wondered, with hollow grief, if the child she had lost would have been a boy or a girl. She thought about Franz and how angry he would be when he heard that his anxiety about her travelling without Paul had been well founded. From there, her mind wandered to the wounded and she opened her eyes.

"I wanted to check on Michael."

"Michael is fine," Paul said firmly. "Adam has just come from there. Stop worrying or I will beat you."

"No, you won't."

"No, I won't. But I will be cross with you. Can you lie on your side?"

"Yes," Anne said puzzled.

"Turn over then."

Anne did so, and a moment later she felt him lift her dark hair from the pillow. Incongruously, she felt the gentle rhythmic stroking of her hairbrush. Paul lifted her hair away from her face. She felt him pause, gentle untangling a knot, then the movement continued.

Anne closed her eyes again. He often brushed out her hair for her before bed and the feeling of him doing so now was wonderfully familiar and very soothing. She lay still, not speaking, and gradually felt her body relax and her restless mind stilled and comforted as she drifted into sleep.

***

When he was sure that she slept, Paul got up, feeling cramped and stiff. Keren Trenlow moved forward to take his place and Paul accompanied Norris outside.

"Talk to me, Adam."

"Paul, I've got no answers. We know that Nan is capable of a healthy birth. She was amazing with Will, I've seldom seen a woman so much at ease with the whole process. She must have got pregnant very quickly afterwards because this was no eight-week miscarriage, it was clearly a child. I'm sorry."

"It's all right, Adam, I'd rather know." Paul took a deep breath. "She was frightened she'd end up pregnant by that bastard Dupres."

Norris went very still. "He raped her?"

"Repeatedly. Could that have caused this?"

"It might, but if she was punched in the stomach, my money is on that as the cause. It could take a few days, she'll have been feeling ill without knowing why. God, Paul, I'm sorry. She's been through so much."

"More than most women could stand. Last night, back together in the tent, we were so happy. I thought it was over. And now this."

"Paul – women miscarry. It's sad but it happens. This is worse because it does seem very likely that it was due to what he did to her, but there is no reason to believe it will affect her ability to carry another child."

"I hope not. Though even if it does, I don't really care, as long as she's all right." Paul smiled painfully. "I've four children, Adam. Nan has one, I know she'd like more, and so would I, with her. But we're luckier than most, my sister in law has yet to carry a healthy child. As long as Nan is all right…"

"I think she will be, Paul. But she might struggle with this. She adored Will, I think she'll want more children. Just give her time."

"She can have whatever she needs. I'm going to check on her but if she's still sleeping, I'm going to walk up and talk to Wellington, he knows nothing about anything yet."

"She'll sleep for a while now, and Keren is with her. Get properly dressed and go and see him. And eat something, you look like hell."

Paul arrived in Lord Wellington's tent to find the commander in conversation with Captain Graham. He looked up as Paul entered.

"Sit down, Colonel." Wellington studied him. "I heard what happened," he said quietly. "Have you eaten?"

"No, sir."

"Captain, ask Bonduc to arrange some food for Colonel van Daan. Hot food if he can manage it. I'll have something too."

"Yes, my Lord."

When Graham had gone, Wellington got up and went to pour brandy into two cups.

"I know it's too early, but you look as though you need it. How is she, Colonel?"

"She's all right, sir. She lost a child. Norris suspects it's due to what he did to her – she was punched in the stomach several times. He thinks she'll make a full recovery, but she's very upset."

"Paul – what I want to do is make a noise about this that will reach Bonaparte himself. This is disgraceful and we both know it. But..."

"No, sir," Paul said quietly.

"I thought you'd say that."

"Dupres is dead. I killed him in a fair fight. But I'd have killed him anyway. She was treated appallingly. He beat her more than once with a riding crop, made her march for miles in bare feet with little food. And he raped her."

Paul saw Wellington flinch. He was aware that most of the army would never have seen even this smallest display of emotion from their distant, unemotional commander and many of the officers considered Wellington to be incapable of any kind of empathy. Paul knew that his chief found emotions difficult and any open display of them could bring on one of his worst episodes of biting sarcasm, but that did not mean he was incapable of feeling. His friendship with Anne had begun with a pleasant flirtation with a pretty girl on the deck of a transport to Lisbon when she had still been married to Lieutenant Carlyon, but he had known her now for four years and Paul knew how much he cared. Anne brought out the best in his undemonstrative chief and the senior officers had learned that approaching him when she was present would often bring a better response to a problem than they would otherwise have received.

"I hope he didn't die easily, Colonel."

"He died. I didn't really think much else about it, although I take your point."

"I was praying it wouldn't be this bad," Wellington said. Paul could read his distress in his eyes. "Are you sure she'll be all right? Paul, at this point you can have anything you want including leave to take her home if she needs it."

Paul laughed in spite of himself. "Christ, sir, that tells me more about how much you care than anything else could. We've talked about it. She wants to stay here with me and get on with her life. I know that would seem strange with most women, but it's how she is. I think she's right. She'll do better here with me and with the people who know and understand her than back in England with people who don't. She's very strong, sir. We had words yesterday because I found her down in the works under fire saving the life of Captain O'Reilly."

"Good God."

"She did it too, Norris says he's looking much better this morning. She's been through hell, but I think she'll be all right."

"I'm so sorry, Colonel. None of this is going to be easy."

"No. There'll be gossip, no question."

"Not within my hearing," Wellington said grimly, and Paul laughed.

"I can imagine. Sir – thank you for letting me go. And for supporting us in the way you always have. She'll say it all herself, I know. We're not going to tell most

161

people the details. They'll have fun guessing, but not anywhere near me, that's for sure. And she'll be all right. She's the most resilient person I've ever met in my life."

"And you?" Wellington said quietly, refilling Paul's glass.

"Me? Oh Christ, that's another matter. It's my job to protect her and I left her to travel back without me. I let her be taken by that bastard. And then when I'd got her back, I left her again to ride down and fight the French. Just now I feel like the worst husband this side of the equator."

There was a sound, and an orderly entered and ushered two men bearing trays into the tent. Paul smiled his thanks, and surveyed the plate set before him.

"Eggs? Sir, are you feeling all right? I've never seen this much good food on a plate in your quarters in my life."

"Eat it, they must have made a special effort for you, Colonel."

Paul began to eat. The food made him feel considerably better. He cleared his plate and set it aside. "I need to get back. Is there any news of General Alten?"

"He is on his way but if he does not arrive by the time we breach, I've spoken to Vandeleur and Barnard, Colonel. You'll command the Light Division when we go in."

"It should be one of them, sir."

"I want you. They're both excellent commanders and could do the job. But if something goes wrong, I want you in command."

Despite himself, Paul grinned. "When something goes wrong, I usually end up in command anyway, sir. I'm at your disposal, whatever you decide. But if you don't need me to do anything just now, I would like to spend some time with my wife."

"Of course. At present it is your job to put her first. Whatever she needs."

"Thank you."

Wellington studied him. "Do you think he would have killed her?"

"Yes. He was not going to risk his superiors knowing what he'd done to her."

"No, it would have finished him. Thank God you were in time. Give her my good wishes, Colonel. And when she's fit to travel, take a few days off. Ride over to Elvas and have some time to yourselves. I doubt we'll breach for another few weeks. If it goes quicker than we expect I can send a message, it's only eleven miles, you can be back in a couple of hours. Look after her."

Paul stood up, recognising his dismissal. "I will. Thank you, sir."

***

Anne slept for almost twelve hours and awoke feeling stiff and sore but surprisingly well. She found Teresa dozing in a camp chair and awoke her.

"Teresa, go to bed. I've no idea how long you've been there but you must be exhausted."

"Señora, I am very well. How are you?" Teresa studied her critically. "You look much better."

"I feel it. I think this has been coming on for days. Where's the Colonel?"

"He went to visit Colonel Fletcher. He was injured in the attack."

"Was he? How about Michael?"

"He is doing well. Weak and very tired but no sign of infection or fever."

"That's good." Anne stretched and winced. The Spanish girl was watching her. "Señora…you do not have to tell me anything. But if you need to talk…"

Anne understood. She met the Spanish girl's serious dark eyes. "Teresa, you already know what happened to me. Danny will have told you."

"He did. I'm so sorry, Señora."

"At least you understand." Anne studied Teresa's face. "How old were you?"

"I was eighteen. A novice, soon to take my vows. We knew so little of what was happening in the outside world. We knew there was a war, that Spain had allied with France. When the French army arrived at the door of the convent, we had no idea that they had turned on us, that we were now the enemy. But I don't think they would have cared. The Abbess opened the gates to them, offered them food and wine. I think she thought it would save us, but it didn't. They drank the wine cellar dry and then they turned on the nuns. Some managed to flee and they shot them down. They killed some of the older ones and they took us into the church and raped us. Five or six of them held me down, one after the other."

"Teresa, that must have been terrible."

"I don't remember it all. Afterwards, those of us who survived made our way to the village but they had already been there. So many dead. So many women crying. And no food left. I needed to survive and soldiers always need women. So I sold myself to the Portuguese soldiers who were marching south. They took me with them."

"That can't have been much better than the French."

"It wasn't as bad. They didn't beat me. They fed me."

Anne squeezed her friend's hand. "Was it hard to tell me that?"

"No, I know you understand. You always did, even without what has happened to you. It does get easier, Señora, although I am not sure it ever really goes away. I never went near a man once I'd found work at the hospital. I never thought I would until I met Danny. He was so patient and so understanding, never tried to rush me into something I wasn't ready for. There are not many men out there like him. But you have one. You will be all right."

"I will. I'm determined to be. I am not letting that creature ruin my life, no matter how bad I feel right now."

Teresa laughed and got up with some difficulty, putting a hand to the small of her back. "Señora, when I think of all the other things you have made up your mind to, and achieved, I have no doubts. Just do not be too hard on yourself, you are still human. Give it time."

"Thank you, Teresa. You've helped. Would you do something for me? Before you go to sleep, will you ask Maggie Bennett if she could get the women to heat up water for a bath? I'm sorry, it's so self-indulgent, but I…"

Her friend was laughing. "Señora, after what you have been through you may have whatever you ask for. I will see to it."

Bathed and fed, Anne walked up to the cottage where the wounded of the 110th were housed. She spent some time with Michael who seemed to be doing well, then inspected the other men, changed several dressings, and left. Outside she was surprised to encounter the young soldier who had been her first patient two days earlier.

"Private Black, what the devil are you doing out of your bed? You should be resting."

He gave her a lopsided smile, the wounds giving him a crooked appearance. "I'm all right, ma'am. Not fit for duty yet, but I offered to help with the wounded, so they sent me up here. Most of the orderlies are out at the hospital in Elvas."

"Thank you, that's good of you." Anne examined the stitching. "That's looking good, it's going to heal well, I think."

"Are you all right, ma'am? I heard you weren't well."

"I'm much better, thank you, Private." Anne fell into step beside him and they walked back down towards the lines. A work party was lined up from the seventh under two officers, a captain and a lieutenant. Anne did not know either of them, but she gave them a pleasant smile and stepped aside to let them march down towards the lines. As they passed she heard the Lieutenant's voice, barely lowered.

"I say, sir, who is that?"

The Captain laughed. "The woman? That's Colonel van Daan's young wife. He commands the third brigade of the Light Division."

"What the devil is a woman that lovely doing out here hobnobbing with the enlisted men?"

There was another laugh. "Good question, Reid, and we've all asked it. He's got no control over her, she runs wild. It's caught up with her, mind, she's just back in camp. She's been held by the French for two weeks or more, and rumour has it that she had a very interesting time with them, if you know what I mean."

"Bloody hell. You mean they…?"

"So I hear, old boy. Surprised she's out in public, but she's got no shame…"

Private Black turned back, so quickly that Anne could do nothing to stop him. He strode towards the two officers who looked startled. Reaching out, he took the Captain by the front of his coat and shoved him backwards, so hard that he nearly fell.

"Show some respect," he yelled.

The Captain righted himself. The shocked expression on his face would have made Anne laugh if she had not been so upset. "Bloody hell! What in God's name are you doing, Private? Assaulting an officer is a hanging offence." He looked over at the ranks of his men who were openly enjoying the drama. "Sergeant, arrest him. Take him…"

Anne arrived on the scene and held up a hand to the Sergeant. "Don't bother, Sergeant, it was just a misunderstanding. Private Black had the Captain confused with somebody else. Nothing to worry about."

"Excuse me for saying so, ma'am, but this is none of your business," the Captain said shortly.

Anne was suddenly completely furious. "Of course it's my business, you imbecile, given that he was defending me. Go ahead and arrest him, Captain, and I will go straight to Headquarters to speak to Lord Wellington. I promise you that within fifteen minutes you will be facing a charge of conduct unbecoming an officer and a gentleman while this soldier will be walking free. How dare you think you can get away with that?"

The Captain's face was scarlet. "Ma'am. Very sorry, just a misunderstanding."

164

Anne stepped forward. She was conscious of a flood of anger and she clamped down on it hard, trying not to allow it to overwhelm her. "Captain, the only thing you've misunderstood is what a loud mouth you've got. I'll be speaking to my husband about what you just said. And if I hear you've given any grief to this soldier, in any shape whatsoever, I'm going to bury you in the breaches so deep you won't even be remembered. Now get your men down to the trenches and do something useful for a change."

Anne arrived back at the tent to find Paul dismounting. He came forward, his eyes on her face. "I didn't expect you to be up and around yet," he said, studying her. "Are you all right?"

"When our lads' wives give birth on campaign, Paul, we expect them to be up and marching again immediately or they get left behind."

He smiled. "True. Although in my regiment they do get space on the baggage wagon. Or occasionally a ride on my wife's horse, I seem to recall. But you're right, bonny lass, there are different rules. I'm not going to confine you to the tent. Just take care. Are you sure you're all right? You look angry."

Anne gave a wry smile. "I am," she said, preceding him into the tent. "I just had a taste of what I can expect from some of the officers and gentlemen of this army. It reminds me why I often prefer the enlisted men."

"Tell me," Paul said. Anne complied and he listened in silence. When she had finished he said:

"Remind me to thank Private Black, I appreciate his defence of my wife. I'm sorry, love."

"We expected it, Paul."

Paul eyed her warily. "Nan, I'm going to speak to them."

"Good. Be very specific."

She could tell that he had expected her to protest and he laughed aloud. "I will. I'm going to see Johnny first. While I'm gone, pack a bag and give some instructions to your medical staff, girl of my heart, we're taking a holiday."

Anne looked at him, surprised. "Another one?"

"Shorter and more local and this time I'm not letting you out of my sight. Wellington has given leave for me to take you to Elvas for a few days. Just us. Can you ask Jenson to pack for me? We'll take one pack horse."

Anne put her arms about him, her spirits soaring. "Thank you, Paul. It's just what I need. I'll be ready."

Paul spoke to Johnny, giving him command in his absence, and then made his way down towards the trenches. In the aftermath of yesterday's attack there were several companies of the 110th and the 95th on guard, their eyes watchful and their rifles and muskets ready. If the French should attempt another sortie, it would cost them considerably more. They had relied on surprise and had been successful, including making off with a large number of spades and other tools which would slow down the working parties until more could be obtained. But they had lost more men than they had expected thanks to the surprise attack by his six companies and he did not think Phillippon would risk another sortie.

He found Captain Elliott of the first company who saluted. "Sir, how's your lady?"

"Much better, Donald, thank you. I'm off for a few days, taking her to Elvas for a break. Lord Wellington has authorised it so I'm leaving as soon as I can before he realises I'll be more than five miles away from him and panics."

Elliott laughed aloud. "Good for you, sir, it'll do you both good."

"I hope so. I'm looking for a work party from the 7th, there's a Lieutenant Reid and an unnamed Captain in charge. Any idea?"

"Over in the far trench, sir. They're still digging out the mess from the other day, it's put us back a fair few days."

"Good, I might get a longer break with my wife."

"As long as Soult doesn't show up."

"If Marshal Soult interrupts my holiday, he's going to regret it."

Elliott turned and pointed. "The officers are over there I think, sir."

Paul turned and surveyed the lines of men digging with grim resignation. Beyond the first trench he saw a small group of officers which included Smith from the rifles, Zouch and Lloyd from the 110th and two officers wearing the blue facings of the 7th Foot. Paul gave a grim smile.

"Thanks, Donald."

Elliott seemed to catch his expression suddenly. "I say, sir," he said quickly. "Is everything all right?"

"Fine, thank you, Captain."

Paul walked over to the second trench, leaping nimbly over a runnel off one of the trenches which was filled with muddy water. Harry Smith saw him coming and saluted cheerfully.

"Morning, sir. Come down to see if we're skiving off?"

"I don't need to do that with you, Captain, I know you bloody will be. Morning George, Davy." Paul surveyed the other two officers thoughtfully. "Introduce me, will you?"

"Yes, sir. This is Captain Brough and Lieutenant Reid from the 7th. They've just been telling us…"

"Thank you, George. Sorry to interrupt your social life."

Paul stepped forward and grasped Captain Brough by the front of his coat. He swung him around, taking hold of the back of his collar with the other hand. He propelled the man forward, hearing a collection of startled exclamations from the other officers, and frog-marched him to the muddy ditch where he upended him head-first into the foul water. He watched as Brough thrashed about, disoriented, and finally managed to turn himself around, spluttering and spitting out mud and water. Paul stepped forward, placed his boot firmly into the middle of the man's chest and pushed him back down.

"Don't get up, Captain. There's no need for formality here, I just wanted a chat. Am I right in thinking it was you giving your opinion on my wife's virtue earlier in front of your entire company?"

There was a silence so thick and heavy that it could have been sliced with a cavalry sabre. Nobody moved or spoke and Captain Brough looked up into Paul's implacable face with an expression of sheer terror.

"Was it?" Paul yelled, and every man jumped.

"Sir. Sorry, sir. No offence intended…"

"No offence intended? You opened your foul mouth to give your view on what might or might not have been done to an innocent girl by the French within her hearing and stood laughing about it with that twat over there and you're telling me you didn't intend it to be offensive? Jesus bloody Christ, I'd like to know what you can come up with if you do decide to offend somebody! Reid, get your useless arse over here and help Captain Brough out of this ditch."

Reid moved quickly, not looking at Paul. Paul was aware of the appalled expression on Captain Zouch's face but he said nothing. As Reid bent, holding out a hand to help his Captain up, Paul kicked him hard in the back of the knee so that he fell on top of Brough in the filthy water with a yell of pain. Paul placed his foot once again, this time on the back of Reid's head, shoving his face down into the water. He stepped back and watched dispassionately as the two men struggled to unscramble themselves. As they climbed out of the ditch he bellowed:

"Get to attention, you sorry pair of useless gobshites!"

They did so, standing rigid with mud streaming off them. Paul wrinkled his nose, noticing with satisfaction that the water had stagnated and smelled foul.

"I don't know how you feel about this, Captain, but you might want to send one of your lads up to get another officer to cover for you while you clean yourselves up because if Lord Wellington rides past and sees you in that state he's going to ask why, and you need to trust me when I tell you that you do not want to have to explain. And when this gets around and the rest of the army are having a good laugh about it - and trust me, they will piss themselves, George over there tells a good story - just think about how bloody lucky you both are that Lord Wellington doesn't allow duelling in his army. I've just gutted a French colonel for looking the wrong way at my wife, and if I didn't value my career, I'd do the same to the two of you and go and enjoy my dinner without giving either of you another thought. In future, when you see her go past you keep your eyes down and your mouths shut and if I hear that either of you has had one word to say about her again, I am going to shoot you in the fucking head and dump you at the foot of these walls and they'll just assume the French shot you while you were taking a piss and use your sad fate as a warning to others. Is there anything about any of that you don't understand?"

"No, sir," Brough said quietly.

"Louder, Captain. Let's make the best of that loud mouth of yours, I know you can when you want to. Understood?"

"Yes, sir!"

"Good. Now fuck off and don't let me see you again until I'm in a better mood."

He turned away and the other officers sprang to attention and saluted smartly. Paul returned the salute and made his way back past the work party. As he approached the three companies of the 110th on guard duty he heard a rumble of laughter, and then somebody cheered. Within seconds they were yelling to a man. Paul stopped, turned and regarded them, trying not to laugh openly.

"Enough!" he roared, and they subsided and at an order from a sergeant, fell into perfect lines as if on parade. Only their faces showed open appreciation and Paul gave in, laughed and saluted.

167

"Your job is to watch for the French, not turn this into Astley's circus. One more yell out of any of you and you'll be in that ditch as well. Get on with it."

***

As Paul walked back up towards the lines, Smith, Zouch and Elliott turned to look at the two officers from the 7th who were trying to wipe mud from their hair and faces. Zouch wrinkled his nose.

"Good luck with getting that smell out of your coats," he said shortly, and turned away.

Harry Smith glanced over at him sympathetically. He had no idea what to say. He was struck by the memory of Anne van Daan when he had laughed with her and sent his men to help her set up her medical tent. She must only just have arrived back in camp and had shown no obvious signs of her recent appalling ordeal. She had seemed her usual charming self and the rumours he had heard circulating since then had shocked him to the core.

Smith was very friendly with George Zouch and had longed to ask him what he knew of the matter, but he did not. George was devoted to his Colonel's young wife and Smith suspected that if he said the wrong thing he might well get a punch. Looking from one face to the other, Smith realised that he had his answer and he felt rather sick. It was clear that the officers of the 110th knew exactly what had happened to Anne van Daan and were closing ranks with formidable determination.

"He's got a bloody nerve!" Brough said furiously. "That's no way for a gentleman to behave. He knows perfectly well we can't challenge him…"

Zouch turned on him. "What did you just say?" he demanded.

"I think he was implying that the Colonel was taking advantage of his position, knowing that junior officers can't challenge him," Elliott said. He had come to stand beside his friend and the tone of his voice made Smith turn and look at him. Elliott was rumoured to have a temper but Smith had never heard him use that particular tone of voice before.

Lieutenant Reid looked up from a fruitless attempt to brush clumps of mud off the front of his red jacket. "Look, I am sorry," he said. "I didn't think. I didn't realise she could hear, I genuinely didn't mean to upset her."

"Glad to hear it, Mr Reid, because I'd hate to have to throw you back in that ditch," Elliott said grimly. His eyes were on Brough. The other man attempted a sneer.

"If you touch me, Captain, I'll…"

Elliott stepped forward but Smith was quicker and he caught the other man's arm. "Elliott, don't. He's not worth the trouble. Colonel van Daan has dealt with him."

"Are you challenging me?" Brough said, his eyes on Elliott's face.

There was a long silence and Smith realised he was holding his breath. Eventually, Elliott said:

"Duels are for gentlemen, Brough, and you don't qualify."

He turned away and Smith relaxed but it was clear that Brough was not going to let the matter drop.

"You'll meet me for that," he said.

168

"Didn't you hear me?" Elliott said, without looking round. "Go and clean yourself up, you stink."

Brough's voice rose. "I'm challenging you. Calling you out. I'll see you at dawn, sir!"

Elliott turned back and Smith braced himself to intervene again, but the Scot shook his head. "Brough, you can stand there yelling challenges until you've no voice left, I'm not interested."

"Are you afraid to fight me, sir? Am I talking to a coward?"

Zouch was laughing. "Stop it, you're giving me a stitch in my side," he croaked. "Don't you know better than to issue a challenge to an officer of the 110th? Christ, you must be green. We don't fight duels, boy, we kill Frenchmen. Now piss off before you end up back in that ditch."

He put a hand on Elliott's shoulder and moved him gently away, and Lloyd followed with a contemptuous glance at Brough. Brough did not move. He looked as though he had been slapped. After a moment he turned to Reid and Smith.

"You saw that. You heard that. I challenged him and he refused to fight. He refused me satisfaction. When they hear that story in the mess..."

"If that story reaches the officers' mess of the 110th, Brough, a swim in a stagnant ditch will be the least of your worries," Smith said quietly. "Go and get cleaned up. I'll cover for you down here; my lads don't need much supervision. You're an arsehole, Brough, at least your Lieutenant has the grace to admit he's done something wrong."

"He'll give me satisfaction, sir, or I'll..."

"You're obviously new out here. He won't accept a challenge, Brough. None of them will. They won't break his rules and they don't need to; they wear that uniform, and you don't. If you've any sense you'll keep your mouth shut and your head down until they've calmed down, and you'd better hope the men of the 110th light company don't hear what you said about their Colonel's wife or you're going to be found dead in that ditch one dark night. Get out of here and try not to be such an arsehole next time."

He watched as Brough turned without speaking and made his way dripping foul water back up towards the lines. Shaking his head, Smith went to join the other officers.

Chapter Thirteen

The town of Elvas was at the top of a hill, five miles northwest of the Guadiana River, a fortress town surrounded by seven bastions and the two forts of Santa Luzia and Nossa Senhora da Graça. It was a town of winding streets and graceful buildings, many of them dating from the fifteenth and sixteenth centuries. Anne was particularly fascinated by the aqueduct, almost four miles long which had been built in the fifteenth century to supply the town with pure water.

Paul and Anne were given a room in a pretty inn, white painted and clean with high ceilings and long white draped windows. For a town which had been variously held by both the French and the English, it seemed remarkably untouched by war. For three days they wandered hand in hand through the narrow cobbled streets, and explored the local churches, forts and shops. They ate in cosy taverns, surrounded by locals who welcomed them with smiles, and slept late, revelling in waking together with no need to rise for early drill.

Sleeping in Paul's arms seemed like a new joy. Anne was reminded of the first days of their marriage. After two years of loving him and needing to keep her distance because of their respective spouses it had been a simple happiness to wake with him by her side and she felt it again now and suspected he did too. Her body was still healing and he made no attempt to make love to her simply lay holding her as she began to feel safe again.

Anne's first husband had believed that marriage gave him the right to make use of her body whenever he chose and had beaten her if she refused him. She had learned, for her own safety, to accommodate Robert's desires, doing whatever he asked her to do. It had stopped him beating her and it had made her feel like a prostitute.

Marrying Paul, Anne had not given much thought to what he would be like as a lover. Their mutual desire was not in question and in the first heady weeks of their marriage she had waited all day to be in his arms. His experience with women was wide and varied while her experience of men was limited to Robert but she had been both pleased and slightly shocked to realise how much she desired her husband and how much pleasure she was capable of giving and receiving.

Anne was also surprised and somewhat amused at how easy Paul seemed to find it to admit when he did not want to make love. She had often felt that Robert had needed to prove something in her bed, as though his possession of a very beautiful young wife gave him something to live up to. Paul appeared to have nothing to prove and she valued the nights spent lying together talking or simply holding one another. He never demanded or expected and never grew angry if she did not want to make love. She had never appreciated this aspect of him so much as now, lying in his arms feeling her battered body beginning to heal and grow strong again and her confidence returning.

Anne dreamed. On the second night she awoke sitting bolt upright, her body rigid with fear and bathed in sweat, shivering in the darkness. He was awake in an instant with a soldier's ability to make a quick transition between sleep and wakefulness, and she felt his arm about her.

"It's all right, Nan, it's me. You're here with me. It's over."

Anne turned to him, burying her face in his shoulder. Paul ran a hand soothingly over her hair. "Stop trying not to cry," he said. Anne gave a watery laugh.

"I'm sick of crying. I've cried more in the past weeks than in the previous two years."

"Well holding it in isn't going to help, bonny lass. Just relax and think about how much I love you."

He drew her down into his arms and she lay still and warm. "Have you cried?"

"Every night. I didn't sleep much. I spent a lot of time digging trenches with the men just to tire myself out, but it didn't help. I cried in bed and then if I slept, I'd wake up and remember you'd gone and I'd cry again. Poor Jenson must be exhausted, he flatly refused to go to his own tent. He sat up with me every bloody night."

"Oh, poor Paul. And poor Freddie."

Paul laughed. "I wrote to you," he said. "I missed talking to you and I wanted to tell you how I felt, so I wrote to you."

"Did you keep them?"

"Yes."

"May I read them?"

"I doubt they make much sense, but yes. I'll find them for you. Just don't show them to the rest of the brigade, they already think I'm soft."

Anne laughed. The terror had receded, and his nonsense made her feel normal again. "You are soft, Colonel."

"I am when it comes to you, girl of my heart. Feeling better?"

Anne nodded. "Yes. Thank you. I hope this stops soon."

"Just let it happen, Nan. It's part of healing and you can't rush it. Go back to sleep, it's still dark. I love you."

***

Knowing his wife would not, Paul had obtained details of the recommended dressmaker. In a small shop, just off the main square Anne was measured by a plump motherly woman for a new riding habit, explaining her requirements fluently and laughing with the woman over the shabby condition of her clothing. She had brought her old velvet robe with her and the woman studied it and then sketched a suggested design. Anne bent over the table with her, gesticulating, describing, and the woman was smiling and nodding, bringing out fabric samples. Paul watched his wife appreciatively, enjoying the relative normality of their activities, and reflected that nobody who had been through these years of war could possibly understand how good it could feel to do something as simple as shopping without waiting for orders or the call of the bugle. Anne was beginning to look well again. She had colour in her cheeks and the dark circles had gone from under her eyes. She was moving more easily and the wounds inflicted on her body were healing well. Paul could feel himself beginning to relax and it made him aware of how tightly strung he had been for weeks.

"I think that's everything," Anne said, and he moved forward shaking his head.

"No it isn't, bonny lass. Since we're here and we've time why don't you see what else Señora Moreno has in stock. You could do with a couple of new day dresses and I don't think you've had a new evening gown since I married you."

Anne was laughing. "I knew you'd do this once you got me in here."

"Indulge me, Nan. Let me spend some money on you for once. And new underclothes, yours have been washed so many times they're threadbare."

"To say nothing of the damage the French do to them," Anne said shaking her head, and Paul spluttered with laughter at the expression on the dressmaker's face.

"I can tell you're feeling better," he said.

The dark eyes lifted to his face and the expression in them made Paul catch his breath. "Thanks to you."

Paul did not respond immediately, partly because of the presence of the dressmaker and partly because emotion made speech impossible for a moment. Anne seemed to understand and reached up to caress his face.

They left the dressmaker with an order which made the woman's eyes shine and wandered through the narrow streets, peering into shop windows. They found a tiny watchmaker, the shop so dark that the proprietor had to take his wares out into the street for them to see properly, and at Paul's insistence Anne chose an elegant watch which he asked the man to engrave for her, his name and hers. She selected a chain and as it was wrapped, Paul saw her studying a man's watch with thoughtful eyes.

"I'm happy with my grandfather's watch, love."

"Not for you, Paul. I was thinking of Francis and Grace. Neither of them has a watch and they're old enough."

He shot her an amused glance. "Why not? Do you know, in all these years I've never sent them a gift before? What is wrong with me? Come on, we'll chose one for Grace and get their names put on them. And then I think we'll need a toy shop for Rowena and Will. There's a woodworker down by the gate, I bet he makes toys as well."

They took their purchases back to their room and Paul watched her wrap them and scribbled a note to accompany them before delivering them to the army post office.

"I wish I could see their faces when that arrives," Paul said. "Thank you, Nan."

Anne smiled up at him. "They're my children too, Paul. You need to tell me when their birthdays are."

"Well you know Will's and Rowena's, girl of my heart. Francis was born on the second of May, and we've tended to celebrate Grace's then as well because I don't actually know her birthday."

His wife glanced at him. "Really? We need to make one up, she should have a day just for her. Work it out, Paul, you must have some idea."

Paul laughed at her determination. "I will, lass, you can write to tell her she has a new birthday. I'm not sure what Patience will make of it, mind, but she'll have to get used to it. Come over here."

Anne moved towards him, looking puzzled, and he handed her a small, wrapped package. Anne stared at it and looked up. "What is it, Paul?"

"Open it."

Anne obeyed, very curious and found a velvet covered box which looked very old. Anne looked up at him and saw that he was watching her. She opened the box.

"Oh."

It was a pendant, not large or elaborate, a delicate gold cross set with pearls on a fine chain. Something about it spoke of age. Anne picked it up and studied it, then on impulse turned it over. The initials on the back were worn away but still legible and she stared for a moment then looked up at him.

"Who was this?"

"My grandfather gave it to his wife on the birth of their first child, my father," Paul said. "It's not a very valuable piece although the pearls are real. He lived in Antwerp, was a merchant on the rise back then but hadn't really made a fortune. According to my father, they adored one another, he told me that my grandfather never really got over her death."

"Where did you get it from?"

"My father sent it for me to give to you when he got back to England. There are a few pieces of very personal jewellery that he's always kept. I was honestly shocked when I opened it. And given that I wasn't sure I'd ever see you again, you can believe me when I tell you that I cried like a baby. It's a very big compliment, Nan, he's never wanted Patience to have his mother's jewellery, we'd always rather assumed they'd go to the girls eventually. But he wanted you to have this."

"Oh Paul." She was smiling, her eyes misty with tears. "It's lovely. And now you've made me cry again, you horrible man."

"Blame my father. Let me put it on for you. It goes well with your earrings."

There was a small mirror above the dresser and Anne studied her reflection. "It's lovely. And it's small enough to wear every day. I need to write to him to say thank you." She glanced at him. "Does he know…?"

"No, I didn't write. I will, although without the details. Do you know, I think that very delicate piece of antique jewellery suits you better than my expensive diamonds and rubies. "

Anne touched the pendant. "I love it. I realise I don't know much about your family, Paul."

"I don't know many of them," Paul admitted. "My father has a brother and a sister still living. Uncle Andries is in trade in Cape Town. I met them once when I was a boy, apprenticed aboard my father's ship. We docked at the Cape, spent some weeks there. It was just before the Royal Navy intervened in my career. I've met my

173

aunt as well, she visited us when I was young, although I don't remember her well. She's some years younger than my father, married into a merchant family in Vlissingen. There were several children but I think only the girl survived."

"The fruits of a well-travelled family. I, of course, know far more of my family than I could possibly wish to; none of them have moved further than Derbyshire. I'm not sure which of us is to be envied."

Paul grinned. "I must say, I'm looking forward to that experience when we finally go home. I wonder if your step-mother will hit me; I'm sure she knew. Come on, let's go to post this and then we'll walk up to the cathedral, you'll like it."

Anne slipped her arm through his. "I think I'll enjoy anything today, Paul. I think I'm finally beginning to feel like myself again."

***

They explored the cathedral. It was not large, but Anne found it extraordinarily beautiful with an immense vaulted ceiling decorated with swirls of gold. She wandered around the edge looking into several private chapels and drinking in the sense of peace. When she turned to find Paul, she saw him standing before the high alter, his eyes on the cross and his lips moving. Anne went to join him and took his arm, quiet beside him as he prayed.

He was silent for a further minute, then slipped his arm about her and kissed her. She smiled. "Are you all right?"

"Very much so. It's just that doing what I do, I ask for a lot of help. I've prayed in ditches and tents and in the heat of battle at times and I'm always asking for something. I feel as though I've done well out of it too, we're all still here. Sometimes it's not a bad idea to say thank you as well."

"For me?"

Paul nodded. "I wasn't sure I was going to get you back alive, Nan."

"Nor was I," Anne said soberly. "It's funny, I never really think of you as a religious man."

"I wonder why that is? I'm not much of a churchgoer. It was more of a chore when I was a boy and since I joined the army I've little chance. But I used to go with Rowena when I could. I find it a comfort."

"It is."

Her husband grinned. "Now that surprises me a little. I distinctly remember the day I met you and we engaged in about twelve hours of conversation about everything under the sun. The thing that shocked me the most about you, girl of my heart, was not your willingness to allow me to make love to you, but your open questioning of traditional religious beliefs."

Anne laughed aloud. "Heavens, you've a good memory, Paul, I'd forgotten that."

"I've forgotten nothing of what proved to be the most important twenty-four hours of my life. What changed?"

"You'll laugh."

"No, I won't."

"General Craufurd. I spent three days with him while he was dying. His belief, his complete faith...I can't explain it, Paul. I prayed with him a fair bit. But I've prayed before. It was different this time."

"I understand."

"Probably you do. And like you I've prayed a lot recently. For you and me. And we're here. Standing here with you in this beautiful church...it's hard not to believe."

Paul studied her and then smiled.

"Come on, I'm starving, and there was a tavern opposite with benches outside. It is the most amazing feeling to be able to do this, I'd forgotten what normal life felt like. Shall we stay a few more days? Wellington will send for me when he needs me."

"I'm not going back until he does, Paul, this is heaven. I love your regiment, but it's made me realise that we've literally had no time alone since we married. I am not missing that wretched bugle."

Paul laughed. "Are we finally getting a honeymoon, lass?"

"It feels like it. Do you know we have honestly never done this? Just been alone. There's always been the regiment or family. It's good to remember how much I just enjoy your company. And I feel so much better."

"So do I, girl of my heart. If this has taught me anything, it's that I should take the occasional break." Paul shook his head. "It's been a point of pride with me over the years that I'm still here when everybody else is taking leave. But I'm not sure it's the best idea." He took her hand and kissed it. "Lisbon is secure now. I'm going to write to Josh and tell him that I want to see the children more often. It's not a difficult journey and a few weeks once a year won't kill Wellington, it's not like I'm asking for months in England. Although next time we are doing that journey together, I am not letting you out of my sight again, you're not safe."

They sat in the sunlight, holding hands across the rough wooden table and the landlady's daughter brought them wine and bread and plates of steaming paella, smiling at their absorption in each other. Most of the other tables were occupied by locals, and Anne tested Paul's Portuguese, getting him to listen in on the voluble discussions about crops and the weather and the price of grain.

"You've got very fluent."

"I have. I don't miss much now. Of course, the lessons from Captain Peso have helped...."

Anne broke into laughter. "Juan has been teaching you?"

"He has. I teach him swordplay in return. I was fed up with you being so much better than me, I'm quite good at languages, it's just laziness. But I've enjoyed it, using my brain again. How are your German lessons coming along?"

Anne gave a gurgle of mirth. "I didn't realise you'd noticed."

"Well either you're having language lessons, bonny lass, or you're intriguing with our charming German recruit, and I don't think that's likely, somehow." Paul took off his coat and laid it over the bench next to him. "Jesus, it's hot."

"I don't know why not, he's very good looking. He's rather a surprising young man, is Private Kuhn. Did you know he'd a degree in Medicine from the university in Halle?"

Paul gave her a surprised look. "Has he? I thought he was extraordinarily articulate, and very confident with the officers. What the hell is he doing in the ranks of the KGL?"

"Military family. Father and two older brothers. All killed during the French invasion. The French took over his family estate, he'd literally nothing, and at that point the Prussian army was destroyed. Dr Kuhn took it fairly badly. He joined the KGL and came to the Peninsula."

"The things you find out about my men. I'm not querying his motives, Nan, and there's no doubt that he's a bonny fighter, but wouldn't he be more use in the medical services?"

Anne smiled slightly and Paul shook his head. "And suddenly your enthusiasm for learning German becomes much clearer. What's his objection?"

"He doesn't want to treat the French."

"Ah. Are you working on that?"

"I am."

"Well good luck, he'd be a godsend. But if you don't think he'll budge, let me know. He should be an officer, I've already been considering it."

Anne laughed and lifted his hand, kissing it. "You know he hasn't a penny, don't you, Paul?"

"Nor have half my officers, love, but for somebody good we can always work something out."

"You mean you can. No wonder they hate you at Horse Guards."

"They actually do. I swear that if they thought they could get away with it they'd have me assassinated just to shut me up. But you cannot be any more popular with the medical board, girl of my heart. You've the tenacity of a terrier in a rat hole and you can write the rudest letters I have ever seen in my life. And the worst of it is, they can't threaten to fire you because they don't pay you anyway. If they ever get you in their sights, you are history."

Anne was laughing hard, suddenly remembering something she had forgotten to tell him about her last communication with the medical board. She related the story as they ate, and he was laughing too, enjoying the sense of peace and freedom from care.

It was rudely shattered by a slight scream. Anne and Paul both turned their heads along with all the other patrons of the tavern. A group of red-coated English soldiers had arrived. Some could be seen at tables inside the tavern and others spilled over outside, sitting or lounging on the cobbled square in the sun as there were no free tables.

The woman who had served Anne and Paul was distributing jugs of wine, and as she had turned to go into the tavern to get more, one of the men had grabbed her around the waist and was trying to kiss her. There was laughter among the troops watching. Several of the Portuguese farmers at the tables were on their feet, shouting and gesticulating. Paul sighed.

"One kiss, Señorita!" the soldier was saying. "It won't hurt."

Two of the farmers moved away from their table, shouting at the man to let the woman go. Paul hesitated. The chances were that in a moment the incident would

176

have passed, but with the other men involved it looked likely to turn into something more.

"Paul, she's really scared," Anne said quietly, and he shot her a look of sudden comprehension. There were too many women in Portugal and Spain, like his wife, who had learned the hard way, how quickly an army could turn bestial, and he looked over at the woman and understood that her terror was greater than might have been expected. He got to his feet.

"That's enough!" he called, keeping his voice genial. The mellow sense of being on holiday had not left him and he was hoping that the sight of an officer would settle the men down without need for further intervention. "No reason for me to kick you out, lads, if you behave. Let the lass go about her business and enjoy the day."

The man holding the woman's arm glanced across. Whether he had recognised the rank of the officer, given that he could not see his insignia on his coat, Paul was not sure, but he seemed to recognise the authority in the tone, grinned somewhat sheepishly, and released her. The woman scuttled back into the inn. The soldier saluted and Paul nodded, smiled, and went back to his seat. The farmers returned to their table, reaching for the wine. Paul smiled at his wife. "Are you all right?"

"Of course, I am. My hero."

"Much more of that, and you'll get a slap, lass."

Anne gave a gurgle of laughter. "That is such an unconvincing threat coming from you."

"You've no respect for a senior officer," Paul said, summoning a waiter for more wine. "I suspect I'm going back to our room to fall asleep. I'm not used to all this relaxation. But I am enjoying it."

"So am I, Paul." Anne met his eyes and gave a smile. "We could go back to our room and stay awake."

She saw his eyes light up with amusement. "Nan, you are aware that if we were at home in England and you'd miscarried like that you wouldn't even be out of bed?"

"Oh yes I would, Colonel. Complete poppycock in my opinion, women are not that delicate. At least, I'm not. And I've missed making love to my husband."

Paul laughed and kissed her hand. "Nan, I am not going to turn down that particular invitation. But only if you're ready, I can wait. Simply going to sleep with you in my arms is good enough for me. I'm not sure I'm ever going to be able to take that for granted again."

Another voice called out, a harsh northern accent, deliberately loud in the drowsy air. "All right for him, boys, playing the big protector. No need for him to go after a tavern wench, he's bought his commission and it looks like he's bought himself a very expensive whore to go with it. Stuck up twat, sends his men out to die and he's sitting here staring at her tits and..."

Paul got up, moving so fast that Anne could not have stopped him if she had tried. She watched as he strode forward. The man who had spoken was a big broad man, solidly built with a nose which suggested that he had spent some time in the boxing ring. As Paul approached, he pushed himself off the wall he had been leaning on and stood ready to fight. Anne rose too and followed her husband. She knew that he could not have ignored the man's words, but she was concerned at how far he might go. He was especially protective of her at the moment, understandably after what she had just been through. She was furious that their blissful afternoon together had been so rudely interrupted.

"Name and regiment," Paul said quietly.

"Why don't you go first, sir?" the man drawled. "If we're going to be mates?"

"Jagger, don't be a prat, he's an officer, you can't hit him!" one of his friends said.

"I don't see any other officers around to see what I do," Jagger slurred. He was clearly drunk. "And this pretty lad isn't getting up by the time I've finished with him, he won't remember what happened anyway. If he's still alive. Who knows, maybe I might give his girlfriend a try when..."

Paul punched once, low and hard, and the man made a strange sound and doubled up, clutching at his midriff. Anne almost wanted to smile at his expression. Around him his friends were moving away slightly.

"Name and regiment, Private. Don't make me ask you again."

The man straightened and the expression in his eyes was murderous. He was clearly one of the leaders in the group and used to dominating by his physical presence and his fighting experience. Anne glanced around at the other men. They were slightly dishevelled, but the uniforms looked in very good condition. She suspected that they had only just arrived from England.

Jagger stepped forward. "You cocky bastard, I am going to fucking kill you. If you think there's an officer out there that can beat me in a fist fight, you..."

Paul hit him again, a four punch combination which sent his opponent reeling. Jagger recovered quickly and charged like an enraged bull, throwing wild punches. Few of them connected. Anne watched her husband with some amusement. The men of his regiment sometimes engaged in friendly boxing and wrestling bouts and one or two of the officers occasionally joined in. Leo Manson was a formidable boxer, and very few of his light company would take him on, but Paul always laughingly refused to join in. She was beginning to see why.

Her concern was the growing atmosphere among the other men. They had been faintly amused at first, waiting to see the arrogant young officer humiliated by Jagger's superior strength and skill. Their reaction suggested that it was not the first time he had struck an officer and she wondered at that. It was rare in the army as the official penalty was death and it spoke of a disciplinary problem beyond the usual. Anne glanced around. Paul's sword and coat were still lying on the table. She went to pick them up and returned. The man who had first accosted the waitress glanced at her, first at the sword and then down at the coat. Anne deliberately held it where the insignia could be seen.

"Jesus Christ, Jagger, back off, he's a bloody colonel!" the man yelled.

Jagger was on his knees, his face battered and bloody. Paul stood before him, unmoving but with his feet apart, his body balanced ready to react quickly.

Jagger suddenly moved, reaching behind him to his belt and the knife that came out was long bladed and looked very sharp. Anne gave a gasp, quickly suppressed as he lunged at Paul, who leaped back out of reach. Jagger was grinning widely.

"Not so cocky now, are you?" he said.

178

Paul did not speak. His eyes were not on the knife, they were on the other man's face. Anne watched, her heart in her mouth, and to her surprise she saw the flicker of his eyes at the same time as Paul did. Jagger moved, but Paul was before him and the man's wrist was in his hands. He twisted hard, put his leg behind the man and threw, and in seconds Jagger lay on his back in the dust, winded, his knife in Paul's hand at his throat.

"If you move, Private Jagger," Paul said in tones of pure ice, "I am going to cut your throat from ear to ear and dump your remains in the woods for the wolves to finish off, because I cannot be arsed with the paperwork. And I'm not only a colonel. I command the third brigade of the Light Division, and you are up to your ugly neck in shit right now."

Jagger stared up into his eyes. For the first time his belligerence was being replaced by fear. "How did you do that...?"

"Don't you mean 'how did you do that, Sir?'" Paul said. "Get up, you pathetic gobshite, and get to attention." He hauled Jagger to his feet and looked around. "And that goes for the rest of you!" he bellowed, and even Anne jumped at the volume. "Into line, now! Christ Almighty, do you call yourselves soldiers, you useless dog turds, my wife's maid can salute straighter than you can. And she can probably fight better as well."

Anne studied them as they scrambled into line and stood to attention. Paul glanced at her finally for the first time since the brawl had begun. "I am sorry," he said, his face finally softening into a smile. "We will continue our holiday, I promise you."

Anne handed him his sword. "It's all right, Colonel. That's army life."

Paul adjusted his sword and took the coat from her. He buttoned it up and Anne could see eyes widening from some of the men who had still not realised his rank. She admitted that nobody seeing him sitting in shirt sleeves laughing with her at the table could have thought him old enough to be a ranking colonel, let alone commander of a brigade.

Paul surveyed the men. Anne could see no sign of an officer or an NCO and as she thought it, Paul pointed to the man who had tried to kiss the Spanish woman and beckoned. The man stepped forward.

"Name, Private?"

"Aycliffe, sir. First company, first battalion, 115th Yorkshire infantry."

Paul's brows flew up and he stared in surprise across at Anne and then back at the man. "I know the 115th, lad, and I don't recognise those facings."

"New, sir. Our new Colonel didn't like the old colour, got it changed to black, sir."

"Well at least it won't show the blood, Private, which is a good thing where you're going. Where are you bivouacked?"

There was an uncomfortable silence. Paul looked at the man steadily. "Private, that was a really simple question. Answer it."

"Officers are billeted at the monastery, sir. NCOs and men up by the watercourse. But it's wet and boggy, and some of us thought we'd do better in town."

Paul took a deep breath. "Are you all out of camp without permission? How the hell are you expecting to get away with that?" he said.

179

Jagger spoke for the first time. "Who's going to stop us?" he said, and Paul looked at him. Anne saw the truth dawn on him for the first time. She had grasped it some minutes ago, but this level of indiscipline was so unbelievable to her husband that it had taken him longer.

He took a deep breath and Anne uttered a silent prayer. Paul did not disappoint her. He gave a faint smile. "All right. We'll look at the billeting situation later. I'm going to walk down to see your officers to find out where you're supposed to be. In the meantime, get yourselves out of here, these people have had enough."

They complied, moving away fairly readily. Paul looked over at the landlady, standing in the door. "I'm guessing they've not paid you a penny," he said in easy Portuguese.

"No, sir."

"How long have they been here?"

"Three days, sir. They forced their way into homes in the town, demanding food and drink. People are afraid, sir. Of what they might do."

"Don't worry about it, Señora. Once they're out of here, I'll send my quartermaster round and find out what they owe. You'll all be paid."

"Thank you, sir. And for my daughter. She was very frightened."

"I know. Best keep her out of the way for now. I should be able to get them out of here tomorrow."

"Sir, their officers are afraid of them."

Paul studied her. "My officers won't be," he said. "I need to know how many we're dealing with and how the hell it got this bad. Nan, I'm sorry...."

Anne laughed. "Paul, we've had three lovely days. Chances are, you were going to get called back soon anyway."

"Yes, we've done very well. But we'll pick this up once we're in winter quarters. One thing this has taught me is that I need an occasional break. Come on, girl of my heart, let's get up to see..."

"Sir."

They turned together to see a stocky man in his forties regarding them steadily across the tables. He was leaning heavily on wooden crutches and his leg appeared to be strapped up as if it were broken. Paul studied him and then broke into a smile.

"Sergeant Barforth. Welcome to Portugal. I was just wondering about you. What the bloody hell is going on? I've left your battalion alone for four years and the whole thing has fallen apart."

Barforth limped forward, shifted a crutch to the other hand and saluted. "Good to see you, sir. I've thought about you a lot, wondered how you were doing. Then we got word that all our best officers were transferring to serve under you in Portugal."

Paul jerked his head. "Come and sit down, Sergeant. I want to hear what's happened before I go and put a rocket up the arses of the officers. After that I'm riding back to camp to collect some help and I intend to give this lot the shock of their lives. Because this looks suspiciously like mutiny to me."

Barforth nodded. "In places. But they're not all bad lads, sir, some of them will remember you from last time. There's a core of wrong 'uns and no mistake, but a good officer could get those weeded out soon enough and the rest would fall into line."

180

"And don't you have a good officer?" Anne asked, pouring wine and passing it to Barforth. The Sergeant looked at her in some astonishment, and Paul gave a slight smile.

"Welcome to the 110th, Sergeant. The lady passing you wine and asking questions about military matters is my wife, Anne."

"Good to meet you, ma'am."

"You too, Sergeant. I have a very clear memory, Paul, of you mentioning at a dinner party in Yorkshire that summer that socialising with your officers, while necessary, was painful, and that the only man in the regiment that you really wanted to socialise with was your new Sergeant."

Paul gave a shout of laughter. "Christ, lass, but you've got a memory. I probably did!"

Barforth was studying her curiously. "You're from Yorkshire, ma'am?"

"I am, Sergeant. Helton Ridge in Thorndale. My father is Sir Matthew Howard."

"Bloody hell!" Barforth said. "Sorry, ma'am, just surprised. But am I confused? I thought you married Mr Carlyon."

"I did. Paul was married at the time. We were both widowed out here. We married over a year ago."

"What happened, Sergeant? And how did you come to arrive here with a broken leg?"

"Interesting story, sir. I'll make it quick, for you'll be wanting to get out of here, I know you. It went all right under Colonel Kincaid. You'd done the groundwork. We were up to strength. Spent some time in Italy, and then did a spell in Malta. When we got home, the Colonel died very suddenly. Heart gave out. They promoted a Scotsman in his place, Colonel Elliott, but he was a lazy bastard, couldn't care less. Second battalion got sent to Cape Town, we were in barracks for a while under Major Walsh. You remember him, sir?"

"I do. Pointless individual. Is he out here?"

"No, sir. Got a post at Horse Guards like his father."

"No wonder nothing works there."

"After him, came Major Stead. He's young and very unsure. Got promoted through family connections."

"That isn't supposed to be happening any more," Anne said.

"Do I need to mention the name Erskine?" Paul said ironically. "Long story, Sergeant, I'll tell you over a few drinks. So nobody takes charge?"

"Well just about that time, sir, some bastard from the 110th cleared out all our best officers in one swoop," Barforth said in matter of fact tones and Anne gave a choke of laughter.

"They are very good, Sergeant," she said.

"I know, ma'am. I helped to train them. Stead can't manage the men, and most of the other officers are young, new or stupid. It got worse when they cleared out the York sessional into our barracks and we got the delightful Jagger and his friends. Former boxer and highwayman. He's a scumbag, killed two men in barracks – I know it but can't prove it – and beaten a lot more. He's gone after a couple of the officers when nobody is around and they're terrified of him. My company wasn't too bad, not as good as when you were there and I admit I was struggling, but they sent me Ensign Raby and he has got to be one of the most ballsy little bastards I have ever come across. My captain is permanently drunk and both lieutenants too frightened to speak, but Raby is a very good lad."

"And where is Ensign Raby now?" Paul said.

"Back in his billet, sir, nursing a knife wound to the back. He's not well. Happened aboard ship. Same place I had this unfortunate accident and ended up with a broken leg. Didn't see a thing, but the deck was slippery. Although I had the sense of a very strong hand in the middle of my back, which is strange because I'd not been drinking."

Anne looked at Paul. "We need to get back."

"Yes. Let's skip the officers until tomorrow. Sergeant, is Raby safe where he is?"

"He is while he stays in bed."

"And you're staying here?"

"Can't move far, sir. They put me in a billet over the road, didn't think I should be out in the open because of this leg. They wanted me in the hospital, but I don't like the look of it."

"That's a good choice, Sergeant. How many companies out here?"

"Only four, sir. The rest are in Ireland. Supposed to be coming out later, but God knows when."

"Where are you intended for?"

"The seventh division I believe."

"Bad idea. They're new and inexperienced and they'll never cope with this. I'm going to see Lord Wellington to ask him to put them with the Light Division, at least until this matter is resolved."

"We're not light infantry, sir."

"Don't worry, Sergeant, you will be. It's what I do, and by the time I've finished with them, they won't have enough energy to mutiny. And if they go for one of my officers or NCOs, they'll find themselves checking to see where their balls have gone. Right, get back to your billet, Barforth and stay there until I come back. I won't be alone and you'll hear me. We're about to give Private Jagger something new to think about."

Barforth saluted and rose cautiously. Anne studied him. The weathered face was unnaturally pale and lined with pain. "Who set that?"

"The bosun, ma'am, aboard the transport."

"When this is over, I'll have a proper look at it for you, Sergeant."

Barforth looked puzzled. "Yes, ma'am."

Paul eyed his former Sergeant with some amusement. "Let her look, Sergeant, she's better than some of the surgeons. Once this is settled, we'll have a few drinks and catch up properly. I'd like to stay but I need to get back and collect my men. I'm going to come back here and kick the living shit out of the 115th for the second time in my life. Come on, girl of my heart, let's get going."

182

Chapter Fourteen

Paul rode back to Elvas the following day with five companies of the 110th, headed by his light company. He had left his wife reluctantly at the temporary hospital, and the absent-minded way that she had bidden him farewell had reassured him that whatever his anxieties, she was more concerned about medical matters than her own recent ordeal. In the centre of Elvas Paul reined in. "Sergeant-Major Carter."

"Yes, sir."

"Skirmish formation, in twos. I want you to check every house in the town. Be polite to the householders and round up the 115th. Buglers in the square, signal them if you need help. I want every man out here, lined up and disarmed. If they really piss you off, shoot them in the foot. My wife can always patch them up later."

Carter grinned. "What if they piss her off, sir?"

"Then they are doomed, Sergeant-Major and it's their own fault. Get going."

He glanced across at Barforth who had limped out from his billet to meet them. "Do you know where Jagger is billeted, Sergeant?"

"There's a tavern at the far end of the road out towards Badajoz, sir, right on the edge of town. Nice little place, and they've picked it for a reason, it's also a local brothel. Six or seven of them there, him and his mates. They all came in from the courts at the same time. They're armed and they'll kill without hesitation."

"So will we." Paul looked at Manson. "Captain Manson, take Sergeant Hammond and whichever men you choose. Bring them back here. Alive or dead. I'm not too fussed with this lot, given that I suspect one or two of them are going to hang anyway."

Manson saluted. "Yes, sir."

Paul looked over at Giles Heron. "Captain Heron, take your company out to the campsite and march the remaining men and NCOs back here. Line them up and we'll have a chat. Once again, if anybody gets in your way you've got Lord Wellington's orders to shoot them dead, although I doubt you'll have much trouble with that lot, they're the ones who stayed where they should be."

"On my way, sir."

Paul watched his men move out, and then walked in through the door of the monastery. One of the brothers came towards him, looking anxious, and he smiled.

183

"Colonel Paul van Daan, I command the third brigade of the Light Division. I'm looking for Major Stead."

"Sir, the officers are at dinner. In the refectory."

"Would you mind showing me the way?"

Paul walked into the long dining room, reminding him of so many similar rooms in convents and monasteries he had visited throughout Portugal. There were ten men sitting around the table. The board was well stocked with dishes; meat and fish and salads, and all the men looked up as he entered, pausing with food halfway to their mouths, astonished.

Paul's eyes rested on Major Stead. He was a tall thin fair man, in his mid-twenties at the most, with pale blue eyes and a nervous expression. "Major. Good to meet you," Paul said very gently. "Don't get up, will you?"

By now Stead had identified the uniform. He scrambled to his feet, saluting, and the rest of the officers followed suit. Paul stood studying them.

"Just at this moment," he said quietly, "four companies of my regiment are going through the village dragging out your men into line ready to march up to do their duty at Badajoz. The reason they are having to do this is that you are sitting here on your arses eating and drinking and not caring what havoc those men are creating in a Portuguese town. Major, can you give me some justification for this?"

"Sir....who are you...."

"Colonel Paul van Daan of the 110th light infantry. I command the third brigade of the Light Division. Is there somewhere we can talk privately, please, Major?"

"Yes, of course." Stead looked terrified. "Unless – have you eaten, sir? You could join us..."

"No thank you, Major. I lost my appetite yesterday afternoon round about the time a private in your first company threatened a brigade commander and his wife in front of half a company in broad daylight and assumed he'd get away with it."

"Jagger," one of the lieutenants said, and then blushed. "Sorry, sir."

"No, you're right. Name?"

The man saluted. "Lieutenant Irwin, sir, second company. But we all know it's likely to have been Jagger. Sir, are you all right? I mean..."

"If you mean did he pull a knife on me the same way he presumably did on Mr Raby, then he certainly did, Mr Irwin. Although I think five minutes later, he rather wished he hadn't. Under normal circumstances he'd be with the provost marshal by now awaiting a quick trial and a short walk to the gallows. And that is definitely where he's going. But I realised rather quickly that without troops I was likely to get into trouble with a regiment this badly out of control and I wasn't going to risk that with my wife there, so I let him go. By now I rather imagine he is in more trouble than he'd like, my light company are on their way there and they have no sense of humour about this whatsoever."

"Sir, how did you find out so much?" Irwin asked. "I'm sorry, but..."

"I ran into Sergeant Barforth in town, he's an old friend of mine. Major, I'll meet you in the hall in ten minutes, I want to see Mr Raby first. Mr Irwin, will you show me where I can find him, please?"

He followed Irwin up the stairs to a small dark room furnished only with a narrow bed, a chest and a chair.

"Thank you, Mr Irwin. Go and finish your dinner, I'll speak to you all after I've seen the Major."

"Not that hungry really, sir. But thank you."

"How long have you been in the army, Mr Irwin?"

"Just over a year, sir. I joined a cavalry regiment but I couldn't afford it."

"Yes, I've a couple of officers who did the same."

"I got the chance of promotion with the 115th so I bought in. Wishing I'd waited, to be honest, sir."

"Cheer up, Mr Irwin, it's about to change and you can relax and concentrate on killing the French instead. The 115th have just been switched from the seventh division to the third brigade of the Light Division, which will mean once we've taken Badajoz there'll be some work to do. But we can do it. Off you go."

Irwin left and Paul pulled up the chair and sat down, studying the young face on the pillow. Raby was slight, with a shock of red hair and freckles across his nose which made Paul think with a pang of his first wife.

"Mr Raby?"

The eyes opened, a surprising blue, and Raby looked confused.

"Who…what…sir?"

"Don't try to move, wounded men are excused saluting a senior officer."

"Could try it lying down, sir. I'm sorry, I don't know…"

"Colonel van Daan, 110th light infantry. I command the third brigade of the Light Division, which makes me your commanding officer, by the way."

"What's happened, sir? Is the Major all right?"

"He's fine. I'm in the process of reorganising your regiment. For the second time in my life, which must be a penance for something although I'm not sure what. Don't worry about it, I just came to see how you were. Sergeant Barforth told me what happened."

Raby closed his eyes. Paul studied him. He suspected the boy had naturally pale colouring, but surely not as white as this. Even his lips were colourless. He was worse than Paul had expected and he wished he had brought Anne with him after all.

"You don't look so good, Mr Raby."

"I don't feel so good, sir. I'm as weak as a mouse, and every time I try to move it starts bleeding again."

"Have you seen a surgeon?"

"One came down from the hospital, sir. He's bled me a few times, but it doesn't seem to help."

Paul opened his mouth to say something vulgar then bit it back. He knew that Anne would not have been so restrained.

"I don't think bleeding helps when you've already lost this much blood, Ensign."

"The surgeon said…"

"I can guess what the surgeon said. I don't know who it was, but I'm going to give orders not to admit him again. Later today I'll get one of our doctors in to see you. Or possibly my wife, she'll know what's best for you. Sergeant Barforth tells me you've tried to deal with this situation."

"Not very successfully, sir, although we were making some progress before this. But there's a man called Jagger..."

"I've met Private Jagger. Don't worry, Mr Raby, Private Jagger is going to regret his effort at mutiny before the end of the day. I won't keep you talking, you need to rest, you've lost a lot of blood. That's about the limit of my medical advice as I don't know what I'm talking about. We'll wait until my wife gets here. She'll get you back on your feet."

"Is your wife a nurse, sir? That's unusual."

"It is rather. I have a lot of respect for Sergeant Barforth's opinion, Ensign, and he tells me you're my kind of junior officer. I'm looking forward to getting to know you better. Try to sleep, I'll be back later."

***

Manson led his men through the streets of Elvas towards the tavern. Behind them they could hear the sounds of the 115th being lined up in the square. It was unlikely that the citizens of Elvas would do much to shield them. There had been no shots fired, so Manson presumed that the men were cooperating. He was not surprised. The 115th had become accustomed to pushing around a few young and inexperienced officers, but Manson did not think they would stand up to the veterans of the 110th, and if any of them tried they were going to quickly regret it.

"How do you want to do this, sir?" Hammond asked.

"We'll give them a chance to come quietly, Sergeant, although I'm not optimistic. I want our six best shots concealed about the place. They can't aim at us easily; they've only got muskets and we have rifles. If they start shooting, give the order to take them down. I'm hoping it doesn't come to that."

"So do I, sir, since if it's me giving that order it'll be because you've been shot."

Manson gave a crack of laughter. "I'm aiming not to. The rest of the men will be armed and ready and visible, half at the front and half at the back. If they come out with their hands up, we disarm them and march them up to join the others."

"And what if they stay right where they are and tell us to piss off, sir?" Hammond asked quietly.

"Then Corporal Blake is going to stand out here bellowing orders very noisily about getting the Colonel and some more men down here. Meanwhile you, me, Dawson and Cooper are going in whichever way we can and dealing with them without further ado. At that point, they're going to get hurt. My aim is to make sure that nobody else in there gets hurt either. In fact..."

Manson broke off as an idea came to him. Hammond studied him with deep misgiving. "I absolutely hate it when you look like that," he said. Manson grinned.

"I know you do, Sergeant, your face says it all. I've had an idea."

"That was what I was afraid you were going to say."

Manson laughed. "Just looking after the locals, Sergeant. Right, get the marksmen into position out of sight. Keep the others back for a bit. I'm going in there alone."

"You are fucking not, sir."

186

"Don't swear at the officers, Hammond. I'm going to ask, very innocently, where I can find their officers. I'll have a friendly chat with them and tell them I've a message for their officers about where Lord Wellington wants them, doing my best to look very wide-eyed and naive. Do you think I can still manage that?"

"No," Hammond said without hesitation. "You were very good at it for the first three months, sir, but you look as disreputable as the rest of us now. Have you seen the state of your uniform? It's got holes in it."

"They match the holes in me. At least this will give me a chance to see how many there are and what civilians are involved."

"And you think they're going to let you walk out of there?"

"They might, Hammond. They've not slaughtered all their officers and deserted they've only gone after the ones trying to enforce a bit of discipline. I reckon army life has been good to these men so far. I'll guarantee they've been robbing both the locals and their fellow soldiers blind ever since they joined. Going to war is going to spoil that, so they're likely to want to know what my message is all about. After that it depends on how stupid they are. If they've any sense, they're going to run for it, they must know the game is over once the rest of the army gets involved. I'm hoping they'll wait for me to leave and then try to get out the door before I come back with reinforcements."

"At which point, we can take them. It's not a bad plan, sir, but there is a very large risk that you'll end up dead or injured."

"It might save some lives."

"It's probably not going to save yours, sir."

"I'll be sensible."

Hammond gave a derisive snort which Manson thought he might have copied from Paul. "Pull the other one, sir, it's got bells on it."

"Well muffle them, Sergeant, this is supposed to be an ambush."

"If the Colonel was here..."

"He would tell me to do it, Hammond," Manson said flatly. "He couldn't go in himself because they know him, but I'd be his next choice."

"That's because you're as stupid as he is. All right, sir. Let me get them into position. Is your pistol loaded?"

"Did you actually ask me that question?"

"Sorry. I'm a bit distracted."

With the men in place Manson walked to the door of the inn. He found himself in a smoky but pleasant tap room. There was a bar at one end and a plump man was standing behind it. Around the room were a variety of wooden tables and benches. Two of them were occupied by eight men of the 115th, most with their coats off. Jugs of ale and wine were scattered around, and two of the men were smoking pipes. One of them had a girl on his lap. All Manson could see of him was the back of his head, as his face was hidden in her bared breasts. She sat immobile, her bored expression suggesting that this was trade rather than an assault. Manson looked over at the barman. He looked nervous and unhappy.

"Good afternoon, I wonder if you can help me?" Manson said brightly. "Looking for your commanding officer. Can you tell me...?"

"Who the bloody hell are you?" a man said, getting up. Immediately the lounging men were coming to their feet, all apart from the one with the girl. The leader, whom Manson guessed was Jagger from Paul's description, glared across at him.

"Ferrars, put that bloody whore down. We've a visit from an officer."

Manson studied them, thinking that they were wary and on edge. He guessed that their encounter with Paul in the square yesterday had rattled the more timid of them. He glanced across again at the barman and gave a cheerful smile.

"Just looking for directions," he said. "Captain Manson, 112th. I've a message from Lord Wellington for your commanding officer but I don't know where he's billeted."

Jagger was studying him. "112th? I thought that uniform was for the 110th?"

"They're the same. We serve with them, the Colonel thinks it makes life easier. Do you know men in the 110th, Private?"

He could sense the man relaxing slightly. "Ran into somebody, no more. You'll be wanting the monastery for the officers. Up this road, through the main square and go up the hill on your right, it's at the top."

"Sounds like a trek in this weather. Still, I'm not risking my horse on these cobbles more than I need to, I can't afford a new one. Ah well. Thank you, Private."

He nodded and was amused when Jagger sketched a salute in response. Manson turned towards the door to leave, his senses alert to the slightest sound. He heard it easily in the silent room and reflected that Jagger could have covered it if he had carried on talking. Putting his hand to his pocket he drew the pistol, swung around and fired in one motion at the man by the window who had lifted his musket to his shoulder.

Manson had known he would have no time to reload, but he did not expect to need it now that the shot had been heard outside. He drew his sword and stood, balanced and waiting. None of the other men had a loaded weapon and Manson did not think any of them was sober enough to load one in time to threaten him.

"You're under arrest for mutiny, lads. What happens next is up to you," he said clearly. "If you put your weapons down and line up over by that wall, your cooperation is duly noted. If you don't, you're probably going to die."

He could sense three or four waverers. Jagger was not one of them. Manson saw his hand moving towards his coat. "You reach for a gun or a knife, Jagger, and you're going to lose that hand, I'm not pissing about here. And the rest of you move. Now!"

"You can't take us all," Jagger said.

"Jesus, you are stupid, aren't you?" Manson said. Jagger moved and Manson leaped forward and placed his sword at the man's throat. "You move and you're dead."

"How's it going, sir?" a voice said from behind him, and Manson was suddenly aware of weapons being dropped or deposited on tables which suggested that Hammond was probably holding a rifle on the men. He lowered his sword and stepped back, and Hammond came forward. Behind him were Cooper and Dawson. Cooper had his rifle trained on the men as they scrambled awkwardly into line.

188

"All right, thank you, Sergeant. Dawson, check them for any hidden weapons and get them outside, will you? I don't want to frighten these people any more than I need to." Manson glanced over at the men. "Don't try anything stupid unless you want to find yourself dead, you've got the Light Division's finest lined up out there. And they've got rifles, not muskets, they are not going to miss. Get going."

He turned back to Jagger. Hammond was methodically checking him for weapons. He removed a knife and a pistol and jerked his head. "Outside," he said. Jagger moved sullenly. Hammond looked at Manson who grinned.

"I'm sorry, Sergeant, did I worry you?"

"Leo, at some point when I've got time, I'm going to bloody punch you for that!" Hammond said in matter of fact tones and slung his rifle over his shoulder. "Did you kill him?"

Manson glanced over at the man slumped against the wall. "Yes."

"You checked?"

"No. Get two of the men to carry him outside, will you, Jamie? Can't leave him here to upset the ladies. Of whom I suspect there are a fine collection here."

Hammond grinned. "Nice billet to choose," he said.

"What is going on?"

All three men turned. A girl was coming down the stairs. Her eyes were wide with fright. She was dressed in an elaborately frilled garment which displayed a good deal of her attractive figure. It appeared to be slit to the thigh, giving Manson, Hammond and Dawson an excellent view of a pair of long shapely legs as the girl descended. Manson glanced at Dawson.

"Private..."

"On my way, sir," Dawson said resignedly. "Glad I hung around, mind. Come on, you worthless sack of shit, outside."

He shoved Jagger through the door to join the others. Manson bowed politely to the girl. "Nothing to worry about, ma'am. Just getting rid of your unwanted guests for you. I'm assuming they were unwanted."

"Since they did not pay for it, Captain, very much unwanted. Maria, come over here, are you all right?"

The woman who had been sitting on the bench sidled towards the younger girl. There were tears on her plump cheeks. The girl looked at her with some concern, which gave Manson an excellent opportunity to study the girl. It was well worth it. She was small and slender, delicately made, with very long straight dark hair and a pair of wide dark brown eyes. Something about her made him think of Anne van Daan, and he reminded himself to keep that particular comparison to himself given the obvious nature of her profession.

Having spoken a few words in Portuguese to the stricken Maria, the girl dismissed her upstairs and looked across at the man behind the bar. "Are you all right, Emilio?"

The man nodded. His face was white, and the girl moved past Manson and went to him. "Why don't you close up? Nobody will be down today. Tomorrow we might get some customers at last."

He nodded again, and Manson realised he had not heard the man speak yet. Hammond touched him on the arm. "I'll get them marched up to join the others, sir."

189

"Yes, thank you, Sergeant. I'll be there in a few minutes; I just want to make sure they're all right. He doesn't look it to me."

"God love you, sir, you're the only man in the regiment who would have been looking at him at all at this point." Hammond grinned, saluted and left.

The man had gone to the door to close it and lock it behind him. He made a slight awkward bow to Manson and then looked at the ground where Manson had shot the mutineer. There was blood on the floor and he pantomimed mopping it. The girl shook her head.

"Leave it, Emilio, I'll do it. Go and lie down, you've had a shock."

Emilio nodded, bowed again to Manson and mounted the stairs. Manson waited until he heard a door click above.

"What happened to him?" he asked.

"He was tortured by the French. He would not tell them where food was hidden for his wife and children. So they removed his tongue."

"I wondered," Manson said soberly. "His family?"

"Dead."

"Poor man. Is everybody all right? I need to get back, but I wanted to check. We'll be round at some point to find out what they owe the various inns and taverns. There are things the army isn't going to pay for but make up a bill for food and drink. And feel free to bump up the price a little, I'll see it gets paid."

The girl turned in a swirl of dark hair. "It is all right, Captain, I don't expect the army to pay for their soldiers' misdeeds. Some things cannot be paid for anyway. But I'll let you have the bill for the food and drink. They drank a lot."

"I am sorry, ma'am. Really. Was anybody hurt?"

"One of the girls got a few slaps because she objected. I told her to think about something else. It's what we do anyway. No point in putting ourselves at risk."

"Good advice. I'll be on my way. I hope your people recover soon, ma'am. Good afternoon."

Manson was sliding back the first bolt when he heard her laughing, an unexpectedly rich chuckle. He turned in surprise.

"You have genuinely surprised me, Captain. I was very sure you were going to at least ask me my name."

Manson studied her. "I'm sorry, was that rude? I thought you'd probably prefer to see less of a red coat for a while."

"Red coats are our business, Captain. But usually I ask for the money up front."

"And this time?"

"This time I did the same and he threw me across the room and told me if I didn't shut up and take him upstairs, he'd cut my face. I can't afford that."

Manson felt a stab of anger, studying the girl's attractive countenance. "He's going to hang. He has a charge sheet so long it would be hard to know where to start. I've no idea if that helps given what he did to you, but I am sorry. My name is Manson, by the way, Leo Manson. I command the light company of the 110th."

"And how did the 110th come into this?"

"My Colonel was in town, a brief holiday with his wife, she's not been well. He intervened when this lot kicked off at a tavern in town yesterday and Jagger made the mistake of trying to intimidate him."

190

"And your Colonel is not easily intimidated?"

"No. Nor is he stupid. He backed off pleasantly and came back with reinforcements. There'll be one or two trials, but we'll get the rest back."

"Floggings?"

"I hope not. I hate flogging. But if they survive the storming, this lot are in for the shock of their lives, they've been placed under his command. It'll do them good. And I realise I've still not asked your name. My manners are all over the place today. Miss...?"

The girl laughed and came forward, holding out her hand. "I actually can't push you into behaving badly, can I? My name is Diana Pereira."

Manson took her hand and kissed it lightly, releasing it immediately. "Miss Pereira, it's been a genuine pleasure. I hope you don't mind me saying so, but what I'd really like is to buy you a drink and have a conversation with you. I'm very curious. But I can't, I'm on duty. When I can, I'll come back if I may. And I actually do mean that I'd like to have a conversation, by the way. I'd also like to go to bed with you, but you must be used to that, so no need to mention it. You should be all right now, but if you have any further trouble from anybody, will you send your lad over with a message to me at Wellington's lines? We're not hard to find, and I'd be happy to help. Go and see to your people, I suspect you've all had a bad couple of days. Good afternoon."

Manson unbolted the door and went outside, looking back at her before he closed it. "Bolt it," he said quietly. "At least until tomorrow."

"I will." The dark eyes studied him. "You are the strangest man, Captain. But thank you. For the rescue and for the unexpectedly respectful behaviour. I am completely charmed."

Manson bowed. "So am I," he said. "Lock the door."

191

Chapter Fifteen

"We're going to attack," Lord Wellington said.

There was complete silence among the senior officers. Wellington had invited all three brigade commanders from the Light Division. Orders about the storming had not yet been given and with no overall commander until General Alten arrived, Wellington had still not formally announced who would be commanding the Light Division. Paul had no idea what Wellington would do and was not sure what he hoped for. He was torn between ambition and diplomacy. If the upcoming engagement had been on an open field, ambition would have won, but Paul had no particular desire to lead his men into the breach at Badajoz.

Paul glanced over at General Picton and saw from his grim expression that he was not the only person present with doubts. Around the tent nobody spoke, but Paul felt a spurt of exasperated amusement at covert glances coming his way. He was aware that the others were waiting for him to object.

"What does Colonel Fletcher say, sir?" he asked.

"Colonel Fletcher is wounded and about to be transported back to England to recover," Wellington said smoothly. "I have no wish to trouble him."

Paul knew that his incredulity was visible on his face and made no attempt to hide it.

"I know he's wounded, sir. I went in to see him yesterday. In fact, I met you coming out."

"I was enquiring about his health."

"Really? Well I was having a conversation about the breaches, and it's my understanding that…"

"Colonel van Daan." Wellington's voice was suddenly frosty. "I am well aware that you see it as your duty at my briefing sessions to question my every decision. Please desist. We are ready to attack, the breaches will suffice. This is not a debating society. If you don't feel able to take your part in this assault, may I remind you that I have offered you the option to take some leave with your wife. Perhaps her recent ordeal is making it difficult for you to…."

Paul's temper flared at the mention of Anne. Around him he heard a collective intake of breath.

"Did I just hear you correctly, sir?" he cut in, and beside him Colonel Barnard physically jumped at the tone of his voice. "Did you actually just question my ability or my willingness to do my duty because of my wife? Who is, by the way, down in a dressing station barely out of reach of musket fire. Or were you under the impression she'd be lying down with a bottle of smelling salts waiting for me to take her home?"

"You forget yourself, Colonel."

"Very likely, sir. I'm not sure what I'm doing here anyway, I'm only a brigade commander. Why don't I just go back to my officers and make sure they've made their wills and got their affairs in order? You can send a note telling me what your orders are, I don't need…"

"Certainly, I think it might be wise if you left until you are able to control your temper better, Colonel. Please do not go far, however. I will see you in half an hour alone. It is probably not appropriate for me to tell you what I think in front of these gentlemen."

Paul saluted. "I'll be outside when you're ready, sir. Although I'm fairly sure it's not stopped you in the past."

He left and stood outside, breathing deeply. After a moment he moved away from the tent and walked down to where Richard Fletcher, Wellington's chief engineer, was seated in a camp chair outside his tent. The engineer's face was pale and drawn and his feet were up on a padded chest.

"Morning, Richard."

Fletcher's dark eyes surveyed him thoughtfully. "That was a short briefing."

"It is still going on. It won't take much longer though. He's not looking for opinions today."

"He seldom is these days, Paul. He's becoming more autocratic as the days go by."

"Those breaches aren't good enough are they, Richard?"

"They're as good as we can make them in the time we have, Paul. Did he kick you out?"

"Yes. He wants me back in a minute to give me a bollocking in private. I lost my temper a bit, but to be honest, so did he."

"He doesn't want to do it, Paul."

"So why is he?"

Fletcher took out a silver enamelled snuff box and offered it to Paul who smiled and shook his head. Fletcher laughed and took a pinch.

"I forget you don't indulge, Colonel. You don't smoke, either do you? Or drink to excess. I've often wondered…"

"No you haven't, Richard, the entire army is well aware what my prevailing vice is, they made enough of it before I married."

Fletcher gave a choke of laughter and held his wound. "Don't make me laugh, it kills me."

"Still bad?"

"Yes, but your wife was wonderful, she probably saved my life. I thought they'd got everything out, but she went back in and found a tiny piece of metal left and since then it's been a lot better. Daniels says she's the most patient surgeon they have when it comes to extracting shot. I'll mend, there's no sign of infection now. But

I've no mobility and won't have for a while so Lord Wellington suggested I go home for a few months. He's been very good about it."

"I notice he's not sent you home until this bloody siege is over, mind," Paul said.

There was movement from the command tent and Paul turned and sighed. "I'd better get back and take my medicine," he said. "Sometimes I'm very tempted just to tell him where to stick it, to be honest."

"You won't, though, Colonel."

"I hope not. But it does piss me off sometimes. We all know it's my job to raise the questions nobody else will ask him; I've been doing it since I was twenty-one. I wish somebody else would take a turn. I miss Craufurd for that, at least he wasn't scared to say if he thought Wellington was getting it wrong."

Paul walked back up to Wellington's tent, acknowledging the sympathetic smiles of the officers leaving. At the flap he smiled at the orderly.

"Does his Lordship still want to see me, Sam?"

"Is that Colonel van Daan, Sergeant? Will you send him in, please?"

Paul ducked into the tent and moved to stand before his chief, saluting. Wellington surveyed him across his folding desk and Paul did not speak. The silence lengthened. Eventually, Wellington said:

"Sergeant?"

"My Lord?" The orderly ducked back into the tent and saluted.

"How many of the commanders are hanging around outside listening?"

Sergeant Hanly turned to look. "A lot of them, my Lord."

"It is interesting how very enthusiastic they all are to hear me lose my temper with somebody other than them," Wellington said scathingly. "Sit down, Colonel."

Paul complied, still not speaking and his chief studied him for a moment and then gave a small wintery smile. "Too early for brandy, Colonel?"

"Yes."

"I am not going to get a sensible word out of you until I've apologised, am I?"

"You don't need to apologise for bollocking me, sir, it's my job to put up with that. But you crossed a line."

"Your wife. I'm sorry, I lost my temper. I seem to be doing it a lot at present."

Paul studied him and relented. "I've been fairly pissed off myself, sir, to tell you the truth. It's not been my best year so far. And it's not looking to get much better this week."

Wellington studied him. "I'm going to delay it for twenty-four hours," he said quietly.

"Is that for me to put my affairs in order, sir?"

"No, you insubordinate young whelp, it's to see if we can create a third breach, we're very close. As you probably already know, Richard Fletcher gave me the same advice. I'll write the orders. But after that we need to go in, Soult is on his way."

Paul studied his chief for a moment then walked to a chest and returned with the brandy. "I thought it might be that," he admitted. "But sir, why can't you just tell them that instead of starting to yell every time somebody asks you a question? You're getting worse."

"Colonel, if I shared every aspect of intelligence in here with them, we would be arguing until midnight. They're not all like you. Surprisingly you don't take advantage of your somewhat privileged position with me."

Paul poured two cups and passed one to Wellington. "Don't I?" he said with a grin.

"Possibly with regard to helping yourself to my brandy," Wellington amended. He seemed to have relaxed. "I don't like this any more than you do. We could have done with another week or two at least. But if Soult gets here and relieves the town, we're going to lose another campaigning season. I pushed my army through winter to get this border secured. I'm not retreating now."

Paul studied for a long moment. "All right. What are my orders?"

"When this interview is over I will be writing all the orders. Fitzroy will let you have them."

Wellington waited and Paul did not take the bait. After a moment, Wellington gave a snort. It was one of his more amiable sounds.

"How disappointing, Colonel. I was sure you would react; you must have been practising restraint in your spare time. I originally intended to have you command the Light Division going over the breach but I'm putting Barnard in command instead."

"I'm happy with that, sir. Do we go in brigade order again?"

"Not this time. The third brigade is not going over with the rest of the division."

Paul stared at him. "You're keeping us in reserve?" he said quietly, trying not to overreact.

Unexpectedly Wellington laughed aloud and sipped his brandy. "I am tempted to say yes, just to test your restraint," he said. "No, Colonel, you're going over by escalade. I'm using the fourth division and the Light Division to scale the breaches. The Portuguese will mount two false attacks as a distraction. I'm also putting in three subsidiary attacks elsewhere – Leith's over at the San Vincente and Picton's third division and your brigade by escalade at different points."

"Do you know where?"

"Where do you think would be most effective?" Wellington asked.

"I'm not sure. Mind if I talk to Fletcher about it?"

Wellington smiled grimly. "As if you wouldn't," he said. "I'm ordering the attack for tomorrow night. We'll keep up the bombardment until just before we go in to make sure they cannot effect repairs. May I infer that you are happy with my orders, Colonel?"

Paul gave a twisted smile. "You didn't make this decision to make me happy, sir, you'd already made it."

"I was testing the waters. We can afford one more day, I think. It might make a difference."

"Sir, I'm never happy about storming a town, that's not actually the joke I make it. But this is an interesting assignment. Philippon's garrison must be stretched very thin, they're not going to be able to defend their position everywhere. They'll concentrate their efforts on the main breaches with a skeleton defence around the ramparts and bastions. With your permission I'll talk to Fletcher and then come back to you. In the end it's your decision where we go in. But I have some ideas."

"If you can give me a good reason, Colonel, you can have your way." Wellington drank. "There's a reason your brigade is doing this, and it's very much the same reason as you were first over the Douro at Oporto. I need men in there who will hold their nerve. Don't let me down. If those breaches go wrong, I will need you."

"Do the others know this?"

"Not all of it."

"Did you stage that fit of temper earlier?"

His chief gave a sardonic smile. "Colonel, it is never hard to lose my temper with you. I simply have to stop restraining myself. Get out of here and send Fitzroy in. Go and see Fletcher and then get on with your reconnaissance, I'll see you back here first thing tomorrow with a plan. And I'm sorry I said what I did about your wife earlier."

"Well you certainly got the reaction you wanted, sir. You'd better hope I don't tell her about it, she's already bored with hearing people whisper as she walks past."

Wellington did not speak for a moment. When he did, his voice was flat. "Nothing I said suggested any disrespect for your wife, Paul, and you ought to know that."

"I do," Paul said, getting up. "I just wanted to remind you that you're not the only one who knows exactly where to set the fuse and light the touch paper, sir. You and I have known each other for a long time now."

"It is not your job to antagonise me, Colonel, it's your job to follow my orders."

"And when don't I? I'll see you in the morning."

He spent the day encircling the town on horseback with Jenson at his heels, careful to stay out of range of the guns. On 25th March, just as Paul had returned from his brief trip to Elvas with Anne, Picton's third division had successfully stormed the outwork at Fort Picurina with losses of around three hundred dead and wounded. Since then, the French had made several raids to attempt to destroy the lines advancing towards the curtain wall but were fought off by the men of the 110th, 112th and 95th who were guarding the works.

With Fort Picurina captured, it was possible to dig more extensive siege earthworks, and the arrival of heavier howitzers enabled Wellington to set up an intensive bombardment of the town's defences. As the cannons blasted away at the stonework a maze of trenches crept ever closer to the walls. Two breaches had been created by 5th April, and a third, on a poorly constructed wall between the two, was being made with deafening gunfire as Paul rode slowly around the walls before returning to Fletcher's tent to look again at his plans and maps.

"What are you thinking, Paul?" Fletcher asked. He had retreated in pain again to his bed, watching as Paul pored over the maps.

"Leith is going to hit the San Vincente bastion by the river, and Picton is going in by escalade over near the San Pedro. The wall along by the San Vincente is tempting but I gather it's mined."

"It is."

"Well I'm not risking that, not after Ciudad Rodrigo. But there's an area here, close to the San Jose, where I suspect the wall isn't as high as it looks. They'll have put defences in place, no question about it, but if we let Leith hit first, he'll distract them. They'll expect us to go in hard at the breaches, but they'll expect us to spread out our other attacks fairly evenly. So I want to follow Leith in, if Wellington agrees. I can use his assault as a screen and see if I can get enough of my lads over that wall."

Fletcher was studying him. "And then?"

"If I get them in there, Richard, the French will have something other to do than slaughter our lads in the breaches, I'll have those guns shut up in minutes. Wellington's not stupid. He knows we'll stand in the breach, but he also knows we can be a lot more use elsewhere. Poor Barnard. He's actually happy about getting command of that slaughterhouse, it makes me want to cry. Me, I'd rather be doing something other than using my lads as cannon fodder."

Fletcher gave a slight smile. "Wellington thought about putting you in reserve," he said quietly.

Paul shot him a startled glance. "Did he? You know, I did wonder. He was bloody odd at that briefing meeting. What the hell have I done to piss him off?"

Fletcher laughed. "It's not that, Paul. He knows this has the potential to be a slaughterhouse. He'll do it because it's necessary."

Paul shook his head. "He doesn't keep his friends out of danger, Richard, he never has," he said positively. "Christ, you're living proof of that one. He's never hesitated to send me into harm's way before."

Fletcher laughed softly. "You can't think this is about you, Paul?"

Paul stared at him in puzzlement then suddenly understood. "Nan?"

"Yes. He thinks she needs you just now."

Paul could not speak for a moment. It had never occurred to him that Wellington's curious indecision about his role in the storming might have anything to do with Anne.

"I'm glad I didn't know that before," he said finally. "I'd have been furious, and I'd probably have said entirely the wrong thing. Who talked him out of it, Richard, was it you?"

"No, it was Colonel Campbell, I believe. He told Wellington it would be unfair if your career suddenly ground to a halt because of your wife, especially since it wasn't what either of you would have wanted. So Wellington came up with this instead."

"I owe Campbell a drink for that. My poor lass would be horrified if she thought he was trying to keep me safe so as not to upset her."

Fletcher grinned. "Lord Wellington is utterly devoted to your wife, Colonel."

"I know, he doesn't even try to hide it. She's attached to him as well, but she would hate to think their friendship was having a detrimental effect on my career."

"How is she?" Fletcher asked.

"She's recovering," Paul said. He was not comfortable talking of Anne's ordeal, but he and Fletcher had been close since they had worked together on Torres Vedras, and he knew the engineer's concern was genuine. "She seems very well most of the time but she dreams."

He broke off, not wanting to say more about Anne's night terrors. All he could do was hold her in helpless sympathy and anger until they passed. He wished, at those moments, that Dupres was alive again so that he could kill him more slowly.

"And how are you?" Fletcher asked quietly.

197

"All right, I suppose. I'm just really jumpy with her. It's hard to let her out of my sight, and I can't stand her wandering about alone. I'd got my junior officers on a rota finding excuses to accompany her but it only took three days before she worked that out and I got a bollocking that Wellington would have enjoyed. She won't let me curtail her freedom and she's right, but Christ, I worry."

"I'm not surprised. Honestly, Paul, no other officer's wife does what she does, it would frighten the life out of me."

"It's worse at the moment because Teresa, her maid, is about to give birth and can't run around with her. I've got Keren Trenlow playing shepherd as much as possible, but it's not really fair on her or on Carl." Paul shook his head. "Enough of my nervous disorders, I'm sure they'll pass. What do you make of this? Will he go for it?"

"Yes, I think he will. I wish I could be out there to help with this, Paul. My engineers will be there to guide them through the defences, but…"

Paul walked over and sat down beside the bed. "Richard, step back. You almost died out there in those damned trenches, it's a bloody miracle it wasn't worse than this. Christ, I remember all those years ago when I was wounded at Assaye. And then at Talavera – lying back in bed half dead worrying about transport and food supplies and a whole lot of other things I could do nothing about." He grinned suddenly. "And about the lovely Mrs Carlyon who had been left behind by her bloody husband when he went south with a supply column and who was wandering about my lines as if she was completely invincible. I was terrified for her."at'

Fletcher laughed. "Even back then, Paul?"

"From the day I met her, if I'm honest, Richard. Not that I needed to worry on that occasion, by the time we marched back to Lisbon she'd got my regiment so firmly wrapped around her elegant finger that they'd have died for her to a man."

"Not much changes. I don't think you need to worry about her in our lines, Paul, she's well liked. Do you want a piece of advice?"

"You say that so warily, Richard. Am I that bad?"

"Well as you said, you're a bit jumpy. And with good reason. Find her an orderly. You've got Jenson."

"She needs another maid…"

"I'm not talking about a maidservant, I'm talking about a man you can trust. Someone who can ride and act as groom to her. Make it his full time job to look after her. And then tell her why you need this. Otherwise, you're going to go into every battle with half your mind on her, and that's not good."

Paul studied his friend for a long moment. "Thank you," he said abruptly. "That's good advice, Richard, and I'll give it serious thought. I'm going back to talk this through with my officers and then I'll take it to Wellington. May I borrow this map? I'll bring it back."

"Be my guest," Fletcher said.

Paul explained his plan to Wellington the following morning and was aware from the gleam of interest in his chief's hooded blue eyes that he had caught his attention. He examined the map and barked a series of short, intelligent questions at Paul and then looked up at him.

"Very well, Colonel, you've leave to go ahead. I'll give Leith his orders."

"I'll talk to him as well, sir, we'll need to get the timing right."

"We're going in at ten o'clock."

"I'll go and let my officers know. Thank you, sir."

With his preparations made and his men alerted, Paul went to find Anne awaiting him in their tent. It was an accepted practice that his officers and men left them alone for an hour or two before he went to speak to his men and check their final preparations before battle. They lay together on the mattress after making love, kissing gently, speaking little. Eventually Paul stirred reluctantly.

"I need to go, Nan."

"I know. I'll get down to the hospital," Anne said in matter of fact tones. She slipped from the bed and Paul lay still for a moment longer, watching her as she dressed in the plain dark gown and white apron she wore when working. She went to get a clean shirt for him, laying it across a camp chair and he found himself smiling at the incongruity of it since he would be filthy before the end of the night. They had developed a familiar routine before he went into battle and Paul wondered if fussing over his clothing and equipment helped her in these last difficult moments. It definitely helped him.

When he was dressed, he took her into his arms and kissed her for a long time. They went outside where his officers and men were making their preparations for battle. Paul looked up at the walls of the town, still under heavy bombardment. Wellington would not halt the guns until he was ready to move in, to give the French no time to attempt repairs on the breaches, but Paul knew that the French would see what was going on in the lines and would be working frantically to put in place what defences they could, including possibly mining the main breaches. Paul was briefly and passionately grateful that his men would not be going over the walls in the most vulnerable spot.

"Are you all right, Colonel?" Anne said quietly and he turned to her and pulled her close to him.

"I am, girl of my heart. Get yourself down to your tent, Daniels will be waiting for you. I'll see you after the battle. Don't worry about me, I'll be fine."

She smiled, her heart in her eyes. "I know you will. You'd better not show up on a stretcher or you'll be in big trouble."

"I love you, Nan."

"I love you too, Paul."

He watched her go and then turned and saw Keren Trenlow break away from Carl's arms and run to join her, falling in beside her to walk down to the medical tent. Conscious of the missing third person Paul looked over and saw Sergeant-Major Carter in line, his face paler than usual, set in grim lines. Paul understood suddenly and walked to join him.

"Where's Teresa, Danny?"

"In labour, sir."

"Oh, bloody hell. That is not good timing."

"She's all right, sir. Maggie Bennett and Sally Stewart are with her and they'll call your lady at need."

"Carter, there is no way on God's earth you can concentrate on fighting a battle with your lass…"

"Yes, I can, sir. It's what I do." Carter gave a grim smile. "It's what we all do. Were you there when William was born?"

"No."

"Well then, sir. I hate leaving her, but she understands. And it's her first, it'll be hours. I might make it back in time."

Paul heard the tension in Carter's voice and knew his unspoken fear that he might not make it back at all to make the acquaintance of his first child. Paul sought for words to reassure him but knew that there were none. Carter understood the risk as well as he did. Instead, Paul strove for normality.

"All right, Sergeant-Major. Let's get this over with and see if we can make it so that you see your child born."

Carter gave a tight smile. "Be good if we can, sir."

Around the camp, Wellington's army made its preparations in apparently high spirits. After the delays and frustrations of the past weeks it was a relief that the assault was finally going ahead. Some of these men had taken place in the abortive attempt to storm the town the previous year and most of them had been present at the taking of Ciudad Rodrigo. The Light Division in particular was still mourning General Craufurd, and Paul was ruefully aware that Badajoz had a reputation for being pro-French and unfriendly to British troops in the past. Whether that reputation was deserved or not, he knew that a town taken by storm was seen as legitimate prey by the rank and file and he suspected that the citizens of Badajoz were likely to have a bad time once the British broke through.

He lined up his men and spoke briefly of the coming assault, making sure they understood what he expected of them both during the attack and afterwards. There was little need to remind the men of the 110th and 112th of his rules regarding the civilian population and both his Germans and Portuguese had behaved well at Ciudad Rodrigo but this was likely to be much worse. Paul ran his eyes over the first battalion of the 115th with misgiving. With the worst of the mutineers removed by the provost marshal and the others split up between companies there had been no further trouble during the past week or more, but they were raw troops and this was not an ideal first action for them. They were not yet used to him or his way of doing things and he was aware that for those who survived the assault, temptation was going to prove too much.

He finished his address and ran his eyes over the neat ranks of his men.

"You all know what I've just been through," he said. "Some of you have known my lady since she was a girl of eighteen, first out here. Over those walls, in that town are lassies just like my wife. They're hiding behind walls and they're praying. Not Frenchwomen. Not enemies. Not soldiers or even soldiers' wives. Just girls, doing their needlework, raising their children, living their lives. Don't put any one of them through what my girl has just gone through. Don't turn yourselves into Colonel Dupres. Every single one of you is better than that. You'll have spent blood kicking the French out of this town, I reckon you're owed a good meal and a bottle or two of wine. But you're not brute beasts. If you get tempted down there, think about my wife and be a man."

He stepped back and saluted. They had been instructed not to cheer, so as not to give warning to the French, but he could sense that he had reached them and although not all of them would have heard him, the words would be repeated, whispered back as they marched down to their forming-up point to the west of the town and he hoped that most of them would remember it.

The main Forlorn Hope was due to lead the attack by the fourth division on two of the breaches, while the first two brigades of the Light Division attacked the third breach at ten o'clock. Forming up in silence in the darkness, Paul was conscious of every sound. Over to his left, the men of the light companies of Leith's fifth division should be preparing their ladder parties, as he was, and he was faintly surprised that he could not hear them and wondered if they had been delayed. Even as he thought it, there was the sound of gunfire in the distance and Paul turned and surveyed the walls. No attack should have begun for another fifteen minutes but it was clear that battle had commenced, possibly from the castle on the far side of the town where General Picton's third division was due to make an assault.

"Somebody's watch not working?" Major Swanson said softly.

"Bloody Picton can't tell the time." Paul said. "And where the hell are the fifth, there's no sign of them?"

Johnny Wheeler moved up to join them. "What are we going to do if he's late?" he asked softly.

"We'll wait a bit, but once they hit the breaches I'm going in," Paul said quietly. "I want to go in while they're distracted in the breaches."

Johnny studied his commander through the darkness. "This isn't just a diversionary attack, is it?" he said. "You think we're getting in."

"Not according to the rest of the army, Johnny. But I've never yet gone into battle without the intention of carrying the day, and this is no exception."

They waited in the darkness, listening to the rising sounds of battle and straining to hear sounds from Leith's ladder party. At ten o'clock there was an explosion of sound from the breaches as the fourth and Light Divisions attacked, and Paul looked again at his watch.

"They're lost," he said grimly.

"How the hell did they get lost, it's barely a mile?" Carl said.

"Don't ask me, Major, but unless they've all dozed off, they ought to be here by now. All right, the main attacks are underway. We'll give it another fifteen minutes and then we're going in."

In the main breaches, Wellington's troops made their way forward with scaling ladders and various tools. As the men of the Forlorn Hope were beginning their attack, a French sentry was alerted and raised the alarm and within seconds the ramparts were filled with French soldiers, who poured a lethal hail of fire into the troops at the base of the breach. The British and Portuguese surged forward and raced up to the wall, facing a devastating barrage of musket fire, supplemented by grenades, stones, gunpowder barrels and bales of burning hay to light the action. The destructive barrage devastated the British soldiers at the wall and the breach soon began to fill with dead and wounded, hampering the attacking troops who had to climb over their own men to continue the attack.

Fletcher's guiding engineering officers were shot down early and in the rubble and the darkness, the first two brigades of the Light Division became confused. So many officers were killed or wounded in the first rush, they lacked leadership and were quickly mixed up with the fourth division, wasting time and ammunition attacking an outlying ravelin which led nowhere.

With the sounds of battle filling the air Paul looked over at Johnny and nodded. "All right, we're going in. Carter, pass the orders back quietly. No sign of life over here, I'm hoping they're looking the other way but they're up there, trust me. Let's get those ladders to the front."

Following their officers, the third brigade moved quickly and quietly over the ground with the ladder parties at their head. Each group had been given very specific instructions about the placement of the ladders and Paul watched approvingly as they ran down towards the ditch.

He had given orders for them to pause at the edge and the men of the 110th and 112th light companies moved ahead throwing lighted bales of hay into the darkness. The flames lit up the ditch garishly and Paul's sharpshooters dropped into position, rifles pointed at the battlements. There were shouts in French from the ramparts as the French realised that their section of the wall was under attack and Paul surveyed the ditches in the flare of the bales.

"Chevaux de frise," he said in matter-of-fact tones. "Major Swanson, keep up that fire. Get the lads to take down as many as you can while we're hanging around. Skirmish formation – one fires and when the French fire back the other shoots at the flash. Ten minutes of that should keep them busy. Hammond, get me some volunteers to go down and haul those bloody things out of the way the minute the flares go out. Preferably men who can see in the dark and have a brain."

Above in the darkness the fire from the defenders was increasing and Paul kept a wary eye on the range as a dozen men scrambled quietly down into the blackness of the ditch armed with ropes to drag the chevaux de frise out of the way. In the distance the noise of battle had grown louder and Paul wondered how the rest of the division was doing in the breaches.

There was a sudden explosion of light and sound and screams of pain from a section of his men and he swore softly.

"They're onto us," he said, and raised his voice. "Hammond, how's it going?"

"Nearly there, sir, we've three men down but they saw us too late."

"Good news." Paul turned to yell orders and his brigade, silent and still in the night, exploded into sudden action. More hay bales were lit and in the flare of their light he looked down and saw the path through the ditch was clear.

"Advance!" he yelled, and the ladder parties scooped up their burdens again and continued their run under covering fire from the rifles of his sharpshooters.

Paul had known that the chances were high that the ladders would be too short to reach the top of the wall for most of its length but one stretch of the curtain wall was much lower, having been previously damaged and not built back up to its full height. It was to the right of his position and the risk of mining was higher, but if he could get a small force up onto the ramparts there, they could hit the defenders in the flank and distract them for long enough to allow the ladder parties to scramble up.

On his orders, his men advanced in immaculate formation. He had sent his light companies ahead to continue their skirmishing, giving covering fire to the ladder parties. Paul's previous experience of storming a wall was that darkness and lack of information tended to mean that the assault disintegrated into chaos very quickly.

There was no way of knowing for sure what defences were in place but away from the main assault, he had time to minimise the risk to his men by taking the attack slowly and methodically and making use of his skirmishers who had rifles and considerable skill. He had seen the French use the technique of firing at their opponent's musket flash both at Ciudad Rodrigo and in the trenches during the previous siege at Badajoz and during the run up to this assault, Sergeant Hammond and Sergeant Stewart had their men out most nights practicing the skill on individual defenders on the walls. His sharpshooters liked a new challenge and they had got surprisingly good.

The main ladders were swung up to the walls with men below steadying them to give maximum height and support, and his men swarmed up at speed. Above him, Paul heard cries in both English and French as the first men reached the top and he realised with a spurt of triumph that the ladders had reached and that his men were fighting at the top. Already bodies were falling and he knew some of them would be English. With the defenders busy he turned and called out to Carl, who began his run towards the lowered section of the wall with his chosen companies.

It was going well. Paul's men were following orders and although many of them were coming down off the ladders, they were replaced immediately by more scrambling up. The sounds from the breaches had faded from his consciousness now that his brigade was engaged and he waited for another ten minutes then moved forward.

"All right lads, I'm going up."

"Not yet, sir…"

"Out of the way, Mr Heron before I kick you. Don't worry, I'm not going to stand at the top waving a flag."

There was laughter amidst the blood and fire and slaughter and Paul set his foot on the ladder and began to climb. Shot rained around him but he kept his body close in and was making good progress when his foot encountered a rung which felt unexpectedly shaky and he heard, from above, a yell of warning and then cries of fear.

"It's breaking up!"

Paul swore. He could feel the wood giving way under the weight of men. It often happened and he knew the danger of falling onto the bayonets of the men below him. Pushing himself back he jumped into thin air and braced himself. The leap took him over the heads of the men below him and back to the edge of the ditch. He felt the impact jar through his body and he rolled over and slid back down into the ditch, feeling the bodies of injured and dead men crashing around him. As he came to a halt something ripped into his hip and he dug his heels into the ground hard to stop his slide and found himself crushed by a press of fallen men into the edge of one of the chevaux-de-frise which had been dragged out of the way earlier.

Cautiously Paul struggled to his feet, feeling pain sweeping through his hip and leg. He eased himself out from between bodies, hearing the groans of injured men and scrambled over them, steadying himself on a man's shoulder.

"Oh God," the man whispered.

Paul stopped and bent over him, gently rolling him over. He recognised him with a stab of pain, as Corporal Finney from the 110th second company, and the man's arm was a shattered mess. Paul stooped and lifted him up, stepping over dead and dying men and back into the darkness of the ditch. He laid Finney down on the grass and reached into his coat, taking out the thin scarf which he always carried into battle. He twisted it hard around the wound to stop the bleeding.

"Corporal Finney, can you hear me?"

"Sir – yes, sir."

"Right. You stay here and you bloody well stay alive, is that clear? Once we're in I'm coming back for you and my wife will sort you out. Don't die on me, that's an order."

"Yes, sir."

"You'll be all right, lad. I'll be back."

Paul rose and as he did, he heard frantic cries from up the bank and on the ladders.

"He went down, sir, I'm going back down to look for him. There's a pile of bodies down there…"

Paul winced and pressed a hand to the wound on his hip. It was bleeding sluggishly but he could walk and his leg felt steady enough. Climbing back up the slope he took a breath to call out and then heard sounds from above, French voices and what sounded like laughter.

"Come into Badajoz, Englishmen," a heavily accented voice mocked. "Come and see what else we have for you. Your Colonel is dead and you will soon join him you English…"

Paul took a deep breath. "Carter, do me a favour and shoot that fucking Frenchman's head off, he's pissing me off!" he bellowed, and from above on the ladder there was a loud cheer. Paul scrambled up the slope then ducked back as a hail of musket fire sought him out. It was a mistake, the flashes identified the shooters and he heard the crack of his rifles, silencing the fire. Paul arrived at the foot of one of the other ladders.

"Can anybody tell me who made these bloody ladders? I am nailing his balls over the top of the gates of Badajoz when I catch up with him," he said. "You all right up there, Carter?"

"I am now, sir, going back up."

Paul set his hand on the ladder, and there was a sudden furious burst of firing from his right at the top. He heard Johnny's voice calling.

"Sir, they're over. Carl's companies are up. And the 115th are on their way."

Paul gave an answering shout and took hold of the ladder. As he did so there was a voice calling his name and he turned and saw one of Lord Wellington's young ADCs approaching.

"Ensign Beaumaris, what news?"

"Hoping for good news from you, sir."

"We're on the ramparts, I'm just going up," Paul said. He studied the young smoke blackened face. "The breaches?"

The boy shook his head. "Sir, they've been repulsed. Huge losses. They keep going back but they're getting nowhere, Lord Wellington is going to tell them to withdraw, they can't take this punishing. I'm just going over to the castle to see how General Picton…"

"Van Daan!"

204

The yell came from the left. Paul swung around and saw men running forward, swinging up ladders towards the bastion. "Leith's light companies," he said. "They must have found a bloody map. Get over to Picton, lad, see how he's doing. But you give Lord Wellington my compliments and tell him we're up and over and in about twenty minutes the lads in those breaches are getting some help. Just hang on. Go!"

The man turned to ride on and reined in as another rider approached. Paul recognised him through the gloom. "Tyler? Is that you?"

"Yes, sir, I'm on my way over to Lord Wellington. General Picton's men are inside the castle."

Paul froze and looked at Wellington's ADC. "Jesus Christ, we're going to do it," he breathed. "And thank God for it because I do not want to have to do this again anytime soon. Get over to Wellington, lad, and tell him to hold on, Leith's men will be over in a minute and we'll clear the ramparts and go through…"

The explosion came from nowhere, causing both horses to rear frantically and knocking Paul off his feet. He lay still for a moment, earth and rock showering around him, and then was up, scrambling to his feet.

"Get moving, both of you!" he yelled to the two messengers and was running forward into smoke and flame and confusion, hearing screams of agony and the cries of dying and injured men.

"What the fuck happened? Somebody talk to me!"

The chaos was coming from his right although the shock of the blast had brought down one of the ladders and those of his men who had survived the fall were scrambling up, trying to help injured comrades. He could see nothing to his right but smoke and flames and he ran forward yelling. A man stumbled out of the chaos and Paul caught him as he fell, his face and body burned and blackened. He tried to speak but no coherent words came out. Paul lowered him to the ground and knelt, but he was already dead, and Paul peered through the darkness and assimilated the thin face of Major Stead of the 115th.

"No," he said softly, getting to his feet. "No.   Oh Christ…"

He was running forward into a scene of horror and carnage. Burned and blackened bodies lay twisted together, some of them unrecognisable, with limbs completely blown off. Looking down at a horrible sound he saw a man trying to drag himself along, sobbing in agony, his face and body black and the ruined and bloody stumps of both legs dragging behind him. Beyond was devastation. The low curtain wall was in ruins and smoke was rising from the piled bodies and Paul felt his stomach churn in horror.

"Carl," he whispered. "Oh please God, no…"

He began to run forward again, understanding now. The inexperienced troops of the 115th, carried away by the success of the escalade and wanting their share of the glory, had swung too far to the right to scale a section of the curtain wall which he had known to be mined. The mine had exploded and the 115th had been blown apart, their bodies lying in the twisted ruins of the wall. Above them the bastion previously taken by Carl's storming party from the 110th sagged dangerously.

"Sir, get back from there, it's going to come down."

Paul felt a hand on his arm and turning, saw Captain Manson, his face blackened and filthy, his eyes wide with horror. "Leo," he breathed. "Jesus, your lads...."

"We're all right. Major Swanson is all right, he's inside, we got over before it blew. But these poor lads."

Paul felt a treacherous relief flood through him and felt immediately guilty. "No time now, Captain. Let's get over. They need our help over at the breaches."

In the main breaches, the fourth and light divisions had hurled themselves again and again into the darkness and chaos and they lay dying in their hundreds, mown down by endless volleys and shrapnel from grenades and bombs. The French were growing in confidence as they held off the assault and the British were becoming exhausted. In just under two hours, some two thousand men had been killed or badly wounded at the main breach and those officers left to lead them were in despair, yelling themselves hoarse trying to take their men back for one more try.

Fighting their way along ramparts and narrow cobbled streets of Badajoz, the men of the third brigade met General Picton's third division who had lost hundreds of men during their assault on the castle. Behind them came the remains of Leith's light companies who had taken the San Vicente bastion with a loss of 600 men to Paul's left. The three forces hit the French defenders in a savage flank attack using bayonet and sword.

There was surprisingly little resistance after the initial shock. General Phillippon did not have enough men to defend the town once the walls were fully breached and with the castle in English hands and the streets swarming with allied troops, the French disintegrated and retreated towards the neighbouring outwork of San Cristobal as the allies overran the defences and took the town in a surge of furious triumph. In the early morning, recognising the impossibility of his position, Phillippon surrendered.

Standing amidst the rubble of the main breach as the sun rose over Badajoz, Paul drew breath, coughing in the thick fog of lingering smoke from muskets and gunpowder. After a long moment, he made himself step forward to look down into the breach and felt his stomach heave at the twisted mass of bodies below, realising for the first time the sickening cost of this victory.

"Colonel."

Paul turned. Carl Swanson was walking towards him, his uniform, face and hair completely black. He was limping slightly. Paul stepped down and went to meet him.

"Carl. I thought you'd gone up with that mine."

Carl indicated his blackened state. "I was too close for comfort," he said wryly. "Jesus, Paul, did any of them survive it?"

"I don't know, lad, I need to get over there and find out." Paul stood still, holding his hand over the wound on his hip which was bleeding sluggishly. Another voice hailed him and he spun around, relieved.

"Johnny. Thank God. I lost track of you."

Wheeler was emerging through the smoke, filthy and drenched. "Glad to see you in one piece, sir."

"You too. Why the hell are you so wet?"

206

"We found a ditch. They'd flooded it. We were up to our necks in filthy water, couldn't see it in the dark."

"Oh bloody hell, did you lose many?"

"I don't think so. Not sure yet, but we were moving very cautiously, skirmishing as ordered. Gervase Clevedon was behind us and realised what was happening. He was so bloody quick, he got half of them giving covering fire and the rest hauled our men out of the water. We did better than the fourth, they had the same problem and lost a fair few to drowning I'm told."

"Is Gervase all right?"

"Yes, sir. But I've lost a dozen officers at least, either dead or wounded. It was bloody awful."

Paul nodded. Around him he could hear rising sounds of splintering glass and the crashing of doors being battered down. "They're rioting," he said.

"They were always going to, Paul," Johnny said. "You're bleeding, what have you done to yourself?"

"It happened when I came down off the ladder, I got caught in a cheval de frise. I hate sieges; I've never yet come out of one unscathed. But this time – dear God, Johnny, our losses are huge. I don't know where to start."

"You need to start by getting yourself up to the surgeon," Wheeler said firmly and Paul shook his head.

"No, I'm all right."

"How the bloody hell do you know without getting it looked at?" Wheeler demanded. "Look, sir…"

"Later, Johnny." Paul raised his voice. "Sergeant-Major Carter. You still alive?"

"Just about, sir. But that was a bloody nightmare, I'm going to remember that one for a long time."

"I'm not sure any of us are going to forget it," Paul said. "Have we got any buglers left?"

"One, sir, although he's wounded."

"Where is he?"

Wheeler looked at Carter and Paul could see the identical expressions in their eyes. He smiled wearily. "You think I'm mad, don't you?"

"Sir, you're not going to get them back. Not after that. They've been given two hours off for plunder, and in two hours time they'll be so drunk…you're not going to get them back."

"Yes, I bloody am, Carter. Who is it? The bugler."

"Freeman, sir. He's over here."

Paul followed his Sergeant-Major. The bugler was young, white faced and bleeding from a savage head wound but as Paul approached, he got to his feet and saluted.

"At ease, Freeman. Lad I'm sorry, you look like hell."

"So do you, sir."

"I feel it. But just at this moment, you and I are the most important men in the third brigade. I'm going to ask you to push yourself. Can you do it?"

"Yes, sir. What do you need me to do?"

"Good lad. All right Sergeant-Major Carter. Where's Hammond?"

"Here, sir." Hammond came forward. Given his apparently suicidal charge of earlier he appeared miraculously uninjured although he was drenched in other men's blood. Seeing Paul's expression, he laughed. "Don't look so shocked, sir. Did you think I'd be off looting already?"

"No, Hammond, you're a sergeant of the 110th. I know you'd wait for my orders to do that. Nearest wine shop?"

Carter shot him a look. "Next street. If you listen, sir, you'll hear that the fourth division have already found it."

"Half the fourth division fell into a ditch and drowned themselves, Carter, they shouldn't be drinking just now. Freeman, get round there with Carter and Hammond. Call them in. Keep calling them. Carter, as soon as you've enough of them, load them up with what they can carry and get them up to the lines. Johnny, Carl, collect as many of your lads as you can and help. If the fourth give you any trouble, thump them. Don't shoot them unless they threaten you, but you can invite them to dinner if you like. As long as they leave Badajoz, I don't care what you say to them."

Carter saluted. "Sir are you telling us to kick the fourth out of the way and loot a wine shop?"

"More than one if you can find it. If my lads are getting drunk, I want them doing it up in the lines. Just at the moment I don't give a damn what they steal as long as we get them out of here."

The sounds around them were rising. Carl looked at his friend. "It isn't going to take long for this lot to get drunk, Paul. And they're mad enough as it is, given what they've just been through. I'll do whatever you want me to, you know that, but if I think this is going to get dangerous, I'm telling you right now that I'm going to hit you on the head and get the lads to carry you out of here."

Paul felt a surge of genuine amusement which he would not have thought himself capable of. "Thanks for warning me, Major, I know to stay out of your way this morning. Who's this, they're ours?"

Two men were running towards him down the narrow street. Coming to a halt they saluted and Paul recognised them under the coating of mud and blood and black powder. "Cooper and Dawson. Jesus Christ, what does it take to kill you two?"

"Captain Manson, sir. He just promised to shoot us if we didn't fall into line."

"God bless Leo. Where is he?"

"Through this way, sir. The church."

"I wouldn't have thought it the time for prayer, but let's go."

He followed Cooper and Dawson through a broken stone arch into a small churchyard and found, to his considerable amusement, that they had not exaggerated. Manson had several dozen men of the light company lined up outside the small white church. Its walls were pitted with shot and several of the windows had been smashed. Paul approached his young Captain who saluted.

"Well done, Captain. Is this all that's left of my light company?"

"No, sir, there are more at the other two doors, guarding them. I've got about half of them still fit to fight and about fifteen wounded that we've found so far. There are a lot of dead. I've never seen so many dead. Those breaches…"

"We'll get to them, Captain. What's in the church?"

208

"Supplies, sir. The French have been using this as a depot. Flour, bread, biscuits and tobacco, and four cages of live poultry. There are also casks of wine, brandy and rum, stacked up right to the ceiling."

Paul met his eyes steadily and began to laugh. "Captain Manson, you are a bloody genius!" he said softly. "Let's get them moving."

"Sir, there are three handcarts we've found. The men have been given leave for two hours, camp, town or wherever else. Most of them will be in the town."

"Not much difference if there's food and liqueur, they might as well be up in camp. Colonel Wheeler, you're in charge here. Get as much of it up to the lines as you can before anybody finds out what we're doing and we need to start fighting our own men. Carl, Leo…"

"I want to get our wounded out," Manson said.

"Do it. If you run into of our brigade, send them down here. Sergeant Hammond, will you stay here with four men. Anybody turns up, load them up with a couple of casks and a bag of bread and send them up to camp. What they do up there is up to them."

"By the time they've walked up there they'll remember what they've just been through and settle down with a bottle and some food," Hammond said quietly.

"That's what I'm hoping, Sergeant. I'm going to go through the streets, to see if I can find any more of our men." Paul had a sudden thought and looked over at his Regimental Sergeant-Major. "Sergeant-Major Carter, I am staring at you and the question I'm asking myself is why the bloody hell are you still here when you need to get your arse up to camp and find out if you're a father yet? Get moving before I start kicking you."

He saw Carter's eyes light up. "Sir?"

"You're relieved of duty. Give her my love and if I'm not named as Godfather I'll take your stripes off you."

He watched as his Sergeant-Major took off at a run and turned to Johnny. Wheeler eyed him. "Paul, if Wellington finds out…"

"If I get my brigade out of here without having to shoot any of them for rape, looting or mutiny, Colonel, I don't give a damn what Wellington says. And I'm going to do it."

Carl gave an exaggerated sigh. "All right, Colonel, I can take an order. But if I end up dead because I've been shot by one of our own in defence of a bunch of Spaniards who made literally no attempt to help us throughout this bloody siege and half of whom were probably hoping the French would win, I am coming back to haunt you. I have actually got something to go back for now, I am not keen on leaving her just yet."

"Duly noted, Major. Get going and take a decent escort with you, don't take risks."

He strode off into the grey morning light and Carl and Johnny stood looking after him.

"Are you all right, Johnny?"

"Yes, I'm fine. Exhausted, but aren't we all? That's the worst I've seen since Assaye. I'm worried about our lads who came down in the assault, some of them will still be alive. But he's right of course, if we can get them out of here before they get

209

too drunk, we'll get them back. Certainly the 110th and probably a fair few of the 112th. I'm not even going near the 115th if any of them survived that mine. They worry me, there will be some of them who hate Paul's guts after that affair in Elvas."

"He's never going to believe that one of his men will take a shot at him, Johnny."

"I doubt one of his men, would, Carl, but not all these are his men. But you're right, he thinks he's bloody invincible. I like the bit where he tells you not to take risks, he was a complete lunatic last night."

Carl gave a wry smile. "You know what, Johnny? He might have been, but his tactics were absolutely bloody brilliant. I've never seen anybody that cool during an escalade. He literally used skirmishers to storm a town and it worked. If the 115th hadn't fucked up so badly we'd have got off very lightly. I'm often impressed with Paul in the field, but last night…"

"I know. I'm so bloody grateful, a lot of our men survived because of him. And it is a good idea to move the party up to the lines. Our lads won't care much where they get drunk as long as they can. Come on, let's get started."

Chapter Sixteen

Within two hours, the ancient city of Badajoz had descended into hell. The men of Wellington's army had suffered horribly during the storming, and they turned quickly into an intoxicated mob who were a danger to themselves, their officers and the hapless inhabitants of the city. Wine and spirit stores were the first target of the rampant soldiers, and once drunk they turned to looting and violence. Men pleading for their lives were shot down without hesitation or beaten to their knees. Children cowered crying in cupboards and under furniture. Women were dragged from every hiding place, sobbing and begging for mercy. There was none. In the hours after the bloody storming of Badajoz, the British army had turned from men into demons.

The officers and NCOs of the 110th and 112th moved through the streets methodically in small groups. To each of them coming to help, Paul had issued the same orders. They were to search for their own men and they were to avoid seeming to give orders or threaten. He was not afraid that the men would turn on their own officers although he was aware that many soldiers did that night. Several officers from other regiments were fired upon when they tried to intervene, and at least one had been killed. His own officers were told to keep calm and pleasant and try to talk their men into returning to camp.

They were, for the most part, successful. Paul had with him Captain Manson and Captain Cartwright along with Sergeants Hammond and Stewart, and Privates Dawson and Cooper who had surprised him by collecting more ammunition for their rifles from the store and returning back to the town after a hasty meal. He realised with some appreciation that they had constituted themselves as his unofficial bodyguard throughout the long day and the sight of their grim, blackened faces caused more than a few drunken infantrymen to back away.

Paul led them first back to the western side of the town. Clambering over the broken walls he surveyed in horror the dead of the 115th lying in twisted, blackened heaps where the mine had exploded. There were no survivors here. Those who lived would be in the town by now, drinking to forget the carnage which must have taken over a hundred officers and men.

Leaving the dead for another day Paul led his helpers back to the ditch behind the ladders then stopped. In the pale early light, a dozen men were toiling through the bodies, all of them from his brigade. A wagon was drawn up on the path above and directing the men as they searched for the living was a slender figure in a dark dress and white apron, her long dark hair pulled up under a scarf. As he approached, she turned and smiled.

"Bonny lass, I'm fairly sure this is somewhere you shouldn't be, they're going wild in there," he said, coming forward.

Anne reached up to kiss his dirty, smoke blackened face. "It's all right, Colonel, I've got bodyguards."

She waved a hand and he looked over and smiled slightly to see half a dozen of his riflemen, weapons ready in their hands. "Yes, you look well protected. I came back to make sure somebody was looking for our wounded but I ought to have known. Have you found Corporal Finney yet? I promised I'd come back for him."

"He's on the wagon. Go up and speak to him." Anne studied him. "You're limping, what have you done?"

"The ladder broke," Paul said succinctly.

"Jesus, Paul, what is it with you and sieges?"

"God knows. I've never yet come through one undamaged, but this isn't too bad, Nan. I want to do a sweep through the town to make sure all my lads are out but then I'll come up to get it looked at."

"Make sure you do."

He kissed her then went up to find Finney stretched out on the wagon. "Glad you followed orders, Corporal."

Finney managed a smile through his agony. "You came back, sir."

"Have you ever known me to break my word, lad?"

"Never, sir."

"Nor will you unless I'm dead. I'm glad my wife got here first, mind, she'll get you looked at."

"I think I'm going to lose my arm, sir."

"You might," Paul admitted. "But our surgeons are the best in the army and you know how good she is at getting men through it. Don't worry about anything, Finney. Let's just get you fit again and then we'll talk about what you do next."

"Didn't do so badly, did we, sir? Lost a few and more wounded, but they're saying it was a lot worse in the breaches."

"It's bloody awful over there, lad, we were better off here."

Finney gave a wheezy sound which Paul recognised was an attempt at a laugh. "The rifles were talking about it earlier. They're all saying it's the first time anybody has tried skirmishing their way through a siege wall, sir."

"Maybe it is, Finney, but it bloody worked, didn't it?" Paul said with a grin. "I need to get off, but I'll be back to see you later."

He walked back to his wife, who was directing two of her assistants to move a corporal with a broken leg. "I need to get back, girl of my heart. Don't take any chances out here, will you?"

"I won't. Once I'm sure we've got our wounded out, I'm going back to the field hospital and I'll work from there. I've been hearing a lot about your tactics last night, Paul. Looking at this, it's a lot better than I thought it would be. Apart from the 115th."

212

Paul pulled a face. "I've no idea how bad that's going to be and I can't face it just now. They were supposed to wait and follow Carl's storming party up but they went too far over. Inexperienced troops and poor leadership. I'm just thankful that Carl's men fought their way through so bloody fast or they'd have gone up with them. Poor bastards. Nan, I sent Carter up…"

She smiled. "And he is the father of a healthy baby girl. They're both very well."

"Thank God. I love you, bonny lass."

"You too, Paul."

Returning to the town, Paul went through the streets methodically, knowing that in other parts of the town Johnny and Carl and his other officers were doing the same. When he came across men of his regiments he would stop to talk, accept a drink, admire whatever plunder they had acquired and then slap them on the back and lead them through the streets to the nearest gate. They went without demur, cheerfully and happily drunk, some of them singing as they made their way up to the lines to continue the party.

Inside the town and castle many animals had been gathered, including sheep, oxen and horses, as Phillippon had hoped they might enable him to hold out for longer. These were herded out and back up to camp and Paul found a contingent of his rifles who were willing, on a promise of brandy, to take a collection of animals back to his lines with instructions to Sergeant Kelly to see to their butchering and roasting for the evening meal. He wondered how Anne was doing. He had seen Dr Norris in the town earlier trying to enlist help with carrying the wounded out to the dressing stations or getting them loaded onto wagons to go to the hospitals in and around Elvas.

There did not seem to be a house in the town which was not ransacked by the rioting troops, and murder, robbery and rape were being openly committed. Paul's senses, already exhausted from the fight and from the pain of his wound, were battered by the sights and sounds and smells around him. Drunken soldiers raced through the streets, firing randomly at anything until their ammunition ran out. Children cried and men shouted and women screamed and over everything was the sound of the animals being herded away, the cackle of geese, the bleating of sheep and the bellowing of oxen thundering through the streets.

Whatever could not be stolen, eaten or drunk on the spot was wantonly destroyed. Houses were smashed up and fires started in the street made of broken furniture. Pipes of wine had been rolled into the street and broken open, and when some of the officers tipped them over to try to limit the drunkenness, the men lay down to drink from the gutters which ran with wine. Doors that were locked were blown open with muskets and charges, and the inhabitants dragged out into the street, their goods pillaged or destroyed.

After the first two hours Paul found very few of his own men in the town. Word seemed to have gone round that the party had been moved up to the camp and meeting groups of his officers in the street Paul was relieved to hear that they too reported no sightings of the 110th or 112th. He did however, find half a dozen men of the 115th lying drunk in a house next to the town hall. As Paul entered, one of them glared at him through bleary eyes and lifted his bayonet.

"I was hoping they'd have blown your fucking head off in that breach," he slurred.

He got no further as Hammond stepped forward, swinging his rifle butt. The man went down like a stone and Paul turned to stare at Hammond in surprise.

"I hope you didn't hit him too hard, Sergeant."

"It would have been a lot worse if I'd used the bayonet end, sir. What do you want to do about this lot?"

"I think we'll confiscate their weapons and leave them to sleep it off. I'm not sure they're much of a danger to anybody in this state and I can't be bothered…"

There was a scream from above, quickly cut off by a blow, and the sound of laughter. Paul was moving before any of them had time to respond, up a narrow wooden stairway and into a room at the top. He could hear Hammond on the stairs behind him, swearing furiously.

"Don't go bloody haring off like that, sir, you will get yourself…oh Jesus Christ!"

There were half a dozen soldiers in the room. The house owner was on his knees, his eyes bulging with terror and a gash across his chest.

"I knew you were hiding something, you greedy old bastard," one of the men said. "I'll take the cash and everything else you've hidden up here and you can die knowing it."

The soldier, who wore the blue facings of the fourth infantry, was armed with a looted French sword. Paul uttered a furious cry of protest, reaching for his pistol, but he was too late. The man slashed once and the Spaniard fell forward, blood gushing from his throat. The soldier looked around at Paul.

"You try and stop us and you're next," he said viciously.

There was a moment of frozen silence. The soldier stood, blood dripping from his sword, his eyes fixed onto Paul. Paul looked back at him. Around the room, the other rioters waited to see what happened next. Paul knew he had only seconds to decide. He could walk away, keeping his own men safe or he could ensure the safety of the other occupants of the house.

Paul raised his pistol, looking directly into the man's face and fired. He saw the bloodshot eyes widen in shock and then the soldier fell, hit directly in the heart. Paul looked over at the other looters, reached for his shot and calmly began to reload.

***

The sound of the shot seemed to reverberate around the panelled room. Manson had drawn his sword, but the crash of the pistol froze him along with everybody else in the room. Only Paul continued to move, reloading the pistol as though he was practicing at the range. Nobody else made a sound.

Predictably, it was Paul who spoke first. He raised the pistol and levelled it at another soldier across the room. The man dropped his bayonet and lifted his hands, backing up quickly.

"My God, you've killed him," he stammered, his eyes on the twitching body on the ground.

214

"I just watched him commit murder in front of me. If any one of you opens your mouth again without permission, you'll be next. Drop your weapons and line up over there. Sergeant Hammond, make sure they're properly disarmed."

"Yes, sir."

Hammond moved forward, along with Cooper and Dawson, to divest the men of their weapons. None seemed inclined to resist and Manson did not blame them. He looked over at his commanding officer, wondering how Paul could appear so unmoved. Shock seemed to have sobered up the five men lined up against the wall. They were staring down at their fallen comrade on the ground as though they could not believe what they had just seen. Manson remembered, inconsequentially, a story Michael O'Reilly had told him when he first joined the regiment about the very young Lieutenant van Daan shooting a man in the head for rape while he was in India. Manson had often wondered if the story had been true or if it had been one of the Irishman's tales, but he thought now that he should not have doubted it.

Across the hallway, a woman screamed. The cry was cut off abruptly by a blow and Paul spun around and was through the door before anybody could stop him. Manson froze, his eyes meeting Hammond's across the room. Next door, he heard his commanding officer give a bellow of rage.

"Go," Hammond said. "He needs help."

"No he doesn't." Manson was already moving.

"Well they need help, then."

Manson paused in the door of the room and was in time to see his commanding officer manhandling a soldier across the room. The man was clad in shirtsleeves and his trousers were around his ankles, displaying a hairy backside. It was the last part of him visible as Paul swung him forcibly into the glass panes of the long window and through it, into the cobbled street below. The crash was enormous, drowning out some of the man's scream. Manson wondered dispassionately how far he had fallen and if he would survive. He looked around the room and lost all sympathy for Paul's victim.

There were two girls. They must have hidden in the long cupboard which stood open but it was as impossible to hide women as it was to conceal wine or valuables from the British soldiers today, and they had been dragged out. Neither had escaped unscathed, Manson realised. The man Paul had thrown through the window had been the latest, not the first. Manson felt a rush of nausea but pulled himself together quickly and stepped between his commander and the other men in the room. Paul had drawn his pistol again and his expression was murderous.

"Sir, wait. There are four of them, and a few more outside. It's impossible to tell which of them has done what and you can't shoot all of them."

"Why not?" Paul said grimly, his eyes on the men.

Manson took a deep breath and wished that Carl, Johnny or Michael was present. They were more accustomed to dealing with their commander in the grip of rage. Manson was angry himself, but he realised that in this frame of mind Paul needed to be stopped. It occurred to him abruptly that given what had recently happened to Anne, Paul was not going to see reason on the subject of rape.

"Sir, we need to get these women out of here, they need a doctor. We can't leave them here unprotected. There are a lot of other drunken bastards out there."

Paul hesitated, and Manson realised he had found the right words. After a long moment, Paul looked directly at him and Manson felt that he was himself again.

"You're right, Captain. Get these men into the back. That room smells rather like a latrine which is where I'd like to drown them. It doesn't matter now anyway. I've seen their faces and I know their regiment and when this is over I'm going to find them and kick the living shit out of each of them personally. Get Hammond to bring the others through."

"It's a very small room, sir."

"Good, they'll be nice and cosy then. Cooper, Dawson, when they're all in there, move that iron bedstead over the door to block them in will you? And then I want you to pile every stick of furniture in this house in front of it. I should think it'll take them a while to get out. Who knows, they might be sober enough to be as scared as they ought to be by then."

Hammond was watching the faces of the men as they trooped into the small foul room. "They look pretty scared to me already, sir. Especially that one." He prodded the man with his bayonet. "He's going to spend the next couple of hours sobering up while he remembers that he just threatened the commander of the third brigade of the Light Division with an unloaded musket. You reckon that's a flogging or a hanging?"

"I don't know. When I've got more time, I might come back and cut his balls off. We'll see."

Paul crossed the room to the corner where one of the girls was huddled, her face streaked with tears, her gown stained with her own blood. They had held a knife to her throat and a trickle of blood had run down while she lay motionless and terrified as one after the other had brutally forced themselves into her. Paul knelt beside her.

"Can you stand?" he asked gently, in Spanish. "We need to get you out of here."

She nodded silently and he took her hand and drew her to her feet. She looked painfully young and frightened. Manson glanced at the other girl who was slightly older. She was getting up, drawing her torn clothing about her.

Paul came forward. "Take my coat," he said.

"No!" Manson said forcibly. "Don't take this personally, sir, but if we have to try and make it out of here with these two without getting shot or gutted, I think your coat with your very shiny insignia should be very firmly on you. Here ma'am, take mine."

"It's all right, sir, I've got it," Hammond said.

The girl came forward, wide eyed and terrified and Hammond put his coat around her. She looked up at him without speaking.

Paul was checking his pistol methodically. He looked at the women. "Don't be afraid, we'll get you out of here. Leo, get them downstairs. Hammond, get young Freeman to call everybody in. I know you're going to be relieved when I tell you it's time to get out of here. It'll be dark soon, even I'm not stupid enough to be wandering around in here at night. We'll see what we can do tomorrow."

Hammond eyed him. Are you in pain, sir?" he asked quietly.

216

Paul nodded. Manson realised with sudden horror that he had completely forgotten his Colonel was injured. He watched as Hammond put down the rifle, moved forward and put both hands on Paul, turning him side on firmly.

"Stand still and let me look at it."

Paul obeyed and Hammond examined the wound. "It's bled a lot, sir, your trousers are soaked. You should have said something before."

"I'd forgotten about it." Paul saw Hammond's expression and held up his hands in mock surrender. "I did, I swear it. I've only just realised how sore it is."

"Well you've done enough, sir. I think our lads are all out of here. You need to get back, get that treated and rest, because if I let you get an infection because you're too bloody stubborn to do as you're told, she'll kill me stone dead. And so will Carter."

"Coward," Paul said with a smile.

"You are so bloody right, sir. I don't mind going over the walls with half the poxy French army shooting at me, but I am not getting on the wrong side of your wife or my Sergeant-Major. Come on."

Manson stood back to let the women go ahead of him. As he moved to the stairs, his Colonel said:

"Leo."

Manson turned back. "Sir."

Paul held out a hand. "Put this in your pocket. Don't say anything. When you get back to your tent, sort through it and divide it up as you see fit."

He moved forward and took the bag from Paul, surprised at its weight. Opening it he looked inside and then up at Paul, startled. "Jesus, sir. I can't…"

"You didn't. I did. It's prize money, Leo. I took it out of the pocket of that bastard I shot."

"It's looting, sir."

"Whoever they took that off of is probably dead. You leave it here and the next mob of rioters who comes through here will be on to it and possibly kill each other over it. And some of them will have come directly from holding down some poor lass like one of these and raping her while she's crying. I'd rather you and the lads share it. I don't need it. We could give it to Wellington, and we'd all get a share of the prize money. So will a lot of other men who aren't in here trying to help. And the likes of Cooper and Dawson, who came with us of their own accord instead of getting pissed up at the lines, will get next to nothing. Take it, work out shares, do it however you want. I know you, it'll be fair. Send it home, save it, buy yourself a new horse or a new uniform and invest some against the day I want to promote you to major, it'll save me the hassle of fighting with Horse Guards over it. It won't be that long, trust me."

Manson smiled uncertainly. He looked into the bag again at the dull gleam of gold and the sparkle of jewellery. Eventually he looked up, nodded, and put the bag into his inside pocket then followed his Colonel down the stairs.

In the street outside, the 110th and 112th were congregating following the bugle call. Manson was surprised at how many of them there were, not only the officers but NCOs and enlisted men. They had collected more than a dozen refugees, mainly women. There was one older man, his head bleeding badly and his arm about his

217

elderly wife. A young girl clung to him, probably a granddaughter. There was a woman with two children, one a girl who was probably no more than thirteen, and Manson looked at her and then looked away realising that his men had reached her too late to prevent what had been done to her. All of the Spaniards looked shocked and frightened and desperate.

"Form square," Paul said to Hammond. "We only need two ranks. We'll put the refugees in the middle and bayonets or swords should keep them out. There's not much shooting now, most of them have used up their ammunition or else they've lost their weapons. Let's get out of here, Sergeant, we all need food and rest."

"And possibly even some medical treatment," Hammond said sarcastically.

The square moved through the town steadily, and although it attracted a good deal of attention from the drunken soldiers, nobody made any attempt to attack. There were even a few inebriated cheers and one man, standing on top of a broken wagon wearing a cockaded French hat, raised a yell.

"Look lively, lads, it's the heroes from the Light Division going through. Got Lord Wellington in the middle there, have you, boys?"

Paul grinned and waved, then glanced back to where Manson was helping one of the two injured girls along. Manson thought his Colonel looked white faced with pain and exhaustion and wished that he had remembered sooner that Paul was wounded.

"Not far, Captain. How's she doing?"

"She's being very brave, sir. They all are."

"We'll get them fed and tended to very soon. I'll be honest, I need a rest myself."

***

It was quiet on the edge of town. Despite his show of confidence, Paul felt an enormous relief that they were almost clear. He was completely exhausted and the wound in his hip felt as though it was on fire.

The lights of the camp twinkled ahead of them and Paul felt some of the tension ease from his body. He had not even tried, yet, to assimilate the extent of the losses that day although looking out over the breaches piled high with dead and wounded, he knew that they were huge. He had many friends in the other two brigades of the Light Division and he wondered how many he had lost today. He wondered too, how much was left of the first battalion of the 115th and thought ironically that the half dozen men awaiting trial and probable execution for mutiny had managed to survive longer than many of their comrades.

Heading up towards the gate he was conscious suddenly of a sound, pushing itself into his tired brain and he paused, the square stopping beside him. Through the roar of rioting soldiers there was a whimpering sound which had, for some bizarre reason, attracted his attention more than any of the raucous sounds of drunken soldiers.

"Keep going, Captain Manson," he said, glancing at Leo. "I just want to check that house."

Manson glanced over at the darkened building. "It looks deserted to me, sir. And a bit rickety, all the houses this side will have been weakened by the bombardment. Are you sure…?"

"I'll be careful. It's probably nothing. Get these people out of here and find where they're putting the refugees."

"Yes, sir." Manson looked at Hammond. "Sergeant."

"I'll wait for him," Hammond said and Paul sighed.

"It's like having a bloody wet nurse at my heels with you lot."

"You need one, sir."

As the square moved on to the gate, Paul went through a crumbling doorway into a dark panelled hall and stopped, listening again. The sound was louder, and he followed it up the stairs, stepping over one which had splintered from a shell, and went into the large upstairs chamber. It was clear that the raiders had been through. Furniture was smashed and turned over and there was a pool of vomit reeking on the floor. Clothing lay strewn about the room. A big tester bed was the only item of furniture left intact although covers and pillows had been ripped open by men looking for hidden valuables. On the floor by the bed lay an expensive, heavy looking quilt and Paul went forward and lifted it up. He stared down in some surprise and then laughed aloud.

"Were you stuck under there?" he asked and knelt as his Sergeant came into the room behind him.

"What is it, sir?"

Paul rose, still laughing. "I thought it was a child," he said, and held out the bundle of fur. Hammond came forward and laughed aloud.

"Bloody hell he's young. What the hell is he?"

Paul studied the puppy. "I suspect mostly mongrel," he said succinctly. "But look at that face. He looks like a shaggy wolf."

Hammond reached out and stroked the dog's head, his eyes on Paul's face. "Sir – are you about to rescue a puppy from Badajoz?"

"Well, I can't leave him here, he's going to starve," Paul said, a little defensively.

"You are so bloody soft it's untrue."

"I know," Paul admitted. "But I actually quite like dogs. I wonder what my wife will make of him?"

"Well, you'd better hope she shares your liking, sir, because I know that look. Come on, let's get out of here."

The puppy was shivering in Paul's hands. He held it reassuringly against his body, unbuttoning his coat to tuck it inside. A sudden noise made him freeze.

"What was that?"

Hammond had heard it too, a creak from the door on the far side of the room. "I don't know, sir. I hope it's not this house coming down, it looks as though it might. I'll check."

He crossed the room and opened the door. It led into a cupboard, probably used as a wardrobe, and it appeared to be empty. Hammond stood listening and heard the sound again. He studied the wooden back and saw what he had missed at first, a thin gap in the wood. Reaching out he hooked his fingers into the gap and pulled and the false door opened. Hammond peered into a dark space and then gave a startled shout as a figure erupted past him into the room.

Spinning around Hammond made a grab at the figure and caught an arm, holding on hard. "Wait!" he said. "It's all right, we're not going to…"

The girl twisted desperately, lashing out with her free hand, catching him hard with her nails across his face. Hammond swore and released her in surprise and she was running to the door. aul dropped the puppy onto the bed and caught her in his arms, scooping her back.

"Lass, no! Stop, it's all right, we won't hurt you. Don't go out there, it's not safe."

He was holding onto her tightly as she struggled fiercely in his arms, a wildcat in her terror. Paul repeated the words in Spanish, but it had no effect. Firmly he caught her arms and pinned them to her side, forcing her to remain still.

"Stop!" he said, raising his voice. "You're going to hurt yourself."

"Let me go," the girl said.

"Not until you calm down. You're safe. If you let us, we'll get you out of here and up to the lines, there'll be a camp for refugees up there. If you go running through this town tonight, God knows what will happen to you."

"I know what will happen to me!" the girl said, and there was a sob in her voice.

"No, lass. It's all right. Be still now, you're safe. We'll take care of you."

"I can take care of myself."

"Not today you can't. Not out there. Calm down."

His words seemed finally to have reached her and she stilled in his arms. After a moment, still speaking in Spanish, he said quietly:

"I'm going to let you go. Please don't run off. I'm genuinely worried for your safety."

He released her and stepped back and she did not move. Eventually she raised her head and looked directly at him and Paul felt a rush of sympathy. She could not have been more than thirteen, a thin scrap of a child with the gaunt, starved look of a beggar. Her hair was long and tangled, a dark blonde mass and her gown was mud coloured. It was filthy and too big for her and it was also ruined. She was clutching it across her thin chest and he realised in appalled comprehension that it had been ripped open to the waist. There was a dark bruise on the dirty face and a pair of huge blue grey eyes regarded him in mute terror.

Paul looked over at his Sergeant and saw his own horror reflected in Hammond's eyes. He took a deep breath.

"All right, little one," he said gently. "We're going to go up to our camp and find you something to eat. And my wife can look at those cuts and bruises."

"No. I cannot go out there. They…they…"

Hammond stepped forward and squatted in front of the slight form. "What's your name, child?" he said in halting Spanish.

"Esmeralda."

"Esmeralda. Pretty name. Do you speak any English?"

She shook her head. Hammond glanced at Paul who came forward and crouched beside him. "Well my Spanish is very bad," he said. "But I will try. Have you family in the town, Esmeralda?"

She shook her head decidedly. "They died. A year since, fever and hunger."

"So who takes care of you?"

"I do. I beg. Sometimes I find work."

"Mostly you don't get enough to eat, do you?" Paul said softly. "All right, sweetheart. Food we can definitely provide and safety. But you need to trust us. You can't stay here. The men have been drinking and…"

"There were two of them."

He had suspected it but felt the horror hit him nevertheless. He met the wide, terrified eyes which were no longer the eyes of the child she should be and could think of nothing to say. Beside him, his Sergeant reached out unexpectedly and took the girl's hand.

"Where did it happen?" he said.

The child pointed. "Outside. In the alley."

"They run off?"

She nodded. Hammond squeezed her hand. "Don't be afraid," he said gently. "If we find them, I'll kill them. I promise you."

Her eyes widened in surprise. Paul studied his Sergeant in some amusement. He knew that Hammond had been taking Spanish lessons from his wife, but he was surprised at how well he was doing. He seemed to have found the right words because the child hesitated and then nodded.

"Good girl," Paul said. "Let's go." He turned and scooped up the puppy from the bed, smiling at the child. "Is he yours?"

The girl shook her head, staring at the dog in some bewilderment. "No. He must have wandered in…"

"It's a good thing he's so noisy," Paul said. "I thought it was a child crying. I'm glad I did, mind, you'd have had to come out of there sooner or later. I'm sorry, I should have introduced myself sooner. Colonel Paul van Daan of the 110th and this is Sergeant Hammond of my light company."

"Call me Jamie," his Sergeant said. He was still holding the child's hand and she seemed content with it.

"Come on, let's go," Paul said, and led the way. Outside it was relatively quiet in this section of the town although the sounds of rioting carried on the still air.

They encountered no trouble on their way out and arrived up at the lines to be met by Johnny Wheeler. "I'm glad you're back," he said. "I was beginning to worry. I've sent the others up to the headquarters tents, Nan has coordinated a refugee camp up there. She's got some of the women sorting out tents and food for them. I've a horrible feeling she might have looted them from some of the regiments still down there sacking the town…"

Paul gave a choke of laughter. "Good for her. Is she up with them?"

"She just got back, our lads are eating roast pork and celebrating being alive. And the creation of yet another legend for the 110th. Apparently, Stewart complimented Wellington earlier on the success of his tactics on the western wall. Graham told me he raised his eyebrows and said "my dear Stewart, you cannot think

I had anything to do with that, even I would never have thought of escalade by skirmishing. Perhaps they will add it to the training manual." Picton nearly choked himself laughing."

"Is Picton all right?" Paul asked. "Somebody said he was hurt?"

"He was, but then so are you. Go up and let your wife take care of you, I'll see this lass over to the camp…"

Paul glanced at the wide eyed child and read the fear in her eyes. "Not yet, Johnny. I want Nan to look at her. She's very young and I'm afraid…"

He saw Johnny's eyes flicker over the girl and read his appalled comprehension but he responded quickly. "Good idea. Come on then…Paul, what the hell have you got there?"

Paul lifted the puppy out from his coat. "Another refugee," he said. "Jesus, this hurts now."

He limped up to the lines of the 110th. As he approached, the puppy began to bark shrilly and Paul smiled. "You hungry, boy? So am I. Come on."

The officers' tents were set up around a large open square and several cooking fires blazed brightly, with oil lamps hung on branches and hooks about the camp. His officers sat around eating and on the far side of the square George Kelly was carving meat from two roasted pigs on spits. Paul realised suddenly that it had been almost twenty-four hours since he had eaten anything, and then a tall slender figure rose and came forward, long dark hair falling about her shoulders, and he reached for her and folded her into his arms.

"Bonny lass."

"I was beginning to worry," Anne said. "Carl said you'd gone back…Paul, what on earth?"

Her eyes were fixed on the puppy. Paul grinned. "Sorry," he said. "This wasn't part of my plan for the day, but I couldn't leave either of them. I heard this lad whimpering and thought it was a child, went to look. And this is Esmeralda. She was hiding in a cupboard. She's been living on the streets, begging. Her parents have been dead a year and I rather think she's had a very bad day. I can't send her to the refugee camp alone just yet, she's so young…"

His wife's face softened. "Lord no. Neither of your refugees are old enough to be left alone. All right then."

She moved forward, took the girl's hand and spoke in fluent Spanish. "Esmeralda, welcome. I'm Nan, I'm the Colonel's wife. I'm so glad you've come. You shouldn't be down there alone. You must be so tired and hungry and very frightened. Are you hurt?"

The child's eyes were fixed on Anne's lovely face and Paul could see her fascination. She shook her head but then seemed to change her mind. "Yes," she said.

"Why don't you come with me and I'll have a look?"

"Señora, I cannot."

The thin face burned with embarrassment and Paul wanted, more than anything else, to find the drunken men who had abused a child and shoot them dead. He looked at his wife, wondering how she was coping with women coming out of Badajoz who had been raped as she had recently been, but all her attention was on the child and he suspected that she was not thinking at all about Dupres.

222

"Esmeralda, I am not going to make you do or say anything that you do not want to. Do you like babies?"

The child studied her with wide, puzzled eyes.

"I do," she said. "I had a baby sister but she died with my mother."

"My friend has just had a baby. A little girl. Would you like to see her?"

The sheer normality of the question was ludicrous in the violence of the evening, but to Paul's amusement the child's eyes brightened. "Yes."

"Come along. Meet them both."

Anne took Esmeralda's hand and glanced over at Paul. "I will be back shortly," she said. "While I am gone you may give some thought to your excuses. And also come up with a reason for carrying a puppy around with you."

Paul smiled. "Nan, I'm fine. I was just…"

Anne pointed at the tent. "Enough!" she said. "Get in there, get undressed and lie down. I will deal with you in five minutes and if that injury is as bad as I think it is, you are going to regret most of your actions today, Colonel."

"Yes, ma'am. May I…"

"You may say or do nothing without further permission."

Paul grinned and disappeared into the tent. When Anne reappeared some ten minutes later, he had obeyed her instructions to the letter and was lying on his side on their mattress with the wound exposed. The puppy lay beside him and he was stroking its ears. Anne came forward, smiling, and knelt to stroke it.

"Well?" she said.

"I heard him crying. I thought it was a child. I'm glad I went back though because it led us to that girl. Nan, she's just a child and I'm fairly sure she's been raped. It makes me feel sick, it's like a dimension of hell down there just now. What have you done with her?"

"I've left her with Teresa. She's feeding the baby and talking to her. Give her some time and then I'll get her to have some supper and try to get her to allow me to look at her. She's terrified. Paul, it sounds awful down there."

"It's a nightmare. They're drunk and running wild and impossible to control. Our lads have been amazing, we've got them all out I'm fairly sure, but even I'm not risking being in there tonight."

"Carl was telling me. Apparently, Wellington is going down tomorrow to see what is needed."

"Personally, I'd hang a few of them, that'll sober them up." Paul was watching his wife's lovely face as she fussed the dog. "Another man with a wife as beautiful as mine would have had the sense to loot a jeweller's shop on the way out, and I've brought you back a puppy. What's wrong with me?"

She looked up at him, her face alight. "Truly? Can I keep him?"

Paul laughed. "Diamonds or pearls would never have brought that look to your face, girl of my heart. Yes, he's yours, but he'll need training, he's going to be a big dog by the look of his paws."

"That's all right, I used to train all George's gun dogs. He was too lazy to do it himself, and my stepmother couldn't abide badly trained dogs in the house. Thank you, Paul." Anne laughed suddenly. "And if he gets that big it might stop you sending your ensigns running after me all the time. Now let me get some water and look at that wound."

He lay still, stroking the puppy and trying not to flinch as she cleaned the long, deep gash which ran down his thigh.

"This should have been cleaned and dressed hours ago, Paul."

"I know, love. I'm sorry. I needed to…"

"Don't give me a list of all the things you needed to do ahead of taking care of yourself, I'll get cross. Lie still and let me clean it properly or it will get infected."

He lay still and quiet, appreciating how gentle she was, wincing a little as she applied salve and then a dressing.

"I'm not going to stitch it," she said. "There's no point unless you're going to stay off it, and I know you better than that. But you're going to be black and blue tomorrow, I can see the bruising coming out already. Does it hurt much?"

"Everything hurts. I jumped to avoid falling onto the bayonets of the men below but it was a hell of a drop. I'm aching all over, I'm surprised I didn't break my neck, or at least my leg. But lass – we did better than most."

"I know you did, Colonel, and you were apparently first over the walls as well. Not bad for a man who hates storming a town."

"I still hate storming a town. And I am so hungry…"

"So am I, I've not eaten yet. Come on, up you get and let's get you washed and decent."

She went for more water as he rose and helped him to wash, laughing as his familiar beloved features emerged from the blackening of smoke and mud.

"I am not sure you have another pair of trousers without a patch until your new ones arrive from Elvas."

"They'll be ready any day now. Perhaps I'll ride over in a day or two."

"If you're fit enough." Anne went for clean clothing for him and watched as he dressed. After a long moment he turned and surveyed her.

"Was it bad?" he asked quietly and she nodded.

"Yes. I was out in the breaches for a few hours with Adam and Dr McGrigor. They got a bit panicked when three drunken men from the third approached me."

"I'll bet they did. I'm glad I didn't know you were there, I'd have died of fright. You all right?"

"Yes, I had a dozen of our rifles with me, I'd no trouble, trust me."

"Is Harry Smith all right, Nan, I've not seen him."

"He is." Anne was laughing. "Looking remarkably pleased with himself."

He caught her tone and lifted his eyebrows. "Why?"

"He's acquired a couple of refugees, a Spanish girl and her young sister, barely more than a child straight from a convent. They managed to get out and up to the camp and the rifles are looking after them. I called in to thank him for the loan of his men and the girl is curled up rather like an adoring puppy at his feet while he practices flirting with her in Spanish."

Paul laughed aloud. "I hope he bloody behaves himself," he said, reaching for her and kissing her with leisurely enjoyment. "I love you, bonny lass. If I weren't so hungry, I'd skip the evening and take you to bed, but I'm truly famished. Come and get me fed."

"What shall we do with this fellow?" Anne asked and Paul scooped up the puppy.

"Give him a drink and some supper along with the rest of us," he said.

They walked outside arms about each other and joined the group congregated about the fire. Paul lowered himself tiredly into a camp chair beside Carl Swanson and glanced at his friend. Carl had been eating and was just setting down his mess tin with a sigh of content. Keren approached bringing food for Paul and Anne and he smiled up at her.

"Keren, thank you. Get a drink and come and sit down, I'll bet you've not stopped."

She obeyed, bringing wine for all of them. Paul sipped his cup appreciatively and smiled at the girl.

"How's Teresa?"

"Very well, sir. Danny has taken her some food down." Keren reached out and stroked the puppy which had established itself in the skirts of Anne's velvet robe. "Does he want some food?"

"I'd say so," Paul said, and she laughed and went, bringing back a mess tin of pork scraps and some water. They watched the puppy eating.

"Does he have a name yet?" Manson asked. "I'm rather assuming he's staying."

"He is," Paul admitted. "It's up to Nan, he's her dog."

"Oh honestly, Paul, how you can say that? You've made more fuss of him than you have of me this evening," his wife said breaking into laughter. "I know what I want to call him, I'm just not sure if it would offend anybody."

"What?" Paul asked.

"Craufurd. Doesn't he rather look like him?"

Paul looked at the puppy, and the dog scowled back at him from under expressive eyebrows. He began to laugh. "Oh dear God, he does. That's perfect, although I'll get the blame for it, for sure. Nan, you're a genius."

They were still laughing, watching the puppy, when Anne glanced up. "What on earth is this?"

A muleteer was approaching the group, asking questions. Anne got up and went to speak to him, exchanging quick words in Portuguese. She turned, her face alight with amusement.

"Leo. This man has a message for you. And two crates of wine."

Manson looked up in astonishment. "For me? What in God's name...?"

He moved forward to take the note and read it as the muleteer unloaded two full boxes of wine and then backed his animal away, a coin from Anne in his hand.

"Who is it from, Captain?" Paul asked, approaching.

Manson looked up from the note, bewildered. "Miss Periera," he said. "In Elvas. When we went in to clear out Jagger and his cronies...she sent it in thanks for what we did and in the hope that we're all well enough to enjoy it."

He folded the note and went to take a bottle from one of the crates. Paul joined him and studied the label then glanced sideways at his junior.

"What services did you provide exactly for Miss Periera, Leo?"

Manson was laughing although Paul noticed a slight flush. "I just did my duty, sir. I was only there for ten minutes, ask Hammond. I wanted to check they were all right."

"Were they? With everything else, I don't think I even asked. I'm not sure having Private Jagger billeted in the house would be that much fun."

Manson opened the bottle and poured into his cup and then into Paul's. "I don't think it was, although she made very little of it. She told me she'd asked for payment, and he'd told her to take him upstairs or he'd cut her face. She did as she was told. But he was bloody rough with her, she'd bruises up and down both arms where he'd held her down."

Paul sipped the wine and smiled, lifting his cup to Manson. "Well, whatever you managed to say to her in ten minutes, Leo, I take my hat off to you, you got it right. This is not cheap wine."

Manson looked over and nodded. "We have a visitor, sir."

Paul turned. Carter was approaching and beside him, wide eyed and wary, was the Spanish child. Anne got up. "Esmeralda. Have you met little Ana? Isn't she pretty?"

The girl nodded. "She is."

Carter met Anne's eyes, smiling slightly. "I think she's hungry," he said.

"Why don't you come into the tent, Esmeralda. Keren will bring you some food through."

Paul sat by the fire, the puppy sleeping on his lap and drank wine. The pain in his hip had settled into a dull ache and his exhausted body was finally beginning to relax, the food and wine warming him. Beside him Manson was unusually quiet.

"Are you all right?" Paul asked quietly.

Manson looked around, startled. "Yes. Sorry, I was miles away. I'm tired."

"We're all exhausted. It will be a long day tomorrow. We need to bury our dead, do roll calls and find out who is missing."

"It's going to be bad," Manson said. He sounded depressed. "Not so much our lads although we lost a few, but the rest of the division. I think I've lost friends out there today. And the 115th, God help them."

"I know, lad. I'm glad this one is over."

"Have you ever been through a battle this bad?"

Paul was silent for a moment then nodded. "Assaye. Slaughter like I've never seen it." He glanced at Manson. "It was my first big battle, I'd made Captain twenty four hours earlier."

"Dear God. How did you…?"

"I didn't. Not for a while. I was wounded and got sent home. A blessing really, I've a suspicion if I'd gone into battle again too soon I might have got my head blown off. It took some time."

"Yes. The bodies piled up in those breaches. I keep thinking about the ones who must have still been alive."

"Don't, Leo. Just don't. It'll drive you mad, trust me. We went back to where our lads fell and any who were still alive there are out and being treated, and tomorrow we'll start burying the dead. One of the things experience has taught me is to do the best you can and then leave it alone. You can't save them all."

Manson smiled and reached out to stroke the silky fur of the sleeping puppy. "You saved him."

"I know." Paul laughed. "Mad, isn't it? But somehow, it does help."

Anne was approaching. She sat down and took the cup he held out. "How is she?"

"She's very battered," Anne said. "Two of them caught her in an alley when she was trying to sneak out of the gate. Pushed her down on the floor and raped her. I think it's a bit of a blur for her."

"Oh bloody hell."

"How old is she?" Manson asked.

"Fourteen. She looks younger, but she's half starved, been living on the streets for over a year. Keren has found her one of her old dresses, she can't walk about in that thing, and she's going to spend the night down with the women, they'll keep an eye on her. Poor little thing."

"There'll be a good few women in there with scars after this night's work," Paul said soberly. "God, I'm tired."

"You look it. Come to bed, Paul."

Anne was quiet as he undressed and slid into bed beside her. A snuffling sound across the tent made him grin. They had found the dog an old blanket and it was curling up trying to get comfortable. "I can bloody hear you, Craufurd. You can stay there as long as you don't move, but you try and get in this bed and you're out on your ear!"

Anne laughed and moved into his arms. "He must be shattered, he'll be fine," she said. "Does that hurt?"

"I don't give a damn if it does. Kiss me."

She reached up to do so and he pulled her close against him, letting the tension drain away. "I love you, Nan."

"I love you too, Paul. I'm so thankful you came through that."

"Me too. Too many of our lads didn't. My Portuguese and rifles were badly hit. We lost Juan Peso, Nan."

"I know."

"He's been with me since Bussaco. And my KGL lost half a dozen officers, killed or wounded. Oh Nan."

She drew his head down onto her shoulder and he felt the tears wet against her skin. He had been holding onto it for the past twenty-four hours and he knew from past experience that it was better to let it go, to lie there in the warmth of her arms and allow himself to feel the grief and the loss. She did not speak, just stroked his head, running her fingers through his hair, and he fell finally into an exhausted slumber.

Chapter Seventeen

The following few days were spent dealing with the aftermath of battle. With grim determination, Wellington dealt with the situation in Badajoz, setting up gallows in the square and sending Paul and the 110th and 112th through to round up the rest of his army. There were no hangings although several of the divisional commanders ordered floggings. Paul did not. Whatever crimes had been committed during those few horrific days were over now and he could see no point in trying to make an example of those of his brigade who had joined in. He collected them together to bury their dead and made a short pithy speech at each service which he hoped at least some of the men would remember.

The burden of his administrative tasks was relieved by the arrival of General Charles Alten back from leave to take command of the Light Division. He received Paul in his tent, a pink faced, dark haired Hanoverian in his late forties with a serious demeanour. Paul gave a detailed report of the siege and the storming and Alten listened, nodding and making the occasional note.

"Thank you, Colonel van Daan. That was very clear." Von Alten studied him for a moment and then waved him to a chair finally. Paul seated himself. "I have talked with Lord Wellington about the division. I believe we need reinforcements badly."

"We do, sir. I've been meeting with the other two brigade commanders. With your permission, I'm going to send an express to our second battalion in Ireland to get as many reinforcements as we can. I'll tell Major Flanagan to start recruiting again immediately. We'll split them between the 110th and 112th. I'll also ask for the second battalion of the 115th to send out what they can – Lord Wellington is suggesting the whole battalion, they've so few left. We had two companies of rifles and we lost half of them. I'm going to combine what is left to make one company. Captain Tregallas was wounded and Captain Bryson is dead so I'll need a new officer…"

"I will speak to Lord Wellington, but I know that General Craufurd trusted you to make your own decisions about promotions and officers, Colonel. Providing you remain within the rules, I am happy to do the same."

"Thank you, sir."

Alten looked up and smiled, and Paul was surprised at how much it altered his somewhat solemn countenance.

"I don't think we have served together before, Colonel, although I can remember talking to you at Headquarters parties a few times. And I very definitely remember dancing with your wife."

Paul laughed. "Doesn't everybody?"

"Is she still with you out here?"

"Yes, sir. We had a son last year, he's gone back to England, my family will take care of him."

"Lord Wellington told me a little of her ordeal with the French. I hope she has fully recovered; she is a charming woman."

"She's doing very well, sir."

"Colonel, I know that you were very close to General Craufurd. In many ways you were similar. You will find me different to serve under. I obey orders and I try to keep my commanders informed."

Paul grinned. "Have you been listening to Lord Wellington, sir?"

"I have taken some time to find out as much as I can about my brigade commanders, Colonel. But in your case, it has not been hard, your name is very well known throughout the army. I know your reputation. I also know that Lord Wellington places a very high value on your capacity to act independently. It is not something he likes to see in an officer, but he has told me many times that in your case, he trusts you."

"I am flattered, sir. Although I am well aware that it still drives him mad at times."

"It does. I suspect it will also drive me mad. He has not chosen me by accident. He wants the Light Division commanded by a man he trusts to follow his orders. But the reason he has felt able to make that choice is because he has you. He does not need another General Robert Craufurd when he has Colonel van Daan."

Paul was interested. "Did he tell you that, sir?"

"Ja, he did."

"He told me that too," Paul admitted.

"Colonel – since I received news of this appointment, I have received some interesting correspondence and a good deal of advice and information. A surprising amount of it concerns you."

Paul sat very still, studying him thoughtfully. "And what do these disinterested people have to say?" he asked.

"Mostly it is gossip. The opinion at Horse Guards seems to be that you and I will find it impossible to work together. You have the reputation of being difficult, insubordinate, and impossible to command and you will despise my very German need to obey the rules and wait for orders. While I will loathe your independence and your refusal to conform to the rules. At least one person recommended that I should make it a condition of accepting this command that Lord Wellington get rid of you, preferably with a command to the West Indies. And I have here a letter from the medical board in London requesting that I step in and remove your wife from all army hospitals and medical establishments."

229

"And what did they have to say about her?" Paul asked, keeping a tight rein on his temper.

"They said that she is a young woman of considerable ignorance and doubtful reputation who should not be received in polite society and who does a great deal of harm to the men in her care and they have suggested she is put upon the next transport home."

Paul took a deep breath. "Yes, they're not that fond of her," he said mildly, and Alten gave a thin smile.

"All of this is very interesting, Colonel, because it has given me a great deal of useful information. It tells me, for example, what some of the people at Horse Guards think of me. They see me as a stiff-necked German with no imagination and no talent who has been given this job because Lord Wellington needs a safe pair of hands and is too frightened to give it to anybody else. It tells me that they think I am not only incapable of commanding the Light Division, but that I am too weak to stand up to either them or you and that I would rather have you removed than learn to work with a man who is very different to me. It also tells me that they are spiteful and have poor enough manners to try to use your wife as a weapon in this very unseemly political power struggle."

Paul was beginning to feel himself relax. "You seem to have picked up a fair bit from a little gossip, sir. I can't wait to see what you make of the Light Division."

"What would you do if you were me, Colonel?"

"Did you want this command, sir?"

"Yes. I was also told that you wanted it."

"I do, but not yet." Paul gave a faint smile. "It takes me too far away from the action. One day I'll be ready for that, but not just yet. And I'm too young. It's hard work managing the resentment and unhappiness of some of the older men when they see me being promoted ahead of them. I've only been a brigade commander for five minutes, I'm still learning. In a few years I'll be ready."

"We could probably manage a very senior post in the West Indies," Alten said, and Paul laughed aloud.

"I'm sure you could, sir. With your approval, though, I'm well suited where I am. With regard to my wife…"

"Your wife is none of my business, Colonel, although I look forward to meeting her. I have written to the medical board telling them to refer any complaints to Lord Wellington or to the Inspector of Hospitals."

"Thank you, sir," Paul said with considerable appreciation. "I'll admit I have been worried. Not about you especially, mind – just about a new commander. After Sir William Erskine I was feeling a bit nervous."

"And now?"

Paul studied him. "I think they've got you wrong. You might be less eccentric than I am, and I'm prepared to accept you'll be a safe pair of hands, sir, but that doesn't mean you've no imagination. As a matter of fact, I think the way you've just handled me demonstrated considerable imagination. I'm looking forward to serving under you."

Alten smiled. "How you manage your brigade is up to you, Colonel, I shall not interfere. I do not think I lack imagination, but I am aware that you have a reputation for being a very talented officer. If you think I am getting it wrong, I hope you will be frank with me."

Paul laughed aloud. "Not much fear I won't, sir," he said. "But thank you. And when I piss you off – because trust me, I will – please be equally frank with me. I have the thickest skin in the army, you might make me angry, but you won't offend me. Have you spoken to Barnard and Vandeleur yet?"

"I shall do so shortly."

"Have I your permission to leave, sir? We've got the last of the dead out of the breach, my men have arranged for burial and I want to be there."

Alten rose. "Ja, I was told of this. You prefer not to have your men buried in mass graves."

"We often have no choice, but even then we'd rather our own mass grave. Their comrades feel better if it's a separate service. Recently the other two brigades have started to do the same thing, it's become a bit of a Light Division custom."

"I like it. Would you inform me in future when there is a burial service? If I am in camp, I would like to attend."

Paul was surprised and touched. "Yes, sir, very gladly. The men will like it."

"Tomorrow, I have invited my brigade commanders and their senior officers to dine with me, Lord Wellington is lending me his dining room over in Elvas."

"Don't let him lend you his cook, sir, he's dreadful. Want to borrow mine?"

Alten laughed aloud. "May I?"

"Yes, I'll send him up to you, let him know what you want, he's very resourceful."

"Thank you, Colonel. Would it be appropriate to invite your wife to join us? I realise it is not traditional with the English mess, but…"

"It is in my mess," Paul said with a grin. "She'd be delighted, sir. Thank you."

Paul was accompanied on his ride to Elvas not only by his senior officers but by Captain Manson. He tried hard to conceal his amusement, but as they approached the town, Manson said:

"You might as well say it, sir. Your face does."

Paul laughed aloud. "Is she pretty, Leo?"

"Yes. Although that's not wholly why I'm going. I should thank her for the wine. And I'd like to make sure they're all right."

"What's her name?"

"Diana Periera. I don't know any more than that, but I am curious, she sounds English. I'll let you know the gossip tomorrow, don't worry. You need to go and be respectable with the German general."

"I rather like the German general, Leo. He's not what I expected at all, but I think we may have done rather better than we thought this time."

"I wondered about that when I heard you'd lent him George Kelly."

"At least dinner will be good," Paul said with a grin. "I like the fact that he invited my wife, it's a very military affair but I think he's making a point. Horse Guards seem to have tried to persuade him to muzzle me and get her sent home."

"Bloody hell. Does Lord Wellington know?"

"I doubt it. But what's interesting is that instead of going to his Lordship to find out what he should do, Alten has made his own decision, and the first thing he does is invites my lass to a dinner to which she should undoubtedly not be invited. He's telling them to piss off in a very German, very correct way. I like him."

"Good," Manson said. "I'll leave you here, then, sir. Unless you want to join me for a drink?"

"If you keep that up, Captain Manson, you'll get a punch in the face. Can you imagine my wife's face if I told her I was just slipping into the local brothel with you?"

Manson laughed. "You never know what your wife will do or say, sir. She might slap your face for you, or she might just invite herself along for a drink."

"So true. Enjoy yourself. If you want to stay the night, feel free, you're owed a day or two off. I hope she is very charming."

"Sir, she might be occupied this evening, I'm not sure…"

"Leo, I am older and more experienced than you and you need to trust me that women are something about which I know a good deal. Whatever you said to this lass during your rescue mission made a damned good impression, that was extremely expensive wine, and you were not intended to reply with a polite note of thanks, you were supposed to go in person and she will be very welcoming. Enjoy yourself."

"Night, sir."

"Good night, Leo."

***

Manson rode into the stable yard of the tavern and dismounted, handing his horse to a waiting groom with a smile. He made his way into the tavern.

It was busy, a thriving trade from the exhausted officers and men, looking for relief after the horrors of the siege. Manson paused by the door, wondering if he should go in. He could see Diana Pereira across the room, talking and laughing with two officers of the 43rd. She looked very lovely in a gown of flowing white muslin, cut to display her shoulders and breasts, and she wore her hair down her back, caught up at the sides with two combs. There were two or three girls around the room, and it was noisy and very amiable. The silent bartender stood polishing glasses, watching with his sad eyes. Manson moved into the room and went to the bar.

"Evening, Emilio. Brandy?"

The man nodded and then recognising Manson, smiled. It was a surprisingly sweet smile and it transformed his face. He poured and Manson reached into his pocket. The man shook his head firmly. Manson smiled back at him.

"One drink, Emilio. After that I pay my way, you've a living to make."

"We might not be alive at all if it hadn't been for you, Captain Manson."

Manson turned. "Miss Pereira, how are you?"

"Much better than last time we met. Although I can see you had a bad time." The girl's eyes were on the healing gash on Manson's face which he had got from flying debris when the mine had exploded. She glanced at Emilio. "I'm going to get some supper, Emilio, I've not eaten since breakfast. I'll let Francesca know I'm not available for a while."

He nodded. Diana turned and went to speak to a fair haired girl by the door then returned to Manson. "Come through to the back, we can't have a conversation in here, it's too noisy."

Manson followed her through a thick door, which she closed firmly behind her, and found himself in a small hallway. One door clearly led to the kitchen, and a second, partly open, seemed to lead to the cellar. Diana Pereira opened the third door and led him into a small clean parlour. There was a fireplace and a wooden settle and several wooden armchairs. A table was pushed against one wall, set out with a selection of covered dishes bearing bread, cold meats, cheese and olives. A bowl of fruit was at one end. The girl picked up a plate and went to the board.

"There's wine over there, will you pour me one? And have one yourself, it's very good. A present from a grateful Major of the cavalry. We will not be serving it to our customers. Are you hungry?"

"No, I ate in the mess. But thank you."

"We always keep food available in here. With tavern hours and what we do, we all eat at different times. Often at the strangest times, to be honest. This room is strictly for the girls and the staff, nobody brings customers back here. It is nice to have a place to ourselves."

Manson wondered if she was deliberately making a point. He poured two glasses and set them down on a small table and she brought the plate over and sat down, indicating that he should do the same. Manson did so. He was conscious once again, of the passing resemblance to Anne van Daan. She was not really like Anne. She was not as tall and her hair and eyes were not as dark, and although her face was very lovely, she did not have the startling perfection of features that stopped every man in his tracks at the sight of his commander's wife. But she did share something of Anne's extraordinary poise in the face of the most surprising circumstances. She also, he realised, had something of her blatant sensuality.

"I was pleased to see you there," Diana said. "Do you know, I honestly was not sure that you would come back. I can usually tell."

"I've been a little busy."

"I know. I've spent the past five days listening to horror stories. And the poor townspeople."

"It was bloody. Both during the storming and in the town afterwards. Our lads were very good on the whole, but some of what's been done up there is going to stay with me for a while. I'm very glad you were out here."

"So am I. Half a dozen rowdy soldiers for three days doesn't seem so bad now."

Manson studied her as she ate. "I rather think, Miss Pereira, that it was more unpleasant than you are prepared to admit. But that's not my business."

She regarded him steadily. "Why do you say that, Captain?"

"Because you'd bruises up both your arms that day, shaped exactly like a man's fingers, lass."

"You're very observant, Captain."

"You've very lovely arms, Miss Pereira, I've been looking at them this evening as well. They look better without the bruises."

"Is he dead?"

Manson nodded. "He was hanged along with two others who had attacked their officers. The rest went over the walls with us and a large number of them are dead, they hit an enemy mine. The ones we have left are out training and we're working with their officers as well."

"Training? So soon after..."

"We can't let that lot sit around, ma'am, they'll only start nursing their grudges, and the Colonel would rather not hang any more of them. Although I think his wife would have hanged the lot of them for interrupting her holiday."

She laughed. "Captain – I believe you are the first man in years to call me ma'am. But it's a little too formal for me, given the circumstances. Would it offend your sense of propriety to call me Diana?"

"Not at all. And I need to thank you for your gift. It was a surprise but a welcome one. You didn't need to."

"I know I didn't, Captain. But I was very grateful."

Manson sipped the wine. "Diana – will you satisfy my curiosity and tell me where you come from, because you've got me stumped. You sound English."

"It gives a nice air of mystery, doesn't it?"

"Yes, I'll bet the officers of Lord Wellington's army love it."

"They do. I am in considerable demand. My mother was Portuguese, Captain, my father English."

"Soldier?"

"No, he was a wine merchant, he had warehouses in England, Portugal and Spain. My mother was his maidservant."

"I see."

"He was good to me when I was a child. I think I was a pretty little thing who amused him and I was no trouble. My mother made sure of that, she needed him to support her. He died when I was fifteen of fever. It took my mother too. It was 1807."

"The year the French invaded."

"Yes. My father's brother took over the business. He did not want to lose money, so he closed down the Portuguese office, dismissed the staff and put me out onto the streets. I had nothing but a portmanteau of nice clothes, a few items of not very valuable jewellery to sell and a pretty face."

"Not a good time to be on the streets, lass."

"No, but I was a very practical child. I knew what was about to happen to me when those armies marched through, so I decided to make it work for me. I approached the most senior ranking French officer that I could find and I offered to sell him my maidenhead at a very reasonable price. He was only too glad to make the bargain."

Manson set down the wine glass. He felt unexpectedly sick. She was looking at him, bright eyed, the epitome of a sophisticated woman of the world, but he could imagine with gut wrenching clarity the frightened child she had been, making the best of an impossible situation. He looked at her steadily.

"And it rather looks as though you did well enough out of it. Do you own this place?"

"Yes. I had a series of protectors. One of them was a Portuguese grandee, actually quite wealthy. But it's a very precarious life. I wanted some stability. I came

234

to Elvas with an English colonel and I liked it here. This place was very run down and I bought it cheaply. I'd met Emilio on the road, picked him up begging. We restored this place together and ran it as a tavern. And I began taking very carefully selected customers. Gradually the other girls joined us. All of them came to this the same way."

"Victims of war?"

She nodded. "Some girls lose all their families, Captain. Or their families don't want them back after they've been used by half a dozen French troopers. They can starve or they can sell what they have."

She got up and went for the wine, topping up both glasses and setting a dish of olives down on the table. Manson took one. It was very good.

"We've some refugees up in camp with us," he said. "Three or four women who had a very bad time down in Badajoz. It sickens me, to be honest. Some of them have families to go back to, but I wonder what will happen to those who don't when we move out."

"By then, Captain, they will very possibly have worked out another way of earning a living," Diana Periera said. "I've five girls living here now. They manage their own earnings and pay me rent for the rooms. We share the food bills. I don't own them, they can come and go as they please, but they stay because it's safer and more pleasant than plying their trade on the streets. We have Emilio, who has a large club behind that bar and will use it if he needs to, but he doesn't often. Our clients are mostly English troops, some Portuguese. We're clean and the girls are nice to them. Many of them are very lonely and a long way from home, and I've taught all the girls English, which they like. We don't rob them or cheat them, so they keep coming back."

"You're a very good businesswoman, Diana, I'm impressed. Would it be rude of me to ask your age?"

"I'm twenty. I've been here for two years now."

"You've done amazingly well. And you've been very, hospitable, thank you. I'm not surprised this place is so popular, it feels very different from a lot of similar places I've been in. The girls seem all right."

"I'm not beating them to keep them here, if that's what you mean? And none of them are children, brought in to please some filthy old man."

"That's exactly what I mean. But not just that. It's the setting. It's very plain and very welcoming. It feels like a man could just come here for a drink."

"He can, and a lot do, the tavern itself makes a decent profit. I've deliberately kept it that way so as not to antagonise the neighbours. And it has worked, they've been very tolerant. They all know what I do, but they can ignore it and a lot of them do come to drink here. I don't encourage my girls to parade themselves half naked through the tap room, they can do that upstairs. And if they don't want to work for a week or two, they don't have to as long as they pay the rent. It makes for a better working relationship, I think. They feel free. And I don't feel quite as bad for making money out of..."

She broke off and Manson realised that for the first time she was upset. Getting up he moved to sit beside her on the wooden settle. Gently he took the empty plate from her, put it down on the table, and took her hand. "It's all right, Diana, I do understand. Every now and again, I run up against the fact that I make my living out of killing people."

She looked up into his face in surprise. "But you're called a hero for that."

"I am but it doesn't change the piles of dead bodies I've just helped clear out of those breaches. I'm very good at what I do, but it's still killing."

She gave a rather watery smile. "You really are the most surprising man, Captain."

"My name is Leo," Manson said. "It's only fair."

"Leo. That's very nice. Are you going to stay, Leo, or is this really just a conversation?"

Manson studied her. "I'd like to," he admitted. "But only if you'll let me pay my way. I don't feel comfortable taking advantage of your gratitude when I was just doing my job."

"Leo, I know you were. But the way you did it, was what earned my gratitude. Another officer would have brought half a company in here, the place would have been wrecked, and some of my people might have died. You walked in that door on your own You must have known one of them might try to kill you, and I am fairly sure you did it to try to protect us."

"I did," Manson admitted with a grin. "My Sergeant was furious with me. But it worked."

"Is that the very good-looking young man who was with you? Most sergeants I've met are forty and bad tempered."

"He's twenty-two or three, I think. And generally in a good mood, although he has his moments."

"You should bring him down one evening, Leo, my girls would be delighted."

Manson laughed aloud. "I might do that, he's earned a treat, he's had a bit of a bad time this week."

"Socialising with the NCOs?" Diana said, lifting her eyebrows. "Is that even allowed, Captain?"

"Not officially. But we work a little differently in the 110th, lass."

"I wondered about that," Diana said. "Because I was at the top of the stairs when he came in that day, and I am fairly sure I heard him call you Leo."

Manson laughed. "Did he? I didn't notice. He wouldn't usually do so but I think I gave him a fright that day."

"I'm not surprised; you gave me one. Why don't we take the wine upstairs? Do you need to get back tonight?"

"No, I'm owed a night off."

"Then I'll make you a deal. I'll let you pay me since you're so insistent on it. But stay the night, and that's on the house."

"All right." Manson picked up the wine bottle and one glass and she took the other and led him up narrow stairs to a large room on the first floor. It was very much in keeping with the rest of the house, clean and fresh with filmy drapes at the window blowing in the breeze and polished bare boards. The bed was large and bore none of the gaudy dressings he associated with a brothel. He realised with considerable amusement that she had furnished and decorated this room to suit her own taste, not that of her clients and he set down the wine and turned and looked at her.

236

"Not what you expected?"

"No, but you're a constant surprise. And you don't need silk sheets and erotic pictures on the wall to make a man want you, Diana, you just have to stand there."

She smiled broadly. "Leo, you are very surprising yourself. Not at all what I'm used to in a young officer. Don't ask me why, but I'm actually nervous about this."

Manson removed his coat, draping it over a chair and came forward. "Don't be. I'm singularly boring when it comes to this, I don't require anything particularly unusual or unpleasant. I am looking forward to kissing you, though, I've been thinking about that for a while. Do you mind?"

"No," she said softly, and he drew her into his arms.

She was, as Manson had expected, a consummate professional. He let her take the lead, sensing that she would be more comfortable that way, and he admitted, as he lay quietly beside her afterwards, that he could not remember the last time he had enjoyed this act quite so much. That it had been an act he was in no doubt. She felt that she had a debt to pay, and she was paying it with interest, and he had no complaints. He turned his head on the pillow to look at her and she smiled.

"You're a very gentle man, Leo."

"Not always. Thank you, Diana. You are without doubt the loveliest girl I've shared a bed with, and I enjoyed that very much."

"I'm glad. So did I."

"You don't need to say that, Diana."

To his surprise, she blushed. "Leo..."

Manson reached out and touched her lips gently. "Don't," he said. "I am very sure you can convince most of your customers that they have moved you in a way that no other man has, but you don't need to put on the performance for me. I really enjoyed making love to you, and I don't think you hated it, which is good. I also like you, which means it would bother me if you felt you had to treat me like everybody else and lie to me to make me feel good. You don't, my self-worth isn't tied up in this one bit. Just relax and hold my hand. It's nice lying like this, knowing I don't have to rush off."

She took his hand and they lay quietly for a while. Manson had thought that she had fallen asleep but suddenly she said:

"It isn't you, Leo."

He was startled. "Christ, Diana, it didn't occur to me that it was. Come here."

He scooped her close and kissed her very gently. "Go to sleep," he whispered and she snuggled closer into his arms.

He slept, curiously rested in the wide comfortable bed with her close beside him. Waking before dawn he was aware that she was not there and he sat up cautiously. She was standing by the window silhouetted against the dark sky and Manson got up and went to her. She was cold to the touch. He put his hands on her shoulders and bent to kiss her cheek, realising suddenly that her cheeks were wet with tears.

"Oh lass, what's wrong?"

She shook her head impatiently. "I don't know. I'm sorry, I'm never like this."

Manson studied the profile of her lovely face in the darkness and had a sudden sense that he had got it badly wrong. He had followed her lead and let her express her gratitude and it had not occurred to him that she had possibly been trying to express something else.

"Diana…"

"I'm sorry, I didn't mean to wake you. Let's go back to…"

"No." Manson held her still, very gently. "Stop trying to brush me off. Why do you think I'm here?"

She looked up at him with a little smile. "I think I know why you're here, Captain."

"Well you're bloody wrong. There's a very accommodating lass attached to our camp, Diana, and if that was all I wanted I'd be tucked up in my tent with her just now, I don't need to ride to Elvas for that. I came here to see you. I was really curious about you. And then I sat downstairs talking to you last night and I wanted to know more. I still do. But I've no idea how to manage that, given what you do for a living. All I do know is that I'm making a complete balls-up of this."

She laughed suddenly through her tears. "Oh Leo, you're not. I can't remember the last time I've been around a man who has been so respectful, so gentle, so…"

"Come here."

He stepped forward and picked her up, bending to kiss her very gently as he carried her back to the bed. She lay back, the dark eyes wide and questioning on him.

"Leo…"

"Stop talking," Manson said, his mouth against her hair. "I'm tired of being gentlemanly here, it's not getting me anywhere."

He heard her give a little gasp at his touch as his hand slid lower and he began to stroke her steadily his eyes on her face.

"You're so beautiful," he whispered. "And I'm damned sure they all say that to you, Diana. But I'm seeing so much more than that."

"Leo…" There was surprise in her voice, and he continued to caress her until he felt her body relax and soften under his hands. He took his time, realising with amusement that in this, if in nothing else, he was the more experienced of the two. It gave him confidence, and he stopped being so careful, letting himself relax as he seldom did, conscious of a response he had not felt from her the previous night.

She shifted her body against his and Manson was aware of a sudden urgency. "Leo…"

He caught her hands very gently, laughing, and brought one to his lips, nibbling gently at her finger. "You ready yet, lass? There's no hurry, you know. I'm enjoying myself very much, can keep doing this for a while."

"I'm ready."

He looked down at her, teasingly. "You sure now….?"

"You're a bastard, Captain Manson."

He moved over her finally. "Not to you, lass. Never to you."

She gave a little cry and he felt her nails digging into his back as he began to move. He did not try to be gentle, sensing that on this occasion she did not want his careful courtesy, and he felt her arching into him, meeting his passion with a fierce response that was not feigned.

She collapsed finally breathless and wide-eyed and Manson shifted his weight from her and leaned over to kiss her with considerable enjoyment. "Diana, that was really lovely," he said, and she laughed.

"You sound as though you meant it this time."

"I meant it both times, love. Are you all right? I got a bit carried away there, I wasn't as gentle as I meant to be."

"Not at all gentle." She pushed herself up and leaned forward to kiss him with obvious enthusiasm. "I am definitely going to miss you when you march away, Captain Manson."

"Good. It gives me an incentive to come back."

"I hope you do. That could probably do with some practice, but I'd be very willing to try."

"You're not going to hear me arguing about that, lass. In fact, if I didn't have to get up and leave, I'd be happy with a couple of hours sleep and another go. But I can't."

"I know. When are you marching out?"

"Within a day or two. We're off to chase Marmont, which brings back not very happy memories of my first campaign when we scuttled around Portugal for weeks trying to chase Massena under the worst general in the army. At least we don't have him to deal with this time." Manson kissed her again. "I've no idea when I'll be back this way, Diana. But I'll make sure I am."

She reached up to caress his face. "Good," she said quietly. "Please try to stay alive, Captain. I've a feeling you're a man who needs that saying fairly regularly, I've seen how reckless you can be."

"Nonsense."

"How did this happen, Leo?" She leaned forward and very gently kissed the healing scar on his face and he felt a shiver of pleasure at the touch of her lips.

"I was a little too close to a mine when it exploded on the walls. Sore, but not dangerous."

"It's not your only scar," Diana said sliding her hand down his body. Manson felt her fingers brush over the long healed scars from the previous year and he lay very still enjoying her touch.

"No. I had an encounter with French infantry during Massena's retreat. And the one you're kissing just now was a cavalry officer at Fuentes de Oñoro who is recently deceased, having pissed off my brigade commander beyond the telling. If you don't stop, darling girl, I am going to forget my duty and he'll be coming after me with a sword. And since he's the only man in the regiment who is better with one than I am, I am not taking that risk."

He tipped her neatly onto her back, leaned over and kissed her long and hard. "I'm going to need to go, Diana. Thank you for this. It's been a rare interlude of peace, and I've not felt this rested in years."

She smiled. "I don't know how you can feel rested, Leo, but you're very welcome. Are you hungry? Grab something from the parlour as you go past."

"Thank you, I will. Don't get up, lass, go back to sleep, it's very early."

Manson dressed quietly in the half light and then went to sit on the bed to kiss her very tenderly. "Goodbye, Diana."

239

"Goodbye. Take care."

He got up and moved away. Diana sat up. "Leo?"

"Yes?"

"Will you do something for me?"

"Probably."

"Don't leave that money on the mantel shelf it will upset me."

Manson studied her and nodded. "If you'll do me a favour in return."

"I'll try."

"It's not that onerous, lass. Write to me. Direct it to the 110th light company, you can drop it at the post office in Elvas and if that closes there's one in Badajoz, just set up. Scovell is in charge of the postal services now, so they run like clockwork, it'll reach me. And I'd like to write to you."

Diana slid from the bed and reached for her silk robe, pulling it around her. "Leo, I'm not sure your commanding officer would approve of you setting up a correspondence with a prostitute."

"It's very clear you've not met my commanding officer, lass."

She shot him a provocative glance. "How do you know?" she said.

Manson gave a shout of laughter. "Because I've seen his wife and you've not," he said.

Diana was clearly taken aback. Then she laughed aloud at her own reaction. "Is she much prettier than me?"

"She's the most beautiful woman I've ever seen. Which takes nothing away from how lovely you are. But it's not that, actually. He adores her and she him. You won't find him in the local brothel, no matter how charming its proprietor is. Although he would like you. The Colonel won't give a damn whom I write to, he wouldn't see it as his business. And if he did, I'd tell him to piss off anyway."

She was still laughing. "I don't understand you at all," she said. "I run a very nice business sneaking young officers in and out the back door so that their commanders don't know they're visiting prostitutes."

"And I'll just bet some of those bastards are using the same entrance and exit so that their young officers don't know what hypocrites they are. Do you need to keep written records so that you don't get it wrong?"

Diana was shaking with laughter. "You are the most irreverent captain in the army, Leo."

"I'm actually not, lass. Have you met Lord Wellington yet? Because he would definitely like the look of you."

"Leo! The commander-in-chief cannot visit a prostitute."

"No, but I am very sure he makes certain there's a discreet entrance into his bedchamber during winter quarters, he is a man with an eye for a lovely woman. And you are just his type."

"How on earth would you know that?" she said, still laughing.

"Because he's had his eye on my Colonel's wife for years, and you are not unlike her at all. Want me to put in a good word?"

"No!" Diana said, throwing a cushion at him. "I am very well as I am. Go away and do your duty, Captain Manson."

Manson caught her to him, kissing her hard. "Write to me," he said. "I want to know you're all right."

"I will. I'd like to hear the same about you."

Manson nodded and left, running lightly down the stairs. In the tap room Emilio was already up, tidying up tankards and bottles after the previous night.

"Emilio, I'm off. I don't know when I'll be back, but I will be. Do you know how to shoot a pistol?"

The man stared at him in surprise. Then he nodded. Manson reached into his greatcoat, took out the pistol and handed it to him.

"Show me."

The Portuguese took it and studied it for a moment. Then he reached for the shot Manson was holding out and began to load. Manson watched him critically. When he had done, Emilio raised the pistol and pointed as if to fire. He lowered it and looked at Manson.

"Partisans?" Manson asked quietly. Emilio nodded. "Is that why they killed your family, Emilio?"

Emilio nodded again. Manson put his hand on the man's shoulder. "I took that from a dead Frenchman. Keep it, I'll send one of my lads over with some ammunition for it. Under the bar."

The man nodded. He reached up and put his hand over Manson's for a moment. Manson smiled.

"I hope you never need it. I doubt the French will make it back this far, they're out of Portugal, however things go with us in Spain. But we both know there's more than the French to worry about. I don't want any of you hurt. And I never want to come in here again and see some bastard's handprints on her arms because he's held her down in her own bed, are we clear? You use that if you need to, and if any trouble comes from it, send to me, she knows how."

The man nodded again, and Manson touched him lightly on the shoulder and then left.

Chapter Eighteen

Over the next weeks Wellington's army began its preparations to march further into Spain. With the border fortresses secured, their commander was awaiting supplies and reinforcements. The dead had been buried and the wounded were being treated, and in many cases loaded up for the long journey back to Lisbon or Oporto and then on to England.

The refugee camps emptied as the citizens of Badajoz returned to their ruined homes and tried to salvage what they could. Anne's heart ached for them. She had seen so much misery throughout Portugal and Spain over the past two years and she wished she could do more to help, but the disaster was too big. She sent their own refugees off with bags of food to keep them going for a short time and prayed that they would find enough left to survive in the sacked city. In particular she worried about young Esmeralda, but the girl seemed to have attached herself to one of the families and she hoped they would continue to help her.

Despite the severity of their losses, Anne was conscious that Paul was more settled than he had been. The weather was turning warmer and as April moved into May, Wellington took up residence once again in Elvas and after consultation with his new commander, Paul moved the third brigade to a camp site on the edge of the town and allowed his senior officers to find billets among the headquarters staff. For a few weeks the army concentrated on provisioning and resting and recovering. Anne spent hours with Captain Breakspear and Lieutenant Fallon working on supplies for the brigade on the march and Paul requisitioned a fallow field half a mile from the camp and lined up his men in battalions and companies and gave a short speech both thanking them and praising them for their efforts since he had taken command.

They cheered him, making officers on their way to and from headquarters rein in to stare at the noise. Paul wondered as he gave his orders and separated them into battalions for training if they would be cheering him at the end of the day. But it felt good to be out there again, watching as they fell into the steady routine of drill and training.

"Colonel van Daan."

Paul turned, surprised, and saw his new commander dismounting. "Morning, sir. You're about early."

"I am an early riser," Alten said. "You also, I see. Mrs van Daan, good morning. I am surprised to see you about so early also."

"I'm used to army routines by now, sir," Anne said, coming forward with a smile. "How are you? I was going to send a message up to see if you wanted to dine with us on Monday."

"I should be delighted, ma'am." Alten's rare smile warmed his rounded features. "You are making my new appointment very easy for me."

"You're my favourite guest along with Lord Wellington," Anne said laughing. "You eat everything, your manners are excellent and you do not bore the company senseless by telling people how important you are. It must be something about the Light Division commanders, General Craufurd was lovely as well."

Paul was amused at the slight flush which stained the Hanoverian's face, but he laughed aloud.

"I cannot believe anybody could display bad manners at your table, ma'am, it is a joy to be there. But I have an invitation of my own. Lord Wellington is holding a reception on Friday. He wishes to thank his officers for their striking endeavours during the past months. I believe he is also inviting some of the local Spanish grandees…"

"I'll just bet he is," Paul said cynically. "Wants to get them on his side if we're heading into Spain. And you are about to tell me that he wants us to attend."

"He is issuing a general invitation, Colonel. But I am his deputy in asking if your lovely wife would consent to act as his hostess for the occasion."

"I notice he sends you instead of coming himself," Paul said with a grin. "He is going to use this as an excuse to spend the entire evening monopolising my wife, sir, trust me I've seen it before."

Anne was laughing. "Tell Lord Wellington I should be delighted. I have a new gown which I have been dying to show off. Shall you be there, General Alten?"

"I shall, ma'am. Lonely among my staff members, all of whom clearly think I am a dunderheaded German who does not understand English fully since they whisper quite loudly within my hearing about how badly I shall do in command of English troops."

Paul laughed. "They've no idea, have they?" he said, amused. "Ignore them, sir. I am becoming daily more convinced that you'll do very well."

"Thank you, Colonel. As I am here, would you mind if I watched for a while? I have heard a good deal of your training methods. I would like to see for myself."

"If you can bear it, sir, I'd be delighted," Paul said. "Let's start with the 110th. You won't see them at their best, we've a hundred and fifty new men just arrived from the second battalion. They're good lads and they know the basics but it will be a while before they're up to speed."

He moved away, talking to Alten who was listening, nodding, his eyes on the men. Anne watched, a smile on her face. The puppy, who was growing at an alarming rate, became bored with her inactivity and stood on his hind legs, his paws on her knee. Anne pushed him down firmly.

"That's going better than I expected," Johnny Wheeler said.

Anne turned, smiling. "They like each other," she said.

"I know. Bit of a surprise. I thought he'd be far too staid to work well with Paul."

"He's not as staid as you'd think. They'll disagree at times, but Alten is a very clever man, Johnny. He knows what he's good at, but he also knows his limitations, and he's going to use Paul to fill that gap. In some ways it will work better than General Craufurd did. Craufurd was every bit as brilliant an improviser as Paul. They loved working together, but it was unnecessary. Alten is a far better fit. He'll bring the stability and the organisational skills and Paul will provide the flashes of brilliance. And this – this is what they share. The work ethic to be up at dawn when the rest of the army is still resting and recovering, training the new recruits. Alten is genuinely keen to learn how this works, and Paul loves the fact that he's down here listening and watching instead of being up at headquarters being nice to Wellington."

"You think Wellington worked this out?"

"I'm sure he did. He's not always the best manager of people in the army. But he is very good at putting the right men in the right place. I think this will be good for both of them."

"What about Vandeleur and Barnard?" Johnny said.

"They're both good soldiers, Johnny, they'll work under anybody. We both know none of this is about them."

Wheeler studied her in some amusement. "Ma'am, I know very few men of your acquaintance would say this. But you ought to have been born a man. You'd have made commander-in-chief and we wouldn't have needed Wellington at all."

Anne laughed and reached up to kiss him lightly on the cheek. "Think what you'd all have missed, though, Johnny."

"I'd better join my regiment, or my brigade commander will be yelling." Wheeler smiled and turned to go and on impulse, Anne said:

"Johnny?"

"Yes?"

"How are you?"

She saw surprise followed by wariness in the velvet grey eyes. "I'm well, ma'am. Thank you."

"I meant…"

"I know what you meant," Wheeler said quickly. "You meant how am I coping without Caroline."

Silently Anne nodded. Johnny smiled painfully.

"I'm all right, ma'am. It's worse at night. Sometimes I lie awake worrying about how he's treating her. Mostly I just miss her. She was part of my life for a very short time, it's amazing how much it hurts."

Anne felt herself flinch internally. His pain was so raw and so well concealed for most of the time. His affair with Caroline Longford, the wife of one of Paul's officers had ended painfully when Longford had been transferred to Dublin and Caroline had chosen to go with him to safeguard the child she carried.

"She's all right, Johnny."

"Has she written?"

"No. We agreed not to. But Major Flanagan has. He's keeping a careful eye on things. No need to worry."

Wheeler smiled faintly. "Thank you."

"You're welcome. I'm going up to the hospital, I'll see you later. Come on, Craufurd, heel."

She had moved away when he said suddenly:

"What did she have? The child?"

Anne turned back, her heart aching for him. The child in question was very likely to be his. "A boy," she said. "They called him Richard."

Wheeler nodded without speaking and turned to make his way down to the brigade.

Anne attended the headquarters reception wearing one of the new gowns Paul had bought for her in Elvas, a masterpiece of simplicity in black lace which highlighted the ivory skin of her shoulders and breasts and caused some consternation, she knew, among those few ladies who had braved the journey to headquarters from the safer areas of Lisbon and Oporto.

Anne was aware that part of her usefulness to the commander in chief on these occasions was her excellent command of languages. She moved among the local grandees, both Spanish and Portuguese, switching easily from one language to another and was deep in conversation with Sir Denis Pack and several of his Portuguese officers when the tinkling of a bell silenced conversation and Lord Wellington stepped forward to present a variety of medals and campaign clasps to some of his senior officers.

Anne stood applauding with the rest of the company, privately amused. She knew that Lord Wellington was not especially keen on medals or awards and shared the faint contempt of most of the British army for the plethora of medals worn by many European officers. There were no medals available for the enlisted men although on a few occasions an unofficial regimental medallion had been struck and awarded for a particular piece of gallantry. The men of the first battalion of the 110th had been awarded one after the action on the Coa back in 1810 when Wellington considered that they had saved the Light Division from possible annihilation.

Anne felt a lift of pride as she saw Paul step forward to receive the appropriate awards. Wellington went on to present a selection of courtesy awards to Spanish and Portuguese commanders, which she knew was to some degree, the purpose of the exercise. The commander himself was then presented with a medal and a local Spanish title by a representative of the Spanish Royal family and there was a smattering of polite applause and Anne hid a smile at the expression of frozen civility on Wellington's face as the medal was pinned to his coat. She suspected it would seldom be seen again.

The proceedings ended with a series of personal awards. Anne was aware that these had a different meaning for Lord Wellington, who liked to give gifts in recognition of some piece of outstanding service. Several of his exploring officers who were present, stepped forward to receive an engraved telescope, including Captain Giles Fenwick, formerly of the 110th. Sir Richard Fletcher, Wellington's chief engineer limped up, still in considerable pain from the wound he had received during the siege, to receive a pocket watch. There were several small gifts for members of Wellington's staff, including Major George Scovell. Anne glanced across at Scovell's wife Mary, with whom she was good friends, and saw her blinking back tears of pride.

Anne was glad for George, who had served for a long time with no promotion and little credit for his amazing talent for both organisation and code breaking. George did not have an especially close relationship with the commander-in-chief, who tended to overlook his quiet competence.

"There is often some delay," Lord Wellington was saying, "in giving credit for courage and service over and above what might reasonably be expected during wartime. So many of the gallant officers I might like to recognise are sadly no longer here to be acknowledged, especially after this recent sanguinary action. I would consider myself remiss, however, if I did not recognise service from previous engagements and I would call up an officer who gave service to his country, to his men and to myself personally during the difficult period of the French retreat from Portugal, often under considerable difficulty and personal danger. Colonel Paul van Daan of the 110th light infantry."

Anne saw her husband's expression. This was different to the medal now adorning his coat, which was the standard award for men of his rank and service. He moved forward and the smattering of polite applause grew louder, not only from his own officers but from those of the rest of the Light Division who understood and gave grateful tribute to the difficulties of his command under Sir William Erskine. Paul bowed and accepted the gift which was in a small box, and she saw him examine it and then look up, his face breaking into laughter.

"You know me so well, sir," he said and stepped back, saluting. He moved to join Anne and she saw that it was a silver flask, elegantly engraved with a simple message. She looked up at Paul.

"Well deserved, love," she said softly. "I'm very proud of you."

"Thank you. Think we're almost done, bonny lass? The sight of you in that dress has been praying on my mind for hours." Paul was leaning in close to murmur in her ear, and Anne felt a shiver of desire at his tone. "I particularly like the way the lace displays those very lovely shoulders, but just at this moment, I'd like to be sliding it down so that I can..."

"Paul, stop it for God's sake," Anne whispered, laughing. "You're making me blush."

"I can see that, girl of my heart. Which is not especially easy for me either, since I know where that blush starts and just what it looks like in the lamplight. Surely he can't go on for much longer? Do you know what I want to be doing just now?"

She leaned into him, laughing, her back to the room and he slid his hand discreetly around her waist, caressing the curve of her hip through the silk and lace of her gown. He was laughing back, knowing the effect of his words and his touch.

"I bet you wish you'd not offered the others a lift back in the carriage," she whispered.

"It's only a ten minute drive. I can wait that long to start taking your clothes off. Although not much longer. Oh Jesus, is he still talking? It's not like him; he's normally done quicker than this..."

He broke off suddenly as the sense of Wellington's words reached him and Anne turned at his expression, puzzled, looking at Lord Wellington

"Without any formal award that can be given to a civilian, I wish, nevertheless to acknowledge her extraordinary work with the wounded of my army, along with the

246

exceptional personal courage with which she has many times placed herself in danger to save the lives of both officers and men. Of the support and encouragement, she gives to her husband I will say nothing more, since it is well known. The assistance she has rendered to me and to the officers of my staff is perhaps less frequently advertised, but her remarkable talent for organisation has more than once rendered an impossible task more manageable. I crave the indulgence of her husband and hope that he understands that this gift is not personal but should be seen in the light of a campaign medal."

Wellington was looking over at them and Paul met the blue eyes in considerable amusement. "It had better be, sir," he said, and gave Anne a gentle push. She looked up at him, confused, and then understood and felt herself blush scarlet. She moved forward to greet Lord Wellington and curtseyed. He was smiling down at her.

"May I?"

Anne nodded and he reached out to pin the brooch to her gown. Anne looked down at it. It was a golden dragon, closely resembling the dragons which supported the Portuguese coat of arms, its one visible eye a tiny emerald. He must have had it specially made and Anne looked up with quick appreciation.

"Thank you, sir, it's beautiful."

Wellington took her hand and raised it to his lips. "So are you," he said, and for a brief moment his expression was unguarded, and Anne smiled slightly, acknowledging it. He smiled back and then released her as Paul stepped forward to claim her.

"Take her home, Colonel," he said quietly. "We march in a day or so. Time I got these fools out of here and got to my bed."

"Yes, sir. Thank you."

Anne drifted in a daze of surprised happiness until they were back in their room, and then stood as Paul carefully unpinned the brooch and put it into her open jewel case. Anne looked up at him and laughed at the expression on his face.

"If you tear this gown, Paul, I am going to slap you," she said and he grinned.

"Better turn around then, girl of my heart and let me get these buttons undone."

She stood still, her heart beating more quickly as he unbuttoned the gown and then slid the lace down, his mouth moving down her shoulder making her shiver with desire.

"Paul," she whispered, and his hands moved, pushing the gown to the floor, unlacing her stays with quick practiced fingers. He slid his hands down over her body under the chemise and she felt his breathy laugh against her ear.

"It this silk?"

"Yes. It's new, do you like it?"

"Very much." His hand stroked her breast through the soft material. "I wish I could have seen the dressmaker's face when you ordered this, bonny lass, it is not an undergarment for a respectable married woman."

"No, it isn't, is it? Perhaps she thought I had a lover….oh."

Paul turned her round and knelt, removing her shoes and then reaching up under the black silk to her garters, sliding her stockings down. She stood, melting with

247

longing as he put his mouth to her inner thigh and kissed it, then bit gently, laughing, his hand moving up and over her, feeling the evidence of her desire.

"Judging by how you feel, I'd say you've been thinking about this as long as I have this evening."

"I have," Anne admitted. "Wait…"

She reached up, taking the pins from her hair and heard him catch his breath as it fell about her half bare shoulders in a silken curtain. Laughing softly she removed her earrings but when she reached for the clasp of the spectacular diamond necklace he shook his head.

"Leave them on," he said softly and she laughed aloud and reached for the black ribbon at the front of her chemise.

"You're not subtle, Paul."

"I don't need to be, bonny lass, you're already mine. That's a very pretty little toy he just gave you, and don't think I didn't see how he looked at you as he was pinning it to your dress. Lie down, I can't wait any longer."

Amused and intrigued Anne obeyed. "Aren't you even going to undress?" she asked.

"Not yet. Afterwards. I've got all night."

"I hope my social exertions haven't tired me out then," Anne said.

His mouth hovered above hers. "So do I, girl of my heart, because you're not going to be sleeping much. We'll do the romance in a minute. Right now I'm very clear about what I want."

Anne gasped as he moved into her, her back pressed hard against the cool wooden boards of the floor, her shift up around her hips. Used to the sense of his skin against hers she was conscious of the buttons and braid and rough cloth of his coat scraping against her body as he held her still, gently but firmly, and took possession of her with a fierce urgency that left her trembling with reaction.

"You all right?" he asked softly against her mouth when he had done. Anne nodded, unable to speak for a moment. He seemed to understand and simply kissed her, very gently at first and then harder, his mouth parting hers. She felt his hands on her chemise and shifted to let him lift it over her head, not wanting him to tear it. His hands on her body sent a wave of desire flooding through her.

"Paul…"

"Get me out of these clothes," he whispered, and she obeyed, conscious the whole time of his eyes on her body. When she was done he lifted her into his arms and carried her to the bed. She lay back, smiling at him.

"You're a brute, Colonel van Daan. I've a row of bruises all down my spine from those boards and that coat is like a weapon."

"I can see it is," he admitted, reaching to touch a scratch on her breast. He put his mouth to it. "I could also feel how much you hated every moment of it."

Anne slid down beneath him. "You had your fun," she said. "I was promised romance."

"I can do that. Might take me a little while, mind."

Anne laughed. "I can probably help with that," she whispered, and he gasped as she reached for him.

248

They lay quietly together some time later, her head on his chest listening with relaxed enjoyment to the sound of his heart beating against her ear. He suddenly gave a little chuckle.

"What is it?"

"I must be the only man in the British army whose wife has a campaign medal of her very own."

"Is that what got you so worked up, Colonel?"

"No. That's what happens when I watch them all drooling over you at a party all evening, girl of my heart. I tend to get the urge to reassert my claim. Sorry, was I rough?"

"No, it was lovely. Although I still prefer a mattress to the floor."

"Even this mattress?" Paul asked with a grimace, shifting his back. Anne laughed.

"Just about. I didn't realise that's what you do."

"Never thought about it that much, but it does happen. It sounds somewhat ridiculous to say it aloud but there's something about other men desiring my wife that makes me realise what I've got."

"It doesn't bother you, does it? It used to drive Robert mad."

Paul glanced at her. "There's a name I've not heard in a while. No. I actually enjoy it. Carl once said it's part of my natural arrogance, that I enjoy having what they all want."

Anne shifted and leaned over to kiss him. "I don't care what the reason is when it feels as good as that did. Welcome back, Paul."

Paul studied her for a long time, taking in what she had said. "Nan?"

"That's the first time since I got back you've really let yourself go. I've missed it."

"Oh Jesus, bonny lass!" He was half laughing, half appalled. "Has it been that obvious?"

"It has to me, Paul, but then I've done this with you rather a lot. I know the difference." Anne smiled. "It was supposed to be me who struggled with this."

"It's not that I've struggled, Nan. It's just that every time I've touched you, I'm watching your face to see if you're all right with what I'm doing. I'm so scared of hurting you or frightening you."

Anne laughed aloud. "Is that all it's been?"

"Yes, of course. Why, what did you think it was?"

"I was rather afraid that every time you touched me you were thinking that he had too."

Paul's eyes widened in horror and Anne felt, fully, the relief as she realised how badly she had misunderstood. "Nan, you cannot have thought that! Oh love, why didn't you say something?"

"Paul, it's not that easy to talk about. And if you had been struggling with that, what could you have said anyway? I didn't want to upset you."

"So instead, you've been upsetting yourself." He regarded her sternly. "I thought we agreed when we first married that we wouldn't do that again."

"We did. But it's difficult to predict something like this, Paul. I'm sorry."

249

"Don't be. I didn't say anything either, I didn't want you to feel I was putting pressure on you."

Anne was laughing aloud. "Do you think we could stop being so careful with one another?"

"It might be an idea." Paul studied her for a long moment. She was still laughing.

"Spit it out, Colonel."

"All right. Although you're not going to like it. Nan - I am not coping well with you wandering around the camp on your own. I know you've always done it and I've not worried about it for a long time. But at the moment, every time I see you ride off on your own, I am going mad until you get back."

There was a long silence. Paul let it go on, knowing that his wife often needed time to think about her reply to something that angered or upset her. She was the opposite to him; he would often explode and say the first thing that came into his head, but he had learned to give her space to think about her response.

"What do you want me to do?" Anne asked finally.

"Well, I am not going to tell you to stay at home and take up needlework, girl of my heart. You'd go insane and shoot me. And that's not the girl I married anyway. I'm hoping that this will pass. But until it does, I want to find a groom for you. Not one of your medical orderlies but someone employed by us whose job it is to look after you. And I know you're going to bloody hate that, but..."

"All right."

His shocked expression made her laugh openly. "What's the matter, Colonel, you've got what you wanted. I've said yes."

"I know you have. Why? I was prepared for you to slap me."

Anne shifted closer to him and kissed him very gently. "I want to tell you that I'm doing this purely for you, Paul. And do you know what? I would. But I am going to be very honest with you and admit that I don't really have all my confidence back yet. I'm a little jumpy myself."

"You don't seem it."

"It's an act. I told you, I am determined that what happened to me isn't going to change who I am. But I've always sailed through the lines completely disregarding the way some of the men watch me. It has honestly never bothered me before, but once or twice recently I've felt uncomfortable. I hate the fact that I'm changing my behaviour because of Dupres, but I think I might be happier with an escort for a while."

Paul smoothed the dark hair back from her face. "Girl of my heart - I don't know if you're making that up to make me feel better and I don't care. Thank you. Do you have any ideas...?"

"Yes. I'm going to ask Juan's orderly."

Paul wrinkled his brow. "Costa?"

"Yes. He's been with Juan since he was a lad, Juan picked him up from a farm near Belmonte. He's wandering the lines looking for jobs like a lost soul."

Paul nodded, his eyes on her face. "I'll speak to him. Thank you, Nan. I feel better for that."

"You're welcome. Are you tired?"

Paul smiled lazily. "Too tired for what you have in mind."

"That was not what I was thinking!"

"Liar. You've got the fidgets, haven't you? Let's dress and take Craufurd down to the river, shall we, there's a lovely moon? It might wake me up a bit."

Anne gave a gurgle of laughter. "It's the middle of the night, Colonel, you're not supposed to be trying to wake up."

Paul rolled over and kissed her with leisurely enjoyment. "Some nights are too magical to waste sleeping," he said softly, and Anne reached up to caress his face.

"You are such a hopeless romantic, Colonel van Daan."

"I am, girl of my heart. Get dressed. Come and drink wine with me in the moonlight while your dog fails to catch rabbits in the undergrowth."

They slept late into the morning and Paul was aware of covert grins when he joined his officers out at training later in the day. He was pleased to see Michael O'Reilly at the head of his company and went to join him.

"Good to see you back, Michael. Has my wife given you permission?"

"No, sir. I'd have asked her, but she seems to have slept awful late this morning."

Paul grinned. "Normally I'd thump you at this point but I'm too glad to see you fit again. Are you?"

"Yes, sir. It's healed well and I'm feeling better in myself. Sorry I missed the party yesterday, mind, Captain Manson tells me it was glory and honours all around for the 110th and the Light Division."

"Including my lady. I wonder if that one will make it into the Gazette or the Times back home?"

"If it does, they'll make something of it that it's not. You should be very proud of her."

"Couldn't be more so. We celebrated by seeing in the dawn with Craufurd and a bottle of wine by the river."

Michael laughed. "Making the most of it, sir?"

"I need to, we'll be marching out the day after tomorrow. Captain Manson, well done. They're looking very good. You've done wonders with them in a short time."

"Major Flanagan had done a lot of work with them already, sir. I wanted to ask if you could spare me for an hour or two this afternoon? We've done kit inspections and they're packed and ready to move out."

Paul studied him in some surprise and then nodded. "Take as long as you want. Not much chance of time off once we're chasing bloody Marmont around the countryside."

"Thank you, sir, I appreciate it."

Manson moved away and Michael glanced at Paul. "What's that about?"

"He is intending to visit the local brothel, Michael."

Michael laughed aloud. "Is he, by God? I can't say I blame him, not much chance of it on campaign. But it's not like Manson, he's usually fairly discreet about these things. Has he been short of funds for a while or something?"

Paul grinned. He watched as the NCOs called the men into line and began issuing final orders to prepare for the march. "I'm not sure he's paying for it, Michael.

He seems to have struck up a friendship with the lass who runs the place. I was asking Hammond about it, he was with Leo that day we cleared the 115th out of town, and they went in to pick up Jagger and his repellent friends."

"She seems grateful."

"That was my assumption. And I don't blame Leo for making the most of it, Hammond tells me she's very lovely. Part English, he thinks. I've not asked, it's none of my business and Leo is so damned conscientious, it's almost a relief to see him playing truant a little. I forget sometimes how young he is."

"He's twenty-one. And I seem to remember another young officer of that age who was over-conscientious years ago."

Paul laughed. "I might have been, Michael, but I don't think anybody could say that I lacked female company along the way. In a lot of ways, he's more mature than I was. In other ways he's a lot less experienced; by the time I joined up at twenty-one I'd fought in the navy for two and a half years, fathered a bastard and taken far too many women to bed. I wouldn't want Leo to follow my example, people tend to get hurt. But I would like to see him enjoy himself a bit more, so if this lass is giving him a good enough time to make him want to slope off and see her in the middle of the day, I wish him well."

Michael looked at his friend and laughed. "When I see you with Manson, sir, I get a glimpse of how you're going to be with your boys as they grow older. I know there's only ten years between you, but there's something paternal about your attitude to him."

"If my lads grow up to be half the man Leo Manson is, Michael, I'll consider we've done a good job. Get this lot stood down. They're as good as they're going to get, no need to push them right up to the march. Issue a general order for an evening's leave, they can go and get drunk tonight, they'll still have a day to recover. Might be their last chance for a while."

"Yes, sir. What about you? Fancy coming out? Colonel Wheeler could do with cheering up, and Carl needs prising away from that lass of his, they're welded together."

"Yes, I think I will. There's a nice place opposite the Cathedral, Nan and I went there. I haven't been out with the lads for a while."

"Will your wife mind?"

"No, she never does. It would be different if I was leaving her behind, but she'll be with me. Speak to Johnny and I'll inform Carl that it's an order."

***

With his kit packed and his company ready, Leo Manson walked down to Diana Pereira's tavern. He paused at the door and the bartender recognised him and smiled. Manson came into the room. "Afternoon, Emilio. Is Diana around?"

The Portuguese nodded and indicated the back room. Manson smiled. "All right if I go through?"

Emilio nodded and Manson walked through to the back parlour where he found Diana occupied with some mending. The scene was very domestic and he stood in the doorway smiling. She got up, setting her work aside.

252

"Captain Manson, welcome. I thought you were on your way north."

"I am, we're marching the day after tomorrow. There's nothing urgent for me to do, my lads are ready to march, and I suddenly wanted to see you. I hope that's all right? If you're busy…"

"No. We've been quiet, probably because the army is about to march out. Not all your men get to play truant like this."

Manson laughed and came forward to kiss her lightly. "Not all the officers do either, I'm somewhat privileged."

"Did you ask your Colonel for permission?"

"I did. He laughed a lot and told me to go."

"Well I'm very grateful he could spare you." Diana reached up and kissed him again, and he felt her body leaning into his. "I've been thinking about you rather a lot."

"It's mutual," Manson admitted, studying her. "I almost didn't come, simply because I can't work out how to be around you. It's confusing…"

"You're not a customer, Leo, if that helps clear it up," Diana said, and he felt a surprising leap of pleasure at the words.

"Are you sure, lass? Because I would definitely like to take you to bed just now, but I don't want you thinking I'm here for a free treat before I leave. At the same time, I don't want to offer you money if it's going to insult you. I just wanted to see you."

The girl was laughing and the sound warmed him. "Leo, you are the most delightfully clear man I have ever met in my life, there is no possibility of confusion with you, is there? This is strange for me too, I've never in my life had a relationship with a man who didn't pay me for it. And I don't know how hard this is for you because I can't give up what I do, I can't afford to."

"No. Well, I can't afford to sweep you off your feet and offer you a new life either, Diana, so it would be unreasonable of me to demand that you give up your means of support after meeting me two or three times. I like you. Rather a lot, I find."

Diana reached for his hand. "I like you too. Come upstairs, I'll let Emilio know I'm not to be disturbed.

Manson waited for her in the simple room and looking around him realised how much he liked it. It reminded him of Diana herself, calming and peaceful and good to be around. The door opened and she came into the room. Standing before him she reached up to remove the pins from her hair and his pulse quickened as he saw it fall about her shoulders. She reached for the buttons of her gown and Manson moved forward.

"Let me do that," he said softly, and Diana nodded and turned so that he could reach. He undid each button slowly, enjoying the sense of anticipation. Sliding the soft muslin to the floor he slid his arms about her waist and swept her hair to one side, kissing her neck. She gave a sigh of pleasure, twisted round into his arms and kissed him then took his hand.

"Come to bed," she said.

Manson had wondered if his memory had exaggerated how much he had enjoyed his previous night with her. He was not a frequent visitor to brothels, both from lack of money and because he had realised early on that he preferred to share a bed with a woman he knew and liked. On his arrival in Portugal his fellow officers had quickly become aware of his lack of experience and Michael O'Reilly had taken it upon himself to introduce him to an attractive widow who ran a local grog shop and supplemented her income from time to time with a few selected officers. Elena was choosy about who she would go to bed with and O'Reilly had been both irritated and amused when she had taken such a liking to the newest lieutenant of the 112th that she had remained his exclusive companion during his time in Lisbon. Since then, Manson had occasionally visited the brothel but preferred the company of Lucia, one of three or four prostitutes who had attached themselves to the Light Division. His friends laughed at his choosiness over his bed mates but Manson did not care.

He did not know this girl well, but he was aware that it felt as though he did. Despite her extensive experience, there was something touchingly innocent about Diana Periera, as though her capacity to enjoy herself was a surprise to her. He lay beside her afterwards in silent content with her dark head on his shoulder and her long shapely leg thrown across his.

"Are you all right?" he asked softly and she stirred, turned her head and kissed his shoulder.

"Yes. Very much so. You're a lovely man, Leo Manson."

Manson tightened his arm about her. "You're a lovely woman, Diana Pereira. And I am not just talking about the way you look."

She was silent for a moment then she said:

"You mean that, don't you?"

"Yes. I wouldn't have said it if I didn't."

"I've never met a man as straightforward as you."

Manson grinned. "Not everybody appreciates it," he said. "Especially when I'm giving my men a bollocking over something. I am so comfortable here, I don't want to move. What time is it - the light is fading."

"I don't know. Something about you makes me lose track of time. Do you have to leave soon?"

"No. There won't be much to do tomorrow, the Colonel will let the lads rest before the march. May I stay the night?"

"Of course you may. But won't he mind?" Diana asked curiously, with long experience of young officers and the importance of pleasing their seniors.

"No, he'll understand. He might give me a roasting, but I'll survive that." Manson ran his fingers lightly over her tummy and she giggled.

"Well you'll need to eat, Captain, or you'll have no strength to march anywhere. Stay here, I'll organise some food."

Manson shifted to kiss her lazily. "You shouldn't be waiting on me, lass, I can dress and come down."

"No. Let's eat up here. I'm greedy, I want you to myself this evening. You won't be here tomorrow, and God knows when I'll see you again."

Manson felt a tug of sadness. "I know. But I will write to you, Diana, I promise. Often."

They ate sitting at the small table by the window, talking of ordinary matters. She asked him about his family and he told her about his father, and a little about his early days in the regiment. She laughed at some of the stories and studied him across her wine glass.

"I honestly can't imagine you being that unsure about anything," she said. Manson grinned.

"Believe me, I was. My father had been lecturing me about how to be a good officer since I was three, I thought I knew. But it was so much harder than I thought. I realise now we were given a poor hand, Will Grey and I. The 112th wasn't as far out of control as Jagger and his friends, but it wasn't that much better, and they sent eight companies with only the two of us in charge, neither with any experience. On board ship we'd little to do with them but when we landed here I suddenly realised they were my responsibility and they had absolutely no respect for us whatsoever. It was terrifying."

"That must have been horrible, given that you wanted to be a soldier so much."

Manson thought about it and then laughed. "Do you know what's so funny, Diana? I don't know that I did. It was what my father wanted for me. So I just did it. I thought if I could be like him, it would make things better."

"And did it?"

Manson sipped the wine. "No. I thought he'd be pleased that I settled so well. All I got were carping letters about the regiment. When I was promoted to captain so young, I wrote to him and he replied that he'd pulled some strings at Horse Guards and they were now prepared to let me transfer into his old regiment. Cavalry. I said no."

"Was he furious?"

"Completely incensed. He wrote to tell me he'd cut me off without a penny if I didn't fall into line. It wasn't much of a threat, really, there's very little money, I've always lived off my pay. He also wrote to the Colonel."

"How embarrassing."

"It might have been, but the Colonel just replied telling him it was up to me where I served. It must have been a shock to my father, he is so used to his family doing exactly as he tells them to, I don't think it occurred to him that I wouldn't give in. And then I had a letter to say that he'd had a heart attack and wasn't expected to live."

"Oh Leo, I'm sorry."

"Yes. The Colonel gave me leave immediately and I went home. First time I'd been since I came to Portugal. I don't know why I was shocked to find him sitting in his study reading the newspaper just as he'd been the day I left."

Diana's eyes widened. "He wasn't ill?"

"No. Probably never had been. He wanted to berate me in person. I'd left my company, possibly to fight and die without me, on the whim of a spiteful old man who couldn't bear not to have his own way. I'm not sure I'd ever been so angry."

"So you quarrelled."

"We did. Spectacularly and finally. He ordered me out of the house and I left. I feel sad for my mother, and for Elinor and Juliet. I can't even write to them; he intercepts any letters. But him...I'm glad it's done with, to tell you the truth, I feel the lighter for it. What amazed me was the fact that he had no idea why I was so angry. I'm not sure he felt any remorse at all and he certainly didn't understand about my company or my regiment, he'd felt no attachment to his own men. Just to the name and the prestige it brought him." Manson drank deeply. "You're the first person I've told," he said abruptly. "I don't usually talk about this."

"Well I'm glad you did, Leo. I feel very fortunate. I may have had my troubles after my parents died, but while they were alive they were very kind to me. In fact, I suspect that if he had not been taken ill so suddenly and so surprisingly my father would have made some kind of provision for me. He simply did not have time."

"No. I rather imagine he'd have been horrified at what you had to do to survive. And also very proud of you."

"Proud?"

Manson put down his glass and reached for her hand. He lifted it to his lips and kissed it. "He was a businessman, Diana. A successful one by the sound of it. And here you are, started with nothing and you own a very successful tavern, you're secure and you're comfortable. I know you had to do things to earn it that you'd rather not think about…"

"How do you know that, Leo?"

"Because I'm not stupid, lass, and not all men know how to behave with a woman. You've got to the point where you can pick and choose for which I'm thankful, but even then you'll get some bastard like Jagger walking in here and thinking he can treat you however the hell he likes because of what you do."

"I'm not sure that had a lot to do with what I do, Leo. I suspect Jagger was a swine with a woman whoever she was. And you're right, I've done well. Mostly I try not to think about what I do. They're men. Some I like better than others. Are you all right talking about this?"

Manson paused for thought. "I need to be," he said. "Because we're agreed I don't have the right or the money to ask you to stop doing it. It's hardly fair to behave as though it's something we can't acknowledge."

Diana smiled and refilled their glasses. "No details, I promise. You were right, I am choosy, I can afford to be now. And that helps, it gives me a sense of control. I try to see it as a job. I'm as nice as I can be but I'm also business-like."

"Officers only?" Manson said, amused by her manner and she eyed him warily.

"Is it going to bother you if I say no?"

Manson laughed aloud. "No. I told you, the 110th isn't like other regiments, you're not going to last long if you've you're nose in the air half the time."

"Then no, I don't base my choice on a commission. I charge more than the other girls which means that most of my customers tend to be officers or local businessmen. The odd diplomat or Portuguese or Spanish grandee. But I've one or two regulars from a while ago when I had less and couldn't afford to be so choosy, and if they show up on their way through, I won't say no, some of them were very good to me when I first started out. It's been my experience that the enlisted men and NCOs can be better behaved that some of the officer class."

"I believe you." Manson studied her, aware for the first time of discomfort. He caught it and looked at it steadily and realised what was bothering him. She was watching his face and he understood that he was testing to see how frank they were able to be with one another. He took a deep breath.

256

"That was a bit of a moment," he admitted wryly. "Because it suddenly occurred to me…my regiment hasn't spent much time here yet. But…."

"No," she said quietly. "I've not come across this particular colour facing before, Leo, it's very elegant. And I won't, not now. Plenty of other girls they can choose from. But thank you for being honest, it makes this very much easier for me. Leo – this is going to sound like a strange question, but how old are you?"

Manson laughed aloud, ready for her reaction. "I'm twenty one. I'll be twenty two in a few weeks."

"Oh dear God – you're barely older than I am. Diana studied him with wide surprised eyes and then laughed and shook her head. "I thought you older."

"People always do. Something about my manner I suppose. And war makes you grow up fast." Manson met her eyes steadily and felt his pulse quicken. "Have you finished?"

"I'm suddenly not hungry any more," Diana said, and he rose and moved around the table, taking her hand as she stood.

"Nor am I. At least not for food."

She was laughing as he slid into bed beside her. "Captain Manson, I am beginning to realise why you're so good at what you do. You never seem to get tired."

"I do, lass. I'm just very good at ignoring it when there's something I need to do." Manson reached for her with sudden urgency. "Or something I very much want to do. I've realised I don't give a damn how many men you go to bed with while I'm not here, but I want you to remember how this feels and look forward to me coming back."

"Leo, there is no danger of me forgetting about you any time soon."

"Good," Manson said, and bent to kiss her.

He was thinking about her as he moved to the head of his company the following morning. Around him the brigade was forming up into marching order. Manson surveyed his men with a critical eye and found, as he had expected that there was nothing to complain of. Further up the lines he could see his commander's wife mounted on her pretty black mare. She wore a new riding habit which Paul had bought for her in Elvas, a dark wine colour which highlighted her vivid colouring and the dark sheen of her hair. She wore no hat and even as the thought entered Manson's head, he heard his commander's voice raised in a bellow.

"Teresa! What has she done with her hat again? Christ, it's like raising a five year old! You get sunstroke and I am sending you back to Lisbon, I'm telling you!"

There was laughter in the ranks as Teresa Carter disappeared and emerged from Anne's deserted billet with her smart black riding hat. She took it to Paul who rode over to his wife and placed it firmly on her smooth dark head. Anne laughed and reached for her hat pin to secure it. Manson was amused to notice that the dragon brooch given to her by Lord Wellington was pinned very openly on the riding dress, standing out against the rich material.

Paul surveyed the chaos of his brigade and Manson looked over at Carl Swanson who was already mounted. Carl grinned back and began to count, silently mouthing the numbers at Manson. Manson responded by silently raising one finger for each number. They had reached six.

"Jesus bloody Christ, I have never seen anything like this in my life!" Paul bellowed, and every head within earshot turned towards him. "I have seen more organisation on cattle market day in Lisbon! Captain Heron, is there a reason why your company can't stand in a straight line? Captain O'Reilly, have you forgotten which company you command and what order we march in? 110th light company, stop standing there and fall in, you look like a bunch of stuffed frogs! Kelly, Jenson, get those supply wagons into line or I'm leaving the baggage behind and the women with them, you can keep each other warm at night like every other regiment in this bloody army!" He watched with a critical eye as his brigade began to move and the chaos resolved itself into organisation within three minutes. Paul did not turn.

"Major Swanson, Captain Manson. I know what you're doing, I can hear you laughing. Just for that, you are jointly in charge of my wife's dog for the day, make sure he doesn't run off and put him in the wagon when he gets too tired. All right, let's get moving or we'll be crossing the Spanish border at just about the time the rest of the army reaches Madrid. Sergeant-Major Carter, give the order, please!"

The bugles sounded and Leo Manson moved to the head of his company and rode out, looking over the long train of the marching army ahead of him. As they approached the edge of the town people had come out of their houses to wave and to stare, and one or two of the women ran forward with flowers or small gifts of food. Manson wondered with some cynicism if the regiments who had marched out of Badajoz that morning had been given the same response. He seriously doubted it.

Then they were passing the tavern with the white walls and olive trees and he looked, feeling foolish, and was disproportionately pleased to see her standing at the gate dressed in yellow muslin with her hair loose. He smiled slightly and nodded and she returned it, her eyes on his face. He was level with her when he saw her move and he turned, startled, and caught the object she had thrown up to him. Looking down into his hand he saw that it was an apple, rich and red, and he looked over and saw that she was laughing. He smiled back, hearing the amusement of his officers and men, and put the fruit in his pocket.

They were passing an almond tree, the white blooms blowing gently in the morning breeze, and on impulse he reached out and broke off a sprig heavy with flowers. Looking back at the girl he raised it to his lips to kiss and then threw it to her. She caught it, still laughing and lifted it to her lips in response. Then he was past and looking ahead towards the Guadiana River and Badajoz and towards Spain.

Author's Thanks

Many thanks for reading this book and I hope you enjoyed it. If you did, I would be very grateful if you would consider leaving a short review on Amazon or Goodreads or both. One or two lines is all that's needed. Good reviews help get books in front of new readers, which in turn, encourages authors to carry on writing the books. They also make me very, very happy.

Thank you.

Lynn

Author's Note - Contains Spoilers

A Redoubtable Citadel is the most difficult book I've written so far. I rewrote it until my head span and even now, revising it, I'm not sure I've got it right. I have nightmares that all the readers who have been enjoying this series will be put off and never read another one of my books. I have visions of angry reviews telling me that I've trivialised the awful subject of sexual assault by including it in a series of historical novels.

But I still wrote it.

There is nothing trivial about rape and the fact that it has happened to my favourite female character isn't an accident. Anne was raped by her first husband, and more than once but there was no comeback on Robert because Anne married in 1808 and there was no such thing as rape in marriage at that time. Anne was expected to provide sex on demand to her husband and if she objected, which she did, he was entitled to force her. During the two years of her marriage, she learned the painful lesson that it hurt less if she gave in. She got tired of being beaten so she gave him what he wanted until his violence escalated to the point where she could no longer hide it from her friends.

Friends and family who have helped by reading and proof reading my books have queried Anne's behaviour over her first marriage because they struggled with the concept of a woman as intelligent and strong willed as Anne putting up with that relationship for so long. I don't struggle with it at all. In a historical context there was nowhere for Anne to go. There were no social services or women's centres, no specially trained police units or counsellors. She was a long way from her family who might possibly have become aware that something was badly wrong with their daughter's marriage and although she had a close friend in Rowena, the two girls had not known one another very long. She would not go to Paul because she was afraid of what he might do.

But outside of the historical context, Anne was no different to many women even today who remain in a violent relationship for a variety of reasons. Abusers don't just use physical violence to control. They use shame, guilt, verbal abuse, financial control and a variety of other methods to make their victim feel worthless and powerless. Despite her hatred of him and her anger at having to appease him, Anne still feels a sense of relief when Robert is kind to her and a sense of gratitude when he graciously allows her to continue her work with the medical staff. It is a myth that all women in abusive relationships are natural victims. Repeated abuse can paralyse even the most strong minded person.

By the time we get to book four, Anne has been in a very different marriage for over a year. She has given birth to her first child and is secure and happy in a loving relationship. People around Paul and Anne doubted that it would work; they thought that Paul would be unfaithful or that Anne's unladylike behaviour would drive him mad. The army's most unlikely couple have enjoyed proving them wrong.

And then Anne is taken prisoner by a French colonel with a grudge against Paul, is held for two weeks and is raped.

When I was struggling with this storyline, I wrote about ten different versions. In several of them, the rape doesn't happen. They didn't work; the last minute rescue was too convenient and as hard as I tried I couldn't manage a scenario where Colonel Dupres acquired a set of scruples at the last minute. In the end I took a deep breath and wrote the scene and I absolutely hated it. I also hated the scene when Anne is rescued and is struggling to tell Paul what has happened to her. When she does so, she apologises. She feels guilty because she wasn't able to fight her way out of it. She feels worse when she loses the child she is carrying because Dupres punched her. She feels defiled and used and despite several brutal beatings, it is the rape which leaves scars. She is terrified that it will affect her enjoyment of sex with her husband and initially, not knowing that she was already pregnant, she is afraid she will end up bearing a child by her rapist.

The scenes between Anne and Paul in the immediate aftermath of the rape were very difficult but they were also some of the most rewarding scenes I've written about them. For once there is little or no laughter between them but there is an enormous amount of tenderness. She needs to tell him what happened and deal with her guilt at not being able to stop it. He needs to listen and to manage his own guilt at letting her travel without him, at not being there to protect her. She worries that it was somehow her fault, that something about her caused this to happen to her. He desperately tries to reassure her, reminding her that in war horrible things have happened to a lot of women and that it is not personal to her. And in the middle of it all, both of them know that there will be talk and that some people will judge Anne and believe that her unorthodox behaviour has somehow brought this on herself.

This story is set more than two hundred years ago but so many aspects of it have not changed. Women still get beaten and raped by men. These days we have more effective laws and a variety of support systems for women in trouble but they don't always work. Moreover, in a war zone, invading armies still behave, at times, with the same careless brutality of the French soldiers in Portugal and Spain and the

British army in Badajoz and San Sebastian. I have read stories of women who have survived wars in Africa and Asia, in Europe and the Middle East, and they are horrific and they make me cry. Women and girls suffer in wartime, even in our so-called enlightened age and to write a story set in the Peninsular War which ignores that fact would be wrong.

Many years ago I worked as a counsellor at a woman's centre with women and children who had experienced domestic violence and I later did specialised training to work with survivors of rape and sexual abuse. One of the things I learned is that people experiencing trauma of any kind react in so many different ways that it is hard to generalise. I've tried to keep Anne and Paul's reactions believable given the people they are. Paul is torn between concern for his wife and an overwhelming need to kill somebody which is inevitable given the man he is. Anne experiences many emotions in quick succession; anger, fear, shame, humiliation and misery. But she is also fiercely determined not to let Dupres ruin the life she has built for herself with Paul.

Paul kills Dupres; he was always going to. I chose to end Anne's ordeal with swift retribution and the historical setting enabled me to do that. Most women don't have that option. Even if their attacker is brought to justice and sent to prison, it does not end their suffering. Like Anne, many of them are aware that they are being blamed for what happened to them. Did they ask for it? Were they dressed provocatively? Did they say or do something wrong? Were they drunk? Walking home alone in the dark? Had they said no loudly enough or firmly enough?

To make it worse, like Anne, most survivors are asking themselves the same questions. They need support and understanding from those around them, not censure. And they need time and help to heal. Anne has little time for any of this. She is catapulted fresh from the trauma of her ordeal right into the middle of a battlefield with men being injured and dying. Initially it is a big help to her, since getting back to work is a distraction and makes her feel normal again. But anybody who has been through that kind of assault or who has worked with survivors knows that she is unlikely to be over it that easily.

She is married to a man who understands that better than anybody, because he is a survivor himself. I'm glad this one is over. In the meantime, there's a war on. Next stop, Salamanca…

In the re-edited versions of these books, I've taken to including one of my short stories as a bonus at the end. All these stories are freely available on my website but I'm aware that not all of my readers spend that much time online and I don't want people to miss out. *The Last Sentry* is chronologically set at the end of book six, but I've included it here because it is closely related to the storming of Ciudad Rodrigo. I hope you enjoy it.

The Last Sentry

The journey from England to Spain was beset with problems and delays, and on arrival in Oporto, when it became obvious that due to a particularly unpleasant voyage, the officers' horses would not be fit to travel for some days, Lieutenant-Colonel Philip Norton listened with half an ear to the complaints of the other five officers who had arrived with him on the *Sally-Anne* and was silently relieved. A week of almost constant sickness had left him feeling weak and exhausted, and he found himself a comfortable inn, ensured that his groom, his valet and his horses were well-cared for and went to bed.

Philip was on his way to take up a new command, in charge of the first battalion of the 115th. He should have joined the regiment during the previous year, but within days of the confirmation of his promotion and transfer to a new regiment, his personal life had fallen apart with terrifying speed, leaving Philip floundering in the chaos of his deceased father's affairs and heartbroken after the death of his young wife in childbirth. He had written to his new brigade commander, guiltily aware that he would miss this campaigning season, and had dreaded the response. It had been kinder than Philip had expected and had given him a good impression of the commander of the third brigade of the light division, making him all the more eager to settle his affairs and get back to his job.

Settling his affairs had taken some time. The death of the Honourable Thomas Norton had come as a shock, though not a grief, to his only son. Norton had died as he had lived, half-drunk and throwing his horse over a fence on the hunting field. Philip was in London, making arrangements for his journey to Portugal while awaiting the birth of his third child. Emma had been well through the pregnancy, and was her usual placid self when Philip apologetically told her that he would need to post down to Hampshire to be with his mother and sister, and to help arrange the funeral.

"Go, Phil. If the baby comes, it comes, it isn't as though this is the first time I've done this. I'm sorry I can't come with you, since I know it will be hard for you, but I shouldn't travel this close to my time."

Philip kissed her warmly. "I'm so sorry, Em, and you're an angel. I'll be back as soon as I can, I promise."

Emma was dead before Philip reached his family estate, having gone into early labour the day he left. The child died with her, leaving Philip alone to manage his two

263

small sons, his mother who was apparently prostrated with grief over a husband who had never been faithful to her, and a sister of twenty trying to conceal her fears for the future.

Mrs Norton raised herself from her bed at the news of the death of her daughter-in-law and made her pronouncement.

"Dearest, it is terribly sad, of course, but it is not as though it was a love-match, after all. Indeed, I have never understood why…however, your duty is now clear. With your father gone, and your two little boys motherless, you will naturally sell out and come home. Nobody would expect anything else."

Philip bit his tongue and took himself from the room. He knew that she was right, and that the army would fully understand and support his decision to sell out. His father's affairs were in disarray, and he had no idea how his wife's money was settled. He had married Emma in full understanding that she was looking for a place in society that her late father's situation could not provide. In return, she had agreed to pay his family's debts and purchase his promotions.

Philip respected his wife's clear-sighted practicality and insisted that she settle her considerable fortune on their sons when they were born, with a dowry set aside for his sister, Amelia, and a comfortable jointure for his mother should she be widowed. He had asked the lawyers, during the negotiation of the marriage settlement, to ensure that Emma's personal fortune remain with her, well out of reach of his feckless father and grasping mother. Philip had made a marriage of convenience to secure his future, but he was not greedy and he had no wish to watch his family bleeding his wife dry.

Emma's will was a shock, and brought with it a fresh flood of grief, as Philip listened to the lawyer's dry tones and understood that alongside the agreed provisions, she had left him a wealthy man. He cried bitter tears alone in his room, hoping that she had known how much she had come to mean to him. Philip had hoped for friendship in this unlikely marriage, but instead, they had fallen in love, and he read, in those brief lines of her final testament, her firm and abiding affection and trust.

It made his job much easier, although no less tedious and painful. Philip told neither his mother nor his sister of his unexpected prosperity, merely assuring them that there was money to support them. Amelia, as he had expected, was relieved and grateful, while his mother was visibly discontented. She was furious at Philip's announcement that he intended to rent out the London house for the foreseeable future, and even more so, when he informed her that when his sister was ready to return to town for another Season, she would do so under the care of her aunt.

"I hope you're happy with that, Ammie. I know you didn't much enjoy London last year. I'd hoped that once the baby was born, you could try again with Emma, but…"

"So did I, Philip. Please don't worry, I'm thankful. I've no wish to do the round of balls and parties just now, I couldn't think of it. Ignore Mama, she would be angry whatever you did."

"I can't give her free rein to run through Emma's money in London."

"You should not, she is very comfortably provided for. At present, I am happier at Hanley. And you, dear brother, will be happier back in the army."

"I will. My new commander has been very generous with my furlough, which makes me all the more determined that I will get back as soon as I have sorted out the chaos of my father's affairs and paid his debts. I am trusting you to look after Tom and Ned for me, they'll have Miss Carling and Nurse, but they're going to miss Emma so much, she was…"

"She was the best mother ever, and I envied them. I'll do everything I can for them, Phil. Just don't do anything foolish. I know how much you loved her, I couldn't bear it if…"

"I give you my word. As far as any soldier can. Take care of yourself, Ammie."

After the turmoil of family drama, it was bliss to don his uniform and to think only of transport and kit and billets and the new campaigning season ahead. Even the misery of the voyage gave Philip something to think about other than Emma. It was eleven months since her death and Philip had begun to believe that he was recovering, but away from England's shores, he missed, all over again, the weekly routine of writing to her.

From Oporto, Philip joined a supply convoy travelling towards army headquarters on the Portuguese-Spanish border. His fellow officers were all veterans of the Peninsula, having been home either on furlough or sick leave. Along with the wagon train of weapons and medical supplies, there were a hundred and eighty reinforcements for the 43rd and 112th, so the officers travelled at marching pace. To Philip, suddenly eager to join his battalion, it felt painfully slow, and he was not at all surprised when they reached the commissary office in Pinhal to discover that Lord Wellington had marched his army into Spain three days earlier.

"There's a supply depot in Ciudad Rodrigo, sir," Captain Jones said helpfully. "Only a day's march from here. Lord Wellington sent instructions that all reinforcements and supply wagons are go there, where he'll have left orders for them."

Ciudad Rodrigo was a small cathedral town situated at the top of a rocky rise on the right bank of the River Agueda. Philip knew it was one of the key fortresses along the Portuguese-Spanish border, and two of his companions had been present when Lord Wellington's army had stormed the town at the beginning of the previous year in a bloody engagement. Philip and the other officers were greeted by Colonel Muir, a depressed-looking Scot in his fifties, who commanded the district supply depot and looked as though he would rather be somewhere else.

"Aye, I've orders for you, I've got details of the quickest and safest route for you to follow to catch up with the light division, it seems you're expected."

"I have been for some time," Philip admitted. "Will the supply column be taking the same route?"

"The supply column is my problem now, Colonel Norton, don't worry your head about them. The reinforcements, now - that's another matter. You'll be staying a few days to rest the horses, I'm guessing?"

Philip eyed him suspiciously, sensing an unwelcome request. "One or two, maybe, but I don't want to delay longer than I have to, sir. My brigade commander has been incredibly generous in granting extensions to my furlough to sort out my late father's affairs, I don't want him to think I'm taking the long way round."

"Van Daan? He's not in my good books just now, he poached two of my best officers on his way out, blast him. He doesn't deserve that I do him a favour, the thieving bastard, but I'm going to. I'm asking if you'll wait a few more days, Norton. We're expecting another draft of reinforcements for the 110th within the week."

"Can't they follow when they arrive?"

"The thing is, Colonel, we've been having a lot of problems with discipline among troops making their way back to their regiments. Half the time, they either don't have an officer with them at all, or the officers are young and inexperienced, or from a different regiment and don't really give a damn about them looting the local population. Wellington's furious about attacks on Portuguese and Spanish farms and villages. You've got a few officers with these drafts for the 43rd and 112th, but they're all very junior, and they tend to take a casual attitude to their duties on the march. If they've a colonel of the 115th to supervise them, it's very unlikely any of the men will try sloping off to raid a wine cellar or rape the farmer's wife."

"Jesus, is it as bad as that?"

"On occasion." Muir eyed Philip thoughtfully. "And not just among the enlisted men. I don't know if the gossip has reached you yet, Colonel Norton, but…"

"If you're referring to the murder of Major Vane, I received a very full letter from Major-General van Daan," Philip said. "A terrible business."

"Aye, it was. Did you know him?"

"Never met the man in my life, I'm new to the 115th, I transferred in for promotion. And I believe Vane did the same. I'd never wish a man dead, Colonel, but I find myself thankful that I don't have to manage an officer like that in my battalion."

"Aye, his conduct wasn't right, that's for sure. All the same, a lot of the officers I've spoken to, don't think it's right that his murderer escaped the death penalty. Sets a bad example to the men."

Philip did not particularly want to get into a pointless argument with a senior officer, so he said:

"So you'd like me to wait until the rest of the light division reinforcements arrive and march them up to the lines?"

"I think your brigade commander would appreciate it, Colonel. We can make you comfortable here, you can join our mess."

Philip could see the sense of it, and firmly quashed his frustration at yet another delay. Now that he was formally, if temporarily in command of the new troops, he went to inspect their bivouac outside the city walls, gave strict instructions to the NCOs about leave passes and behaviour and rounded up the few junior officers who would be marching with him, to remind them of their obligations. His duty done, he decided to make the most of his enforced leisure to see something of the town and the surrounding area.

Ciudad Rodrigo was a walled city, dominated by its solid medieval cathedral. Narrow streets opened up into wide squares with houses and churches built in mellow local stone, and although there were still many signs of the destruction of the previous year, the citizens had already made good progress with rebuilding damaged houses and there was scaffolding up at several of the fine churches. Philip could see damage to the walls and tower of the cathedral caused by artillery, and the Spanish garrison of the town were out daily to supervise work parties who were close to completing the repairs to the town walls, where Wellington's guns had blown two enormous breaches in the ancient stonework.

It was hot during the day, and Philip rode out with one or two of the Spanish officers to shoot game in the countryside. None of them had been present during the siege and seemed more interested in complaining about delayed pay and poor leadership in the Spanish army than talking about the recent history of the town. Muir, when applied to, was more helpful, and provided Philip with Sergeant Griffith from his department. Griffith had lost an arm and an eye during the storming and proved a willing guide, walking out to the Greater and Lesser Teson with Philip, to explain the placement of Wellington's troops and the direction taken by the storming parties.

Dinner was a protracted affair, with a good deal of wine and brandy, and afterwards Philip developed a habit of going for an evening walk through the pretty cobbled streets of the town and up onto the walls. The sentries along the walls were all Spanish, and Philip thought that they seemed to take a relaxed attitude to their duties, although he supposed that with the French a long way off, they probably had little to do other than drink, smoke and complain. He spoke Spanish fairly well from his time in South America, and he stopped to chat to them, listening to their stories of battles fought and friends lost and wives and families left behind.

Philip lingered late one evening, watching the sun go down from the Citadel, colouring the slate roofs of the outlying villages with a dazzling palette of rose gold and brilliant orange. He had drunk a little too much wine in the company of some Spanish officers in Colonel Muir's cosy dining room and realised it was becoming a habit. It was too comfortable here and felt a long way from the war. Philip walked around the walls to clear his head, pausing to look out over the old Roman bridge and smiled at himself as he realised he was willing the new troops to march in over the bridge, leaving him free to do his job.

Further around the walls, he climbed down a flight of steep stone steps and stood looking up at the repaired section of wall where the men of the light division had fought and died on that bloody night in January. The different colour brickwork reminded Philip of a scar, and he felt a connection standing here, even though he had not been present and his new battalion had not even been part of the light division at that point.

Walking back along the walls to his billet, Philip noticed that the sentries were out of position again. He had observed it several times, and although they were not his men, and the town was in no danger of attack, it irritated him as a breach of discipline. Four or five men were grouped together, a lazy spiral of cigarillo smoke rising into the air, while only one man, dressed in a dark cloak, stood in position above the breach. Philip paused to watch him, standing completely immobile looking out over the countryside. He did not appear to have his musket with him, and Philip wondered if he should go back and speak to the man but decided against it.

Philip remembered the incident the following afternoon at the dinner table. He was seated beside Colonel Ramirez, determinedly avoiding a third glass of port, when Colonel Muir said:

"Are you still having trouble with the men on the northern wall, Ramirez?"

Ramirez rolled his eyes expressively. "Always, Colonel. Only last week, I have two men on a charge for deserting their post. I tell them that if Lord Wellington comes back, he will have them shot for their cowardice. I hope to make an example of them, so that we have no more problems."

"Cowardice?" Philip said, surprised. "Surely it can't be that they're miles from the French lines with the whole of Lord Wellington's army in between. Perhaps they've just got sloppy, sir. I admit, I walk the walls most evenings, and they're often not in position, particularly along that wall. They tend to gather together in groups, smoking and talking. I suppose they're bored, but you're right, it's poor discipline."

"They are not afraid of the French, Colonel Norton, they are afraid of the ghosts."

Philip spluttered on the last of his port and set his glass down. It was immediately refilled. "Ghosts? Surely, you're not serious?"

"I am not serious, Colonel," Ramirez said. "Me, I do not believe in ghosts. But my officers tell me that the men complain that sometimes they hear things up there after dark. Screams and cries and the echoes of guns that have not fired since that night.

Muir snorted, reaching for the bottle. "Drunken bastards. If they're hearing things that aren't there, they're coming from the bottom of a bottle, if you ask me."

"I have told my officers to search them for drink, Colonel, and they assure me they go on duty sober."

"Over-imaginative, then. A lot of you Spaniards are, I believe."

Philip blinked at what felt like an astonishing lapse in good manners. He shot an apologetic look at Ramirez and was relieved that the Spanish Colonel seemed amused rather than offended. He winked at Philip, then said smoothly:

"It is possible, I suppose, Colonel, but we do not pay them to feed their imagination with ghostly tales. I will tell my officers to make frequent inspections again."

"There was one man up there last night," Philip said. "You're right, sir, the others were all huddled further round by the steps, but one brave soul didn't mind the ghosts, he was standing right above the breach. Although it looked as though he'd forgotten his musket, I couldn't see it."

"On sentry duty without his weapon?" Muir said scathingly. "Wouldn't catch an English sentry doing that."

Philip wished he had not spoken. "He probably had it, sir, he might have just leaned it against the wall while he was having a smoke and forgotten to pick it up. Look, why don't I take a walk around there after dinner and have a chat with the men? They might speak more freely to me, given that I'm not their commanding officer."

Ramirez studied him thoughtfully for a moment, then gave his charming smile. "Thank you, Colonel, it is a kind offer. I fear, if they do not improve, I will be obliged to take more drastic action against them."

It was pleasantly cool as Philip began his nightly circuit of the walls. The Spanish sentries had grown used to the sight of him by now, and greeted him cheerfully, although without the formal salutes and springing to attention he would have expected from an English garrison. Philip took his time, stopping to chat. One group on the eastern wall offered him a drink from a bottle concealed in a coat pocket, and Philip took a swig, then reminded them pleasantly that their own officers might not be so tolerant.

It was beginning to grow dark as he approached the section of the northern wall above the lesser breach, and Philip could neither see nor hear the sentries. He paused, listening, peering ahead into the dim light. This entire section of the wall appeared to be unguarded, and Philip quickened his step. He had been inclined to take a light-hearted view of the Spanish garrison's dislike of manning this section of the wall at night, but to find no guards at all was beyond a joke.

It was cooler now that darkness was falling, and there was a faint summer mist. Staring ahead in search of the missing guard, Philip caught his foot on a jutting piece of masonry and stumbled a little, catching the edge of the wall to steady himself. The fall brought him up short. The ramparts were not high, and it would be easy for a man to tumble over the edge. Philip made his way forward again, but more cautiously.

The sound of footsteps made him pause again. Clearly somebody was up here after all, although Philip still could not see him. He wondered if it was the lone sentry once more, the stocky figure who seemed the only member of the garrison willing to patrol this part of the wall. Philip waited, as the footsteps came towards him, puzzled by his inability to see the man. The steps were firm and confident and were growing very close. It was not yet fully dark, and Philip could easily see through the mist, but there was no sign of the Spanish sentry.

A sudden breeze ruffled the feather in Philip's hat, and he felt it, cool on his face. The footsteps were inexplicably fading again, as though a man had walked briskly past him and onwards down the walkway, but there was nobody there. For a moment, a shiver ran through Philip, then he heard voices from below. Going to the inside edge of the walkway, he peered over, and thought he understood. The foot of the wall was paved all the way up to the next bastion, and the footsteps must have been below him, the sounds distorted by an echo in the quiet evening air. Philip grinned at his momentary superstitious folly and ran lightly down the bastion steps, surprising the Spanish guards who were huddled in the shelter of the small tower passing a bottle between them. They turned in surprise at Philip's abrupt descent from above, and one put the bottle behind his back. Philip was suddenly angry.

"To attention!" he barked, in Spanish. "Give me that bottle, that you're so pointlessly trying to hide. Why aren't you at your posts?"

There was a scramble into line, and Philip held out his hand and took the bottle. "You have deserted your posts," he said. "I am not your officer, is not my job to walk the wall and ensure you do your duty, but I am here to tell you that Colonel Ramirez is well aware that you are not where you should be. He has declared that it is enough, and your officers will be checking on you each night. If you continue this way, you are going to be disciplined, possibly flogged. I will not be here to see it, I will be leaving in a few days, but it is sad that I leave with such a poor impression of Spanish troops. You - step forward. What is your name?"

"Garcia, sir."

"What's going on, Garcia?"

The Spaniard threw out his hands in a dramatic gesture. "It is not our fault, Colonel. Time and again we tell the officers that we cannot be on that part of the wall at night. All other places, we will guard. From this bastion to the further tower only. But they will not change the location of the sentry posts."

"Why can't you be on that wall?"

"Because of what we see and hear, Colonel. That place belongs to the ghosts, it is not for men."

"Nonsense," Philip said firmly. "At least one of your men has been up there, I've seen him twice now, the man in the dark blue cloak. Clearly it holds no fears for him."

There was a long, awkward silence. Then Garcia said:

"He is not one of our men, Colonel, and he has no reason to fear a ghost."

The tone of his voice brought a momentary chill to Philip, but he mentally brushed it aside. "Well, if he isn't one of yours, it must be one of the townspeople," he said. "Either way, it isn't a ghost."

"How do you know it is not, Colonel?"

"Because I don't believe in ghosts, Garcia. And a ghost isn't a good enough reason for you to shirk your duty. I'm going to talk to Colonel Ramirez, but I'm warning you, you'll need to improve your behaviour if you don't want to get into trouble. For tonight, get yourselves back up there. One picket at the top of this bastion, the other along the wall at the further tower."

Garcia sprang to attention and gave a dramatic salute. "Yes, Colonel. That, we can do."

Philip watched them go, not sure whether to laugh or be irritated, but the Spanish garrison was not really his problem. He walked back to his billet, giving the bottle to a surprised old man who was smoking on his doorstep, and grinned at the extravagant thanks and blessings that followed him up the narrow lane as the man realised it was more than half full.

A message arrived as Philip was writing a letter to his brigade commander the following day, to say that the new troops had arrived. Philip finished and sealed the letter quickly and sent his groom to add it to the daily post, then took himself out to the bivouac by the Agueda, to ensure that the new men had set up camp properly and had rations. There were six junior officers from various regiments who would join him on the march to Wellington's lines, and Philip ran an experienced eye over the camp, spoke to one or two of the NCOs and decided that it would be a fairly easy command. Most of these men were new recruits, and although there would be the usual sprinkling of troublemakers, either criminals who had come through the courts into the army, or simply men who found it hard to learn discipline, there would be no time for idleness on the march. Philip gave orders to his juniors to make regular inspections of the camp, ordered a forty-eight hour rest period before the march and went to see the quartermaster to make sure that rations would be issued. Once he was on the move, Philip wanted to reach the army as quickly as possible.

Philip dined with Colonel Muir and some of the Spanish officers, who drank enthusiastic toasts to his journey and his new posting. Going outside into the warm evening air, he hesitated. Knowing he would be on the road in two days, he had asked both his valet and his groom to check his kit and his horses, and to let him know if he needed to make any last minute purchases. He wrote to his brigade commander informing him of the date of his departure and wrote a dutiful letter home to his mother and his sister, and missed once again, the writing of a long letter to Emma, filled with army news and gossip and the trivia of his daily life. For the first time since arriving in Ciudad Rodrigo, Philip felt lonely, and he realised he was longing to reach his new battalion, to get to know his fellow officers and to make friends with the easy facility which was an asset in the shifting relationships of army life. Philip recognised the importance of this extended journey, as a pause between his old life and his new, but it had gone on for too long and he wanted it done with.

Almost without thinking, Philip passed his billet and walked down into the Plaza Mayor, where lanterns hung outside every shop and tavern and the people of Ciudad Rodrigo went about their business as though no war had ever touched them. Philip knew that after the bloody fighting in the breaches, the English and Portuguese troops had run wild for a while, looting the town and terrorising its inhabitants. Returning the smiles of men and women at the sight of his red coat, he marvelled at their resilience and their forgiveness.

Philip was approaching the cathedral when the sight of another red coat made him pause. No leave passes had been granted to the English troops, as Philip wanted them sober and fit to march. The officers were free to wander through the town unless they were on duty, but this was not an officer. Philip stopped and surveyed the man. He was of medium height and compact build, with curly dark hair, and the insignia on his coat told Philip that he was a sergeant.

Philip stood watching with considerable interest, laced with admiration, as the Sergeant went through the process of bartering with the elderly Spaniard selling wine from a market trestle. It was clear that the Sergeant spoke Spanish fairly well, and it was equally clear that this was not the first time he had done this. Most of the newly arrived troops were raw recruits, but there was a sprinkling of old hands returning from sick leave, and after ten minutes, three bottles of wine had been neatly stowed in the battered pack, and Philip was certain that this man was not new to this.

The Sergeant seemed in no hurry to return to camp. With his purchases made, he wandered through the market, stopping at a food stall to buy a hot tortilla wrapped in vine leaves, which he ate as he paused to watch a juggler giving a performance outside the convent. Philip stopped too and looked up at the windows of the house. He was not surprised to see a flutter of white at the window, proving that the novices were not above enjoying a glimpse of the outside world. He also observed that the Sergeant looked up as well, noticed the girls, and gave an impudent wave, sending them scuttling away in maidenly confusion, and probably, if they were unsupervised, a fit of irreverent giggles.

Philip realised that he was delaying approaching the Sergeant because he was enjoying watching the man. There was something about him which spoke of happiness, and a sheer love of life, and Philip was reluctant to end his illicit holiday too soon, although he was definitely going to. He kept his distance, shadowing the Sergeant through the town, until it was growing very dark. The townspeople were beginning to gather their children and their purchases and head for home, and some of the shopkeepers were putting up their shutters. By now, the sentries on the walls would have changed over and Philip wondered if the deserted stretch of the northern wall was properly manned tonight.

It was clear that the Sergeant was in no hurry to get back to camp. He stopped at a tavern and sat outside with a cup of wine for a while, watching the people of Ciudad Rodrigo head home to their beds with a benign expression. Philip hesitated for a moment, then gave in to his baser self, slipped into the tavern, and bought his own cup of wine, then walked outside and approached the Sergeant's bench from behind.

"Lovely evening for it, Sarge, mind if I join you?"

"Not if the next drink's on you, my dear, it's good to…"

The Sergeant broke off as Philip walked to the bench opposite him and set down his drink. The expression on his thin, pointed face almost made Philip laugh out loud. He scrambled to his feet, tripping over the bench, managed to right himself and stood rigidly to attention, saluting, staring straight ahead, his dark eyes fixed on a point above Philip's head.

"Sir. Very sorry, sir, I didn't know it was you. Many apologies."

"I'd rather guessed that, Sergeant. Sorry to disturb you, but I wanted to see your leave pass. One of the officers clearly didn't understand my orders about no leave granted, I need to see who signed it."

The Sergeant shifted his gaze to Philip. Philip held out his hand and waited, and the sergeant did not disappoint him. He clapped his hand to his breast pocket, then shoved both hands into coat and trouser pockets, rummaging industriously. Coming up empty, he reached for his pack, opened it, and rustled around inside it, skilfully concealing the clink of bottles. Eventually he looked up, wide-eyed.

"Well I don't know how I've done that, Colonel, but it looks like I've lost it," he said, and his voice was rich and mellow with the rounded vowels of the West Country. "Maybe I left it in my tent, but I don't think so, I've got an excellent memory, and I'm sure I picked it up. Now, I wonder if some thieving brat has picked my pocket for me in this crowd, knowing I'm new here and taking advantage…"

Philip held up his hand. He was enjoying the performance, and recognised in the Sergeant a natural comedian, but he did not have all night. "That's enough, Sergeant, you'll have me weeping into my wine cup in a minute. Name and rank?"

"Sergeant Nick Coates, sir, 110th second company. Was under Captain Elliott, but I've been away for a while now."

"Wounded?"

"Aye, sir. At Badajoz. Been convalescing ever since."

"That's a long convalescence, Sergeant Coates."

"It was a bad wound, sir. More than one. They bayonetted me in the chest as I reached the top of the ladder, then I broke an arm and a leg when I hit the ground."

"Christ, you're lucky to have survived that with all your limbs."

"We've good doctors in the 110th, sir."

"And now you're on your way back and thought you'd give yourself a night off as a treat. Don't start searching for the leave pass again, it never existed. What I do want to know is where you got the money for three bottles of good wine. Have you been looting, Coates?"

"No, sir." Coates hesitated, then took the plunge. "Not my money, sir. It's more of a commission."

"A commission? For whom?"

"A gentleman, sir, new to Spain, and with none of the language. They'll fleece the youngsters something awful, sir, when they first get here."

Philip was beginning to understand. "So you did have permission."

"Informally, sir."

"Which officer?"

"I don't rightly know, sir. They're not my officers, you know, and he didn't approach me directly. One of the men brought the money and said I could keep the change as an incentive to get a good price. They must have heard I'd been out here before and could speak Spanish."

Philip shook his head. "I suppose if I asked you to point out the soldier in question…?"

"Not one of my men, sir, I didn't know him. They all look very much alike, don't they? I was to put the wine outside the officers' billet, I was just on my way to do that, sir. Sorry I'm not more help."

Philip studied Coates for a long moment. "I think you know bloody well who ordered that wine," he said softly. "Do you think he realised that you could end up flogged and demoted if you got caught?"

Shrewd dark eyes met his. "Oh yes, sir, I expect the young gentleman knew that all right. But I didn't have to say yes, of course."

"Why did you, you bloody fool?"

Coates looked around the darkened square, where only the taverns remained well lit, men sharing wine on rough benches outside. "I liked this place. Met a girl here. Army hospitals weren't that much fun, and it was a bloody awful journey, mopping up puke from the new lads and running out of food on the march because the greenhorns don't know the ropes. I fancied a night out, sir. Didn't expect to get caught."

Philip managed to bite back a grin at the other man's matter-of-fact tones. Picking up his cup of wine, he sat down. Coates remained standing to attention. Philip waited for at least two minutes.

"All right, Sergeant. Sit down and drink your wine, and then we'll walk back to camp together, I want to check on them. When I leave, I'll take those bottles and deliver them personally, with a word or two about using the NCOs as errand boys and hanging them out to dry afterwards. Next time, make the young bleater give you a permission slip and then you're covered, and it'll be him that'll get the bollocking."

Coates stared at him in astonishment, then lowered his compact form onto the bench with a broad grin. "Thank you very much, sir. Your very good health. I'm guessing this is not your first time out here either, you're not new at this."

"By no means, Coates, but not out here. Alexandria, Walcheren, Ireland and Naples, with a spell in South America, which is why I was able to admire your bartering so thoroughly."

Coates sipped the wine. "It's good that you're going to Van Daan's brigade, sir, you'd get cashiered anywhere else, drinking with the NCOs like this."

"I don't usually drink with the NCOs, Sergeant, so don't get any ideas. It's my night off. And besides, you looked as though you were enjoying yourself."

Coates looked up and grinned. "I was, sir. Am I on a charge?"

"Not this time, although you were a bloody idiot. But I'm looking for experienced men to help out on this march, since I seem to have been landed with two hundred and fifty raw recruits and half a dozen officers so wet behind the ears they need a nursemaid. I will do you a deal, Sergeant Coates. I will forget all about this little escapade, and in return, I get your unqualified support in getting these sorry specimens up to Lord Wellington's army."

Coates studied him for a moment, then picked up his cup and raised it. "Sir, you have yourself a deal."

"Excellent. You can start tonight. On the way back to camp, I want to walk via the walls. The Spanish are having trouble with ghosts."

"Ghosts, sir?" Coates sounded bewildered. "What ghosts?"

Philip explained, and Coates seemed to enjoy the story. They sat late into the evening. Philip was aware that his conduct in drinking with an NCO was reprehensible and would bring at best a stern reprimand and at worst, a conduct charge, but there were few English officers presently in Ciudad Rodrigo, and those would be up in the mess with Colonel Muir. Philip had missed his friends in the regiment badly and Coates, although only a sergeant, was intelligent, very funny and shrewd. Philip was careful to keep some distance but enjoyed Coates' colourful account of his entry into the army seven years earlier, through the agency of a magistrate in Truro.

"Smuggling was it, Sergeant?"

"I prefer to call it free trading, sir. It was my job to provide the gentlemen with their port and their brandy and the ladies with their silks and tea."

"And sugar?"

"No, sir, I didn't deal in sugar, on account of the slaves. Nasty business, slavery."

Philip stared in astonishment. "A Cornish smuggler who is an abolitionist? I might need another drink to hear this story, Coates."

"It's not a long one, sir, though I'll happily stand you another drink. I was fifteen and on my father's boat, running brandy and tea into a cove near Marazion when we picked up a body in the water. Younger than me, he looked, half-starved and beaten bloody, poor little beggar."

"Oh Christ. Slaver gone down?"

"Not as such. Runaway page boy, caught in Plymouth and sold back to the West Indies. He could remember life on the plantations, preferred to drown himself."

"He was alive?"

"Yes, sir. Algy, his name was. Crewed that boat with me for nigh on ten years, until we got picked up on a run from Roscoff, and after a spell in gaol found ourselves with the choice of the army, the navy or a trial which could have ended much worse. Algy chose the navy, safer for him. Often wonder how he got on, he was a good mate, was Algy."

"It sounds as though you were too. Right, come on. Time to earn your parole all over again, Sergeant Coates. Let's get up there and put the fear of God into those sentries, then I will take the officers' wine and let them know I want a word with them in the morning."

"You could always confiscate it, sir. Good wine, that."

"You were born to be hanged, Coates. Get moving."

There was no sound or movement along the town walls. This late, the sentries were in position, huddled together for warmth and companionship, the air around them hazy with cigar smoke. Philip paused by each group in turn as they saluted and spoke a few words. It was the last night he would do this, and he hoped he was making enough noise to get the sentries on the northern wall into position so that he could

274

give a favourable report to Colonel Ramirez. They approached by the small bastion, and Philip was pleased to see four men, albeit on the wrong side of the tower, muskets shouldered. They looked grim and miserable, but they were there, and he stopped to compliment them on their fortitude, although he was aware that he could not see the next picket.

The night was very clear, with a full moon, and Philip heard the clink of bottles from Coates' pack as the sergeant followed him onto the wall above the breach. He wondered suddenly if this place held painful memories for Coates, but the Sergeant showed no signs of discomfort.

Further along the wall, Philip caught sight of a lone figure and immediately recognised him. He knew by now that the man was not one of the garrison, but must be a townsman, probably from one of the houses directly below the wall, who came up each night for a breath of fresh air before bed. Philip had not been this close to him before, and as he drew nearer, he realised that what he had thought was a cloak, was actually a dark blue caped great coat. He wore a simple bicorn hat, and Philip wondered if he was in fact an officer, either on sick leave or visiting, although he was surprised he had not met him during his week in the town, as the English officers all knew each other socially.

Behind him, Coates echoing footsteps stopped abruptly. Philip paused and looked round in surprise. The Sergeant's face was clearly illuminated in the moonlight, and his expression chilled Philip to the bone. The thin face wore an expression of utter terror, the dark eyes wide, and Coates was backing up so fast that Philip sprinted to grab him by the arm, worried he might tumble backwards over the low parapet. He realised as he grasped Coates, that the Sergeant was shaking violently.

"Sergeant, what the hell is wrong with you? Look stand here for a moment and catch your breath. Are you ill?"

"No. No, no, no, no. It can't be. He's not here, he's not here. He's dead. He's bloody dead, I saw them bury him."

Understanding was slow to dawn, and by the time Philip understood, the brisk footsteps along the walkway were coming close. Suddenly, he was afraid as well, and it took all his courage to turn around to see what had caused the Sergeant's sheer terror. The sight was so ludicrously normal that Philip felt completely disoriented.

For the first time, he could see the face of the stocky man who guarded the lesser breach every evening, and although there was nothing spectral about it, it was formidable. He was not old, possibly in his fifties, with very dark hair under his hat, and a pair of piercing dark eyes under thick, beetling brows. His complexion was swarthy, as though he had spent many days in the saddle under the hot Spanish sun, and he walked with deliberate authority, his sword belt jingling slightly as he moved. There was a sense of power and controlled energy about him, and Philip found himself standing to attention and saluting even before he saw the glimpse of a red jacket beneath the swinging coat. Unquestionably this was a senior officer.

The man turned to look at him as he passed. Dark eyes flickered over Philip, as though to check that he was correctly turned out, and then the officer nodded in approval and saluted. He walked past the shivering Sergeant without comment. Philip watched his retreating back, feeling as though he had just passed an inspection from a difficult commanding officer, and turned to Coates.

Coates was white in the pale moonlight and looked as though he might be sick. Philip took him firmly by the arm. "Come on, Sergeant, let's get you off this wall before you kill yourself. No, don't try to speak. We'll go back to my billet and if necessary, I'll call the surgeon."

Philip waited until they were inside his warm little room. He pushed Coates into a chair and went for brandy then realised that he had run out. Making a mental note to send Barlow, his valet, to buy more before the march, Philip went to the Sergeant's pack and removed one of the bottles of wine. He poured for both of them and set a glass down in front of Coates.

"I'm going to get cashiered, drinking with a Sergeant twice in one day. If I'd not been with you earlier, Coates, I'd have thought you were half-sprung already, but you're clearly not. What happened, were you ill?"

Coates was beginning to regain his colour. He drank half a glass of wine without taking breath and set it down, then looked up at Philip.

"Thank you, sir. Sorry. Must have taken a turn. Won't happen again. I'll leave the wine here, you can give it to the gentlemen in the morning."

He made as if to rise, and Philip pushed him firmly back into the chair and refilled his glass. "What happened?"

"Permission not to talk about it, sir?"

"Not granted. What were you on about - he's dead. Who's dead, Coates? Was it the breach - did you lose friends up there?"

The Sergeant drank more wine and did not reply. Philip sat down and sipped his own wine. "Look, I understand. I know what it can do to you sometimes, although we all pretend it doesn't affect us. I don't need the details, Coates, but if this is something…"

"You said you'd served in South America, sir," Coates said abruptly. "Mind me asking when?"

"I was with Beresford during the first invasion, but I developed fever and was sent home, so I missed the worst of that shambles. What on earth has that to do with anything?"

"Because he was out there afterwards. Major-General Craufurd. But you won't ever have seen him."

Understanding flooded through Philip along with a chill of horror. He stared blankly at Coates, not wanting to believe what he was saying. "Don't be funny, Sergeant, I'm not…"

"Did it look as though I was joking up there, sir?" Coates said furiously. "It was him. I know him, I've seen him a thousand times. I served in the 110th and we fought under him at Fuentes d'Onoro and at the Coa, and in a dozen skirmishes out on the border. And before then, I marched in his column during Moore's retreat. I saw that bastard flog the skin off a starving man's back for stealing a turnip and then give the same man the remains of his own rations later in the day. I was out there, climbing over dead and dying men into the breach last year and I saw him go down. I was at his burial, at the foot of the wall, in the breach. I know him. It was Craufurd."

Philip believed him. He sat in silence, drinking wine, shocked and feeling slightly shivery. Neither man spoke until Coates set down his empty glass and got to his feet. He saluted.

"Permission to return to camp, sir."

"Granted. Don't go that way again."

"I'm going nowhere near it, sir."

"Get your kit and the men organised, Sergeant, and be ready to march out the day after tomorrow. I'm counting on you to make my life easier along the way."

"My word on it, Colonel." The Cornishman hesitated. "Sir?"

"What is it?"

"I'd prefer not to speak of this to anyone else, sir."

Philip gave a small, grim smile. "Not a chance of it, Sergeant. They'd think I was mad. Look - are you absolutely sure? It couldn't have been another man? A trick of the light, maybe you were thinking about Craufurd up there?"

"I saw him, sir. As clearly as I can see you now." Coates shook his head. "He was a bloody good general, his men thought the world of him. I'd have been glad to see him again, but he shouldn't have been there."

Philip thought about it. "I'm not sure about that, Sergeant. Maybe he should."

The following day was taken up with preparations for the march, and by dinner time, Philip was fully packed and had inspected the men and the baggage wagons, spoken to the Spanish guide allocated to him and said farewell to his hostess. He dined in the mess as usual, but rose early from the table, as he hoped to be on the road at dawn and did not want to set off with a hangover. Colonel Muir shook his hand and wished him well, and Philip was engulfed in a wave of handshakes and good wishes from both English and Spanish officers.

When Colonel Ramirez shook his hand, he said:

"Did you visit my idle sentries last night, Colonel?"

"I did," Philip admitted. "I've been thinking about it, Colonel, and it's possible the problem is easier to solve than we thought. It seems there's one stretch of that wall that they hate to patrol. It's right above where the breach was, and I'd guess they imagine horrors when they're up there. Perhaps if you moved the pickets a little further apart to either side of that stretch, they'd be better behaved."

Ramirez studied him thoughtfully. "It is an interesting idea, Colonel Norton. I will think about it. Goodbye, and good luck."

Outside the mess, Philip hesitated. He had things to do, but the wall was there, still and quiet in the sleepy late afternoon air. After a long moment, Philip turned away from his billet and walked down to the small bastion, going up the steps onto the wall. He walked along the stretch between the two small towers, then turned and walked back again. Nobody was there, but it was early, and he would not expect to see a ghost in broad daylight.

The thought made Philip smile it was so ridiculous. He turned again, to go down the steps, and saw him immediately, the stocky figure in the dark coat and hat, staring out over the countryside to the position where almost eighteen months ago, the Light Division had formed up, ready to storm the walls of Ciudad Rodrigo.

Philip did not move or speak. After a moment, Major-General Robert Craufurd turned towards him and began his brisk, confident march along the walkway until he reached Philip. As before, he turned his head to look at him, and Philip straightened and saluted. It should have felt ridiculous, saluting a man who was not and could not be there, but Philip did not care. Whatever shadow of Black Bob Craufurd that lingered on in the place where he had fallen, deserved his respect.

Craufurd returned the salute with the same quirk of his lips and walked past Philip. After a moment, the footsteps could no longer be heard. Philip turned to look, but both the bastion and the walkway were empty once more.

It was barely light when the two hundred and fifty men formed up under their temporary officers and set off at a brisk march around the outside of Ciudad Rodrigo towards the Salamanca road. Philip rode at the head of the small column, with the walls rising to his right, bathed in rose pink and golden rays from the awakening sun. The repaired wall was clearly visible, looking more than ever like a scar, and Philip looked up and was not surprised to see the lone figure standing above it, watching them leave. He reined in to allow the troops to march past him, until he was at the back of the column. Unobserved, he took off his hat, and saluted for a long, silent moment. Then he replaced it and cantered forward to the head of his men, setting his horse and his thoughts firmly towards Wellington's distant army.

By the Same Author

The Peninsular War Saga

An Unconventional Officer (Book 1)

An Irregular Regiment (Book 2)

An Uncommon Campaign (Book 3)

A Redoubtable Citadel (Book 4)

An Untrustworthy Army (Book 5)

An Unmerciful Incursion (Book 6)

The Manxman Series

An Unwilling Alliance (Book 1)

This Blighted Expedition (Book 2)

Regency Romances

A Regrettable Reputation (Book 1)

The Reluctant Debutante (Book 2)

Other Titles

A Respectable Woman (A novel of Victorian London)

A Marcher Lord (A novel of the Anglo-Scottish Border Reivers)

Printed in Great Britain
by Amazon

28076730R00159